W9-DCO-017

CHILL FACTOR

OTHER BANTAM BOOKS BY CHRIS ROGERS

Rage Factor

Bitch Factor

CHILL FACTOR

CHRIS ROGERS

BANTAM BOOKS

New York • Toronto • London • Sydney • Auckland

CHILL FACTOR

A Bantam Book / February 2000

Library of Congress Cataloging-in-Publication Data
Rogers, Chris
Chill factor / Chris Rogers.
p. cm.
ISBN 0-553-10661-9
I. Title.
PS3568.O424 C47 2000
813'.54—dc21   99-046455
                                                  CIP

Published simultaneously in the United States and Canada

Bantam Books are published by Bantam Books, a division of Random
House, Inc. Its trademark, consisting of the words "Bantam Books" and the
portrayal of a rooster, is Registered in U.S. Patent and Trademark Office and
in other countries. Marca Registrada. Bantam Books, 1540 Broadway, New
York, New York 10036.

PRINTED IN THE UNITED STATES OF AMERICA
BVG   10   9   8   7   6   5   4   3   2   1

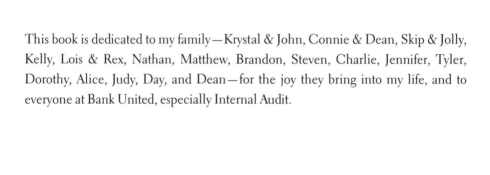

This book is dedicated to my family—Krystal & John, Connie & Dean, Skip & Jolly, Kelly, Lois & Rex, Nathan, Matthew, Brandon, Steven, Charlie, Jennifer, Tyler, Dorothy, Alice, Judy, Day, and Dean—for the joy they bring into my life, and to everyone at Bank United, especially Internal Audit.

ACKNOWLEDGMENTS

I take pleasure in acknowledging the folks who made a difference:

Reverend Rosemary Behrens, for more than pecan farms;

Sylvia Bradley, for good hair;

Howard Bushart, author of *Soldiers of God*, for professional advice;

Dorothy Ruth Carter, for Ryan's failure;

Mike Farrand, for Italia;

Mikael Gordon, for instruction in krav maga;

Leslie McCartney, for rhinestones;

Charlie Montgomery, for true belief;

Mary Rich and Carole Jose, authors of *Evil Web: A True Story of Cult Abuse and Courage*;

Kelly Rogers, for sound effects;

Paul Wunsch, for ranges;

Sandra White, for rich monkeys; and

Sally Yates, for her lending library.

Margaret Anderson, Mary Armeniades, Candace Caley, Kay Finch, Glenn Gotschall, Ann Jennings, Janet Miller, Robert Miller, Linda Posey, Connie Rogers, Barbara Schwartz, Amy Sharp, Charlie Soparker, and Leann Sweeney, for their time, energy, and generous support.

It is also my sincere pleasure to acknowledge Peter Miller and Kate Miciak, for their continued interest in Dixie Flannigan.

CHILL FACTOR

Prologue

Monday, 3:00 P.M.

Lucy Ames, a plump fifty-five-year-old divorcée, swept into the Texas Citizens Branch Bank on a crisp May afternoon and waited her turn in silence, not chatting with other patrons as was her custom. Instead, she hummed "Bad Moon Rising" and spent the brief wait noticing the rich viridian carpet, rose marble counter, and Ms. Darlene Flores pecking away at her computer. Lucy didn't usually bank at the Webster branch. Nevertheless, she'd come to make a withdrawal.

When the woman ahead of her, wearing an outrageously short, poppy-print dress, turned from the counter to exit through the glass doors, Lucy laid an empty book tote in the window and smiled at the teller. The tote was empty now because Lucy had removed the only item it carried, a .38 Police Special.

She pointed the gun at the teller. The young man had worked at this branch two years, Lucy recalled, long enough to know the rules and not panic, long enough to know how to act during a holdup, although this branch had never been robbed. At six-month intervals, the bank's security officer instructed branch employees in proper robbery procedures. Lucy knew the young teller would not try to be a hero.

"I will shoot you, Jonathan," she said amiably, "if anyone in this room makes a stupid move. Do you hear what I'm saying?"

Jonathan nodded, his Adam's apple doing a little bob as he swallowed. He wore too much Paco Rabanne cologne, and someone had ironed his shirt without enough steam, leaving a wrinkled patch on the left shoulder.

"I don't want anyone pushing alarm buttons." Lucy raised her voice so the other employees would listen up. "And I don't want any of that messy bait money smearing dye all over me."

The murmur of speculations faded to silence.

Lucy beamed a smile around the room. Her dazzling smile was her best feature—the Shepherd had told her so repeatedly.

"What I want you to do, Jonathan, is scoop all the real money from the teller drawers—never mind the change or that clever tracking device—and stuff the bills into this bag. I want you to do this without ever blocking my view of your movements. You hear what I'm saying?"

He nodded again, Adam's apple bob-bobbing.

"Good. That's very good. I really don't want to hurt anyone, but I've been practicing with Mr. Colt here." She raised the .38 a tad, level with Jonathan's nose. "I want you to know I can put ten rounds out of ten in the bull's-eye."

She waited for the young man's skinny face to register that he understood. She felt certain the other employees and the two patrons would understand as well. The bank did not retain an armed guard, because an independent study had determined guards were less cost-effective than video cameras. After today, no one in this town would see Lucy's face again, so video cameras didn't worry her.

"But before you begin, Jonathan, I want everyone except you and Ms. Flores and Mr. Simpson over there to lie facedown on the floor, arms and fingers extended." When no one moved, Lucy flashed her dazzling smile again. "You can do this *now*, folks. *Right now.*"

The air rustled with movement.

"Excellent. Now, Ms. Flores." Lucy flicked her gaze from assistant to manager. "I know that you and Mr. Simpson hold dual keys to the vault. I'd like you to open it and bring me the bags you've prepared for the Brinks pickup that's due later this afternoon."

Darlene Flores' eyes widened with surprise at this insider knowledge. Brinks pickups were supposed to be randomly scheduled, but routines surfaced nonetheless, and the truck could be counted on between three and four o'clock on any Monday. The assistant manager would've been even more surprised to know that she herself had divulged this tidbit one morning when she and Lucy chatted over the phone.

If they'd been speaking over the phone now, Darlene would undoubtedly recognize Lucy's voice. During the past few years they'd chatted often, usually about bank business. Lucy Ames worked in the wire room of Texas Citizens' main office, communicating at one time or another with all the branches to verify wire transfers.

"You can omit the change bag," Lucy told Darlene Flores. "Too heavy, and the bursitis in my shoulder has been frightful lately." She waved the gun a fraction. "Go ahead now. Let's get this over with so we can all relax and go home."

The entire transaction took less than two minutes. Lucy was proud of everyone for playing their parts so well — off-the-cuff, so to speak. After all, she was the only one thoroughly rehearsed.

Three minutes after she left the bank, Lucy drove through the back parking lot of a deserted strip center and dropped four money bags out the car window to the pitted asphalt, confident that another car would follow moments later and pick them up. Back on the street, she drove toward home at a reasonable speed, singing "Proud Mary" with the radio and thinking about her neighbor's daughter's wedding shower later that evening. Lucy had promised to bake her famous Gin Fizz Cake. A "regrets" note, claiming a migraine, would travel with the cake by messenger, while Lucy headed to a new life. She decided to stop at the grocery and buy fresh strawberries for the frosting.

When blue-and-red lights flashed in her rearview mirror, Lucy was only mildly alarmed. She'd hoped this wouldn't happen. But she was prepared.

A second police car turned on its siren ahead of her. A third flanked from the left, forcing her to the curb.

So many, so soon . . . One of the bank personnel must have triggered an alarm, although Lucy felt certain she would've noticed.

She picked up the .38 she'd laid on the floor mat. Her temples dampened with perspiration. This part of the plan wasn't nearly so well rehearsed as the actual robbery, but Lucy knew her role. The gun shook in her hand as she stepped from the car.

A wall of blue encircled her, patrol cars parked at odd angles, police officers aiming their side arms from the cover of metal doors or fenders. Despite her instructions, Lucy couldn't bear to shoot one of those young officers. Aiming between two cars at a Rubbermaid garbage container across the street, she drew an arm-steadying breath, blew it out . . . then, as she had been trained, squeezed the trigger.

As the container flew backward, Lucy heard the *pop — pop — pop — pop — pop* of return fire. A thudding blow spun her sideways. Her gun hand cramped — the spasm spit another bullet from the .38.

A bolt of searing pain slammed through Lucy's chest. Her legs buckled beneath her. She sank to her knees.

As she knelt, swaying, on the gritty concrete, Lucy's thoughts scudded over the lonely year following her divorce, through recent months of joyous companionship, into the present moment . . . and she smiled. Everything had gone terribly wrong, but she had played her part exactly right. The Shepherd would be pleased.

Her gaze locked on an earnest young officer as she crumpled to the pavement, smile frozen in place: They would *not* take her alive.

Chapter One

Skip tracing in Houston is a game of hide-and-seek, bail jumpers as dumb as ostriches about hiding. More often than not they could be found bending an elbow in one of their favorite haunts, vegging in front of the tube, or hanging with an old flame. Dixie Flannigan approached a bungalow at 221 Burning Oak Drive expecting the skip she was after to be no more imaginative than average. But sometimes they fooled you.

She eased her tow truck to a halt, turned off the headlights, lowered the windows, and inhaled the heavy fragrance of magnolia blossoms from a tree skirting the road. A tepid breeze flushed the remnants of air conditioning from the truck cab and ruffled her brown hair across the collar of her camp shirt. Dixie'd been growing her hair longer the past three months, and now she wondered if this was a good idea, with summer approaching.

Behind her, nocturnal traffic hummed along the Southwest Freeway. City music. In the distance ahead, the downtown skyline glittered against the spring night.

Burrowing under a handful of mail and a copy of the *Daily Law Journal* on the passenger seat, Dixie grasped a thermos of cold raspberry tea. She opened it, drank as she tuned the radio to soft jazz, then settled back to watch the house. Waiting for a skip to poke his head up was the relaxing part of a job, a chance to sit idle without guilt nipping at her.

In a front window, a television flickered. The other houses were dark—after all, it was three A.M.—but the resident at 221 had only recently returned home.

When Dixie drove by an hour earlier, the driveway had been empty. Now, moonlight shimmered on the roof of a shiny new Camaro: the girlfriend's car.

Dixie's hunch meter said Jimmy Voller was snuggled up with his girlfriend in front of that television. If not there, he could be headed for Mexico, and Dixie wanted desperately to avoid a long-distance haul to bring the skip in. Voller was the last of five she'd traced over the past two weeks. Amazingly, all five skips had surfaced in a single day, and now she was nearly thirty-six hours without sleep.

Eyes trained on the lighted window shades, she reflected on what the pair might watch at this hour. One night recently, Dixie'd settled down with her remote control and a bad case of insomnia. A few clicks had taken her from late-night hucksters to TV evangelists, sitcom reruns, and skin flicks. Nowhere had she found the cozy, classic movie she sought.

After several minutes passed with no shadow crossing the window shades, Dixie stretched, yawned, and braced the thermos on a cup holder that didn't quite fit. She switched on her penlight to examine her mail . . . utility bills . . . check from a bail bondsman . . . bank statement, along with another envelope that looked suspiciously like an overdraft notice . . . and an invitation to The Winning Stretch, a health retreat.

She ripped open the bank notice.

Normally, her checking-account balance bobbed along at five hundred bucks, give or take a few. Overdraft protection enabled the bank to dip into her savings if the checking account dropped too low, which it did on occasion, when Dixie needed travel expenses to chase a skip out of town. Right now she felt certain her checkbook would confirm a reasonably healthy balance. But the bank notice she held in her hand showed a startling overdraft of twenty-six dollars and forty-seven cents. That should *never* happen—unless her three-thousand-dollar savings account had been drained. Where the hell had her money gone?

A light winked out in the front window at 221. A moment later, the television went blank, then a light appeared at the driveway side of the house, near the back.

Dixie aimed the penlight at her watch, checked the time—twenty-three minutes gone—then rolled her shoulders to work out the kinks. Didn't want her reflexes going sluggish while she waited. Jimmy Voller, a brawny, ill-tempered truck driver, out on bail while awaiting trial for drunk and disorderly conduct, had been known to get mean when cornered.

She considered retrieving the .45 semiautomatic from the locked tool safe in the truck bed. A license to carry and a contract with Voller's bonding agent gave her the credentials she needed. But Voller's arrest sheet hadn't included a weapons charge, and ten years as a State prosecutor had taught Dixie that the best way to get someone hurt was to use more force than necessary. She could handle Voller without the heat.

Ignoring a wimpy little voice that said, *Yeah, but why risk it?*, she wedged the penlight in the crook of her armpit as she skimmed the bank statement. Her check for a pair of new tires had apparently caused the overdraft. But the tires cost less than four hundred dollars. No way that one check could be the problem.

Opening her checkbook, she flipped through the carbonless copies. As usual, she'd neglected to carry the balance forward, but a quick mental tally verified a hundred-dollar balance, even *after* subtracting the amount for the tires, and without touching her savings account.

Had she made any large ATM withdrawals? Not that she recalled. Certainly not enough to deplete her savings account. She hadn't even gone out of town this month.

The window at the back of 221 went dark.

Dixie dropped the papers, snapped off her penlight, and eased the truck door open. She stepped out, into the still night. Her boots crunched gravel as she crossed the blacktop. She veered to the grass to deaden the sound.

Reaching the back window where the light had blinked off, she silently attached a listening device to the pane. Over the background hum of an air conditioner, she heard a murmur of voices accompanied by an occasional squeak of bedsprings. Dixie waited until the voices grew quietly urgent and the music of the springs beat a steady rhythm, then she removed the device from the cool glass and walked swiftly, silently, to the tow truck.

Revving the truck's rumbling engine, she backed into the driveway, behind the girlfriend's Camaro. Then she grabbed a halogen flashlight from the floorboard, hopped out of the cab, and slammed the door. She stamped down the gritty driveway to the rear of the truck, rattled the tow hooks down on their chains, and attached them to the Camaro's frame.

The miniblind flew up.

Just as Dixie flashed the spotlight at the glass, a woman peered out, red hair frizzed into a halo.

"Jimmy!" The windowpane muffled the woman's shriek. "Baby, someone's stealing my car!"

Dixie flipped a switch to start the hydraulic winch. With a metallic *thunk*, the Camaro's tail eased off the ground.

"Jimmy!"

The window slid up with a bang.

"What the hell's going on out there?" A man's voice, thick and gruff.

"Jimmy, baby, do something! They're ripping off my new car!"

"Repo," Dixie called brightly, slapping the Camaro's fender. She aimed the halogen at the beefy male face now glaring furiously from between gauzy curtains. Then she strode to the truck cab, swung up inside, and dialed the nearest police station.

"Flannigan," she said softly. "I've got Jimmy Voller at 221 Burning Oak Drive. We'll wait for you."

By the time the bail jumper yanked his pants on and stormed out the door, a patrol car should've been zipping down the street toward the house. Earlier that night, Dixie had alerted the beat cop that she expected to get a bead on Voller. But as he stomped down the front steps, a hairy hulk in the moonlight, the road remained empty.

Dixie pinned him with the halogen spot.

"Hold it right there, mister. This is a righteous repo. You don't want any trouble." Bluffing. The Camaro was paid up, and Dixie didn't repossess cars, anyway. The tow truck was one of four vehicles she'd acquired cheap from guys like Voller who wouldn't be driving for a long while.

He shaded his eyes against the glare, hesitating. Then he charged toward the truck, shoulder muscles bunching as he knotted his fists.

Watching him storm at her like a raging javelina, Dixie mentally flashed on the .45 in the tool safe—too far to reach. Anyway, Voller wasn't armed. She could handle him. She could.

Snapping open the glove box, she kept one eye on the skip as she grabbed a pair of handcuffs.

"Jimmy!" the girlfriend screeched from the front door. "Baby, don't let them take my car!"

Through the open truck window, Dixie kept the spotlight shining in Voller's eyes. He blinked but charged onward, fists swinging like sledgehammers.

Leaving the window down, Dixie locked the door. She slid backward on the truck seat, snapping the handcuff open.

The thermos fell over. Iced tea soaked her crotch. *Shit!* And still no sign of that patrol car.

Voller seized the door handle. Dixie lunged forward, reached through the open window, and clamped the cuff around his wrist.

"What the fuck!!!?" He jerked his arm back as if stung.

But Dixie yanked the handcuff tight and snapped the other end to the steering wheel.

"Forget your court date, Jimmy? The judge suggested someone should drop by, see you don't forget again."

"Goddammit to hell! This ain't no repo!"

His menacing free hand shot toward her. She ducked out of reach. He kicked the truck door but, barefooted, didn't quite dent it. He howled.

"Jimmy, baby? What's happening out there?" The girlfriend, in a T-shirt and panties, minced across the yard swinging a butcher knife.

Oh, great. "Back inside, lady! Jimmy Baby's going to jail." Dixie cranked up the window until it trapped Voller's shackled arm. His curses grew more colorful.

For a butt-numbing hour, with Voller snorting like an enraged bull and his girlfriend alternately cursing Dixie and pleading tearfully for her to let him go, they waited. Dixie's cell-phone inquiry brought the curt assurance that a patrol car would be dispatched as soon as possible. Finally, a blue-and-white whipped into the driveway.

"Sorry," the officer muttered. "Bunch of 911s came in. Your call shuffled to the bottom."

Six minutes later, with Voller on his way to jail and the Camaro back on the ground where it belonged, Dixie pointed her tow truck down the twenty-mile stretch of highway toward home. Recalling the look on Voller's face when he realized he'd been duped, she couldn't help grinning. Skip tracing did have its moments of satisfaction.

More moments, perhaps, than her decade on the DA's staff. The realization always saddened her. She'd entered the study of law with an expectation of making a difference. Although law certainly was fallible and susceptible to human error, Dixie'd been callow enough to expect truth and justice would prevail.

Truth, she soon discovered, was a pale ghost roaming lost in the courthouse halls. While Dixie sparred with legal swashbucklers over petty technicalities, confirmed criminals swaggered through revolving jailhouse doors. When she could no longer stomach the futile fencing, Dixie'd tucked her sword and shingle into a briefcase and drifted.

Now, three years later, she still drifted, winning minor skirmishes like the one tonight. Her efforts didn't count for much, but at least she could look her five-foot-four-inch self in the mirror and see truth standing behind her.

Truth and the occasional bail bondsman with a fat check.

Dixie clicked on the dome light and snatched up the bank statement from the passenger seat. Holding it so she could watch the deserted road and still scan the page, she tried to recall some withdrawal that would explain the overdraft. Obviously, she'd used the ATM on the fly, without jotting the amount in her checkbook, and the bank had neglected to apply her overdraft protection. Banks *did* occasionally make mistakes.

The only other explanation she liked even less: Someone had snatched more than three thousand dollars from her account. Shot one hell of a big hole in the fee she'd earned that night.

Chapter Two

Historic Richmond awakened like a lazy cat as Dixie stopped her Mustang in front of Texas Citizens Bank. Once a fort, when Stephen F. Austin's vanguard of colonists landed at a bend in the Brazos River, the small town now melded into the fringe of Houston's southwest suburbs, where increasingly more urbanites sought greener, safer, quieter lifestyles.

Despite growth pains, the town's heritage landmarks remained intact. Morton Street, where Dixie now parked, had floated rescue boats during the Great Flood of 1899. A clerk at the county courthouse six blocks away had issued a marriage license to Barney and Kathleen Flannigan, Dixie's adoptive parents; at that same site, a doctor had registered their deaths. And five minutes down the farm-to-market road lay the family home and pecan orchard Dixie'd inherited from them.

This morning she'd cut the trip to *three* minutes. Her overdraft problem loomed like a toothy monster.

She loathed handling money and only sporadically balanced her checkbook. To counter her shortcomings, she used direct-draft banking, carbonless-copy checks, a single credit card, a CPA—inconveniently out of town this week—and a financial planner to handle her investments. She'd rather wrestle the meanest water moccasin on a Texas bayou than haggle over the money missing from her account, but she wanted the problem gone before her self-defense class later that morning.

Ignoring the blinds still drawn shut across the bank's expansive sweep of glass, she stepped from the Mustang and tugged on the door. Locked.

Brown eyes, road-mapped from too little sleep, glared back at her from the sun-silvered glass. Her hair looked as spiky as a clump of swamp weeds in a drought—she'd been too impatient to use the hair dryer—and her hastily laundered jeans and shirt felt damp. Not one of her best grooming days.

As soon as the lock clicked open, she pushed through the door, bank notice gripped in one determined fist—

Three thousand dollars!

—zipped past the startled young woman behind the new-accounts desk—

Gone! How in Hades had a bank with thirty-odd years' experience lost track of her hard-earned money?

—stalked past the teller windows, past the loan desks, past the branch manager's latest painted and coiffed secretary.

"Ms. Flannigan, good morn—wait!" The secretary popped up from behind her desk. "You can't go in there."

Facing Dixie's glare, she backed off.

Len Bacon, a phone at one ear, leaned back in his executive swivel chair, desk as clean as a new notepad. When he saw Dixie, his hound-dog jowls worked his mouth into a smile.

"A customer just came in," Len said into the phone. "Let me call you back." Rising, he glanced behind Dixie to the secretary following at her heels.

"Sorry, Mr. Bacon. I couldn't stop—"

"It's fine, Dana, fine. I'll handle it."

The secretary backed out, closing the door.

Still smiling, Len offered a handshake.

Dixie slapped the bank notice into his palm.

"Three thousand dollars disappeared out of my account."

"Dixie, Dixie, Dixie." The jowls shook amiably as Len wagged his unperturbed head. He patted the air toward a chair, which Dixie ignored. "If there's a discrepancy, I'm sure it's merely a computer error. Computers are wonderful at unexplained mischief." When she continued to glare, he added, "Sit down, sit down. Let's take a look at your file."

Grudgingly, she sank onto a tweed guest chair. Len settled his portly rump onto his leather executive model. The chair *whooshed* in protest.

Turning to the computer on his credenza, he tapped a few keys. Over his shoulder, Dixie watched bright green numbers scroll on a gray screen and recalled the day she'd started banking here—the day after her thirteenth birthday. Barney had brought her in with twenty-seven dollars gift money stuffed in a pink vinyl purse.

"You'll never beg a loan, lass," Barney told her, "if you remember the rule o' thirds. One third o' every dollar goes into a principal account. You daren't touch it, even when wind howls through your roof and you've only one cold potato to fill your belly. You don't touch it."

Before being adopted at twelve, Dixie'd known a day or two when she wouldn't have turned up her nose at a cold potato.

"The second third you tuck into a wishes-and-treasures account, mounting it up for a special treat, a vision that makes your innards quiver when you think about it."

As she wrestled with dividing twenty-seven dollars by three, Dixie's wayward thoughts drifted toward a pair of white boots she'd seen in a magazine —

"And the final third you spend on daily necessities."

"Like what?" Dixie blurted. Carla Jean, her birth mother, had considered hair ribbons and nail polish necessities, though Dixie's underpants might pinch and only a layer of cardboard kept dirt from creeping through the soles of her shoes. At the Flannigans', food, clothes, books, and anything else Dixie needed were hers for the asking. Not that she'd think of asking for something as frivolous as white boots.

"What are necessities, lass? Well, whatever you think they are. Birthday card for a friend? Strawberry sundae with Amy after the movies?"

Fifteen-year-old Amy, Dixie's adoptive sister, had bought her a sundae just last week. Dixie hadn't thought about where the money came from. Should she pay Amy back?

Money . . . her own money . . . money of her very own. Dixie's teenage head suddenly ached. She opened the pink purse and shoved the bills into Barney's broad hands.

"Please. You take care of it for me."

Despite Barney's patient counseling, she'd avoided dealing with money ever since. And the bank officer who'd opened that first "principal" savings account had been a much younger, much thinner Len Bacon.

"Here it is," Len said now. "Here's the problem. A two-thousand-dollar check you deposited, Dixie, was returned from the payee's bank, marked insufficient. My dear, when you made the deposit, you apparently withdrew a thousand dollars of the money in cash." His voice dropped into the sympathetic zone. "When the check was returned to us unpaid, we had to debit your account for the cash you received."

A handful of unopened mail lay in a basket in Dixie's kitchen, where she'd tossed it before her thirty-six-hour skip-chasing flurry.

"That's *one* thousand. What about the other two?"

He scrolled through the numbers and hit a couple of keys.

"More of the same . . . yes, more of the same. You deposited four more checks . . . hmmm, that's interesting, at four different branches in one day . . . each time withdrawing part of the funds in cash. All five deposited checks were returned insufficient."

Five deposits? Hell, she hadn't received that many checks last month. And she never used another branch, except for ATM withdrawals.

"Who are the checks from?"

"Hmmmm, let's see . . . here it is—Cook. All five checks—for different amounts—were written on the personal account of a Mr. James Cook."

"Never heard of him."

Len swiveled to face Dixie. "You're saying you didn't make those deposits?"

"No, I—"

The office door popped open, and Dana stuck her head in.

"Mr. Bacon! This . . . this lady says you're to come out here immediately!"

Through the glass wall separating Len's office from the lobby, Dixie could see people lying prone on the floor. At the teller's window, a smiling, middle-aged woman pointed a revolver at a teller's head. *A holdup?*

Watching Len scurry to comply, Dixie mentally ticked off a half-dozen stupid tactics that might stop the robbery and would likely get someone shot. Her gaze took in the video camera near the lobby ceiling, the frightened teller, the woman with the gun.

She looked familiar . . .

Then Dixie's gaze locked on the desk phone, inches from her hand. Her fingers flexed toward it—

No . . . wait for the right moment.

Through the glass partition, she studied the bank robber. Five-three, late fifties, blond-gray hair stylishly combed. Pleasant, round face. Blue silk dress, matching shoes, gold earrings. Impeccably groomed. Hell, she was the TV version of every kid's Aunt Bea.

Aunt Bea wouldn't actually pull the trigger and blow a teller's head off.

But then, neither would she rob a bank.

Two other Texas Citizens branches had been robbed recently, Dixie recalled—one just yesterday. In both cases, the thief was a woman over fifty—but that woman was *killed* after the second robbery. The police shoot-out had been all over the evening news. One middle-aged female bank robber seemed impossible, but *two?*

As Len hustled behind the tellers' counter to the vault, the robber shifted slightly to watch him. Dixie waited a beat, then reached across the desk, eased the receiver up to open the line, and tapped 9 — 1 —

Something crashed through the glass, *zinged* past Dixie, and slammed into Len's leather chair. *A bullet!* She dropped the phone.

Her heart thumped hard enough to break a rib.

The bank robber, smiling her sweet Aunt Bea smile, shook her head at Dixie and motioned her down to the floor. As Dixie knelt, glimpsing the woman's face from a new angle, she recognized her: not Aunt Bea but Aunt Edna, her own neighbor!

Memories flashed through Dixie's mind: She'd gone to school with Edna Pine's son, Marty. Dated him in high school. Every summer, Edna and her husband Bill had taken the three teenagers—Marty, Dixie, and Amy—camping at Brazos Bend State Park, bowling at Richmond Lanes. The last time Dixie'd seen Edna—a year ago, at Bill's funeral—she'd hugged the widow as she sobbed into a handkerchief.

But even at Bill's funeral Edna hadn't been gussied up as she was now—looking not a day over fifty-five when she must be a decade older. No wonder Dixie hadn't recognized the woman.

Gussied up or not, the Edna Dixie knew was a loving mother, a gentle soul. Kind. Thoughtful. A good neighbor. *No way was Aunt Edna a gun-wielding bank robber.*

Yet, pressed to the floor, Dixie watched through the glass partition as her neighbor of nearly twenty-eight years carried away three canvas bags bulging with stolen money.

Chapter Three

Humming "The Merry Widow," fingers marking perfect waltz time on the steering wheel, the Shepherd of The Light watched for Edna's blue Subaru to exit the bank parking lot. Balanced on his knee was a small, gold-edged notebook where he'd recorded the subject's progress. The careful jottings included phrases he knew would brighten the widow's smile or cause her pain, key words that, used in the right order, would entice her into a lion's cage should he choose to suggest it.

He'd tuned Edna like an exquisite piano. In precisely ninety-two seconds she'd sail past him, eagerly delivering the bank's money.

The only hitch had come when the Shepherd arrived to find a Houston Lighting & Power crew working on a transformer near the drop point. *Subject will realize she must drop the bag outside the workers' line of vision*, he penned, in his precise style. *The minimal script change will not cause her any confusion.*

But as he capped his pen, the Shepherd's pulse quickened. No subject was entirely predictable. Yet, he felt certain his merry widow could easily handle such an insignificant correction in the script, and each test she passed reinforced his belief in the power of positive — or negative — persuasion.

Outside his car window, a brown spider dropped a thread from the splayed fingers of a mimosa leaf and hung suspended, swinging gently in the morning breeze. The Shepherd watched, fascinated, as the slender, jointed legs worked at casting a second thread.

Sometimes the Shepherd liked to imagine himself a mighty arachnid, commander of a giant web spanning the underbelly of the country's control centers, touching the most powerful offices, the most influential homes. Thrum any strand and the entire web vibrated.

He'd learned about vibrations on an October afternoon when he was nine years old. School let out early. Whooping with glee and bounding with energy, he rode his bike the long way home, knowing his mother wouldn't arrive from her Bible study group until later. She'd promised to decide today whether he'd get the new racing bike in Johnson's shop window.

But passing the Cactus Bar, he noticed something that caused him to brake hard and pull over into the shadows, the gossamer fabric of an idea materializing in his brain.

During one of his parents' arguments, loud enough to hear throughout the house, his father had promised to stop gambling. Yet, here he came now, out of the Cactus Bar & Truck Stop. And the scowl dragging the corners of his mouth southward suggested his pockets had been plucked clean.

A moment later one of his father's gambling buddies exited, shoving a wad of bills deep in his pocket. A woman clung to the man's arm like a sand burr to socks. Both laughed, heading toward a row of cabins. His father tossed a hard look after the pair, then staggered to his Plymouth sedan.

The bike seemed to move on its own. Rolling right up to the car, its front wheel bumped his father's leg.

"What the hell?" His father's billfold fell to the dirt.

"Sorry, Dad." But as he picked up the empty leather wallet, he resisted a smile, recalling his mother's words during the noisy argument . . . *If I hear you're gambling again, I'm calling a lawyer and filing for divorce.* "What's wrong with a friendly poker game," his father had whined. *Friendly? Your friends lining their pockets with* my *money? I won't have it.*

Dusting off the billfold, he asked, "Did Mom talk to you about the blue racer?"

"The blue what?" His father's words sounded mushy and smelled of the Scotch whiskey he liked to drink. "You mean that bicycle you've been on about?"

"In Johnson's Sport Shop. She'll buy it if you say to." He let his gaze drift toward the bar, where two more of his father's gambling pals had stepped out the door.

"You've got a bicycle. Perfectly good one." But his father darted an anxious glance at the two men, another at the couple, still laughing as they entered a cabin, then back at his son. "That racer, boy, that's a lot of money," he added, as if the cost hadn't already been discussed at length.

"Yes, sir. My birthday's only a month—"

"Your mother worries you're not mature enough to take care of a bicycle that expensive. Not a toy, it's a responsibility."

"Yes, sir."

"What do you know about . . . *responsibility*?" His father spit the word at him, harsh and biting.

"Keep my room picked up. Get good grades." Ever since the blue racer appeared in the shop window, he'd been cleaning his room and doing his homework without being nagged. "Take out the trash." He'd only missed one night this week.

The crease between his father's eyes sharpened like a hatchet mark. "Your mother has a great deal on her mind these days, church studies, the new housekeeper. I don't like worrying her about . . . things."

"No, sir." Some of his parents' noisiest arguments concerned the amount of time his mother spent at church. "But the racer—" He stopped suggestively.

"There's no need to trouble your mother about my stopping off here. For one *drink*."

"No, sir."

"Boy your age, old enough to understand *responsibility*, doesn't worry his mother. You won't be bothering her about . . . anything?"

"No, sir."

They stared at each other in the afternoon heat. Sweat beads hung from the bristly hairs above his father's ears; his eyes, small and green and hard, did not blink. Finally, his father looked away.

"Guess I can put a bug in your mother's ear about that bicycle, tell her you're grown-up enough. I'll talk to her tonight."

"Great! Thanks, Dad!"

Later that week, as he zipped along on the gleaming blue racer, the situation between his mother and father and the gambling popped repeatedly into his mind. He suspected his mother would've reached a different decision about the new bike if not for his father's encouragement . . . if not for that chance ride past the Cactus Bar & Truck Stop. He filed away the experience to examine again from time to time. To squeeze every bit of learning out of it. *Thrum.*

A week later, at lunch, he sat beside Penny Hatcher, the most awkward, smelliest girl in his fourth-grade class. No prize himself—short, skinny, with big ears, freckles so dark and numerous he looked diseased—he knew well how it felt to be snubbed. When Laura Shane, the class beauty, strolled by their table and "accidentally" tipped over Penny's milk, ruining her sandwich, he offered Penny half his lunch.

At first, she was dubious. No one *ever* treated Penny kindly, probably not even at home. When she realized he wasn't going to snatch the sandwich back at the last moment or tease her in some other monstrous way, she turned to him with the most astonishing look.

"Grateful" was how he eventually tagged it, as his father had been grateful that his mother never found out about the continued gambling. But at that moment he only knew, instinctively, that Penny Hatcher would do practically anything he asked because he'd shown her that small courtesy. *Ask her for something*, the voice nagged, the voice he'd come to think of as his racer voice. *Ask her now.*

But he couldn't think of anything.

"I'm failing arithmetic," he'd stammered, finally. "And you're the best in class. I wish I was as smart as you."

"Really?" Penny blushed. "I'd be glad to help you."

Thrum.

Over the months ahead, he thought of Penny as a banjo that needed only a talented hand at the strings. He learned exactly what to say and do to intensify that look in her pale eyes.

"Is that a new dress? The color looks great on you."

Penny started washing more often after that and doing something different with her hair.

"I like it curly," he told her. "You could be in the movies."

She laughed, but walked prouder and spoke up more often in class.

"Your oral report," he promised, "will be the best of anyone's. Read it to me again for practice."

By the end of the school year, Penny had earned respect from the teacher as well as her classmates. She'd never win any beauty contests, but she no longer sat alone at lunch. And the look in her eyes when she gazed at him bordered on worship.

In return, he rarely asked anything of Penny. A week before summer break, he decided it was time.

"Did you see that catcher's mitt at Johnson's Sport Shop? I can't believe Mom won't buy it for me. I need that mitt for tryouts next week."

Of course, Mom *would* buy it—he knew by now that all it'd take was casually mentioning the Cactus Bar & Truck Stop when Dad was in the room—but he wanted to test Penny's gratitude. Three days later, she gave him the catcher's mitt wrapped in a brown gift box. He never asked how she got it.

Over the following summer, he thought a lot about that experiment with Penny, never doubting that his friendship and coaching had elevated her from class embarrassment to class monitor. If he could do that with Penny, why not with someone more . . . promising? *Thrum.*

During the next four years, he singled out seven classmates for special attention. The girls were by far more compliant than the boys, but he sensed the key lay not so much in gender as in some other quality he hadn't quite identified, at least not consciously. Operating mostly by instinct, he created a network of devoted disciples, learned to play each one like an instrument, discovering when to strum a chord and when to thump it. By the end of grade school, his network had helped him acquire answers to a number of math tests and kept him supplied with the latest sports equipment.

In high school, he discovered similar tactics that worked with select teachers. And he remained ever watchful for opportune situations. He found the gym teacher's peephole into the girls' dressing room. He caught Jane Greer letting other guys feel her up while her boyfriend ran laps at football practice. He discovered the marijuana hidden in Ms. Skinner's bottom desk drawer.

At college, his web encompassed every department on campus. Powerful enough to amass him a sizable bank balance, it got him laid as often as he wanted, prompted an associate professor's dismissal, and encouraged a sophomore's suicide. That last unfortunate incident forced him to relocate, sever all connections with his past, and change his name. Now his web reached from coast to coast and deep into the national bureaucracy. Every experiment captured another gossamer layer of knowledge toward assuming control of more power than any U.S. president had ever dreamed of.

The brown spider swung a strand from a third mimosa leaf. The shimmering threads defined an area roughly thirty inches in diameter—ambitious, for such a small arachnid.

When Edna's blue Subaru zipped out of the bank parking lot right on schedule and passed through the intersection, the Shepherd meticulously penned the fact in his notebook. He waited ten seconds, allowing a pickup truck and two cars to pass between them, then pulled into the street. The Subaru turned at the boarded-up strip center as planned, to circle behind and exit on the side street.

Would she drop the money in the clump of weeds behind the old pharmacy, as rehearsed? Or would she make the adjustment and drop it outside the workers' line of sight?

Spying the canvas bags lying in the shadows four yards beyond the original drop spot, he smiled, braking just long enough to pull the bags into his car. The merry widow had performed outstandingly. He recalled how determined she'd been to succeed at this assignment. All in all, Edna had been much happier over these past months than when he'd first met her: He prided himself on that. Too bad her usefulness had come to an end.

Thrum.

Chapter Four

The officer interviewing Dixie couldn't have been more than thirty days out of the academy, she decided. His shirt, so crisp it could stand on its own, retained the absolute blue of uniform fabric not yet faded from laundering. And judging from three fresh nicks on his face, he'd shaved after a bad night. His voice held the slow twang of East Texas. Officer G. Tobler.

"You said your name is . . . ?"

"Dixie Flannigan." *For the third time.*

Dixie's mind hadn't yet assimilated the rush of events following the robbery—tellers babbling, a customer sobbing, Len Bacon patting the air, assuring all would be "fine, folks, absolutely fine," if everyone simply remained calm. The young officer's attention kept straying to his equally young partner communicating by radio with a patrol car on the Southwest Freeway—where the real action was unfolding in a high-speed chase. Apparently, someone had triggered an alarm, and a Richmond patrol unit had locked on to Edna's Subaru. When she refused to pull over, the chase left Richmond, picking up patrol cars in two additional jurisdictions before entering Houston city limits. HPD assistance brought more units, including a helicopter—against one Subaru and a sixty-something woman who must've gone totally nuts.

She hadn't a prayer of outrunning them.

Pull over, Edna. But as Dixie continued eavesdropping on the chase, a nasty, undisciplined little voice deep down inside her cheered, *Go, Edna, go!*

"Ma'am, what were you doing alone in the manager's office?"

Dixie'd answered this question before, too, but she repeated her explanation, her gaze drifting toward a clock. Fifty-six minutes until her self-defense class. Not that Officer G. Tobler's interview wasn't important, but the women Dixie taught were all victims of abuse or, for other good reasons, fearful of attack. The unexplained absence of their instructor could send them wailing back to their support groups.

"And you say the perpetrator fired through the glass after you dialed 911?"

"Before I could finish—"

The radio captured the officer's attention again. From the crackling communication between patrol cars, the dispatcher, and Tobler's partner, Dixie deciphered that the Subaru had exited the freeway and finally pulled over. *Good, Edna. Now, tell the nice officers it was all a mistake. The devil made you do it, or late menopause craziness, or—*

POP! POP! POP! crackled from the radio, then "OFFICER DOWN!"

Dixie groaned. "Oh, Edna, no!"

Officer Tobler stared at her.

"Ma'am, are you acquainted with the suspect?"

Before Dixie could answer, more shots sounded. She held her breath. The next words were like stepping from a humid, sunny day into an open freezer.

"SUSPECT DOWN." Dixie's stomach turned queasy. *Down . . . did that mean dead?*

"I have to get there," she told Tobler in a voice she hoped held the snap of command.

Maybe it was the rookie's own eagerness to be involved in the drama, or maybe it was the fact that Dixie knew most of the senior officers in the Richmond Police Department, but Tobler radioed the patrol officer who'd originally tagged the Subaru. After a moment, a voice came back with a brusque order to escort the witness to the scene of the shooting. *The suspect has no identification,* Dixie figured. *They need my assistance.*

Praying she'd been mistaken, that a trick of light had betrayed her into seeing Edna's face on the shoulders of a stranger, Dixie hurried with Tobler to his car. Then realization finally trickled through to her resistant brain cells. If the suspect were still alive, Tobler would've been instructed to take Dixie to the hospital.

Her steps faltered beside the police car. When the officer opened the door, the sharp scent of floral freshener engulfed her, and Tobler's earnest young face suddenly looked too eager, his black shoes too shiny, too new. He was too goddamn ready to sharpen his experience on the death of an old lady who'd baked the best peanut-butter cookies ever stolen from a cookie jar. Dixie didn't want to stare down at her neighbor's dead face and pronounce her a thief—or worse—if the wounded officer had died, too, a capital murderer.

Tobler's insistent grip on Dixie's arm urged her onto the passenger seat. He shut the door and circled to the driver's side, speaking quietly into his cell phone.

Does he think I'm an accomplice?

Dixie shrugged it off. On the drive, she almost convinced herself it would not be Edna. *Whoops, sorry, guys. Sure looked like my neighbor, there in the bank, but out here in daylight . . .*

It was Edna. Even without seeing her face, Dixie instantly recognized the heart-shaped mole scar on her neck. Marty had insisted his mother have the mole tested after Dixie's adoptive mother died of cancer. An inch-long, gray hair grew from the scar. With Edna's snappy new clothes and expert makeup, the hair looked grotesque.

A bilious knot lodged in Dixie's throat. She looked away from the corpse, scarcely hearing Tobler's comments to the ranking sergeant. Her gaze slid around the secured area. When any HPD officer discharged a side arm, especially if injury or death resulted, a crime scene instantly became enormously complicated. The officer's supervisor appeared, along with his union lawyer, Internal Affairs, Homicide, and the DA's Civil Rights Division. The HPD training team, self-billed as Heckle and Jeckle, occasionally showed up. Today the whole gang had gathered.

Outside a yellow-tape perimeter, the media crowded close with cameras and microphones. Civilian vehicles rolled slowly along the nearby freeway, rubbernecking, causing traffic to back up. A few cars had pulled off and stopped.

Dixie realized she stood at the center of the crowd, still grappling with the idea that the neighbor she knew growing up could be the same woman who now lay dead at her feet, the same woman who just minutes ago had calmly held a gun to a teller's head. The images refused to merge.

A few feet away stood a tight blue circle of officers: the shooters. Male. Female. From a medley of jurisdictions. Some appeared stunned. A few looked as ill as Dixie felt. Others wore hard, insolent veneers.

Taking two long strides, Dixie confronted a male HPD officer who looked totally alert, yet horrified.

"Nine hotshot shooters against one old lady?" The words felt puny leaving her lips, shoved out by a cold rage. "Isn't this how that robbery ended yesterday in Webster?"

The astonished officer opened his mouth to reply—

But Dixie pressed on. "Don't you idiots *talk* to one another between jurisdictions?"

A hand grasped her upper arm.

"Flannigan, what's going on here?" HPD Homicide Sergeant Ben Rashly tugged her away from the officer.

Dixie tried to yank her arm from his grip. When he didn't let go, she allowed herself to be pulled aside.

"They could've handled it better, Rash! She didn't have to goddamn die."

He glared back at her. "You know that woman or not, Flannigan?"

"I've known her family since I was a kid." The sharp burst of words had loosened something inside her. "Her name is Edna Pine. Next of kin is Marty Pine, her son, owns an art gallery in Dallas—Essence or Pleasance or something—and Edna wouldn't do this, Rash, not the robbery, not the shooting, and she never wore high-heeled goddamn shoes in her life, at least not . . . not . . . *Shit!* She was a good person. Something's wrong here, Rash. Totally wrong!"

"Okay, okay." His scowl softened. "Let's move along now and let these people finish up." Taking her arm, he led her toward his unmarked sedan. "We can talk downtown, if you want."

"I can't go downtown. I have a class to teach in fourteen minutes. We can talk here."

The sight of Ben Rashly's strong, square hands filling his pipe, and the familiar scent of Middleton's Cherry Blend tobacco, dropped a layer of normality against the morning's horror. Dixie'd worked with Ben while she was with the DA's office. They'd developed a mutual respect as he bounced from Fraud to Sex Crimes to Accident Division. A year ago, he'd transferred to Homicide.

"Actually, Flannigan, we're glad to have the quick ID, so we can move on this." He took her statement and let her go, knowing where to find her if he had more questions.

And he *would* have more questions. Dixie only wished she had more answers.

Chapter Five

Rose Yenik perched on a straight-backed chair in a plain room, two feet from her tiny television, and watched a news flash that had interrupted her favorite soap. For a sizable chunk of the year, Rose's sixty-fifth year on God's earth, she had occupied this room at appointed intervals. She found the plainness soothing. Natural pine furniture, white bedding, and a single garden window provided a blank canvas for thought. Rose spent hours at that window. But her church allotted only an hour a day for television, so when the dolly-faced news anchor broke in with a flash report, Rose was at first annoyed.

Now she stared at the screen, unwilling to believe her ears. First Lucy, now Edna . . . how the dickens had both women failed so pitifully? Of course, the newswoman didn't yet know it was Edna she reported about so dispassionately. But Rose knew.

And what good were those roving videocams when all they showed of the shooting scene was another reporter, with the crowd milling behind?

A little square picture of Lucy popped onto the screen.

"*Last week a similar robbery occurred at a Houston branch of Texas Citizens Bank. Yesterday a robbery at the Webster branch ended in the shooting death of Lucy Aaron Ames . . .*"

"Oh, my good friends," Rose murmured, reaching a trembling hand to touch the screen. The first stickup had gone without a hitch last week. Lucy's insider information came through as good as gold . . . as good as the sixty-seven thousand and change that now lined the church's coffer.

"It'll be a snap," Lucy had promised in her matter-of-fact style. "Bank employees are trained not to risk lives. We go in quiet, we go out fast. The money is government-insured, and we'll certainly make better use of it than Uncle Sam ever has."

Amen to that.

But then the bank's security people must have wised up and changed tactics. Lucy was dead, and now Edna. Dead.

Rose pondered that for a spell, her myopic gaze resting on the TV screen, where the pretty anchor chatted earnestly with the off-site reporter. Rose realized she would never see Lucy or Edna again, not even at the funeral. The Shepherd would not allow it. Too risky.

A chilly fear wormed insistently into Rose's head. Her eyes misted, and she felt suddenly alone.

Retrieving her eyeglasses from beside the television—she preferred watching up close rather than through the trifocal lenses—Rose placed them on her face. As she stood, an old back pain she hadn't felt for months gave her a pinch.

"I'm strong enough to do what needs to be done," she whispered.

Her leather slippers *shush*ed on the pine floor as she walked to the closet.

I can do what needs to be done.

She removed a gray plastic case from the closet shelf and opened it on the bed. Inside, in a rubber-foam nest, lay her own Colt .38 Special, cleaned and ready to load.

I can do . . .

Her hands trembled as she lifted it, though she'd held the nickel-plated revolver many times in her hours of practice. Steadying the gun in both hands, she aimed at the television.

. . . what needs to be done.

And squeezed the trigger.

"Bam," Rose said.

Chapter Six

"Were you scared?"

Bettye, a high school librarian, was Dixie's most dedicated student. Twice a week Dixie volunteered a ninety-minute class at a women's health center. The center provided space and students. Thanks to one of Dixie's corporate contacts, the space now sported mirrored walls, bright blue workout mats, and a heavy punching bag for practice.

News of the robbery had already reached the center when Dixie arrived.

"Scared?" Dixie addressed the librarian, but it was impossible not to feel the weight of the demanding eyes of all five women. "Of course I was scared. People were in danger. *I* was in danger."

"Why you didn't kick the effin' gun out of the mofo's hand?" This from Lureen, class smartass, cleaning up her language just enough to comply with center rules.

But her question was legitimate. Dixie taught them to defend against knives and guns.

Bettye, the librarian, had joined the class after stumbling upon a pair of students engaged in a gun sale one evening. Her sudden appearance sent the seller scurrying away, but the buyer had whirled in rage and struck Bettye repeatedly, breaking her collarbone. In the weeks it took the bone to heal, the librarian lost forty-two pounds, applied for a concealed-weapon permit, and signed up for defense lessons.

Lureen, mother of two fatherless kids about the same age as the one who'd attacked Bettye, ran a convenience store on the graveyard shift. Barely five feet tall but strong and savvy, Lureen had joined the class at the store owner's insistence.

"Maybe Jackie Chan, with a twenty-million-dollar movie budget," Dixie told her students, "would try to kick through a glass wall. But that's not the real world. Besides, what's the first thing we learned?"

"Ain't no effin' fool come at us with a gun or a knife who *deserves* to live."

"Well, yes, that's one thing, Lureen, but not the first thing."

Silence, as the five women sitting on blue mats stole glances at one another, searching for the right response.

"C'mon, guys," Dixie prodded. "Defending yourself starts with head muscle."

Joan, the battered wife of a prominent Houston physician, spoke up. "Knowing *when* to act is every bit as important as knowing what to do."

Joan had learned that lesson the hard way, refusing to leave her husband until one of his drunken assaults cost her an eye.

"*When* to act," Dixie said, "is usually instantly. The faster the better. But not always. And when the choice is between losing money or losing a life—there's no choice. No amount of money or property is worth getting killed." *Especially when it's bank money. Insured money.* In the end, though, someone *had* gotten killed: Aunt Edna.

"Ain't no granny bandit robbin' my effin' store." Lureen jumped to her feet and shadow-boxed the mirror.

"Why would she do it?" Bettye asked. "A woman of her class? Her age?"

"Her *class*?" Lureen threw a shadow punch at Bettye. "What *class* you think be robbin' banks?"

"There were *two* women robbers," Joan interjected. "And *three* robberies. Do you think the two women worked together?"

"Course they workin' together. Effin' Dumb and Dumber."

"No, Lucy Ames taught school before she worked at that bank," Bettye pointed out. "I'm sure she wasn't dumb."

"Oh? How the fuck she goan spend that money—sorry—how she goan spend her effin' money dead?"

"Maybe it was some kind of suicide pact," Joan said quietly.

The statement stunned everyone silent. The theory made a strange kind of sense, Dixie admitted. Edna may not've been a schoolteacher, like Lucy Ames, the robber gunned down the previous day, but she was smart enough to know that aiming a weapon at a police officer amounted to suicide. Had Edna been so lonely after Bill's death that she no longer wanted to live? Barney Flannigan had mourned his dead wife for only eighteen months before passing away, dying of what Dixie still believed was loneliness.

"Enough chatter, ladies. Twenty-seven minutes and only your jaw muscles are moving." Dixie strapped on a padded helmet. "What's your best weapon?"

"Our minds," Bettye mumbled.

"And your best advantage as a woman?"

"Surprise. No effin' bastard expects a pussy to stomp his ass."

Dixie couldn't have put it better. Less crudely, maybe. "Where do you aim?"

"His nuts," Joan said, with more anger than usual. "Smash his coconuts, he won't be thinking about sex."

"Coconuts?" Lureen hooted. "Filberts is more like it. Show me a man wit' coconuts, maybe I don't fight too effin' hard."

"The crotch is okay, if you have a clear target," Dixie told them. "But a man instinctively protects his manhood. Joints are better targets. Knee, elbow, wrist. Joints are fragile. Sweep a knee and he's down."

Lureen feigned a kick at Joan's knee, barely missing. Joan came back with a side kick to Lureen's hip, connecting.

"Hey! Easy there," Dixie told them. "Screw around and somebody will get hurt. Take that energy out on the bag. We'll pair up later."

But Dixie was glad to see Joan getting some spunk. For the next ten minutes, she watched them all take a turn kicking and punching the heavy bag.

"Don't make the mistake of thinking only men can be dangerous," she reminded them. *Hadn't Edna proved as much that morning?* "Or that every man is out to hurt you. Being prepared means not having to run scared."

"Fuck, girl, *you* were scared." Lureen feigned a jab at Dixie and grinned. "Whyn't you kick Granny in the knee?"

Dixie let a weary sigh escape, then grasped Lureen's arm and whipped her around into a choke hold. Slipping a revolver from her pocket, she pressed it to the woman's temple.

"One flinch of my trigger finger and brains splatter the wall. What do you do?"

Lureen tensed to break the hold, but Dixie kept her in check. "Huh-uh, not you. Them." She faced the other four women. "How do you save your friend?" she demanded.

Joan shifted her weight, telegraphing the coming kick. Dixie pulled the trigger.

Snap! The mirrored room amplified the tiny sound of the gun's hammer harmlessly striking the disabled firing pin. Instantly, all five women sobered.

Dixie released Lureen and reviewed the value of knowing not only what to do but when *not* to do it. She glanced up to find Mike Tesche and two of his students watching from the doorway. Mike taught yoga, meditation, and a lot of touchy-feely crap — useful as hell in a civilized society, but on mean streets none of it kept a woman from getting killed.

Wearing his usual navy-and-white baseball cap to control a mop of unruly curls, blue tweed blazer over a Dallas Cowboys sweatshirt, jeans, bulky white gym shoes, he grinned at her, teacher to teacher. Then he rolled his eyes comically at her dramatic demonstration. Dixie couldn't help grinning back.

Mike dressed like a kid who'd never quite left college, although Dixie felt sure he was close to her own age. She appreciated his friendly good humor, providing the first cheerful moment she'd had all morning.

But his students' frowns suggested that Dixie's teaching method might, with improvement, measure up to barbaric.

Minutes later, as Dixie ambled toward the showers, Mike fell in step alongside. He'd changed into his workout clothes.

"You were tense in there. Come join us and chill awhile."

"Thanks." Dixie could hear the mellow strains of Mozart—or was it Bach?—seeping from Mike's meditation-and-exercise room. She felt tempted. But her pager had recorded seven calls during class, five from the house of Amy and Carl Royal. Her family had probably seen the news. "Another time, maybe. Right now I need to check in with my sister."

He grinned, a lighthearted, boyish flash of perfect white teeth in his not-so-perfect face. Mike wasn't at all handsome, but he had a sincere smile and remarkable green eyes that sparkled with merriment while at the same time radiating intelligence and understanding.

"If Sis is half as intense as you are, Dixie Flannigan, I wouldn't keep her waiting. Did you receive our invitation?"

Dixie paused, then recalled the card from The Winning Stretch lying with the other mail on her kitchen table. The overdraft notice had eclipsed Mike's invitation.

"I got it," she told him. "Some kind of health . . . thing . . . going on this weekend?"

He chuckled. "Sundown Ceremony. You *will* come, won't you?"

If the invitation had been for lunch or a beer or a racquetball game or practically anything one-on-one, Dixie might've taken him up on it. For the past three months, the important man in her life had spent more time at his beach house communing with seagulls than he'd spent with her. Dixie liked Mike, what little she knew of him, and this wasn't the first time he'd invited her to one of his weekend gatherings.

"Mike, today is not good for making decisions." Continuing toward the showers, she told him briefly about the robbery and shooting.

He touched her arm. "Your neighbor, Dixie, you said her name was Edna Pine. Blond hair? Sixtyish?"

"You knew her?"

He nodded thoughtfully, and rotated a ring on his right ring finger. A single garnet surrounded by diamonds, the design looked custom-crafted and exquisitely masculine. Dixie liked it.

"Edna was a student for a while. A good student."

Dixie's surprise lasted only long enough for her to remember that Mike instructed classes at most of the health club chains in the city, and Edna hadn't lost all that weight sitting on her duff.

"When did you last see her?"

He pursed his lips in a soft whistle, deepening the cleft in his chin. "A month ago? Seems about right, but I'd have to check my records."

Questions tumbled into Dixie's mind. *Did Edna seem despondent? Was she friendly with any of her classmates? Did she ever mention knocking off the local bank?*

"Mike," a girlish voice called down the hallway. A trim woman with shining blond hair stood outside his training room. "I've finished the warm-up exercises. Ready to take over?"

He hesitated, turning back to Dixie. The blonde stood her ground, watching.

"Go ahead," Dixie told him. "I need to talk to my sister before she starts phoning the hospitals. Can we chat later?"

"Anytime." He touched her arm again, lightly. "And, Dixie, you've a friend here if you need one."

"Thanks," she called as he jogged back down the hall.

Nice man, Dixie thought. *Damn* nice body.

Chapter Seven

"Why didn't you kick butt and take the gun away?" This time the question came in the adolescent bullfrog voice of Dixie's twelve-year-old nephew, Ryan.

"Never got close enough." Over the previous semester Dixie'd trained Ryan and his schoolmates in a gentler version of the same Israeli defense techniques she taught to women. The private school her nephew attended remained blessedly free of violence, but Dixie believed children should learn to take care of themselves as early as possible. "Guess I needed you there, kid, to snap-kick that glass wall out of my way."

"Yuh!" He jumped from his chair and shadow-kicked his bedroom wall, then popped a series of jabs at a Grim Reaper poster. "Hee-yuh!"

Dixie looped an arm around his neck to wrestle a cheek smooch, which was getting harder now that the imp had learned evasive moves. And jeez—he'd grown since Christmas! Why hadn't she noticed? She succeeded in planting a nice wet one on his temple.

"Aunt Dix!" He eeled out of her grasp and plopped onto his chair.

As she knuckled his head, Dixie caught a glimpse of her name on his computer monitor.

My Aunt Dixie made those bank robbers eat their shorts.

"Ryan, only *one* bank robber—a woman, and—"

"You saved the manager and all those people from getting killed!"

"Hey, guy, I know you want me to be the hero in this story, but that's not quite the way it went down." After the bullet smashed through Len's office wall, Dixie'd stayed on the floor. Later, as she left the shooting scene after identifying

Edna's body, a news photographer had captured her face on video, and her family had indeed seen the TV coverage. Three of the seven pager messages during defense class had come from Ryan, two more from his mother. Returning the calls, Dixie'd calmed Amy with a few reassuring words, but Ryan refused to be satisfied with less than a play-by-play account—and now Dixie knew why: He'd bragged to his E-mail buddies that he had "inside" dope. Ryan's enthusiasm for his aunt's escapades never flagged.

"One bank robber," she reaffirmed now. "And no heroics. If I did anything smart, Ryan, it was staying still, allowing the woman to take the money and go, so that no one in the bank got hurt."

"Was she like Juliette Lewis in *Natural Born Killers*, all crazy and mean and waving her gun around?"

Crazy and mean?

"No, Edna was . . ." *An off-key voice leading goofy camp songs when their two families drove to Brazos Bend. A sturdy arm stirring a pot of stew over the open fire or knocking spiders off the tent. A nervous thumb whisking dirt from Dixie's cheek after a bad fall.* "Edna Pine was someone your mother and I knew growing up, Ryan." Someone Dixie had loved like an aunt. "Someone who must've taken a very wrong turn . . . or had a very good reason for what she did this morning."

Her nephew's face screwed up in concentration. He craved juicy details to convey to his friends.

"The robber was coolheaded and determined," Dixie admitted. "And a pretty good marksman." That bullet had missed by a hair. Was the miss intentional?

Ryan's fingers danced over the keyboard. When Dixie saw him type "cold-blooded killer" in his E-mail message, she thumped the back of his head and left the room.

In the kitchen she found her sister sliding chocolate-chip cookies from a baking sheet to a platter. Amy baked only when she was upset, then she turned out enough goodies to give the neighborhood a sugar high for weeks. Through the oven window Dixie saw a sheet cake rising. A pecan pie cooled on the counter. And the three-course lunch Dixie'd been promised looked ready to eat. A busy morning in the Royal kitchen.

"It *wasn't* Aunt Edna," Amy declared, offering Dixie a warm cookie. "You were mistaken. We all have twins, don't we? Didn't I see that on A&E? Look-alikes. James Dean, Marilyn Monroe, all those Elvises? Why not an Edna Pine look-alike? I called Marty in Dallas and told him not to worry, it was *not* his mother, no matter what the police say. This is all a terrible mistake. You'll sort it out, Dixie, and he'll see."

"*I'll* sort it out? You didn't really tell Marty that, did you?" Amy's constant big-sister complaint since Dixie left the DA's staff was the danger of working as a bounty hunter. She claimed it would someday get Dixie killed. Now Amy *wanted* her sister meddling in a robbery-shooting investigation?

"Marty's like family, Dixie. He was on his way to the airport, and he's coming straight over here for a late lunch, as soon as the cops stop rubber-hosing him."

"Amy, get a grip." Gently, Dixie took the egg her sister was about to break into a bowl and set it back in the carton. "It was Edna's car, Edna's mole scar. It was Edna." *With two bullet holes in her chest and a piece of her cheek missing.*

Dixie swallowed back a sudden surge of bile as she envisioned Aunt Edna lying in a pool of blood beside her Subaru. *Wasn't there anything you could've done, Ms. Butt-kicking Instructor?*

Dixie blinked away the image. Though thinner and younger-looking than she'd been a year ago at Bill Pine's funeral, the dead woman had definitely been Edna Pine. Grasping Amy's arm, Dixie guided her toward the den.

But Amy jerked away and lifted the receiver on the kitchen phone. "Edna is no bank robber. I've left messages for her to call us as soon as she gets home. She's probably at a movie—you remember how much Edna likes movies."

With the phone to her ear, Amy tucked Dixie's unkempt hair back, plucked lint off her shirt, smoothed her collar. Fussy, even for Amy. Dixie found herself praying that Edna would miraculously pick up the phone.

"Hello! Aunt Edna, this is Amy Royal. You won't believe the awful thing that's happened here—"

For one dizzying instant Dixie thought Amy was right: The whole episode *had* been a weird mistake. Then she realized Amy was talking to Edna's answering machine.

When her sister banged the phone down in frustration, Dixie wrapped an arm around Amy's waist and once again tugged her toward the den—less forcefully this time. Amy's warm, cushiony body smelled of vanilla. Her blond hair, cut neckline-short for the rapidly approaching summer, already showed sun-bleached streaks from working in the yard. Fiddling with a silver pendant, she relaxed into Dixie's embrace as they walked.

"Remember the weekend Aunt Edna took us all to Astroworld?" Amy asked. "You, me . . . Marty. She wouldn't get on the roller coaster, but Marty teased her until she agreed to try it, trembling like a wet Chihuahua—"

"Then we couldn't get her off the thing. I believe she had more fun than we did."

"*You* didn't have much fun. The rides made you sick."

"Edna gave a lot of her time to us kids," Dixie recalled.

"She's been lonely since Bill died. Edna needs people around. Shame on us for not going to see her more often. Carl!" Her husband's balding head barely showed above his leather recliner. "We're going out to visit Edna tonight, as soon as she calls back."

"Amy—" Dixie wished her sister would stop speaking about the woman in the present tense. Amy's ability to dismiss anything she didn't want to believe could be mind-boggling at times.

"Keep it down back there," Carl groused, turning up the TV volume. "I want to hear the news."

"*In a police shoot-out today a second Granny Bandit . . .*"

Amy tried to pull away and head back to her kitchen.

"No, sit!" Dixie tugged her onto the sofa. Brutal truth might be the best medicine.

On the screen, patrol cars clustered around Edna's Subaru. Reporters, uniformed officers, and plainclothes investigators obscured the camera's view of the body on the asphalt as paramedics wheeled a gurney to a waiting ambulance. *The wounded officer*, Dixie figured. They'd whisked him away just as she arrived on the scene.

But police were either keeping the details of the robbery under wraps or were as dumbfounded as the media claimed.

"*A suspect in the Texas Citizens Bank robbery that occurred in Richmond this morning engaged police from four jurisdictions in a twenty-two-mile pursuit that ended in Houston. The suspect was pronounced dead after police returned gunfire. The stolen money has not been recovered.*"

"Branch that size wouldn't have but sixty, seventy thousand on hand," Carl commented. He fancied himself another Rukeyser when it came to money. "Not enough cash to go to jail for, let alone get yourself killed. Common crook, maybe, needing his heroin fix, might risk it. A woman *might*, I suppose, if she'd let the taxes run up on her property and expected to be put on the street. What I'm saying, a *desperate* woman. You were there, Dixie. Did Edna look desperate? And what happened to the dough?"

Having been on the scene, Dixie was naturally expected to know such things.

"I saw her carry the bags out. I guess she got rid of them somewhere."

"When?" Carl pointed to the television. "Said they caught sight of her a mile from the bank, stayed behind her all the way into Houston. Richmond's not a big town. If she stopped off, someone would've noticed."

"Would they? People drive around locked in air-conditioned vehicles behind tinted windows."

"Amy, didn't the woman live right in the neighborhood all those years? I'm saying people *knew* her, knew her car. In small towns, people still howdy their neighbors."

A phantom of guilt edged into Dixie's thoughts as she recalled the night Barney and Kathleen brought her home from a halfway house. Edna, Bill, and Marty had immediately bustled over to meet Dixie. Fresh from a sexually abusive environment, Dixie'd found love and healing among the Flannigans and the Pines. Now that she'd moved back into the Flannigan farmhouse, Dixie once again lived next door to Edna, yet she'd howdied her neighbor no more than a half-dozen times in the past two years. *A woman you loved like an aunt . . . and that's all you could manage?*

"Carl, these days most Richmond residents are busy driving to and from Houston," she muttered. Besides, what did he know? Semiretired, her brother-in-law spent most of his time on the golf course or at home playing the stock market on his personal computer.

"The dough from that second robbery in Webster," Carl persisted. "They haven't found that, either. And that Ames woman *worked* at Texas Citizens. She and Edna must've been in cahoots."

Dixie couldn't disagree with his reasoning. If both women managed to dump the money bags before police caught up with them minutes later, it must've been part of the plan all along.

"I'd wager the cops are swarming all over Edna's house right now," Carl continued. "Searching for the loot."

"They wouldn't!" Amy looked horrified. "Tramp through her home?" She swept a frantic gaze around her own den, as if expecting to see storm troopers crashing through.

"If they'd found any money at the Ames house," Dixie mused, "we'd have heard about the recovery. Which means there must be at least one other person in the—"

"Don't say it!" Amy slapped Dixie's thigh.

"Ow! Say what?"

"That awful name the newspeople are using."

"Granny Bandit Gang." Carl chuckled.

Amy batted his arm. "It's not funny!"

"You thought it was funny yesterday, couple of aging female gunslingers making off with a bundle. What I'm saying, it's like that *Apple Dumpling Gang*, only women."

"No, it isn't," Amy insisted. "Women have better sense than men."

Her husband cocked his head down to peer at her through the tops of his trifocals. "The hell they do. What're we talking about here if not *females* robbing *banks?*"

"Well, then—they must have good reason!"

What reason? Carl's property-taxes scenario made as much sense as anything.

"Bill Pine had insurance, didn't he, Carl? And I don't recall Aunt Edna being a big spender. Why would she need to rob a bank?"

"Here's what I'm saying, a bunch of senile old biddies without enough to do—"

"*Edna wasn't senile!*" Amy protested.

"—got fed up with Texas Citizens making mistakes in their accounts. A person can't argue with those damn computers. Once they start messing with your money, watch out."

Recalling her own account problems, Dixie wondered if Carl might be on to something. If not need or greed, why not frustration as a motive? Hadn't she been frustrated enough herself that morning to shout at poor old Len Bacon?

"*We* use Texas Citizens, Carl!" Amy's tone suggested they remedy that situation immediately. "And you said it was my checkbook that was out of balance."

"It was. You wrote down the deposit wrong. I'm saying these women—"

"Are all muddleheads like me? That's—"

"Hold it!" Dixie raised a palm to halt the squabble. "Anybody can write a number down wrong. And the women who pulled off these robberies were not muddleheaded. They've stolen probably a quarter million dollars, total."

Carl chuckled again. "Sure do have the cops scratching their heads. You have to give it to ol' Edna—"

"It wasn't Edna!" But before Amy could swat him again, the doorbell rang. Forced to settle for a lingering glare, she stalked off to answer it.

The visitor was Marty Pine.

Impeccably urbane in a charcoal double-breasted blazer and gunmetal-gray slacks, Edna's son swept past Amy, granting her a quick hug and kissing the air near her cheek. The artistic abstract design in the gray tie he wore matched his pale blue eyes perfectly. Gracefully graying hair retained a fullness a lot of women would envy. Marty looked thinner, possibly, than at his father's funeral, but then Dixie had seen him only briefly that day, before he shuttled Edna away to her sister's house in Galveston and zipped back to his ritzy art gallery in one of the Dallas supermalls.

"Dixie, you can't know how glad I am to find you here. Hello, Carl." Marty's Italian loafers whispered across the carpet. He shook Carl's outstretched hand, then whirled on Dixie and embraced her. "Maybe you can make some sense out of all this. The police are no good. But you—well, there you are, living right next door. Dix, you had to know something was amiss."

Amiss? Dixie supposed buddying up with brilliant artists and wealthy collectors was bound to result in some affectations. She hoped his were only syllable-deep.

And speaking of syllables, she and Marty hadn't exchanged more than a few dozen in over twenty years, yet here he was hugging her as if the time had melted away and they were still high school sweethearts. Had his mother's death shocked him into the past? He still smelled of the citrus cologne she remembered.

Finally, Marty pulled back to study her. The anguish etched in the lines of his narrow face reminded Dixie of the day someone let his pet rabbits out of their cage. He'd found them inside the fenced yard, all dead. He'd been fourteen at the time and doing his best not to cry.

Dixie felt his hand tremble where he touched her.

"Oh, Marty. I wish I did know what was going on with your mother."

Amy patted his arm. "Carl, pour Marty a glass of wine."

"I'll pour us all one," Carl mumbled.

Beyond the expected stress, Marty looked wired, Dixie noticed, his eyes as bright as new marbles.

"The police were all over me." He perched on the edge of Carl's vacated recliner. "They won't let me have her . . . body, you know."

"They will," Dixie assured him. "They'll release her as soon as they clear up some of the questions about . . . how Edna died."

"How she died?" He sprang off the chair. "They know exactly *how she died*. They shot her down, they—" He paced around the chair, then sank back onto it. "They gunned her down like some rabid dog in the street."

Carl brought a tray with four glasses of white wine, handed one to Marty and another to Dixie.

"I—I—I had to look at her." Tears glittered in Marty's eyes. "They said I needn't make, you know, an identification—you'd already handled that, Dixie. But I had to see for myself that it—it was really her."

He tossed back the wine in three gulps. A few drops fell on his pricey jacket, but he seemed as unaware of those as he was the tears now sliding down his face.

"Poor Marty." Amy, her own cheeks damp, took a second glass from Carl's tray and traded it for Marty's empty one.

"I looked at her lying there, and I . . . she looked so different I hardly knew her. How could I not know my own mother?"

Dixie recalled Edna's appearance as she'd stood in the bank lobby that morning, slender, sophisticated. "When was the last time you saw her?"

"I don't know—Christmas? Sure, Christmas. I dropped in a couple days early, took her to *The Nutcracker*. She'd lost a few pounds—taking aerobics classes, she confessed—but she still looked like . . . like *Mom*."

He drained the second glass. Amy took Carl's untouched one and traded with Marty again.

"Did Edna mention new friends? New interests?" Dixie asked.

"Friends?" He rose abruptly, paced past a shelf of framed photographs, and snatched one up. It showed the Pines and the Flannigans on one of their camping trips. "You were her *friend*, weren't you?" His pale, damp eyes smoldered with sudden anger.

"Of course I was, Marty, but—"

"What was she doing there? Did she even bank at Texas Citizens, for Christ's sake?"

Dixie met his glare frankly. "Edna was *robbing* Texas Citizens Bank, Marty."

"That's a lie! A story the police trumped up to cover their murdering asses."

"I was there, Marty. I saw her."

"*You?*" His anguished gaze roved over her face. "The police said there were witnesses. But . . . if *you* were there, you could've stopped it. Could've told them she was no bank robber."

"She had a .38 that spoke louder than I could've."

"That's crazy! A handgun? Can't you hear how crazy that sounds? Where the hell would Mom get a handgun?"

"Any sporting goods store," Carl put in. "No problem buying a gun."

"Well . . . she'd never have used it."

He looked so miserable, Dixie wanted to hug him again, assure him this was all a mistake. But she couldn't do that.

"She used it, Marty. She fired at *me*."

"No." His shoulders sagged. Amy hugged him silently as he stared down into the wine. "What happened, Dixie?" Marty's lips looked stiff around the words. "You lived right next door. How could you not know—not *see* that something was wrong? What does that say about you as a neighbor?"

"Marty Pine!" *You* didn't know, she wanted to shout. *What does that say about you as a son?* But she bit back the reproach. "Except for today, I haven't seen your mother in nearly a year."

"A *year*."

"A busy year," she added lamely.

"You're some sort of investigator, aren't you? Since you dropped out of law?"

Dropped out? He made it sound like skipping school.

Dixie shrugged. "I look for people, sometimes runaways, mostly bail jumpers."

"Naw, I saw it on television." He nodded at the TV, playing mutely, a *Matlock* rerun. "You found out who murdered that friend of yours. That attorney."

"A special case. I'm not a licensed investigator." *But I do want to know what happened.* The month after Dixie arrived at the Flannigans', forbidden to climb the pecan trees, she'd climbed anyway and fallen. Aunt Edna had gingerly run her hands over Dixie's arms and legs and head.

"Don't tell," Dixie'd begged tearfully. She couldn't bear Barney's disappointment that she'd disobeyed.

"Shhh. The important thing is whether you're hurt." Edna scooped her up— twelve years old but scrawny—and carried her into her own house. "Why did you climb up there? You know better."

"I was Robin Hood, on lookout." With her blood mother, Dixie had rarely felt young enough to play childish games. She was so embarrassed she longed to die. "*Please* don't tell."

"Shhh-shhh-shhh. Our secret. As long as you never climb those pecan trees again."

"Special case?" Marty demanded now. "*Special* friend? Exactly how long did you know that friend? Long as you've known me? Long as you knew Mom and Dad?" He looked at the photograph he still held.

"There's no mystery to how Edna died, Marty. There were witnesses."

He stared up at her, pain bracketing his lips. When he finally spoke, his voice was a whisper.

"Doesn't anybody care *why* she died?"

Yes. But four local law enforcement agencies and the feds will be all over this case. No way I can get close. "The police—"

"The *police* gunned my mother down in the street—a sixty-six-year-old woman who never hurt anyone in her life."

A woman with a ready smile for any kid, who loved roller coasters and pitched in at fund-raisers . . . and—

"She wounded a police officer," Dixie said quietly.

"She *never* would've done that! *Never!*" he shouted, squeezing the wineglass so tightly Dixie thought the stem would snap.

Carl cleared his throat self-consciously and rescued the glass. Then he motioned to Amy and they slipped out of the room, leaving Dixie to steer Marty's emotional warpath.

"Somebody changed her," Marty blurted. "That Lucy Ames woman, maybe, and . . . Dixie, *you were right next door.*"

Dixie knew he'd laid the guilt on her because it hurt too much to shoulder it himself. Marty loved his mother, yet, caught up in his own life, he'd lost touch. And how could Dixie blame him for asking the same questions she'd asked herself all day?

"Why would she steal money?" he demanded miserably. "She didn't need money. Dad left plenty, and I gave her a gold Amex card. I took care of her. I *did.* I swear, I took care of her." His voice broke.

Dixie coaxed him back to the recliner. In his grief, Marty hadn't asked the one question dominating every newscast: Where had the stolen money gone?

But another question niggled its insidious way into Dixie's mind. *Who was the one person a mother might steal money for?*

Chapter Eight

In a quiet neighborhood, in the back bedroom of a three-story house on Houston's historical registry, Philip Laskey raised himself off the floor with the help of a steel pull-up bar mounted overhead. He had finished fifty push-ups, twice as many sit-ups, four sets of reps with the free weights, and twenty minutes of t'ai chi after a forty-minute run. His slender body glistened with sweat in the floor-to-ceiling mirror.

He could hear a television playing in another part of the house and his mother humming as she puttered in the kitchen. Philip liked the sound. It meant she was healthy and happy.

The only one of her six children living in town, he felt responsible for making sure his mother stayed healthy and happy; so far it hadn't been a burden. Sixty-three years old, forty-four when Philip was born, Anna Marie Laskey had more fortitude than most. But bearing him at such an advanced age had been a sacrifice, and Philip understood that.

Finishing his reps on the bar, he reached for a sports bottle filled with distilled water. The compact gym was one of Anna Marie's concessions to Philip's exacting disciplines; another was meal preparation. He ate twenty-four ounces of protein a day—beef, fowl, or fish—and drank six glasses of fresh-squeezed vegetable or fruit juice plus six glasses of water, distilled. Nothing else. Ever. Food was fuel.

The hot shower reddened his freckled skin. He soaped his close-cropped red-blond hair, then rubbed the same bar of Dial soap over a vegetable brush and scrubbed from his hairline to his long, thin toes. After rinsing, he turned the shower from hot to skin-tingling cold.

Seven short-sleeved, crew-neck shirts, in various shades of blue, and five pairs of khaki trousers marched precisely one inch apart across the clothes rod in his closet. He selected one of each, adding blue socks and running shoes. The leather belt he slipped through his belt loops contained a narrow pocket with a thirty-inch length of piano wire inside, handles neatly taped. Philip had never used the wire to kill a man.

He removed a Sig Sauer Pistole 75 from a locked drawer, checked the nine-round magazine already in place, and slipped it into a quick-release holster at the back of his belt. In the mirror, he looked like any other nineteen-year-old, especially when he smiled.

"That smile could melt the heart of a hangman," Anna Marie often told him, and Colonel Jay encouraged Philip to use it. "Our most secret weapons," Colonel Jay instructed, "are the most valuable. An enemy expects guns and knives and explosives. But he'll always underestimate the force of a smile."

Philip shrugged into a loose, lightweight khaki windbreaker to cover the pistol's bulge. From a polished wooden box, he extracted a triangular lapel pin, blue and red enamel with a gold letter "P" in the center: blue for loyalty, red for the blood of the enemy, and gold for the golden future of The People. He pinned it to the jacket, above his heart.

Then he closed off the gym by sliding two floor-length panels in place and locked his bedroom on the way out. In the kitchen, he popped a stick of sugar-free gum in his mouth—his only vice—and kissed Anna Marie on her left cheek.

Chapter Nine

A ten-minute drive and a three-minute elevator ride brought Dixie from Amy's house to the forty-seventh floor of the Transco Tower and the offices of Richards, Blackmon & Drake. She found Belle Richards staring out her spacious corner window. Most of Houston stretched below like a giant Monopoly board, the most expensive properties dotted with skyscrapers, but the tiny segment holding Belle's interest lay directly below the tower, at the base of the Water Wall.

Brave the Galleria area traffic, find a legal parking place within walking distance, plant yourself in front of the sixty-four-foot, semicircular wall of cascading water, and you escaped city bedlam instantly into absolute tranquility. Each minute, eleven thousand gallons spilled over the gabled surfaces, playing a symphony of splash and trickle. Dixie had spent many late-night hours on the pebbled walkway in front of the Water Wall when a knotty problem held her thoughts hostage. Right now she found Belle's composed presence plenty soothing enough after the range of emotions she'd dealt with all day. Dixie was glad she'd stopped by instead of phoning.

"What're they doing down there?" she asked Belle, referring to a half-dozen people milling below.

"Brainstorming the Mayor's Memorial Day bash. Blackmon's on the committee. He got the harebrained idea that some of the festivities should take place in that minuscule park. Guess what that will do to traffic."

Belle wore her red power suit today—Austin Reed, Bill Blass, or Donna Karan—Dixie couldn't recall and couldn't tell the difference, but she'd helped Belle's husband shop for it as an anniversary gift. Standing on a stool to offset the defense lawyer's three-inch height advantage, she'd even modeled the suit—looked darn good, too, but not as classy as Belle did today—then helped him choose accessories. With the amount Belle's husband spent on one outfit, Dixie could've stocked up on jeans, shirts, and boots to last a decade.

"What traffic?" Dixie asked now. "Isn't Memorial Day a national holiday?"

"How soon you forget. What lawyer with a heavy caseload doesn't spend the holidays catching up? And all the retail stores around here will have major sales."

"Oh." The Galleria Mall attracted shoppers like a mud puddle attracts tots. "You paged me earlier. What's up?" In a roundabout way, some of Dixie's most lucrative jobs came from Richards, Blackmon & Drake. Their clients jumped bail, skipped town, and Dixie hauled them back.

"In your two seconds of TV fame today, I noticed an absence of your usual mule-headed, media-scorning composure." Belle turned from the window, and her wide gray eyes made a slow study of Dixie's face. "In fact, you looked upset."

"I did come across pretty spacey, didn't I?"

"What were you doing there?"

"Identifying the body—oh, you must've seen an early newscast, before they released the name." Edna and Bill Pine had been clients of Belle's partner Ralph Drake, who handled all the firm's estate and property law. Dixie had recommended Ralph years earlier, when the firm was struggling. When Marty opened his gallery, Ralph handled some paperwork. A year ago Ralph had probated Bill's will; now he'd have to probate Edna's. "Maybe we'd better sit down," Dixie told Belle.

Over coffee, she walked the defense attorney through the morning's disasters, beginning with Dixie's overdraft problem and ending with Marty's accusation that she should've been a better neighbor.

"You aren't buying that, are you?"

Dixie shrugged, suddenly uncomfortable in the red leather guest chair. She stretched her legs out and studied the scuffed tips of her boots.

"How is it that months can zip past while we aren't looking?" she grumbled. "When you and I were in law school, a year lasted forever. Now a year lasts fifteen minutes."

"Dixie, you aren't responsible for every old chum who decides to go postal."

"Even you?"

"Trust me, when I go it'll be by aneurysm during an ingenious closing argument. No mystery. No gunning down cops."

"That's the part I can't get a grip on. I saw Edna rob that bank—calm as a rock, everybody on the floor, poor old Len handing over the money. I saw Edna take the bags out to the car. Unless she's lost a bundle in the stock market, I know she didn't need that money, so it had to be some bizarre sort of suicide scheme, and I can even understand that, in a way. It would account for her being as spruced up as I'd ever seen her, wanting to go out looking her best. But Edna Pine never even raised her voice to one of us kids, never hurt anybody. I can't believe she intentionally shot that officer."

"She fired at you, didn't she?"

"She shot the *chair*," Dixie said firmly.

Belle's scrutiny became more intense. "Loss, grief, loneliness, shame, despair—Flannigan, if people could handle their emotions better, I wouldn't have so many clients."

Dixie polished the top of one boot against her other jeans-clad leg as she considered Belle's comment.

"Is there any chance Edna was about to lose her home and property? For tax liens, maybe?" Perhaps Carl was closer to the truth than she'd given him credit for.

Belle punched a button on her desk phone. "Not my department. But we can ask Ralph."

Ralph Drake, Dixie's least favorite of the three law partners, had lustrous silver hair that undoubtedly came from a bottle and sported a tan so dark he could pass for a swarthy Italian—an image he promoted by tossing Italian phrases into every conversation. Tall, thin, moderately attractive, he'd recently married for the seventh time in his forty-six years, and was rumored to be window-shopping already for *numero ocho*. For any woman under thirty, Ralph revved up his relentless Casanova act; any client who wasn't rich, female, or famous he managed to royally piss off. Nevertheless, he supported his share of the corporate overhead by being damn good at civil law. He also was superb at attracting clients, mostly female, who were occasionally somewhat famous and always somewhat rich.

He flashed his swarthy Italian smile at Dixie.

"*Cara mia*, Ms. Flannigan." He actually kissed her hand in greeting. "*Che bella sei oggi*—how beautiful you look."

Dixie looked as ratty as she had on entering the bank that morning, possibly worse. Yet, even though she knew Ralph was ladling bullshit, the sincerity in his voice made her feel *engagingly* ratty.

"Thanks, Ralph." When he sat down in one of the uncomfortable white sling chairs Dixie always avoided, she repeated a shortened version of what she'd told Belle earlier. At the part where she mentioned identifying the body, Dixie underscored the overwhelming transformation in Edna's looks.

Ralph and Belle exchanged a glance.

Dixie sat up straighter. "Why do I get the idea you two aren't as shocked as I am?"

Ralph's gaze flitted from Belle past Dixie to the expanse of sky beyond the windows. "Evidently, you hadn't talked with Mrs. Pine in a while."

Dixie shook her head.

He glanced at Belle again, who nodded.

"Mrs. Pine came to the office in . . . February," Ralph said guardedly. "To redraft her will. And the transformation, as you say, from the last time I'd seen her, during the probate of her sister's will—"

"What? Edna's sister died?" Her *younger* sister, if Dixie remembered right. Divorced, she'd turned her home in the Galveston historical area into a bed-and-breakfast. The one time Dixie stayed there, she'd been impressed. Her neighbor's sister was gregarious . . . and very different from Aunt Edna.

"Died of a massive stroke," Ralph said, "barely a month after Mrs. Pine buried her husband."

Why didn't I know this? Dixie shrugged away the guilt phantom that attempted to slither into her mind.

"Edna would've inherited her sister's business, assuming the IRS and creditors left anything." Dixie was guessing, but as she recalled, Marty and Edna's sister had been the only family at Bill's funeral.

"Mrs. Pine came out all right on that," Ralph admitted.

In Ralph Drake terms, *all right* when applied to money meant "very well indeed." So Edna's estate when she elected to rob Texas Citizens Bank should've included any retirement money she and Bill had saved up, plus the insurance settlement for Bill's death, plus whatever amount her business-savvy sister had bequeathed her, and possibly a second insurance payment.

"You say Edna came here in February. Why? Her sister's death would've left her with only one heir. Her son, Marty."

Ralph shrugged, crossing his legs as if uncomfortable.

"Didn't you counsel Edna to draft a new will after she inherited?"

"Of course." Ralph looked indignant. "We handled that immediately."

"Then what changes did she make in February?"

"*Madonna mia!* You know I can't tell you that."

"Something must've struck you as unusual, Ralph, or you and Belle wouldn't look like you'd swallowed sour milk."

He shook his head.

Absurd to expect a lawyer to part with client information, but dammit, Dixie was practically family to Edna. She was certainly Aunt Edna's friend. And Marty's friend. And *Belle's* friend. *And* a fellow lawyer.

"Ralph, if you allowed Edna Pine to do something irresponsible—"

"It's not my job to tell a client how to distribute her estate."

"How much money are we talking about?"

Again, he shook his head.

"Didn't you also handle some business transactions for Marty? That makes *him* your client, too. Did you at least notify Marty that his mother made 'unusual' modifications in his inheritance?"

Ralph raised an eyebrow in a manner that suggested Dixie had "dolt" branded on her forehead. Telling Marty—or anyone—the terms of Edna's latest will would've been highly inappropriate. Dixie knew that, but dammit, wasn't it equally inappropriate to let Edna throw her money away?

"Your client Edna Pine just robbed a bank," Dixie reminded him. "She shot and seriously wounded a police officer—not what I'd call rational behavior, Ralph. Are you saying she was totally rational when she came in here three months ago?"

"I saw no reason to believe otherwise."

"Then why are you squirming in that chair like a kid about to pee his pants? What bothered you about the changes Edna made?"

"*Niente!* Nothing, I tell you."

"You smarmy sonofabitch, if you let Edna write Marty out and give the money to a stranger—"

"Did I say that? And what makes this *your* business?"

"Hey, you two!" Belle slapped her pencil on the desktop. "Flannigan, calm down. And, Ralph, Dixie's right about one thing—we *were* concerned about Mrs. Pine's decision. A dollar retainer puts Dixie on our payroll—as a consultant. Now tell her what you told me."

The lawyer shot Belle a disgruntled look, but then he sighed and turned a thin smile at Dixie. Belle's name came first on the law firm's letterhead for a reason.

"In late February, Mrs. Pine bequeathed a significant portion of her estate to a church—which is *not* particularly unusual. When a person gets on in years, losing one family member after another, it's not uncommon to worry about the afterlife, to try and . . . pave a path, so to speak."

"What church?" Dixie didn't recall the Pines ever being especially religious. Bill was Methodist. When Marty was young, Edna usually took him to the Unitarian Church.

"I'd have to refresh my memory," Ralph replied. "Not a church I'd heard of. And that's all I'll say until probate."

"Ralph, Edna was a generous woman," Dixie explained reasonably. "But her family always came first. She wouldn't willingly deprive Marty, her only son, of his inheritance."

"*Basta!* Enough." On his way out the door, Ralph directed his response to Belle. "I'm not answering any more questions until the heirs are notified."

Dixie made a face at the door as it clicked shut behind Ralph Mule-headed Drake. *Heirs.* Plural.

"When do you think your pseudo-Italian partner will change his name to something with too many vowels?"

Belle picked up her well-chewed yellow pencil and tapped the point on a notepad.

"Dixie, I saw Mrs. Pine that day. Spoke to her. Ralph called me in to make sure he wasn't missing anything. Trust me, your friend seemed completely reasonable and happy with her decision."

"So, why were you concerned?"

"Anytime an elderly client makes abrupt money decisions, my loony-alarm goes off."

Dixie nodded, reluctantly. Giving a few bucks to a church didn't qualify as a big reason for concern. As Ralph said, Edna could parcel out her money any way she wanted. But if Aunt Edna didn't need the money she stole, and if she didn't steal it for Marty, then her actions pointed more and more toward suicide. That was the thought that saddened Dixie.

"Ric . . ." She deliberately used her nickname for Belle to underscore that loyalty came before business. "A reasonable, happy woman—with money—doesn't rob a bank at gunpoint."

"*Flannigan* . . . what do you want me to say? When she came here in February, Edna Pine looked a thousand percent more together than she did the previous time I saw her—"

"Was that right after her husband died? Or after her only sister died? She was *grieving*, Ric."

"She wasn't grieving this past February. If anything, I'd say she was in love."

"*Love?!* Edna was old enough to remember Rudolph Valentino, the Charleston, and penny bread loaves."

"Not quite, but since when does love have an age limit?"

"Bill's only been dead a year. If Barney had died first, Kathleen would *never* have fallen in love with another man."

"How did your parents get into this?"

"Barney and Kathleen, Edna and Bill—they were the same. Same age, same lifestyle, same values. Marriage to them was special, dammit. A very close, very *special* partnership. After Kathleen died, Barney mourned himself to death."

"The woman I saw in this office three months ago was not ready to stop the world and get off. She looked calm, happy. She'd turned back the clock a few years."

"I'd say 'stop the world and get off' describes precisely what Edna did this morning."

Belle's pencil tap-danced on her notepad. "A woman in love with the wrong man, a woman *jilted*, perhaps, by a man—heartsick, humiliated, after having already lost two important people from her life—might decide the world had taken one cruel turn too many."

Dixie frowned, not liking the picture Belle painted. Standing abruptly, she looked through the glass expanse at a city filled with men as deceptively charming as Ralph Drake, with his roving eyes and six-going-on-seven divorces. Then she turned and headed for the door.

"So, Flanni, what are you planning to do?"

"About the will? I guess that's up to Marty." She reached for the fancy brass doorknob on the richly polished mahogany.

"About this whole business," Belle persisted. "You were there when the robbery took place. Did Mrs. Pine act nuts?"

Dixie paused, her hand on the knob, and looked back.

"She wasn't raving, if that's what you mean. She knew exactly what to say and do. She didn't waste any time taking the cash and getting out. She certainly didn't hesitate to shoot—but I think she might've missed intentionally. Fired a warning."

"Nice old friend turned bank robber—and you're willing to let it go? Doesn't sound like you, Flannigan."

Dixie sighed. She did want to know what made Aunt Edna go bizocko, but she didn't want to discover a senile-in-lust story. "What is it you think I should do?"

"I haven't a clue. But if I ever rob a bank at gunpoint without any explanation, I hope someone cares enough to find out why."

Riding down in the skyscraper's art deco elevator, Dixie considered Belle's comment. Was it possible Edna had been swept off her aging feet by a man? That would explain the physical rejuvenation. The excitement of being in love gave a woman renewed energy and an outer glow that could take years off her appearance. A woman in love was likely to buy new clothes, change her hairstyle—

Dixie raked a hand through her own spiky mop.

As a kid, her hair had been an embarrassment—thick, long, frizzy. Combing the tangles out each morning hurt so bad Dixie longed to chop it off. For her tenth birthday, Carla Jean, her birth mother, allowed her to go to a beauty parlor alone, expecting her daughter's waist-length locks to be done up in corkscrew curls—a style Carla Jean associated with pretty little girls in romantic old movies. But a cute boy at school had made a snide comment about the frizz, and to her mother's intense disappointment, Dixie coaxed the beautician to cut it chin-length and blunt.

Almost three decades later, she'd finally allowed it to grow past her collar. She'd also started wearing lipstick and occasionally slipped into clothes more feminine than her usual jeans and boots. All because of a man.

The man responsible for her new interest in girly stuff was also responsible for the seventh, and final, message on her pager that morning during defense class. Parker Dann. The only man Dixie'd ever seriously considered snuggling down with for eternity. Not that he'd asked. Their relationship remained a part of Dixie's life she couldn't quite make work.

Having lived in the Houston area all her life, Dixie had no desire to go elsewhere. But Parker thrived on change, and three months ago, when he moved to Galveston, she hadn't been sure she'd ever see him again. After a bodyguard job she was working turned sour—Dixie and the principal nearly killed—Parker had decided that being romantically involved with a woman who repeatedly courted danger only invited heartbreak. In addition to the eighty miles that separated his new house on Galveston beach from hers in Richmond, Parker maintained an emotional distance: They were "just pals."

Over the months, they'd progressed from chatting daily on the phone to also enjoying a casual dinner together each Friday night. Yet, before his move, they'd spent six fun and intimate weeks under the same roof—for Dixie, some of the most sensational weeks of her adult life. At thirty-nine, she'd enjoyed her share of long- and short-term relationships without ever desiring more permanence. Parker changed that, and she wasn't ready yet to give up the intimacy.

When the elevator spit her out at ground level, Dixie returned Parker's page, briefed him on the bank robbery, assured him she'd escaped with no injuries, and promised to elaborate later.

"How about over dinner tonight?" she suggested. "My calendar says Tuesday's a fine day for seafood. I'll buy."

His hesitation told her he wasn't going for it.

"Tonight, I need to take care of some paperwork. For a fifty-footer that ships tomorrow."

"Sounds better than 'I need to wash my hair.' "

"Dixie—"

"It's okay, Parker. I'll call you later."

Another hesitation. "How about if I call you? About eight?"

"Okay. If I'm not there, leave a message." She powered the phone off before he could say another word and piss her off even further.

Chapter Ten

"Another balmy spring evening," the radio weather girl predicted as Dixie drove home. *"Enjoy it."*

"Easy for you to say," Dixie grumbled.

A stained-glass bauble dangled from her rearview mirror. Shaped like a sunburst, it bore the sentiment, *My day begins with your smile, your scent, your touch. Without those I would be cold and dark inside.* The sun catcher had arrived in a Valentine the day before Parker decided to end their intimacy.

He owed her no explanation now about his private life. For the three months they'd been apart, the "just pals" arrangement had remained rigidly intact. And she respected his concern over her choice of occupation. Hell, it wasn't even a choice, merely something that needed doing. Something she did damned well. She refused to sit idly at home until a new career decision struck her. If Parker couldn't accept who she was, then so be it. But if he was dating someone else, Dixie wished he'd be forthright enough to tell her.

Before she closed the gate and started down her long driveway shaded by rows of pecan trees, a hundred pounds of canine energy loped to meet her. She braked, opened the passenger door, and Mean Ugly Dog, her half Doberman, lumbered onto the seat. His larger, uglier half had never been divined.

"Hey, there, boy. Nice to know someone's glad to see me." She scratched his ears as Mud sniffed out the various aromas she'd acquired during the day.

Dixie parked the Mustang in the old pecan-shelling barn, no longer in use since the year Kathleen turned ill, when Barney farmed out the physical end of the business. Also in the barn, alongside the tow truck, sat a taxicab and a van with magnetic side-panel signs—plumber, exterminator, delivery service. In the skip-tracing business, all four vehicles came in handy at times.

As they exited the barn, Mud ran ahead to retrieve his Frisbee from the back steps, then turned and blocked her path, his great ugly face eager.

"Okay," Dixie agreed. A brisk game of fetch might work off her own tension. "Just give me a five-minute bathroom break."

Mud dropped the Frisbee beside the steps and plopped down to guard it.

With her other mail on the kitchen table, Dixie found the invitation from Mike Tesche to visit The Winning Stretch. She opened it envisioning his unruly hair and lighthearted grin.

Please join us for a Sundown Ceremony.
Last Sunday in May, five p.m.

On the back, a map showed the location, marked by an orange dot, in a far north Houston area near the town of Kingwood.

Dixie propped the invitation near the phone, and shed her clothes on her way to the bathroom. Outside again, dressed in shorts and running shoes, she played twenty minutes of hard Frisbee with Mud, while a frozen pizza baked in the oven. When Parker's phone call came, she was draped over her favorite club chair watching a rerun of *The Rockford Files* and scanning through a stack of last week's newspapers for coverage on the first Granny Bandit robbery.

"Saw you on television," Parker told her.

"Can't believe they're still running that same footage. Barred from the secured area, the photographer shot the first person who looked miserable." Dixie heard dishes rattle. "What are you cooking?"

"Swordfish, angel-hair pasta. Guess you're totally convinced it was Edna, huh?"

"I wasn't at first. But yeah, it was her." *Swordfish for one?* Parker never resorted to frozen pizza, but Dixie couldn't help wondering who might be dropping by to share one of his delectable dinners. "You talk as if you'd met Edna."

"Borrowed some spices once. Visited with her a couple times after that."

No big surprise. Parker met people easily, wherever he went. And he'd lived at Dixie's house during January and February, about the time Edna metamorphosed and decided to change her will.

"How was she when you last saw her?" Dixie asked.

"Busy. Cheerful. Thought maybe she and her boyfriend—"

"Boyfriend?" Maybe Belle was right. "Did you meet him? Get his name?"

"Saw him only once, and no, I didn't meet him—and before you ask, he was about forty-five years old, maybe five-ten or -eleven. Wore a topcoat—I couldn't see his clothes. Gray hair and good shoes."

"Parker, Edna was in her sixties. Are you sure this guy wasn't a tad older?"

"Younger, if anything. But then, I'd have guessed Edna at fifty-eight, tops. I usually peg people better than that. Guess age is in the attitude. She worked out every day and watched her diet—shared a great chef's salad with me once."

Parker's description didn't fit the Edna whose ritual Sunday dinner had been Southern fried chicken and lumpy cream gravy, whose grilled burgers turned out raw inside and black around the edges. Her peanut-butter cookies were tops, but loaded with butterfat. People did change, though, especially after losing a spouse.

When Dixie's thoughts caused a brief silence, Parker said, "You're going to snoop around in this robbery thing, aren't you?"

His voice held only a hint of disapproval.

"The cops won't appreciate a nosy bounty hunter getting involved. They'd probably think I was scrounging around for the missing money—like every other treasure hunter in town."

"Your two families, the Pines and the Flannigans, were close when you were growing up, according to Edna."

"Her son Marty and I went to school together. What are you getting at?"

"One thing I know about you, Dixie, is you don't turn away from people you care about. I liked Edna. Anything I can do to help, just tell me."

"Three months ago you would've tried to convince me *not* to get involved."

"Might as well reason with a stone."

Was that an edge in his voice? "Sounds like you've given up on me."

"I've finally figured you out—you call yourself a bounty hunter, but you're really a paladin. Heroic champion, righter of wrongs—"

"That was Richard Boone in the old TV western. Do I look like Richard Boone?"

"—warrior against injustice—especially when an injustice is done to someone you're close to. Have you ever let me talk you out of anything before?"

"Not when it's something I have to do, but—"

"This time I won't try."

When they ended the conversation a moment later—to the sizzle of baked swordfish in the background—Dixie had the miserable feeling she'd sacrificed a once-in-a-lifetime relationship merely to preserve her stubborn independence.

She glanced down at the newspaper she held, folded to a short piece about the first holdup at Texas Citizens Bank in northwest Houston, and read the bank robber's description: *five-three to five-eight, medium build or thin, thirty-five to fifty-five years old, brown hair, wearing a pink or green dress.* Apparently, the witnesses disagreed on almost every point. Typical. Even discounting the age difference, though, the brown hair didn't sound like Edna. And the morning *Chronicle* had described Lucy Aaron Ames, the woman responsible for the robbery yesterday in Webster, as *a petite, fifty-five-year-old, blond grandmother.*

A third woman would account for the missing loot in the second two robberies. Lucy Ames and Aunt Edna could've handed the bags off to the third woman before the police caught up with them.

In the obituary section, Lucy Ames' funeral was listed for the following day. The police would be there, no doubt. And if Dixie wanted to find out how Aunt Edna and Lucy Ames cooked up the idea of becoming kamikaze bank robbers, that'd be the place to start.

She considered calling Parker back and asking if he'd like to go along. He *had* offered to help. Before his move to Galveston, he'd once suggested they team up and form an investigations firm to search for missing kids. Dixie had nixed the idea, knowing he'd suggested it only as a means of protecting her. Besides, she had no interest in acquiring an investigator's license and all the accompanying regulations, and she preferred to work alone.

For that same reason, she didn't call him back, but she did note the time and location of Lucy Ames' funeral.

Chapter Eleven

At the outskirts of northeast Houston, a defunct dance studio presents to passersby a dark and silent front. Plywood sheets batten the doors and windows. Tonight, the fifty-gauge chain that usually blocked the driveway lay heaped on the asphalt as Philip Laskey drove around to the rear.

Security and acoustics had been upgraded in the old building, but otherwise very little construction proved necessary to convert the studio to an excellent training, meeting, and operations facility. Inside, greeted by a familiar medley of male voices and the pungent odor of cordite and warm bodies, Philip lifted a folding chair from a rack along the wall of what had originally been the ballroom. He straddled the chair at a table beside two of his friends.

Nelson Dodge tipped his chair back and leaned against the wall.

"Ho, Philip." Nelson's voice, as smooth and rich as his mocha-brown skin, came almost as a whisper. He had the solid physique, steady moves, and self-confident attitude that marked a black-belt winner. Tonight, only a glitter in his dark eyes revealed any excitement.

But Rudy Martinez, lighter and quicker in both build and temperament—and a crack shot with an M40—jiggled one leg up and down beneath the table.

"So, what d'ya think?" Martinez swept a glance past Philip to the rear entrance. His pink tongue flicked over a meaty lower lip. "Think we'll get some action tonight?"

The two men were dressed much like Philip and the other twenty-seven in the room, in casual blue shirts, khaki pants, and light jackets. Everyone wore the blue, red, and gold lapel pin.

Surprised to be one of the last to arrive, Philip checked his watch against the big round clock over the old bandstand. His was three and a half minutes slow. Tomorrow, he'd buy a new battery. For now, he reset the time.

"Action?" Philip sat down. "What kind of action?"

"Hell, man, any kind." Rudy's fingers drummed the tabletop, marking cadence with his jiggling leg. "What's the use of all this training if we don't use it? Use it or lose it, man."

"We use what we need," Nelson told him. "When we need it."

"Yeah, well. Looks of what's coming down in this town, man, cops wasting little old ladies, we need it *now*."

Philip reached over and put a finger on Rudy's knee to still the jiggling. "We'll go into action when the Colonel says. Meanwhile, work off some of that energy tonight in the training room."

"Shit, man—"

"And clean up your language." Philip gripped Rudy's knee between his thumb and fingers and pinched the nerves behind the kneecap. "The People don't use obscenities."

"Yeah, hey! I get the message."

Philip released Rudy's knee but not his gaze. "*Lose* the rough language."

"Okay, man, but don't handle me. I get that kind of shi—*treatment* enough at home. You touch, Laskey, I touch *harder*."

Philip slowly turned his gaze to Nelson. "You think Colonel Jay called this meeting because of today's shooting?"

"I think he don't like cops killing senior citizens. Not much else happening to rile him up, make him call a special meeting." At twenty-three, Nelson had been one of The People for nearly a year, longer than any of them.

"You want a drink?" Rudy asked. "I need a drink." He sprang from his chair and headed for an Ozarka dispenser at the side of the room, where several of The People stood talking.

Philip glanced at the raised platform where gray-haired gentlemen had once played big-band music. Now the stage held a single lectern wired for sound, lights, and audiovisual presentation. Behind the lectern, The People's triangular symbol emblazoned a wall as blue as the background of stars in the American flag posted at the left of the platform.

Above the bandstand, the clock said two minutes before eight. Philip could feel the tension rising in the room as the time neared for the Colonel's arrival.

When the outer door opened, the men closest to the entrance stood. The scrape of chairs and the shuffle of feet accompanied a low murmur as others rose. Philip slid his chair back and strode to the front of the room. A jumble of hearty greetings floated forward.

The Colonel shook outstretched hands on his way to the bandstand. When he reached the lectern, all noise ceased. Every man and boy in the room stood at attention.

"Good evening, gentlemen." Colonel Jay flashed his broad, soul-warming smile. "I believe you have the lead, Mr. Laskey."

Philip stepped one pace forward and turned to face the flag.

"We The People of the United States, in order to form a more perfect union, establish justice, insure domestic tranquillity, provide for the common defense . . ."

The room filled with the voices of thirty-one ardent seekers of a perfect world. Like others in the room, Philip had memorized the Preamble to the Constitution in grade school, but had never really listened to the words until he said them in this room, among this congregation. He no longer noticed the two words that were changed.

". . . promote the general welfare, and secure the blessings of liberty to ourselves and our posterity, do uphold and defend the Constitution for the United States of America."

Beneath the voices, "America the Beautiful" played so softly it could be heard only when the recitation ended.

"At ease, gentlemen."

He looks different tonight. Philip took his seat among the others. *His eyes burn like coals.*

The Colonel had a trim, compact strength, like Philip's own, and they stood exactly the same height, five-ten and a half. But no one ever guessed Colonel Jay at less than six feet.

His naturally strong voice sounded fuller tonight—or maybe it was only Philip's expectations for the evening. If so, his wasn't the only body keen with anticipation. The room hummed as if thirty hearts beat in unison. As the Colonel began to speak, Philip's palms felt cool, his body wired.

"We stand at the brink of a new world, just as surely as this nation did when those precious words were penned. We have a mission." The Colonel paused, using silence the way he used his voice—as a magnet, drawing his listeners in. "Our first business of the night, however, is to welcome a new soul."

Nelson had silently taken a position near the corner of the bandstand. At Colonel Jay's nod, he mounted the short staircase.

"Recruit! Step forward," the Colonel commanded.

A boy of about fifteen stepped up beside him.

"Do you desire to be one with The People?" the Colonel asked softly.

"Yes, sir."

"Who sponsors this recruit?"

"Nelson Dodge, sir," Nelson said.

"Has this recruit completed orientation training?"

"He has, sir."

"Has this recruit been evaluated by the Committee?"

"He has, sir."

"The recruit's name?"

"Wynn Cronin, sir."

Colonel Jay turned the full power of his gaze upon the boy, and Philip sucked in a breath, recalling the first time he'd felt the ferocity of the Colonel's eyes burning into his own. For an instant, he'd believed his soul was on fire. That night had been the most exhilarating of Philip's life.

Quietly, the Colonel said, "Repeat after me." Then he paused, and his audience held its breath. "With my soul I pledge commitment to the rights of The People . . ."

The boy's voice echoed the words.

". . . and eradication of any who, singly or in collusion, would violate those rights."

As Cronin repeated the phrase, Nelson moved forward with a small wooden box. The Colonel lifted out a fourteen-karat gold-and-enamel lapel pin. He fastened it to the boy's jacket.

"Be one with The People, Wynn Cronin."

"Thank you, sir."

The room filled with applause, then a shuffle of footsteps, as the assembly formed two lines, perpendicular to the stage.

"Do you trust in The People, Wynn Cronin?"

"Yes, sir."

"Stand at the edge of the stage."

The boy walked hesitantly to the edge and looked down at the double line of men, his eyes troubled. Philip knew what he was wondering now: *Was this to be some sort of hazing ritual? Would he be expected to endure pain?*

The recruit didn't have much to worry about now. Discipline would begin later.

Nelson tied a blindfold around the boy's eyes.

"Turn around," the Colonel commanded.

Tentatively, testing the edge of the stage with his foot, the boy turned to stand with his back to the men below.

"You have pledged your soul to The People, Wynn Cronin. Do you also trust them with your life?"

"Yes, sir."

"Show that trust. Fall into the arms of The People."

"You want me to lean backward, sir? Until I fall?"

"Trust in The People, Wynn Cronin."

Philip swiveled to face the first man in the opposite row, then reached out and grasped his hands. All down the line, the other men followed suit, until the two rows were joined down the center.

The moment stretched, Philip recalling the ache of uncertainty, the dread of losing face. The drop to the hardwood floor was only a few feet, but backward, head first, it could easily break a man's neck. Finally, the boy began to lean away from the stage.

"Let go," the Colonel instructed softly. "Trust in The People."

"Trust," someone echoed, and the others joined in. "Trust, trust, trust, trust, trust . . ."

The boy's body twitched with hesitancy.

"Trust, trust, trust . . ."

He leaned, teetered—

"Trust, trust, trust . . ."

—and fell across the first four pairs of arms.

"Trust in The People!" They swung the boy up, tossing him along the line until he reached its end. *"Trust in The People!"*

They lowered him gently to his feet and removed the blindfold. Then one by one, twenty-nine men hugged him.

A rush of emotion dampened Philip's eyes. He enfolded the boy, recalling his own glorious moment, the moment he no longer felt alone in the world. When he became one with The People, he'd finally belonged.

The room settled down; chairs were pulled back into rough crescents facing the stage. Philip dimmed the lights.

"The mission," the Colonel said, and all the sound in the room flew into his voice. "Uphold and defend."

He pressed a button on the lectern. A twelve-foot screen descended behind him, a video already queued up, filling the wall with images of the police execution of Edna Pine.

"The crime in our streets today is exceeded only by the crime among our protectors. In our government. In our courts. In our back alleys. Between criminals and members of our own law enforcement teams." The Colonel's voice thundered over the grisly images moving silently across the screen. "Corruption is spreading faster than the worst virus. It's more insidious than unsavory sex. Who can we count on to stop this horror? Certainly not this man."

The film cut to a head-and-shoulders shot of Avery Banning, Houston's new Mayor. "Or this one." Another cut, and Edward Wanamaker, Houston's Chief of Police, stood beside Mayor Banning. Both men were laughing.

"These elected leaders are no solution, they are the problem. If not for their weak, indecisive command, women would be safe on our streets. If not for their mishandling of city business, our senior citizens would not be so desperate as to turn to theft. If not for their inept investigation, the *ringleader* of this so-called Granny Bandit Gang would be found and brought to task.

"The time has come," the Colonel said quietly. "Who can we count on?" Then he stood silent.

After a moment, Philip rose and, from his position in the back of the room, saluted his idol.

"We, The People," he said.

Beside Philip, Nelson pushed to his feet. "We The People," he boomed.

"We The People." Chairs scraped and feet stamped to attention.

"We The People." The words rolled like a mounting wave around the room.

"We The People. We The People. We The People . . ."

Chapter Twelve

Restless after her talk with Parker, Dixie took Mud out for a walk in the direction of the Pine residence. Past an acre of pecan trees, a hedge of holly shrubs, and a forty-year-old wisteria, they reached her neighbor's driveway. The house sat nearer the road than her own, and no gate blocked the entrance.

The porch light was on, as well as a light in the living room, another toward the rear of the house. Bill had installed timers back in the eighties, when electronic security became popular. But the police car in the driveway suggested a search in progress—not for the money Edna stole and wouldn't have had time to drop here, but for other evidence.

The house, built of pink brick and light gray vinyl siding, trimmed with charcoal-gray shutters and roof, boasted a wide sun porch across the entire front. Dixie noted the gabled windows marking the upstairs bedroom that had been Marty's. Like the Flannigan house, this one had once been a single story with a large attic. Bill and Barney had pooled their woodworking skills and turned their attics into extra rooms. Amy had already claimed the upstairs bedroom before Dixie arrived.

The porch drew her forward, and stepping up onto it, Dixie recalled the day only a few years past when Bill replaced the worn screens and added jalousie windows. Funny how some things lay in the back of your mind, gathering dust.

A chair swing hung from the rafters—not the same one Dixie'd sat in as a girl, but its twin, slatted back and arms, solid seat, all painted creamy white and softened with daisy-print cushions. Battleship gray coated the wood floor. Pots of coleus and red geraniums perched along the window seats. Ivy cascaded down the wall. *Had Edna watered the plants before taking off for her bank heist?*

Dixie peeked in a window. No cops in the living room; they must be searching the back of the house. She sat down in the porch swing. Mud, far too large to snuggle beside her, investigated every flowerpot and spiderweb before curling up at her feet. Dixie pushed gently against the porch floor. To the creak of the swing chain, the music of the wind through dogwood and oak, and the occasional croak of a frog on the Brazos River, she allowed fond memories to invade her mind. When she finally rose to return home, she'd more or less decided that whatever had led Aunt Edna to her bizarre demise should remain the woman's secret. What right had Dixie to dig around in her friend's final decisions?

At home, Dixie's answering machine showed five new messages. She punched the PLAY button and listened as she kicked out of her shoes.

Click. Beep! "Dixie, you have to help me. I can't battle this thing alone, and I can't let Mother go to her grave labeled a 'Granny Bandit.' Call me . . . uhhh, this is Marty." He left a number with a Dallas area code.

Dixie jotted it down on the back of a grocery receipt, hit PLAY again, and unbuttoned her camp shirt.

Click. Beep! "Dixie, the police say I can't get into my own mother's house. Is that crazy? How am I supposed to clear this up? Call me." Marty left the same number and an additional number, which she added to her note.

Click. Beep! "Where are you? You can't abandon me like this. I just listened to a voice mail from Ralph Drake, Mother's lawyer. There's something screwy with her will. Drake says he's contacting other heirs. What other heirs? Do you know anything about this? Call me. Please?"

Dixie stared at the machine as she slipped out of her shorts. What could she tell him? Nothing. The small amount of information Ralph had given her was disclosed in confidence. Being in the middle of a dispute between Marty Pine and Belle's firm would be like walking barefoot through a patch of prickly pears. Reluctantly, she punched PLAY again, glad she hadn't been at home this past hour to catch Marty's anxiety firsthand.

Click. Beep! "Okay, I convinced the police that we *must* get into Mother's house to settle her affairs—hell, I don't even remember the name of that funeral home we used for Dad—but the cops won't be finished with their search and pilferage until tomorrow evening. Will you meet me there, love? For what we once meant to each other?" After a brief silence, Marty's voice came back, less frantic and more anguished. "What if it were *your* mother, Dixie? What if it were Kathleen?"

Dixie grimaced and turned away from the machine. *For what we once meant to each other?*

She poured a tall glass of ice water, carried it into the living room, and slumped in a chair. Mud roused from his napping spot. Deciding she needed a head to scratch, he padded over, gave her hand a thorough licking, then settled beside the chair, his wide mug resting on her bare leg.

"Thanks, guy." Idly, she ran her fingers over the short silky fur covering his ear. Her gaze fell on a photograph of Kathleen Flannigan. Taken the year before she died, it showed the fine-boned face—with its narrow nose and strong jaw—surrounded by a fringe of white hair as fine and glossy as spun glass. *What if it were* your *mother?*

Beneath the photograph stood a row of albums—thirteen, in all—occupying the bottom shelf of Kathleen's bookcase. She'd faithfully recorded the Flannigan family history in the pages of those albums, each photograph positioned with corner mounts and captioned in a neat, flowing script. Dixie gave Mud's ears a final scratch and lifted book number seven. Nudging Mud's head off her leg, she opened the heavy album.

Along with snapshots and school photos, Kathleen had included favorite birthday cards, special report cards, pressed flowers from her daughters' prom nights. Dixie flipped to a page featuring a grainy color snapshot of herself in a white chiffon dress and Marty in a white dinner jacket. Twelfth grade. Rhinestone straps sparkled at Dixie's shoulders, an innovative but disastrous modification she'd made after learning that several of her friends had ordered the same dress. The straps looked terrific, one skinny string of rhinestones attached to each side of the sculptured neckline in front, crossing the shoulder, then widening into three strands as it connected to the chiffon again, low in the back. Sexy. Even sexier as the rhinestones began snapping apart. Before the evening was out, a string of safety pins held the straps together, and Marty's grin had stretched ear to ear.

Beneath the photograph, Kathleen had penned, *My precious daughter Dixie & my best friend's son, Marty Pine. Could there be a more delightful match?*

The year that she and Marty dated had certainly been fun. Even then he'd been interested in the visual arts and had dragged Dixie to gallery openings all over greater Houston. Surprisingly, the scuzziest places offered free wine and usually didn't discriminate against underage art enthusiasts.

My best friend's son. Kathleen and Edna, best friends. None better, looking back at all the good times the two families enjoyed together.

A pair of Kathleen's many cross-stitched samplers hung over the window. In green and yellow threads the first suggested: "One of the Most Beautiful Truths of This Life Is that No Man Can Sincerely Help Another Without Helping Himself."

Is that true, Mom? What if Edna robbed that bank to help Marty? Makes no sense—she had money to give him, but perhaps not enough. And Marty's not the same young man I dated in high school. What if he only wants my help to find and cover up any connection between him and the missing bank loot? You know I can't turn my back on incriminating evidence, but he's self-centered enough to think I'd do it. What I don't know won't hurt him. And if I did uncover a lead to that third woman, how would that help Edna?

Over the window, a matching green and yellow sampler balanced Kathleen's sappy sentimentality with: "Truth Is Real Enough to Hang Your Hat On."

In Dixie's experience, truth often brought sorrow and rarely guaranteed justice. Hadn't she quit law because of such dilemmas?

She closed the album, picked up the phone, and tapped in Parker's number, pausing before the last digit. What if he was entertaining a . . . friend? Did she really want to know? With a sigh, she hit the final digit. He *had* offered to help.

His answering "hello" sounded husky with sleep . . . or something.

"Hey, I'm meeting Marty, Edna's son," she said brightly, "to go through her records and things. And what you said about her boyfriend might be important."

"I've been reconsidering—guess I could've jumped to conclusions about their relationship."

"Based on what?"

"When I walked over one day, a man was leaving. Edna answered my knock, obviously thinking he'd returned—and her expression was . . . well, elated, maybe? Like a woman . . . enthralled, I guess, is the only word to describe it. But that could've been one-sided. I only had a brief look at her visitor. Maybe he was just a salesman."

"First impressions are intuitive. If you're right, Edna may have a snapshot of him." She asked Parker to repeat his description of the man leaving Edna's house.

"He looked like money," Parker replied. "If he came into the showroom, I'd take him straight to the luxury models."

He agreed to check out any snapshots they found of an unknown man fitting that description. Then she called the Dallas number Marty had left. Getting his answering service, she agreed to meet the next evening at Edna's. When she noticed her message light still blinking, Dixie realized she'd never listened to the fifth call that came in during the short time she was walking with Mud—probably another from Marty.

Click. Beep! "Dixie, my dear, Len Bacon here. I don't want to alarm you . . ."

Shit. Why did people utter those six little words? How could you hear them without being alarmed?

". . . but I've taken the liberty of checking further into your account problem. Call me tomorrow. The sooner the better, I'm afraid."

The sooner the better. But the bank wouldn't open until nine.

Shit.

Chapter Thirteen

Wednesday, 9:00 A.M.

"Dixie, Dixie, Dixie." Len Bacon sighed. "I pray that we have nipped this problem before it escalated into a real horror. Do you recall disposing of any old checkbooks that might contain unused personalized deposit slips?"

"I don't think so. My CPA uses them in figuring my taxes."

On the other side of Len's glass wall, a glazier took measurements. The wall hadn't shattered from the gunshot. Safety glass, probably. Dixie'd been so focused on Edna at the time that she hadn't noticed the bullet hole, or the two fracture lines working their way north and west.

"And when your CPA returns them to you, what happens?"

"I file the records in a box and store the box on a shelf in the garage." Among a mountain of similar boxes, a layer of dust, and several hundred dead bugs. "Why, Len?"

"My dear, I'm afraid someone has a supply of your deposit slips. Do you have any accounts other than the ones here at Texas Citizens?"

"No."

"Excellent." He opened a manila file folder. "Then perhaps we'll fare better than poor Mr. James Cook."

"The guy who stole my money?"

"The name that appeared on the fraudulent checks deposited to your account," Len corrected patiently. "The criminal apparently got hold of Mr. Cook's canceled checks and washed them—that is, removed the written information except the signature—then used them to extract all the funds from

Mr. Cook's account. Additional checks were deposited to your checking account, and a withdrawal made, using one of your personalized deposit slips."

He showed her a page from the file, a photocopy of five deposits, each with a withdrawal amount on the appropriate line.

"Wouldn't a person have to show identification to make a withdrawal?"

"Apparently, the woman did have identification. False, obviously, but quite convincing. Perhaps the teller only gave it, ah"—he cleared his throat—"a cursory examination, considering a deposit was also being made."

Dixie felt a pang of sympathy for James Cook, who'd lost more than a few thousand dollars.

"So what do we do?" she asked.

"First, we'll close out all your accounts and open new ones. We'll issue a code word unavailable to anyone besides you and me. This criminal, whoever she is, will not be taking any more funds from you directly."

Len's soothing drawl worked like music, calming her. But that word "directly" didn't sit well.

"Ms. Sticky Fingers is still out there with my ID, Len, committing who knows what crimes—hell, she could *kill* somebody in my name."

"Now, don't borrow trouble, my dear. Your investment accounts are safe. And the funds you lost are federally insured. But in the future, you'll want to be careful about tossing out old records of any kind—credit card receipts and solicitations for credit cards, expired licenses, old health records—even photographs."

They spent the next half hour filling out paperwork and filing the police report, which she dropped at the Richmond Police Department. Dixie tried to feel the relief Len projected, but knowing a crook carried ID in her name unsettled her. She itched to *do* something about it—hunt the thief down, confiscate the ID, then deposit the crook at the nearest jail. To get a description of the woman, Dixie could question the five cashiers who took the fraudulent deposits—that seemed a more positive action than searching for a box of old records. Finding that one box would probably mean cleaning the whole garage.

Scanning the list of Texas Citizens branches Len had given her, she saw that all five were located in the west Houston area. Might take a couple hours. But she had nothing else on her calendar until she met with Marty at six. And the garage would stay right where she'd left it, just as much in need of cleaning. When she exited the bank's parking lot, Dixie turned the Mustang toward Houston.

By lunchtime, she'd questioned all five cashiers, and none could give a description of the woman passing herself off as Dixie. The bank's security department had already removed the videotapes from the overhead cameras. Frustrated, yet admitting she could do nothing more about the theft, she decided to trust Len Bacon's assessment that her accounts were now out of danger. The money she'd lost would be reimbursed, and all the branches were alerted in case the woman attempted another bogus deposit.

None of this practicality appeased Dixie's emotional need to ferret out the thief. Driving toward downtown, and mentally grumbling about how easily a usurper could assume control of a person's life, her thoughts turned to something she *could* investigate.

She recalled Marty's comment about no one caring *why* Aunt Edna died. Edna had died because she shot at police after robbing a bank. But the real question was *why* she committed armed robbery. With a wounded officer in the hospital, the shooter dead, and a quarter-million dollars in stolen bank loot to find, just how much effort would anyone focus on answering Marty's "why" question?

Dixie had a theory about obtaining information: Start at the very bottom or at the very top. From where she sat now, in the shadow of skyscrapers, the office of Houston's top guy was only a few blocks away. That garage-cleaning chore would have to wait a while longer.

Chapter Fourteen

Houston's City Hall overlooks a reflecting pond and corners on Tranquility Park. Since the building's completion in 1939, its lightly veined marble walls and floors have aged gracefully, and the bronze and silver inlays usually command a second look. Dixie'd seen the artistry often enough not to be impressed. Since relocating to Richmond, she could no longer vote in Houston elections, but that didn't prevent her from speaking her piece at council meetings or campaigning for favorite candidates.

She swept through the lobby, bound for the third-floor Mayor's office, knowing she'd have no problem gaining an audience. She'd met Avery Barton Banning while prosecuting a fraud case. As an expert witness on business real estate, he'd impressed her as both judicious and innovative. More recently, during his election campaign, Dixie'd stuffed envelopes, arranged speaking engagements, co-hosted a fund-raising event with Amy, and then had danced briefly—not particularly well, but nobody noticed—with Mayor Banning at his inaugural ball.

In many ways Banning fulfilled her image of a career politician. His savvy attitude attracted voters of all ages. He came from new money, while his wife Kaylynn boasted membership in the Daughters of the Republic. Youthful good looks placed him right up there with JFK or George W. Bush. His podium presence would rival the actor-president Ronald Reagan's. And Banning had a knack for remembering useful details about everybody he met. If Houston's new Mayor didn't have an eye on the big chair in Washington, Dixie figured he needed glasses.

Despite all the political muscle-flexing, Banning came across as sincerely interested in doing a good job. That put him a stroke above average in Dixie's book. She chose to ignore the recent rumors of problems in his marriage and finances—every politician had to deflect a share of mud.

Today she found him swinging a putter at a golf ball on his office carpet and listening to the soundtrack from *The Good, the Bad and the Ugly*. This didn't strike her as showing proper concern for the city's turmoil of the past two days.

"Tell me some good news, Dixie." He tapped the ball with a gold-headed putter. "Everybody else today has brought gloom and doom." The ball rolled smoothly across the five-foot expanse but missed its destination, marked by a paper cup lying on its side.

Dixie shrugged. "I saw Gib leaving." Councilman Jason "Gib" Gibson had been Banning's most outspoken opponent—after abruptly deciding not to run for the office himself. Now, he shot political arrows at every issue Banning supported and, by extension, at the Mayor's appointed Police Chief. "Looks like the HPD shootings have given Gib his big chance to see the voters repent."

Banning scooped up the golf ball and replanted it five feet from the paper cup.

"Gib's a thorn that keeps me hopping, all right, but in the Councilman's shoes I'd be just as prickly. These robberies, and the unfortunate deaths that followed them, make our police look untrained and unprofessional."

Unprofessional. Untrained. Unfortunate. Hollow words. A politician's words.

Dixie struggled to rein in her irritation. Maybe Gib's visit had rattled Banning more than usual. Despite the Councilman's unrelenting attack, the Mayor's response—at least in public—was always dispassionate and amiable. That had to be difficult. And now she'd come to question him, probably about the same topic he'd addressed with Gib.

Banning offered Dixie his putter. She'd never played golf, but she did play pool, which involved a ball and stick. How much different could it be?

Hefting the club, she lined up on the ball, then tapped it—*whack*—harder than she expected. It missed the cup by a foot and bashed into the wall—certainly not the first ding in the sixty-year-old paneling. Nevertheless, she apologized and retrieved the ball. Then she looked Banning in the eye.

"Downstairs, inlaid in the marble floor of the lobby, is a bronze medallion, Avery, that you walk across at least once a day. It says, *Government Protects The People*. After the shootings this week, have you noticed that medallion tarnishing a bit?"

Avery returned her gaze, his cobalt eyes filled with shadows. "I know that Edna Pine was a friend of yours, Dixie. I'm sorry about what happened."

"What're you doing to stop it from happening again?"

His appraising gaze shifted from her eyes to her unsmiling mouth. Dixie recalled that one of Avery's college degrees was in psychology.

"First," he said, "Chief Wanamaker has issued a general order to avoid fatalities if we have another occurrence—"

"How? Tasers? Tranquilizer darts?"

The slight dip of his head couldn't quite be called a nod.

"And second, the FBI is taking additional measures within the banks—"

"What measures?"

"You know I can't discuss that."

True. In fact, the feds probably hadn't shared that information. Dixie placed the golf club and ball on Banning's desk. The ball rolled and stopped against a gilt-edged journal that lay open, neat blue script filling the pages.

"Does the Chief or the FBI have any idea what would prompt women who are old enough to know the consequences to commit armed robbery?" she asked. "Have similar robberies happened in other cities?"

"That's being investigated, of course." Banning closed the journal, slid it into a desk drawer, and picked up the ball. "No similar cases have turned up so far, certainly no recent cases."

"Avery, when Edna Pine made up her mind, she was as strong as horseradish. With the right provocation—and Jesus, I can't imagine what that would be—she might've pulled off that robbery yesterday. But she didn't do it alone."

"I'm sure you believe you knew her, Dixie." He dropped the ball into the same drawer. "Yet, think about it—even people we live with can surprise us. Secret drinkers . . . runaways . . . suicides. We live in desperate times—"

His phone rang, saving Dixie from the rest of the soliloquy. Avery could compose and deliver on demand a speech about any topic you tossed him. Dixie enjoyed his verbal dexterity on occasion, but not today.

"That's another reporter," he said, pushing the HOLD button. "I'll have to talk to him. Avoidance only adds fuel to their suppositions. But, Dixie—" He took her arm lightly. "Chief Wanamaker, his men, the FBI task force—we're all taking this very seriously."

Maybe. But why did she suddenly see his words like dialogue bubbles in a political cartoon?

"I hope you *are* taking it seriously, because in the voters' eyes, Wanamaker's men slaughtered Lucy Ames and Edna Pine."

"They had no choice—"

"*I* know that. But what voters will remember is that *you* appointed Wanamaker, *you* reduced the budget line item for increasing the number of HPD officers, and *only* after you took office did previously law-abiding senior citizens begin robbing banks and being shot down in the streets." Seeing the spark in his eyes that revealed she now had the Mayor's full attention, she said, "Avery, I believe there's more behind all this than three greedy women without a reasonable brain among them."

The spark turned appreciative. "Point made," he told her. "I'll have a talk with the Chief."

Finding herself at the door, Dixie realized he'd been easing her in that direction, a trick every good hostess and politician discovered about the time they learned to walk. He moved his grip from her arm to offer a handshake.

Dixie accepted it, and his manner seemed as sincere as ever, even when she caught his appraising glance sliding over her figure. After advocating Avery Banning to Houston voters, Dixie prayed now that her judgment hadn't been skewed by a winning smile and a glib line of bullshit.

"Good luck with the media," she told him.

As she walked out, Banning's junior assistant, a serious young man with a buzz of red-blond hair, looked up from his Dictaphone. Dixie had seen him before, a fellow volunteer on the Mayor's election campaign. A whiz at the keyboard. Working his way through college, no doubt. Casual but neat in a blue shirt and khaki pants, the kid reminded her of a stone in a brook, scarcely noticed in the ripple of activity, while steadily and efficiently directing the flow.

Flashing a gentle, cheerful grin, he whisked a yellow flyer off a sizable stack.

"Take this coupon and you'll get a free soft drink at the Mayor's Memorial Day celebration on Monday."

She glanced at the flyer and tried to hand it back. "Thanks, but I'm not big on crowds."

"Neither am I. Except, some occasions are worth it."

Ignoring the proffered flyer, he scooped up a pack of sugar-free gum. Alongside his keyboard sat a silver-framed photograph of a woman far too old to be a wife or sweetheart.

"Okay," Dixie relented, sifting through her mental file cabinet for the kid's name. He was probably required to hand out the entire stack of promotional material before Monday. "I'll take it. Maybe I'll even show up."

"Great! Here, give one to a friend."

Who could resist that grin? She folded the yellow pages into her back pocket, planning to toss them later. *Philip*, she recalled. Philip turned studiously back to his typing.

Chapter Fifteen

Dixie raised the brass horseshoe knocker on Edna's door and let it fall with a *clank*. Unless the cops had left every light on inside the house, Marty must've already arrived.

After her frustrating morning, throwing out the accumulation of junk in her garage proved almost as therapeutic as a rousing game of racquetball, and the shelves now held orderly, labeled boxes. She'd found the records in question, with one checkbook missing. Apparently, it was missing when she'd turned the box over to her CPA, because that group of checks had not been entered on the spreadsheet she found. At least she'd accounted for where the thief obtained her deposit slips—each checkbook contained five, and Dixie rarely used them. She usually grabbed a generic slip from the bank's supply counter and filled it out on the spot.

Banging the horseshoe again, she wondered if Marty had fallen asleep. Then she peeked in a window, and her brain sorted through memories of the home's interior for places that might yield useful information. She recalled that Edna had kept a memento box in a hall closet. Vacation snapshots, postcards, invitations—everything went into the box until she found time to stick them in albums or frames. Her bookshelf, too, collected memorabilia.

After several minutes, Marty answered the knock.

"Sorry, I was on the phone with my partner. We have a show for a new artist opening this week." He looked distracted. "Hell of a time for me to be gone."

Right. Damn your mother for being so inconsiderate. Dixie swallowed the sarcasm and braced herself for the nostalgia that hit as she entered the living room.

Edna's fondness for flowers showed everywhere, from wisteria-printed draperies to hand-stitched bluebonnets on the sofa pillows. But the place had a just-scrubbed look Dixie didn't associate with Edna. Marty's mother, friendly, generous, and comfortable as an old shoe, had never wasted energy keeping a spotless house. And it was the new Edna she needed to learn about.

"Did the cops take anything?"

Marty shook his head. "Unless I'm overlooking it."

"They'd have left a receipt."

"They asked a lot of questions about the hunting rifles—wanted to know if Mom owned any handguns, which I'd already told them she didn't."

Marty had tossed his jacket and tie on a chair and rolled up his shirtsleeves. A lock of hair tumbled across his ear. Dixie liked him better this way. Less pressed. He raked the hair back.

"Did your mother ever fire those rifles?"

"Dad taught both of us to shoot when I was about ten. After years of hunting, and bagging only one small whitetail buck, he lost interest and the rifles stood unused in the case. Come on back. There's a desk in the dining room where Mom paid bills. The bank and tax records should be there, too."

Fine. She'd get to those. Did he expect to discover a Caribbean bank account containing money from previous robberies?

"What I want to see first are the rooms where your mother spent her time." To get to know the personal side of the new Edna.

Marty shrugged and led the way to the kitchen. A new juice maker gleamed on the counter. A wire basket held carrots, onions, and peppers—probably from Edna's small garden—all still looked fresh, except for the drooping carrot tops. The vinyl floor appeared recently polished—another sign of the neatness and order Dixie didn't associate with her neighbor.

"Did your mother hire a maid?"

Marty peered around at the tidy kitchen. "She might've."

He opened the refrigerator and absently stared inside as he'd done thousands of times when he lived here. His features slackened into a sadness that alleviated Dixie's annoyance with him. She turned toward the bedrooms, Marty's first. It looked exactly as she remembered. His bed, updated during his college years, was flanked by a matching cherry-wood desk and chest with brass hardware. His college pennant sagged over the mirror. Two paintings he'd done in high school decorated one wall. In the master bedroom, a fluffy cream-white comforter replaced Edna's antique crocheted bedspread. Plump pillows in shades of white were layered three deep against a wooden headboard, carved with angels. A sisal carpet took the place of a colorful braided rug Dixie remembered.

"What happened to all the stuff on her dresser?" Marty demanded. "All the paintings I gave her? The pottery vases I made while I was growing up? Look at this."

Seven white candles in an array of sizes, each on a simple wooden holder, scented the air with a light citrus fragrance. Otherwise, the dresser top was clear. The walls were bare. She opened a drawer. Bottles of creams and oils and jars of makeup lined one side. A fancy art deco tray of brushes and combs lined the other.

Dixie lifted out a jar to read its lavender-and-silver label. Ornate letters spelled the name "Artistry Spa" and boasted "custom-blended," which, to Dixie, meant pricey. All the cosmetics bore the same label. A business card with the spa logo and the name LONNIE GRAY, PROPRIETOR lay beneath one of the jars. Dixie slipped the card into her pocket. Before closing the drawer, she carefully ran her fingers along the wooden surface above it. Nothing taped there.

"No pills," Marty reported from the bathroom. "Not even a bottle of aspirin or liniment. Just vitamins. What happened to her blood pressure medicine?"

"Maybe she kept it in her purse," Dixie suggested. "If she took it frequently." She opened another dresser drawer. Not much there. A simple nightshirt, champagne white. Several bras. A third drawer held cotton underwear, the next, cotton socks and three unopened pairs of panty hose.

She eased the mirror away from the wall to check behind it, then moved to the nightstand. The drawer held reading glasses, pens, and, toward the back, a single-dose package of Tylenol. Behind a door in the lower compartment, she found a stack of volumes, each about six by nine inches, all covered in identical fabric. She lifted one out. The cotton cover, with its tropical flower design, felt almost like satin.

"I remember those!" Marty snatched the book away. "I gave her these blank journals on her fiftieth birthday. One a year, enough to last until she reached a hundred." He opened the volume and flipped rapidly through the pages.

"I only count fifteen," she told him.

"She kept them in the attic, brought a new one down each January."

"Edna was what, sixty-five?"

"Sixty-six. This one's dated last year."

Dixie recounted. Fifteen. "There's one missing." She checked the dates on the others. "This year's would be less than half filled. It's not here. Maybe it was in her car, along with her purse."

"Which the cops have," Marty grumbled. "Maybe they stole the journal from this cabinet."

"Marty, they wouldn't take it without leaving a receipt."

In the closet—remarkably free of clutter—warm-up suits, leotards for working out, and a pair of denim jeans lay folded on shelves. Cotton shirts, two plain cotton dresses, both white, and a coral silk dress similar to the blue one Edna had worn during the bank robbery hung from the rod.

"Where's all the *stuff*?" Marty said irritably, coming up behind Dixie. "Mom never threw anything away. Always planning to patch it or hem it up or dye it and wear it a couple more years. She had sizes from twelve to sixteen, for all the diets she tried and the weight she lost and regained. This stuff looks new."

Indeed. Dixie checked the tags inside a few of the items—all size ten. Several came from one manufacturer, "Unique Boutique," a private-label women's shop Dixie'd seen in the Galleria area. Tracing all the flat surfaces with her fingers, as she had the dresser and nightstand drawers, Dixie found no hidden caches.

"Marty, where does she keep her address book?"

"The desk in the dining room."

He led the way. Opening a drawer, he removed a well-thumbed, spiral-bound book. A bouquet of sunflowers decorated the cover. Years of use had abraded the edges and softened the colors.

Dixie opened it to A. No Ames listed. Then to B, for Bacon, in case Edna's attack on the bank had been directed at Len in particular. No dice. No "Texas Citizens" listed under T, no gun shop under G. She hadn't really expected to find anything that easily. Scanning the pages one by one, she did notice a difference in the writing over the years. Bill had no doubt made some of the entries. Erasures, with new information penciled over, indicated new addresses or phone numbers. Some erasures hadn't been reentered. Numbers no longer needed? Deaths? You couldn't live to be nearly seventy without people around you passing away.

"How about going through this and jotting down any names you don't recognize?" she asked Marty. "I want to look through her canceled checks."

"Yeah, okay. But shouldn't I help you?"

"We can cover more ground quickly working on separate tasks."

He gave her a grudging nod, then turned over a paper-clip holder, removed a key, and opened a locked drawer. Dixie wondered if people really expected burglars to be fooled by such tactics. Boxes of checks filled the drawer.

"Here are the more recent ones." Marty indicated a date scrawled on a box lid.

"Okay. I can take it from here."

He shrugged, grabbed a pencil from a cup on the desk and a tablet from one of the drawers. Dropping onto a chair at the dining table, he bent diligently over his task.

Edna's checks, carbonless duplicates, the same kind Dixie used . . . *with a blocked-out signature on each copy . . . a diligent forger with a single checkbook would have dozens of examples to practice . . .*

With a mental nudge, Dixie turned her thoughts from her own account problems to Aunt Edna's records. The current checkbook was probably in her purse, now in the hands of the police. The most recent checks in the drawer, dated eleven days earlier, were written to the grocery store, health food store, drugstore, a gasoline credit card payment. Apparently, Edna had gone into Houston on May tenth to shop. On that date, she wrote several checks to department stores and one to a Terrence Jackson, for consultation. Dixie jotted the name down, along with Artistry Spa and the Unique Boutique. Any new people and places in Edna's life could be revealing.

On May third Edna paid for six months' car insurance. Dixie wondered if the comprehensive covered bullet holes. In December and January, Edna issued four checks to "Fit After Fifty," a popular health club chain. The notation on a November payment to Southwest Airlines read "Dallas, Marty's art show."

Closing the last box, Dixie dropped it back in the drawer. The desk blotter had shifted, and now a folded newspaper clipping peeked from beneath it. The article, dated the previous November, featured a band called "Meanstreak" playing at a club in the Heights. Folded inside the clipping, a ticket bore the club's name and address.

Meanstreak? Curiouser and curiouser. She added the health club and night-club to her list.

Edna's calendar started with January of the current year. The letters "FAF" marked every Tuesday, Thursday, and Saturday through February. May fifth was circled without an explanation. She'd circled Marty's upcoming show in red. The only other marked date, May tenth, bore a penciled notation: Vernice Urich, four P.M. The same day as Edna's shopping trip to Houston. No address or phone number. Dixie wrote down the name. She glanced through the other desk drawers, meticulously running her hands over the backs and bottoms, and then moved to the bookshelf.

The Zen of Eating. Fit for Life. A booklet titled *An Ounce of Wheat Grass.* Recalling the chef's salad Edna had served Parker, Dixie thumbed the *Zen* book to a recipe section about halfway back. *Spinach, shredded apples, bok choy?*

These cookbooks were all new, compared to *Fanny Farmer* and *Good Housekeeping.* Another new book, *Work It On Out,* stood behind three framed five-by-seven photographs.

The first snapshot, of Edna, Bill, and Marty in front of a Christmas tree, had been taken the Christmas before Bill died. The second picture, one of those glamour photos Dixie'd seen advertised at malls, with professional makeup and soft focus, showed Edna as she'd looked at the bank, hours before her death.

"Seeing the changes in your mother before and after her new fitness regimen, I'd say she was on to something," Dixie said.

Marty rose from his chair and snatched the glamour shot from Dixie's hand.

"That's *Mom?*" He plopped back down like a deflated balloon.

"That's not the way she looked last time you saw her?"

"No. But I guess I didn't realize . . . I mean, she dressed nice for the art show, and she looked great, but she didn't stay over, flew right back that night . . . I mean, how often had I seen her in party clothes? She and Dad never went places as upscale as my gallery . . . except that one time, when we first opened."

The third photo, at least twenty years old, had been taken on a golf course. Bill, curled over a putter, had apparently sunk a winning ball. Marty held the flag, while Edna and two men applauded.

"Your mother looks as trim in this recent photograph," Dixie said, "as she did way back then." She studied the men with Edna on the golf course. "This is your father's old army buddy—what was his name? And his son."

"Hager," Marty said quietly. "J. Claude and Derry Hager."

"That's right—Bill always called him J. Claude, never just Claude. And Derry caddied for them—although you and I usually chased the balls."

"Yeah, that was Derry." Marty abruptly stacked all three photographs on the desk. "And his father."

His eyes had turned evasive. Dixie recalled hearing whispers in the Flannigan household that Bill's old friend had a crush on Edna. Dixie looked back at the photograph. Edna and J. Claude were standing together.

"We didn't exactly come here to dig up old memories," Marty said. "Did you find anything *useful*?"

"Won't know until we follow a few trails." She checked her notes. "Do you know a Terrence Jackson? Or Vernice Urich?"

"No, but I saw Jackson's name in her book, a financial consultant."

"What about this date?" Dixie pointed to May fifth circled on the calendar.

Marty's face tightened.

"Aw, nuts." Stiff-lipped, he turned away. "Her birthday. I forgot it."

They continued to search, including the box of photographs and mementos in the closet, but found nothing else "useful." Dixie pocketed her notes and strolled back through the house, one last sweep for anything they might've missed. This time, she particularly noticed the dichotomy between the colorful, flowered decor in the living room and the white, unembellished decor in the kitchen, bedroom, and master bath. This difference, more than anything she'd seen, epitomized Edna's personality change, from a warm and caring country mother to a cool sophisticate who could dispassionately commit armed robbery.

Dixie departed for the walk home. With a distracted wave, Marty flipped open his cell phone.

Chapter Sixteen

When Dixie entered her house, the phone was ringing. Mud met her at the door with a single bark, then pranced toward the instrument as if to hurry her along. The clock suggested it would be Parker calling—this was their usual time to talk.

"How'd the snooping go?" His baritone voice resonated with restrained sexuality.

Or maybe that was her own hormones backing up. Whichever, it sent a shudder of longing through her.

"I didn't find a picture of Edna's boyfriend," she admitted. She heard a TV commercial playing in the background.

"Like I said, could've been a salesman."

"You don't believe that, Parker. The man didn't strike you that way at the time."

"No."

Mud put his front paws on the kitchen counter and whined softly at the phone.

"Is that my good buddy?" Parker asked.

"He misses you." *And so do I.*

"Let me talk to him."

"Parker! He's a dog. He does not do telephone."

"Sure he does. Just lay the receiver down."

She did as he asked. As soon as it *thunk*ed on the Formica, she heard him say, "Hey, boy!"

Mud chuffed happily.

While her two best friends *conversed*, Dixie hooked a Shiner Bock from the fridge and drank half of it. Finally, Mud dropped back to his feet and chuffed at Dixie.

"Oh, it's my turn again?" She looped an arm around his great ugly head and gave him a smooch, then picked up the phone.

"So, tell me what you *did* find at Edna's," Parker said.

Dixie gave him an abbreviated rundown on the clothing and cosmetics, the checkbook notations, the photographs—including Marty's peculiar reaction to the snapshot of J. Claude Hager—the fitness books, and the circled birth date on Edna's calendar.

"What a guy. Forgets his mother's birthday . . . doesn't notice she's become a glamorous Ma Barker." The fierceness in Parker's words seemed excessive.

"How long since you called *your* mother?"

"Too damn long. And I can't remember if I sent a birthday card."

"So you and Marty have something in common."

"Yeah. We loved the same woman."

"Come again?"

"You and Marty made a handsome couple. I saw the prom photo on Edna's bookshelf."

A duplicate of the photograph in Kathleen's album—Dixie had scarcely noticed it tonight.

"That was taken a long time ago, Parker, and Marty was only a minor-league boyfriend." Parker's mixed messages were damned confusing. For three months it's "let's just be pals." Yet now he's jealous of a high school sweetheart? And Dixie hadn't missed the past tense, ". . . *loved* the same woman."

"Guess I don't like anybody you kissed before you kissed me," he grumbled, as if surprised at his own words. "Or maybe I don't like him on general principles—like being an inconsiderate son."

Or maybe Marty's oversight reminded Parker of his own maternal neglect. *Please pass the guilt.* Nothing to do with Dixie at all. Not really.

"Hey, what's that on the news?" Dixie'd heard the words "Texas Citizens Bank."

He turned up the volume, and Dixie finished her beer as they listened.

"*. . . all managers have been briefed on new procedures in the event another branch is targeted by the Granny Bandits. In a related interview, Houston Police Chief Edward Wanamaker stated that police response to the robberies was neither reactionary nor unnecessarily violent.*"

The newscast cut to an interview with Wanamaker.

"*Chief, the first robbery occurred in HPD jurisdiction and did not result in an exchange of gunfire. Do you care to comment on that?*"

"*The suspect of the first robbery was not apprehended.*"

Wanamaker's tenor voice, which Dixie admired when she'd heard him sing in Christmas presentations, sounded pitifully immature on television.

"*Would you say then, Chief, that the shootings were justified?*"

"*I can't speak for the Webster Police Department. In yesterday's incident, a Houston officer was critically wounded. The other officers had no recourse but to return fire.*"

When the newscast switched to a commercial, Parker lowered the volume.

"What does that idiot reporter expect cops to do when they're shot at?" Dixie demanded. "Call time out?"

Mud responded to her indignant tone by nudging his head under her hand for scratching.

"She's doing what all reporters do these days," Parker said. "Playing to the audience."

"Well, I hate it."

"I know." Their bedtime ritual while Parker lived with Dixie had been watching and arguing over the news together. "So what's next? Will you follow up on those names from Edna's records?"

"Might as well. I might stumble on something interesting."

"Or dangerous."

Now they'd hit the point where their conversations usually ended. Dixie refused to respond this time, allowing silence to stretch the moment. She spied the invitation she'd received from Mike Tesche, folded tent style near the phone.

"Seriously, Dixie, will you call me if—?"

"If I get another .38 pointed at my face—absolutely." She opened Mike's invitation to the map inside.

"I know he's an old friend—"

With her thoughts on Mike, Dixie felt confused for a second before realizing Parker meant Marty.

"—but this time maybe you should consider letting the cops handle it. Edna got herself involved with a radical bunch of women, these Granny Bandits, and whatever her reason, she paid for it with her life. I don't want that to happen to you."

"I don't plan to rob a bank, Parker."

"I'd bet my next sale that Edna didn't plan to rob a bank when I saw her last. Anyway, you know that's not what I meant."

"Yeah, I know. What happened to, 'This time I won't try to talk you out of it'?"

"I reneged." He sighed. "But you *will* call if you need help?"

"Yep."

After they said good night, Dixie stared at the phone awhile, Mike's invitation still in her hand.

Chapter Seventeen

Thursday morning

The baby was crying.

Officer E. Arthur Harris shoved his cereal bowl into the dishwasher and listened for his wife's footsteps. Hearing no sound from the bedroom didn't surprise him—she'd been socked in pretty hard. Ann liked her beauty sleep.

Checking his watch, he saw that he could spare a few minutes this morning before leaving for his shift. He sprinted down the hall toward Peggy—christened Margaret, after her paternal grandmother, but much too small and feisty for such a heavy handle. They'd been arguing—*discussing*, as Ann insisted—whether to call her Maggie or Meg when the old Buddy Holly song "Peggy Sue" came on the radio. Then they'd looked at each other and started laughing.

He peeked in at Ann as he passed the bedroom. Though the baby's cry sounded louder on the monitor than here in the hallway, his wife hadn't stirred. Art worried about that at times, worried that he'd be gone and Ann would sleep right through an emergency.

"Honey, Peggy's awake," he called. "And I have to get out of here."

The doctor said a mother's instinct kicked in when her baby really needed her, but Art had a hunch Ann's genetic mix didn't include motherly instinct.

The instant he leaned over the crib, Peggy stopped crying.

"Hey, kiddo, what are you fussing so hard about so early in the morning?"

A tiny bundle of energy, she responded with one of her heart-melting smiles, waving and kicking like he'd just told the best joke in the whole world. She liked her daddy.

The crib sheets were printed with bunnies wearing eyeglasses and reading storybooks. A brightly colored "busy" toy hung from each corner of the crib, and a mobile of baby seals danced overhead. Art lifted her out and carried her to the changing table.

Somebody should have told him what a joy babies could be; maybe he'd have given in years ago — well, a couple of years, anyway. He and Ann were approaching the big five, anniversary-wise. He cherished their first years together, when they couldn't get enough of each other. But with Peggy, the days seemed fuller, even more satisfying than before.

Ann, on the other hand, seemed to resent these months away from her career. Art almost wished he was the one to take time off and stay home, especially considering these past couple days.

He wiped the sleep from Peggy's eyes with a damp cloth and changed her wet diaper. Then came the good part.

Tossing a blanket over his shoulder to protect his fresh uniform shirt from her slobbery mouth, he snuggled her on his shoulder, next to his heart, which she'd stolen the moment she popped into the world squalling and bloody and full of life. Hearing about it from other guys, he hadn't thought it possible to feel anything but relief that the ordeal was over and he hadn't done anything to screw up. And now, nuzzling her soft baby hair, smelling that sweet, distinctly Peggy smell, feeling the silken skin and the five perfect fingers of her hand clutching his big thumb, he figured he'd done damn good.

Ann had managed her part pretty well, too. It was afterward that wasn't going so well for her.

"Honey! I need to go." He'd be screwed for sure if he didn't leave soon. After the shooting, and the endless interviews, they'd put him on desk duty — standard practice — but he knew Internal Affairs wasn't through. No matter that his wasn't the only bullet that had taken down Edna Pine.

And Lucy Ames.

Damn, that'd been freakish. Even when she got out of the car with the gun in her hand, Art had thought sure they could talk her down. Nobody wanted to shoot—

Except Ted Tally had charged out of his unit like the lady was one of America's most wanted.

And then she'd started firing. How could that happen twice?

He carried Peggy in and laid her in the crook of Ann's arm. Ann stirred, frowning. "Why don't you call in sick?" she asked sleepily.

"Can't." He kissed them both, Peggy still holding tight to his thumb. "You have a good day, pretty Peggy, you hear?"

She smiled and kicked, and he brushed his lips across the tiny fingers.

Minutes later, in the driveway, as he opened the door of his Cougar, Officer E. Arthur Harris felt a blow to his head. He hadn't heard the sniper's bullet, and he didn't feel a thing as he fell to the concrete.

Chapter Eighteen

Dixie entered her Thursday morning classroom frustrated, irritable, and late. After a restless night reliving a troublesome day—reclaiming her financial identity, snooping through a dead friend's personal effects, and feeling a whole lot like Parker's emotional yo-yo—she'd scarcely dropped off when the alarm sounded. Slapping it silent, she closed her eyes for a few extra minutes . . . and when she finally stumbled out of bed two hours later, there was no time left for her own workout.

She arrived to find most of her students already stretching in front of the mirrored walls. Curbing her peevishness, Dixie walked beside the blue mats, murmuring encouragement.

"Looks good, Ruth, but keep it smooth. Don't bounce. Nice, Janice, now this time twist harder. That's it, that's perfect."

The good turnout lifted her spirits. Dixie's only compensation for teaching this class came from seeing the women take control of their own safety. When they failed to show up, or put forth less than their best effort, she could think of a dozen ways to make better use of ninety minutes. Today her students were in good form. By the time Dixie approached the end of the room, her irritability had nearly vanished.

Then she saw Joan's face, marked with fresh bruises.

"You went back to your husband," Dixie said. Not much of a guess. Joan's marriage was a series of close encounters with a mean fist. Dixie'd seen the woman messed up worse than today, and with even more makeup covering her injuries.

Joan glanced away, caught her own image in the floor-to-ceiling mirror, and lowered her eyes.

"We went to dinner. You know, just to talk. I can't help loving him, Dixie."

"Talking doesn't bust your lip."

"After dinner, I went back to the house with him, to get some of my things. Have some coffee."

"Just coffee?"

"You know, some brandy in it. I was so nervous, he said a little brandy would relax us both." She smiled with one side of her swollen mouth. "He's the doctor, I told him."

Joan was not a stupid woman. Dixie didn't understand why smart women made stupid moves when it came to dealing with the men in their lives. But she needed to understand, to get past her own anger before they began practice. Seeing that busted lip, knowing Joan had gone back to the bastard again, made her itch to slap some sense into the woman. Where was the logic in that? The guilt phantom cackled at her even thinking it. Is that what Joan's husband did: try to batter his own brand of sense into his hardheaded wife?

"I just wanted him to, you know, hold me a little. It'd been so long. I *needed* him to hold me."

Dixie felt the ghost of a tingle where Parker's hand had touched hers last Friday during dinner. In the past three months they'd spent a lot of time *not* touching. Some mornings she awoke with a mangled pillow and her arms aching with emptiness.

"Did you talk with a counselor?"

"She's not in yet." The relief in Joan's voice suggested she might conveniently disappear if a counselor did come in today. Why had Joan even bothered to show up for defense class?

"Are you planning to see your *loving husband* again tonight?"

"We have to work this thing out between us, Dixie. He promised he'd go to counseling."

"Did he promise that before or after he hit you?"

Joan's torn lip quivered. "He can be so sweet. . . ." Tears slid from her eyes, and she wiped them away roughly with the back of her hand. "You just don't know. I've never met a man more thoughtful, when he's not . . . you know, stressed out. An anesthesiologist is under so much pressure. Why, he's more responsible for a patient's life than the almighty surgeon."

Or so he tells his wife repeatedly. Dixie was getting in deeper here than she wanted to be. She hadn't the training or the patience to be a psychologist. All she could do was teach Joan how to defend herself physically and pray the woman used that knowledge before her husband beat her to death.

"Stretch," she told Joan. "We've got a hard workout today."

Most of the other students had started horsing around, shadow-kicking the mirrors and each other. Time to focus that energy.

Lureen came in from the changing room, went straight to the heavy bag, and threw a battery of jabs without warming up first. Working off a load of frustration, Dixie figured, all too familiar with the feeling. She ambled over to talk.

"What's up?"

Lureen struck the bag with a backfist. "Some mofo out there sold my kid shit." Another fierce volley of jabs.

Dixie slipped behind the bag to steady it. Up close, she could see the woman's puffy, bloodshot eyes. "Your oldest boy?"

"Yeah."

"How did you find out?"

"Found it in his effin' drawer, stuffed in a sock."

"Any other signs he might be using?"

"Using, dealing, alla same in the end. What I been working my ass off for? So he can kill hisself wit' shit? Kill his bro wit' shit?"

"How deep is he in?"

Lureen finished another twenty jabs before answering. "Let the effin' cops figger it out. I turned the little pissant in."

Chapter Nineteen

On her way to the shower, Dixie heard familiar music coming from Mike's class and peeked in. About thirty women, varying sizes and ages, sat in the lotus position.

Bach's "Air," wasn't it? Baroque music, anyway. Soothing. The same music Dixie used for meditation, which she hadn't done now in far too long. At one time it had been part of her daily routine. After Kathleen died, especially. Meditation and hard physical exercise helped her deal with the loss of her adoptive mother. Why had she stopped?

New priorities, probably. Six months after Kathleen's death, while Barney moped around, not eating, Dixie had moved into her old bedroom on the pretense that she was short of cash—no longer on the State's payroll after quitting the DA's staff. She devoted her days to Barney, trying to jolly him out of his misery. But he'd died anyway, a year later. Dixie managed to get in enough physical exercise now, but she'd never gone back to meditating.

Easing into the softly lit room, she took a place in the back row and assumed the lotus. Maybe what she needed right now was some of Mike's touchy-feely crap. And maybe after the class, she'd ask what he'd noticed about Edna during the time he worked with her.

Closing her eyes, she let the music enter her body . . . felt the rhythm like soothing hands stroking her . . . let all the tension of yesterday flow out like water whirling down an endless drain.

Breathe . . . two . . . three . . . four . . . five. Hold . . . two . . . three . . . four . . . five. Relax . . . two . . . three . . . four . . . five.

When the music ended, she'd been sitting twenty minutes, muscles limp as wet string. She opened her eyes, saw Mike watching her from the front of the room. He grinned. His Mel Gibson hair curled around his sharp-nosed full-moon face. Admittedly not handsome, that face was still easy to look at, oddly expressive, and enormously friendly. She grinned back and began stretching. She'd needed that bit of relaxation. And the movement felt good, too.

The lights brightened. Mike faced the mirror and led the class in basic warm-up routines. His lean body had been through the moves so often he made it look as effortless as breathing. Dixie followed the pace, enjoying it.

The music's tempo increased to about seventy beats a minute, and he led them through some slow aerobic movements. Dixie hated aerobics. But leaving now would seem rude. At least these weren't the silly dance steps she associated with spandexed airheads. She gritted her teeth and kept moving.

A few minutes later, the tempo increased again, then again. Some of the older students appeared visibly taxed.

Mike signaled a woman on the first row—the same blonde who'd called to him in the hall on Tuesday—to take his place. Trim and tanned, wearing white shorts, an abundantly filled tank top, and a faint sheen of perspiration, she eased her gorgeous body into place beside Mike without missing a beat. Her moves had the supple agility of a teenager's. A scrunched white scarf held her glossy hair high off her face. Dixie wished she had a scarf like that to keep her own hair from slapping around.

As Dixie had done earlier in her own class, Mike began walking the room, observing. He stopped beside each student, touched her shoulder, and murmured something. With the ones struggling most, he spent extra time.

As he drew nearer, Dixie heard some of his coaching.

"Excellent, Julie. Good work. Bend deeper, now. Once more, but still lower . . . good."

"*Almost* perfect, Myra. With your strong back muscles, you can do better. That's it. Watch the mirror, see how fine you look? Now do it again, with even more stretch."

After each brief encouragement, his students looked more confident. *Good technique.* Dixie tucked away a few ideas to use later. When he stopped behind her, he said nothing. Just watched.

Unlike the room Dixie taught in, this one had mirrors only on the front wall. She could see him, leaning back, studying her movements. Couldn't tell by his expression what he thought. What the hell did it matter? She was a visitor. But his scrutiny disconcerted her.

"Welcome, Dixie Flannigan." He had a rich, sexy voice, and her name, the way he said it, sounded almost lyrical.

They were doing high kicks, now, the music at maximum beat.

"Higher," he told her. "You can do it."

Fat chance. As limber as she was, her leg was already almost vertical. But she stretched the kick anyway, feeling the pull in her hamstrings. A river of sweat snaked down her ribs. Her lungs started to seriously resist, when suddenly the music slowed, the lights dimmed, and they began some cooling-down stretches.

Mike made the rounds again, saying a word or two to each student. Then the beat slowed to a largo, the class almost over. The unusual mix of meditation and movement was obviously Mike's own innovation. When the music ended after the cool-down, Dixie felt a hell of a lot better than she had an hour ago.

"Dixie . . . could you spare me a few minutes?"

"Sure. After I shower."

"Before . . . if you don't mind." Mike's green eyes, so remarkably attractive in his homely face, held her captive. He smiled. "Gotta dash out of here in about ten minutes."

The room emptied swiftly, everyone headed for showers. Dixie nodded, and she and Mike sat facing each other, cross-legged, on a single exercise mat. After the long workout, she felt deliciously exhausted.

He folded his hands together, steepled his forefingers, and pointed them like a pistol.

"After so many weeks of asking, I finally rate a visit. I'm delighted, but also intrigued."

She shrugged. "Right time, right mood."

"I see. Dixie . . ." He raised his eyebrows, as if struck by a wild idea. "Why do I think that's not the name your mother gave you?"

"It's the name I prefer."

"I watched you during the workout. Your quiet strength tells a lot about your discipline and commitment, but something's troubling you, Dixie . . . a problem, a fear—a disturbance, let's say, in your psyche." His voice resonated, low, mellow, and soothing.

Dixie said nothing. These touchy-feely guru types all wanted to get inside your head. At least this one was easy to take, and her head did feel absolutely relaxed for the first time in weeks.

He grinned and crossed his eyes, comically, as if aware of her thoughts. "Would you tell me something?"

She shrugged, feeling so damned contented she might lie down on the mat and take a nap. After Mike left, of course. Meditation definitely would return to her daily regimen.

"Your given name, the name on your birth certificate. Tell me."

Dixie rarely gave anyone her real name, except on legal documents. Carla Jean must've come straight from seeing *Gone With the Wind* when she chose it. But what the hell.

"Desiree Alexandra."

"Perfect . . ." he said softly. "It's beautiful! It suits you."

Sure it did. "Now, let me ask *you* something. When Edna Pine was in your class, how did she seem?"

Mike frowned, as if searching his memory. "For a woman her age, obviously not accustomed to physical exercise, she shaped up fast and caught up with some of my long-time students. I'd say she seemed driven."

"Anything else you can tell me? How she found you? Who her friends were?"

"She didn't buddy with anyone, though she seemed friendly enough. And how she found me . . . I don't know, but my flyers are everywhere."

Dixie'd seen them posted: *Michael J. Tesche, The Winning Stretch, stretch to win.*

"Did Lucy Ames attend your classes?"

"The other woman robber?" Amusement flickered over his face—then he must've realized this was important to her and grew thoughtful. "Not as a regular student, Dixie, or I'd remember the woman. She might've attended briefly at one of the facilities on my rotation schedule. The gym managers sign up all beginners—but we can find out, I'm sure. Why did you want to know?"

"I'm wondering where she and Edna met." *Assuming Edna didn't merely copy Lucy's MO.*

"Take one of my flyers. It lists all the facilities and the phone numbers." He stood and offered a strong hand to help her up. "You won't forget the Sundown Ceremony this weekend."

"I don't know if I can make it."

"I'll keep asking until you do." He winked and turned to walk away.

Nice muscles, Dixie noticed once again. Not as bulky as Parker's but compact and well defined.

Nice body. Nice buns.

Damn, woman, you're just horny.

Chapter Twenty

Terrence Jackson Associates occupied a penthouse office in a modern building about five minutes from the women's center. A wide elevator rose silently to the top floor, stopping without a hint of bounce. Dixie stepped out onto luxurious, custom-designed carpet.

After showering at the center, she'd changed into a black suit brought from home, suitable for attending Lucy Ames' funeral later that day. Then, considering how infrequently she wore a skirt and panty hose, she'd decided to make the most of the occasion and drop in on Terrence Jackson, the first name on her list from Edna's records.

The company logo, sculpted in shades of green pile, embellished a twelve-foot expanse of carpet approaching the receptionist's desk. The desk itself appeared to be solid marble, greenish black, with the company name engraved across its curved front and underscored with a fine gold line.

A rich, exotic scent, soothing after the choke of exhaust fumes outside, reminded Dixie of an oriental rug salon where she'd once dropped more money than she could afford on a carpet she didn't need. The receptionist might've stepped straight from a Neiman Marcus catalog. Sniffing the air, Dixie asked her, "What is that wonderful smell?"

"Ylang-ylang, an imported oil." The woman's gaze flicked candidly over Dixie's clothes. "Did you have an appointment?"

Feeling abruptly penniless, not to mention dowdy, though her black suit had been fashionable and a shade pricey five years ago, Dixie pictured the expensive oriental rug in her home office. The image bolstered her daunted self-esteem.

"Not yet. Is Mr. Jackson in?" She handed the receptionist a business card from a box she'd never gotten around to tossing out. It read: D. A. "DIXIE" FLANNIGAN, ATTORNEY AT LAW. "I'd hoped he might have a minute between appointments. One of his clients referred me."

"That would be . . . ?"

"Edna Pine."

"Oh!" The red lips remained shaped in the exclamation for a second or two. "If you'll take a seat, I'll see if Mr. Jackson can squeeze you in." She picked up the phone, touched a button, murmured something Dixie didn't quite catch, then nodded. "It'll be a few minutes, Ms. Flannigan. Would you like something to drink? Coffee, tea, juice, water?"

Hell, why not? She'd skipped breakfast. "Tea sounds good."

"Earl Grey, Oolong, Apple Spice, or Chamomile?"

Dixie hadn't a clue, but only one sounded like it might have caffeine. "Earl Grey."

"Lemon, milk, sugar? Artificial sweetener?"

"Plain." Dixie tried to keep the exasperation out of her voice. Did the woman always offer four choices?

When the receptionist rose and slipped through a swinging door, Dixie scanned the opulent reception area. A large Miró—an original?—hung on one wall. In a corner, a stylized bronze horse rose to the ceiling. Four identical side chairs, uphol-stered in black-and-cream-striped silk, faced an apple-green Italian sofa.

On a wall near the desk, Dixie spotted an eight-month-old framed *Financial Times* article touting Jackson as "Houston's Millennium Midas." The excerpt was titled "Seen Any Rich Monkeys Lately?" with a subhead: "Financial Wizard Terrence Jackson Warns PC Investors to Beware of Gambler's Euphoria."

In an accompanying photograph, the silver-haired wizard leaned across a gleaming desktop, head well in front of his custom-tailored shoulders: the power pose. "Handsome" didn't even come close.

After a quick summary of the stock market's fluctuations over the past year, the writer presented the Jackson interview in Q&A style. Apparently, several of Jackson's clients became overnight millionaires because of his astute invest-ments. His success in picking undervalued stocks had inspired investors all over the country to follow his lead. One of the stocks mentioned was an importer of exotic oils. Jackson's success had also piqued the interest of the Securities and Exchange Commission, "who walked away scratching their heads," Jackson claimed.

His message, however, was aimed at cautioning neophytes that investing on-line with their own money could be as perilous as tossing it on a craps table. "The word out there is that even a monkey can get rich in today's market. I haven't seen any wealthy monkeys, but I've counseled a number of unhappy investors after they lost a bundle on speculative stocks."

Questioned about the investment clubs cropping up around the country, Jackson said, "So, all these ladies get together, read *The Wall Street Journal*, listen to a few TV experts, and pool their capital. It's like playing Bingo-for-Broke. I tell them, 'Go ahead, have fun. Just don't risk more than you can afford to lose.' "

The interviewer's next question—"Would you share some of your picks for future gains?"—had the greedy part of Dixie's mind picturing thousand-dollar bills flooding her account. But before she could get to the good part, the receptionist appeared beside her, footsteps muffled by the thick pile carpet.

"Mr. Jackson's free now, Ms. Flannigan. I placed your tea in his office."

Dragging her gaze reluctantly from the magazine article, Dixie followed the woman. Down a silent hallway, they entered an office as crowded as an auctioneer's warehouse. *Tastefully* crowded—with exquisite furniture of various periods and countries.

The carved ebony desk appeared to be antique and probably cost more than Dixie's yearly earnings. A pair of guest chairs faced it, but the receptionist motioned Dixie to a conversation area in one corner, where the "silver-haired wizard" closed a notebook he'd been writing in and stood to greet her.

Adorning the wall behind him was an African mask, four feet tall with scowling mouth and raffia beard. Brutal and primitive, the mask framed the man so dramatically, Dixie wondered if Jackson posed there for all his first-time visitors. In comparison, he appeared even more elegant than in the magazine photo.

"Hope you don't mind getting comfortable," he said. "It's cozier over here."

"Fine." Dixie shook hands, certain she only imagined the hint of electricity when they touched. She sank into the chair he offered—the kind she hated, all fluff and air.

His own, firmer chair placed him a few inches higher than her, and it struck Dixie that he wasn't a tall man, possibly five-ten or -eleven. He composed himself to appear tall. And the chair differences allowed him to lean back, cross his legs comfortably, and still retain the advantage of height.

"Mrs. Pine's . . . death must be terribly traumatic for her family," Jackson said. "I keep thinking it had to be some horrible mistake . . . that lovely woman . . . all those eager police officers." He picked up his gold-rimmed porcelain teacup.

Dixie's identical cup sat gleaming on the table separating them. When she reached for it, her gaze met his, and her breath caught. *You're the most exceptional creature in the world*, his look said. *I've waited all my life for this moment with you.*

She stared down at her tea. *How did he do that?* All thought of what she'd come for had escaped her. She concentrated on the amber liquid swirling in her cup.

Oh, yes. "Your receptionist told me you were between appointments," she said. "So I won't waste your time. How long were you associated with Edna Pine?"

He stirred his tea, rhythmically, tiny back and forth *clicks* with his gold-plated spoon. When she looked up again, his gaze rested on her face.

Charisma is in the eyes, a religious philosopher had once told her. *Everything else, the mannerisms, the clothes, even the voice, can be cultivated. But when a pair of eyes can nail you to your seat, watch out.*

Jackson had the sort of charisma that didn't go on each morning with his thousand-dollar suit and diamond pinky ring. It dripped from his baritone voice and drifted like exotic oil from his exquisitely tanned skin. And it did beckon from his eyes—wide, direct, espresso-brown, and filled with the promise of excitement. Adventure. Passion.

Get a grip, woman. Dixie focused on the primitive African mask.

"I can have Sherry get the file," Jackson was saying, "and give you the exact date. Are you representing the Pine estate, Ms. Flannigan?"

Dixie had hoped the word "attorney" on her card would take them past this part. Maybe she should've accepted that dollar retainer from Belle.

"I represent Edna's son, Marty Pine. We're trying to piece together his mother's life during the months before she died. You handled Edna's investments?"

"Some of them. After her husband's death, we assessed his investment decisions. We were gradually converting the low-performance assets."

"Like . . . ?"

"Again, I'd have to look at the file. Am I to assume that Mr. Pine inherited his mother's entire portfolio?"

Here they were in the sticky part again. Marty's inheritance surely included *some* investments. To Dixie, finances remained a mystery.

"He's her only living relative," she hedged.

"I see. Well, as I said, her husband handled the portfolio until his death. Like many widows, Mrs. Pine didn't have a clue what to do with it before she came to me. Money languishing in a bank is a waste, wouldn't you agree?"

"A waste?"

"In the right place, money attracts money. In the wrong place, it's like a freeloading cousin. Have you ever found money stuck away in a drawer or a pocket, money you'd forgotten for years?"

"I suppose—"

"It feels like found treasure, doesn't it? But the truth is, the money lost value while it sat in the drawer. Invested wisely, it might have doubled or tripled. Tucking money in a savings account is only slightly smarter than hiding it in a drawer." He let the sentence hang there a moment, his eyes never leaving Dixie's. Then, "Does an intelligent woman like you have money languishing, Ms. Flannigan?"

Dixie had a compelling urge to dash home, scoop up all her financial records, and dump them at Jackson's feet, the same way she'd pressed her birthday money into Barney's hands all those years ago. *You figure it out,* she wanted to say. *Take care of it for me.*

"I'd rather stick to the subject of Edna's money," she replied.

Jackson leaned over to a phone on a side table and touched an intercom button.

"Sherry, locate the Edna Pine file, please." He smiled at Dixie as if everything were perfectly settled now. "Once I have verification of the transfer of ownership to your client, Ms. Flannigan, my secretary will deliver the file. And if Mr. Pine has questions about future investments, I'll be happy to discuss them." He set his teacup on the coffee table and started to rise. "Unless there's something else . . . ?"

With an effort, Dixie remained seated, ignoring the part of her that wanted to jump up and bow out of the room, now that she'd been dismissed by the king.

"Where did you and Edna Pine meet?" she asked.

His eyebrow rose a fraction as he settled back in his chair. "That's an unusual question."

"Mr. Jackson, I don't have time for subtlety. You undoubtedly know the circumstances of Edna's death."

"Of course. The police asked similar questions. I couldn't tell them much, either."

They'd probably found Jackson's name the same way Dixie had and wanted to know if Edna came into any sudden cash following the other bank robberies.

"Your name appears in Edna's records for the first time last May," Dixie said. "Surely there's nothing confidential about how she came to choose you."

"We were introduced by a mutual friend."

"The friend's name?" Dixie sipped her tea to avoid meeting Jackson's eyes. She couldn't be mesmerized and insistent at the same time. "I'm sure Mr. Pine will appreciate your cooperation when he decides whether you'll continue to handle the Pine portfolio."

Another second or two passed before Jackson replied.

"I met Mrs. Pine when she and I both attended a Fortyniners event, the Houston Grand Opera's opening of *Rigoletto* at Wortham Theater."

"Fortyniners?" The name sounded vaguely familiar.

"A church-sponsored club for singles old enough to enjoy being single. I notice you're not wearing a ring."

Jackson made his observation sound almost intimate. Dixie resisted rubbing her ring finger. "Which church?"

"Uptown Interdenominational. Do you know it?"

She shook her head. "I thought singles clubs went out with the eighties. Replaced by find-a-mate columns."

"Not at all. Some of us appreciate the finer points of *not* mating. We enjoy one another's company without necessarily expecting to take a friend home for . . . closer communication." Jackson gazed at her steadily. "I can see you're on the young side of forty, Ms. Flannigan, but we're flexible. Would you like to drop by our happy-hour fiesta tomorrow night, meet some of Mrs. Pine's friends? I'm sure they can tell you much more than I can."

Friends, the magic word. Exactly the sort of information Dixie needed.

"Yes, I'd like that. Do you suppose I'll meet the person who introduced you to Edna?"

"Vernice Urich," Jackson said, somewhat grudgingly. "Yes, I'm sure she'll be there."

Another name from Edna's calendar. In the phone book, a string of letters followed it, including "Ph.D."

Accepting the card Jackson offered, Dixie felt the brush of his hand and that same subtle tingle. She noticed his nails, as smooth and well groomed as Marty's. Wanting to shove her own hands into her pockets—and realizing belatedly the black suit had no pockets—she slid the card into the black handbag she carried. She hated handbags.

"One more question. Was Lucy Aaron Ames also your client?"

"Ames . . . I know that name . . . Oh." He shook his head, managing to look offended without losing composure. "Do you suppose I make a career of dealing with bank robbers?"

"Did you *know* Lucy Ames?"

His phone buzzed. "No, I didn't. Now, if you'll excuse me . . ."

Dixie couldn't decide if he was lying. "What if I can't make it tomorrow night? Can I drop in another time, without a special invitation?"

"Anytime," he said absently. He glanced at the blinking telephone button, yet made no move toward it. "Fortyniners has a different event nearly every night, but only one happy hour a week. Edna never missed it."

Edna? So they'd been on a first-name basis, after all.

The door opened and the receptionist stepped in.

"Your client has arrived, Mr. Jackson."

"Thanks, Sherry." He reached for the phone. "Please make sure Ms. Flannigan takes a brochure on her way out."

Then his eyes caught Dixie's again, and although his gaze never dipped below her mouth, a sudden warmth registered at the V of her blouse. If he controlled money as well as he controlled the room temperature, Dixie decided, maybe she'd have a look at that brochure. She couldn't help wondering how Terrence Jackson's dazzling demeanor would've affected her had she been sixty-six and groping for a scrap of self-esteem.

She saw no one waiting in the reception area. Of course, Sherry might've shown the caller to another room. Was Jackson that secretive about his clients meeting one another? According to the *Financial Times* article, some of them were moderately famous. Or notorious.

Once she crossed to the elevator, there'd be no opportunity to snoop into other rooms.

"Sherry, where is the ladies' room?" she asked as she accepted the promotional folder.

"Left at the end of the hall, then it's the first door."

Dixie tried the knob on the only door besides Jackson's that opened into the hall. It held a conference table, an audiovisual wall, and no secrets. Beyond the rest rooms, two more doors were locked. To the right of the hall, a single door opened into a small room with a sofa and chairs, as richly appointed as the main reception area, but more intimate. No one was there.

As Dixie left the offices of the "Millennium Midas" thirty-eight floors behind her, the heady scent of ylang-ylang slowly dissipated. The power of Jackson's presence took a while longer.

Chapter Twenty-one

"I told Marty he could stay with us as long as he wants," Amy informed Dixie, spreading a layer of pecan halves on a baking sheet. "Flying back and forth to Dallas, he can't be staying in hotels. He needs family around."

Amy's kitchen smelled of cinnamon and chocolate. A pecan fudge pie cooled on a rack. While Dixie was in Mike's exercise class, two messages had come, one from her sister, one from Marty. She'd stopped by to bring Marty up to date and found him on the phone, arguing with someone at his gallery. A few words floated into the kitchen now, all of them concerning money.

Spying a pie-filling pot about to sink into sudsy water, Dixie rescued it. Her sister's pecan fudge was good to the last scrape.

"I suppose we're as close to family as Marty has now," she admitted, plucking a tablespoon from the drawer.

"And we're nearer Hobby airport than Edna's house. Anyway, he doesn't need to be around all those dusty old memories."

Obviously, Amy hadn't seen Edna's newly spotless home.

"Did he go back to Dallas last night?"

Her sister nodded. "Flew right back again this morning." She poured cake batter over the pecan halves.

"Amy, how much weight has Carl gained in the past three days?"

"He's at golf now, working it off. I'm the one fat sticks to. Twenty minutes a day on that rowing machine or I'd be a tubby."

No point in telling her to stop baking. Without that, Amy's nerves would never hold up to having Marty around, keeping the whole robbery-shooting episode fresh on everyone's mind.

"Don't you have any low-fat recipes?"

"They're no fun. Dixie, we need to plan Edna's funeral, and Marty refuses to hold it until you clear her name."

"I don't know that we'll ever 'clear her name.' Regardless of why she robbed the bank, or who ended up with the money, she shot a police officer."

"That was an accident. She wasn't shooting *at* the officer. She shot in the air and just got, I don't know, startled, and one of the bullets hit something and hit something else—what's that called?"

"Ricocheted."

"The Channel 13 newspeople were talking about it, only the cops won't say, but a newswoman interviewed some of the people watching from their homes and they swore Edna wasn't shooting *at* those officers."

Dixie'd heard that hypothesis, too. It certainly lent more credence to the suicide theory. Perhaps some crackpot worked out the robbery details, then located desperate people who wanted to save their families from the guilt associated with suicides, or wanted to beat the suicide clause in their insurance policies, or were just too chicken to kill themselves.

"Doesn't matter," Dixie said. "It was Edna's bullet. If she hadn't started shooting, nobody would've been hurt."

"It's obvious whose side you're taking," Marty remarked, coming up beside her.

"I never claimed I could undo what happened. Only that I'll find out what chain of events *led* to what happened."

He looked dejectedly away from her, his shoulders as low as if Atlas had just handed him the world.

"Where are you with that?" he muttered. "Anywhere?"

Dixie related the results of her visit with Terrence Jackson—that Edna knew at least two of the names on her calendar from a group called Fortyniners. She also mentioned that she'd made an appointment with Artistry Spa and found a phone listing for Vernice Urich, but got only a machine when she called.

"I'll follow up on those leads tomorrow," she told him. "This afternoon I'm going to a funeral. For the woman who preceded Edna in the bank robberies."

"Good, I'll go with you. But first, I have an appointment with Mom's lawyer. I want you there."

Oh? Since when do I take orders from you? Dixie bit back the sudden anger. Marty was stressed and not thinking clearly.

"How can I help with lunch?" he asked Amy.

"You're company," she told him.

"No, no, no. I either help or I don't stay. You agreed."

Having no desire to help with lunch *or* to join in their squabble, Dixie slipped away to cool off and to see what Ryan was doing. A year ago, he would've met her at the door, bubbling over with news of school, sports, awesome computer games he wanted her to learn. Of course, his private school was out now for summer vacation. And Ryan was growing up. Almost thirteen. Was that the cut-off age when kids stopped hanging out with old-maid aunts? Well, he might try, but she wouldn't be shrugged off so easily.

A hazardous-waste emblem on Ryan's closed door covered the Super Rangers nameplate he'd talked Dixie into buying three years ago and now wouldn't want his friends to see. She knocked, and when she got no answer, put her ear to the door. He couldn't be asleep—she heard computer noises. Hadn't he mentioned a new game?

"Ryan?" She turned the knob and peeked in. The computer hummed and the printer slowly spit out colored pages. But no sign of her nephew. She stepped into the room. "Hey, guy, don't I even rate a hello anymore?"

She glanced at the page sliding from the printer, a photograph. With sick surprise stirring inside her, she lifted it for a closer look. Just then she heard the rushed footsteps of a twelve-year-old thumping down the hallway. Ryan must've been in the bathroom, never expecting his aunt to open his bedroom door and cruise in—didn't a kid have any privacy? He certainly wouldn't have wanted her to see the filth spewing out of his printer. Or maybe he didn't know, maybe—

"Aunt Dix!" Ryan shoved the door wide and stormed in.

When he saw what she held, his face screwed up like he'd been slapped.

Chapter Twenty-two

"Pornography? Ryan, where did this come from?"

His cheeks turned red and he wouldn't look at her. "The Internet."

Of course. Didn't everything?

"Why would you download this?" Dixie's computer savvy enabled her to type a letter and pick up her E-mail when she remembered, but she had only a hazy idea of how the Internet worked.

He swallowed, looking too miserable to speak.

Surely this level of porno didn't come free. "Did you use your parents' credit card?"

"No!"

"Then—"

"Ryan . . . Dixie . . ." Amy called, her voice growing nearer. "Time for lunch."

He grabbed for the photograph. When Dixie held it out of reach, he opened his mouth to protest. Panic sparked in his eyes. Then he closed down on whatever he'd started to say and snatched the remaining pages from the printer rack.

"Don't let Mom see that," he begged.

"All right. But we're talking about this later." Having no place to put it, she shoved the photo at him, then swept through the door to head off her sister.

"Ryan's clearing some things away," she told Amy. "He'll be right out. What smells so good?"

"Garlic bread. I made spaghetti. I know, I know, it's too heavy for lunch, but Marty looks so thin."

"Spaghetti's great. Come on, I'm starved."

The food probably was great, but pondering what she'd walked in on, Dixie didn't taste a bite. Kids Ryan's age were curious—no harm in that. He knew about sex. Dixie remembered the day he confessed to flunking "ovaries" in health class. He probably passed around copies of *Playboy*, *Penthouse*, hell, maybe even *Hustler* among his friends. So why was she so shocked?

Some mofo out there sold my kid shit. Dixie appreciated Lureen's rage much better now. After working hard to teach her boy what was right and good and worth caring about, Lureen couldn't control the unknown elements that infringed on his teenage world. Finding a hidden copy of *Hustler* wouldn't have shocked Dixie like seeing those disgusting photos sliding out of his printer had. She wasn't naive. She'd seen raw porno before. But was it really that easy for kids to get the hard stuff these days?

She pushed her spaghetti around her plate. She needed to talk to him about this. In private.

"Ryan and I thought we'd go see the new Van Damme film Saturday night," she announced. "If that's okay."

Amy's eyes lit up. "A movie? Marty, maybe we should all go. Edna wouldn't like us moping around."

Ryan ceased staring miserably at his food and slid a grateful look at Dixie. "Mom, you sure you want to see Van Damme?"

"Oh, is that one of those karate movies? Wouldn't you rather see a nice comedy, Ryan?"

"We could go to the cineplex, split up to different films," Dixie offered. Not at all what she had in mind, but she could drag Ryan out to the lobby for a private talk.

"I don't know where I'll be on Saturday," Marty said absently. "But we'll see. . . ."

After lunch, Dixie agreed to drive Marty to his meeting with Ralph Drake. The lawyer gave him a copy of Edna's will to read, but Marty wanted the shorter oral version. And although Dixie tried to stay out of the conversation, he kept pulling her in.

"You're a lawyer, Dixie. Tell them. Mother was obviously not herself. She *never* would've given her money to—what was it? The Church of The Light? Who's ever heard of that? You heard of that?"

Dixie shook her head.

"It's a legitimate church, Mr. Pine. And your mother was adamant. She even told us she'd talked this over with you."

"She didn't tell me anything about a church. Giving her money—*my money*—to a church. How much are we talking about?"

"About nine hundred thousand dollars," Drake informed him, straightening a sleeve on his Italian suit jacket.

Marty looked as if he were going to be sick.

"You receive an equal amount," the lawyer added, "plus the family home and acreage, and your mother's personal effects. Of course . . . you can contest."

"You're damned right I'll contest!"

At Marty's assertion, Drake's chin kicked up defensively, but his voice remained detached. He took an envelope from the file and handed it across the desk.

"Your mother also left this letter for you."

"A letter?" Marty's face paled as if Drake were handing him a trick package that might explode in his face when he opened it. "When . . . um, when did she write that?"

The envelope was blank except for a cluster of bluebonnets printed in one corner and Marty's name written in blue ink. Drake consulted his file.

"In February. The same day she signed her new will."

Marty accepted the envelope. His gaze flickered at Dixie, and the pain she saw made her wonder what that envelope might contain that he expected to be so terrible.

Drake slid a silver letter opener across the desk.

Marty swallowed visibly. "Could I get some water?"

"*Certamente.*" Drake stood, then raised an eyebrow at Dixie.

She shook her head. She wasn't thirsty, but she was curious as hell now about that letter.

When Drake left the room, Marty carefully slit the envelope open and unfolded a single sheet of writing paper. As he read, his face sagged like soft clay. When he refolded the paper, his eyes were moist. His lips twitched into a brief, sardonic smile.

"We can go," he said.

Drake had returned with a glass of water. Marty stood and nodded his thanks, leaving the water untouched.

"I have a few papers you'll need to sign before you leave," Drake told him.

"Sure." Without sitting, Marty signed the documents unread, answered Drake's questions concerning the money transfer, then started toward the door. "What I said about contesting the will? Forget that. But be sure to tell the Church of The Light not to contact me for any future donations."

In the hall, headed toward the elevator, Dixie had to lengthen her stride to keep up with him.

"Marty, did Edna say anything in that letter that might be . . . useful . . . in what we're trying to find out?" She didn't want to pry into a personal message between him and his mother, but he'd asked for help and she couldn't work in a vacuum.

"No," he answered curtly. He punched the elevator button. After a moment, he added, "She asked me not to question her bequest to the Church, said they were building a better world and the money would be used for a good cause."

"You accept that?"

"Yes."

"It might help if I could read the letter."

After another pause, he shook his head. "She said she wants to be cremated. And she wants us to have a party instead of a memorial service."

"That's all?"

He nodded. But he hadn't once looked at her since leaving Drake's office. When Dixie headed for the parking garage across from the Transco Tower, Marty veered toward the Westin Hotel.

"Where are you going?" Dixie called.

"I have some business to take care of."

"What about the Ames funeral? You might recognize someone there that Edna knew."

"I'll catch up with you," he promised. But his tone held little conviction.

Chapter Twenty-three

Philip Laskey rose from a seat at the back of the chapel to join the end of the viewing line. Fingering a brass disk in his pocket, he lightly traced its three-word engraving, WE THE PEOPLE. The woman who led the line past the coffin stood tall, rigid, and dry-eyed. He'd heard the minister address her as Carrie Severn, Lucy Ames' daughter.

Tom Severn stood close enough to comfort his wife but didn't bother, Philip noticed. He wondered how the man could resist. His own hands twitched with the need to stroke the pain from the woman's brow, to massage the stiffness from her neck. How hollow Carrie Severn must feel, losing her mother.

Philip glanced toward a noise issuing from a first row pew. *Bump, bump, bump.*

A boy of about five slumped on the seat, legs stretched in front of him, heels thumping the hardwood floor. In the high-ceilinged room, paneled with oak and accented with beveled glass, the sound reverberated over the hushed voices and soft shuffle of footsteps in the viewing line.

Bump, bump.

"Troy, stop that!" Carrie Severn whispered harshly.

Her son, then. Lucy Ames' obituary had mentioned two grandchildren. Beside the boy sat a girl a year or two older, grinning at Troy from under blond bangs, jaws working at a wad of chewing gum. The boy's navy-blue suit looked a size too big. *Big enough to grow into,* Anna Marie would say. Philip's mother believed in buying well and making a thing last.

The girl shoved an unwrapped stick of gum toward her brother. When he reached for it, she jerked it back and popped it into her own overfilled mouth.

Bump, bump. Bump, bump.

Carrie Severn, from her place at the casket, aimed her hard brown eyes at Troy and scowled. Her husband ignored the whole scene, staring over the heads of the congregation as if he'd rather be anywhere but here.

Bump, bump, bump.

Philip understood the boy's fidgeting. The minister's melancholy eulogy had been lengthy enough to set the entire audience on edge.

Moving away from the dais, Carrie Severn took her children, each by a hand, and ushered them from the chapel. Tom Severn strolled toward several men standing near the back of the church. Pallbearers, Philip guessed. He considered helping them, but instantly rejected the idea. Colonel Jay would be upset knowing he'd even attended the service; he preferred keeping a low profile.

As Philip approached the casket, an image of Anna Marie slid into his inner vision, a bullet hole through her forehead. Philip blinked, to banish the image from his mind, and steadied himself.

Lucy Ames looked nothing like his mother. And no bullet hole marred her wrinkled forehead. The casket's pink satin lining cast a rosy glow on her cheeks. She appeared to be smiling. No sign at all of the damage from police bullets. He blessed the undertaker's skill.

Philip glanced quickly around the room. No one had joined the viewing line after him. He slipped the brass disk from his pocket and touched the cold hand. What terrible grief had prompted this mother, this grandmother, into such a hopeless action?

At Philip's request, Rudy Martinez had brought him the spent shell casing. Philip had flattened it, hammered it smooth, and engraved it. Now he slid the brass disk from his own fingers to Lucy's.

"We, The People, have avenged you, Lucy Ames," he murmured. "Rest well."

Chapter Twenty-four

A somber classical melody drifted from invisible speakers as Dixie followed the viewing line away from the dais. The odor of cut flowers seemed stifling. A few gardenias peeked from a spray of yellow roses covering the pearl-gray casket. The heavily scented blossoms must've been a Lucy Ames favorite. Most florists avoided gardenias.

Studying the crowd, she tried to separate the real mourners from the gawkers. Funeral services were not her idea of a good time, especially the dismal sort this one had turned out to be. Edna had the right idea: cremation, ashes tossed to the wind, followed by a rip-roaring party. Life was a tough road—death ought to be the traveler's reward.

Dixie didn't believe all these people actually knew the deceased. They'd come to see the Granny Bandit.

She spotted Ben Rashly from HPD Homicide and a pair of FBI types lurking at the edge of the crowd. Their purpose for attending was obvious—they expected a third gang member to show up, possibly in a shiny new sports car purchased with part of the missing loot.

At the front of the church, Lucy Ames' daughter, the chief reason for Dixie's attendance, guided two children among the congregation. Except for a son in California, who apparently had elected not to fly home for the funeral, Carrie Severn was Lucy's only direct kin, according to the newspaper. She and her family lived in Austin.

Dixie wasn't quite sure how to approach Lucy's daughter to ask if her mother had ever mentioned Edna. It seemed disrespectful to start a conversation here, and during the entire service, Carrie Severn's mouth had remained a tight, angry slash in her perfectly groomed face.

But if not here, where? The daughter would know more than anyone who her mother's friends were, and she might head straight back to Austin after the service.

When Dixie reached the steps outside the church, Ben Rashly fell in beside her, tobacco drifting to the ground like brown snow as he filled a curved pipe. Dapper as usual, he wore a charcoal-gray suit and matching striped tie, his fine white hair combed neatly across his bald spot. The lines in his face seemed more deeply etched today. Working with FBI agents could do that.

"Isn't this a little out of your jurisdiction?" Dixie asked him.

"Do I look like I'm on duty?"

"You're always on duty, Rash." And she certainly couldn't approach the Severns with him here.

Ahead of them, a black limousine stood ready to drive the family members to the cemetery. Maybe Rashly would skip the grave site.

As the crowd parted, making a path for the coffin and pallbearers, he stepped back a pace. Dixie joined him.

"Did you know the deceased?" she asked.

"That's supposed to be my question." He flicked a lighter on, held it sideways to the pipe bowl, and drew several short, quick puffs. "What're you doing here, Flannigan? What do you know about Lucy Ames?"

"I know she didn't look like any bank robber I ever saw."

He squinted at the coffin being boosted into the back of a hearse. "Short career."

"Really, Rash, what's a Houston Homicide cop doing at a Webster funeral? Are you on the task force?"

He shook his head and plucked a tobacco leaf from his lower lip. "My wife and Lucy Ames were in the same sorority. Ida's visiting her sister in Arizona. She heard about the Ames robbery and called me, all torn up about it. Feeling guilty, like if she'd been a better 'sister,' kept track, maybe Lucy wouldn't have taken to knocking off banks. Whatever sense that makes."

"So you promised to come and represent her?"

His steady eyes moved around the crowd.

"From what Ida said, Ames worked at Texas Citizens Bank since the day it opened. Her divorce didn't leave her hurting for money, and she was never wild and crazy. Married right out of college, did her stint as a mother before starting on a career. She and Ida worked with their sorority sisters at Christmas every year, collecting food and clothing for the homeless. This past Christmas, Lucy didn't show. Ida feels bad for never calling to find out why."

Dixie considered that for a minute. She didn't recall whether Edna had attended college, much less whether she'd been active in a sorority. She made a mental note to check it out.

"What about them?" Dixie nodded toward the FBI agents. "Are they sharing information?"

Rashly scowled at her.

"Flannigan, this case is already a mess. The feds won't be nearly as understanding as I am if they catch you sticking your nose in." Turning away from the two agents, he knocked his pipe against the heel of his shoe to clear it. "When you get through here," he said gruffly, "maybe you should drop by my office and tell me what you've learned."

"Not much to tell."

"Flannigan—"

"Okay, okay." She'd wondered why he was giving up information so easily. Naturally, he expected tit for tat.

The pallbearers had shut the hearse doors. Carrie Severn and her family were ushered into a limousine.

"Have you talked to her?" Dixie asked Rashly.

He shook his head. "Glad I don't have to. Spent this morning with another bereaved widow."

Dixie realized who he meant. Just before the funeral, she'd heard about the sniper killing of an HPD patrolman. "Did you know the officer?"

"Personally?" His face was tight and gray. "I know he got up every morning, strapped on a piece, and put himself on the line. That's all I have to know." He glanced at the FBI agents. "I meant what I said about coming by later."

"I'll be there. Aren't you going to the cemetery?"

"Hell, I've had about all the fun today I can stand."

After twenty minutes of oratory at the grave, Dixie wished she'd taken her cue from Rashly. The minister managed to drone on without repeating anything he'd said at the chapel, but the generic message didn't convince Dixie he'd ever met the deceased.

Contrary to his promise, Marty hadn't shown up. Dixie continued to puzzle over his reaction to Edna's letter. He'd gone from contempt at Drake's handling of the will to complete acquiescence. Had something Edna wrote caused him to lose interest in discovering what drove his mother to bank robbery?

Dixie scanned the faces of the assembly—which far outnumbered the crowd at the church. Some of them may have known Lucy at the bank, although, according to the news coverage, she hadn't worked directly with customers. Several women in the bunch were middle-aged or older and might've been Lucy's friends. Dixie couldn't talk to them without missing her chance with Carrie Severn. Yet, one figure standing alone at the edge of the crowd drew Dixie's attention. A shriveled-up prune of a woman, thin, well dressed, she seemed entranced with the minister's every word.

Finally, he began to wind down.

Dixie sidled toward the front row where she could approach Lucy's daughter after the hugging was over. Tom Severn had started moving his children away from the open grave.

"Daddy?" The girl, a miniature female copy of her father, including a grown-up frown, tugged at his hand. "Will the police kill us, too?"

"No!" His glance caught Dixie's. "Where do children get such ideas?"

"When you don't have answers, I suppose imagination fills in the gaps." Dixie longed to move on, to leave this family to grieve in peace. Instead, she placed herself in Carrie's path. "Mrs. Severn . . . ? I'm . . . awfully sorry for your loss. May I speak with you for a moment?"

"If you're a reporter—"

"No, I'm not." Dixie spoke gently but firmly. "I didn't know Lucy, but I knew Edna Pine—"

"Who?"

"The other woman who was . . . shot by police officers."

"What *is* this? Who are you?"

"My name is Dixie Flannigan. I was Edna Pine's neighbor. She and your mother must've known each other. I thought, if we could figure out how—"

"The police already went over all that. I don't know how they knew each other, and I don't care. I just want this whole mess to go away."

Carrie tried to move off, but Dixie blocked her. "It won't go away until the police find—"

"Look, I don't know *anything*. The police should do their job and leave us alone."

"You must have some idea why your mother—"

"Why she held up a bank? She did it because she was *insane*. You got that? Nuts. Cuckoo. My mother *had* to be insane, didn't she? To pull such a ridiculous stunt and get herself killed? First the divorce, now this. She wanted attention, that's all. Well, she got it. Now my children will grow up knowing their grandmother was a thief."

Tom Severn appeared beside her.

"Come on, Carrie." He urged her toward the limousine.

"Leave it alone," Carrie called back. "You got that? *Just leave us alone!*"

Chapter Twenty-five

The weather is all wrong for a funeral, the Shepherd of The Light penned in his notebook. *Warm. Sunny. Fragrant with spring.*

Anyone who went to the movies knew the best funeral weather was rainy and bleak. Go see *Harold and Maude,* all the graveside scenes filmed against dreary skies dotted with black umbrellas. Nutty old Maude getting her kicks attending funerals for people she'd never heard of. Young Harold trying to hang himself. The two of them as unlikely a pair as peaches and vinegar, but it made a good flick.

Humming a dirge from *Harold and Maude,* he watched the crowd break up and head for their cars. Only a handful, he estimated, had ever heard of Lucy Aaron Ames until her debut performance at the Webster branch made her famous. Like nutty old Maude, they'd all come for a good show.

Lucy would be pleased he'd remembered the gardenias. His anonymous donation ensured she'd have a fine send-off, but he also felt the importance of paying his personal respects. After all, Lucy had been his most loyal disciple, the first to follow his guidance to the ultimate reward.

"You have an ancient soul, Lucy," he'd told her at their first meeting. "Long-suffering. Evolved. Strong as steel."

"You can see that?" Her face radiated joy. "I've always known . . . well . . . I'm not sure how to say—"

"You don't have to say anything. The wisdom in those incredible hazel eyes tells all."

Later, in his carefully appointed studio, under soft light filtered through green branches, he had touched Lucy for the first time. Not sexually; merely the gentlest brush of his fingertips across her hand. A woman too often accepted sex when what she wanted—*needed*—was to be stroked, comforted, cherished. To be appreciated. Since Penny Hatcher, he'd learned to recognize a certain longing around the eyes and mouth.

At that first touch, Lucy's hand had fluttered beneath his own.

"I know it sounds self-important," she whispered, "but I've always sensed that God—"

"Had something special in mind for you? I'm sure He does, Lucy. You've suffered sorrows and suppressed passions that would drive lesser souls mad."

"You *do* understand. I've dreamed that someday . . . someone—" Her eyes flooded, adoration glimmering through the waterworks, and he knew she was his instrument to finely tune.

"Drink your tea." He'd patted the hand that showed a trace of liver spotting. "It's a special blend. You'll like it."

His special blend came from a trio of aromatic herbs discovered in Shanghai and Zaire. One of the herbs enhanced a subject's suggestibility. Taken together, they brought about a deep openness and trust but also an incredible loneliness, a need for human contact, a desire to be understood. Smoldering in an incense bowl, a spicy aromatic root he'd discovered in Hong Kong sweetened the air with a mild sedative. After prolonged or repeated doses—the aromatic root along with his specially blended tea—a subject eagerly accepted ideas she once would have rejected, and even moderate periods of isolation became intolerable.

These herbal drugs were not secret. The Shepherd had merely discovered specific uses for what pharmacologists and physicians considered side effects. For optimum results, however, the project required an ideal subject, a subject like Lucy Ames, already experiencing the melancholy of isolation, the hunger for a kindred soul. The Shepherd filled that hunger instantly, with appreciation, compassionate touches, whispered reassurance. He'd learned, since that first experiment with little Penny Hatcher, that the right word at a vulnerable moment could seduce the stoutest heart.

Over the years, he'd studied every technique on record and invented a few of his own. And over the past months, he'd conditioned Lucy to crave his carefully metered attention as a junkie craves a daily fix. The time hadn't been wasted. Lucy's knowledge of the bank's practices paved the way for lucrative ventures. More important, the Lucy Experiment had proved that kindness, discipline, and isolation could shape a weapon more powerful than a bomb, more guided than a missile.

"Align with me, Lucy." He had tucked a scented handkerchief into her hand. "With your wisdom and grace we shall lead the pure at heart to glory."

Lucy was unaware, the Shepherd penned, *that she'd be the first soul to arrive.*

He closed the book, and instead of driving away, as he should, he watched groups of mourners walking together from the grave site. Only a very few walked alone. His gaze settled on a solitary woman in a black suit.

In recent weeks, although he still drew his greatest strength from solitude, he had felt a pressing desire to share his discoveries with a companion of similar intellect, similar passions. His current partner could be counted on in the smaller picture, but since his college days—and a colleague's betrayal—he'd confided in no one. Not a single person appreciated the full scope of his power. Somewhere, there had to be a suitable mate, a partner who would appreciate his discoveries and embrace his vision.

The Shepherd of The Light opened his notebook to a fresh page and wrote: *Seek out a subject who understands the beauty of patience, the value of power, and the strength of kindness.*

Chapter Twenty-six

Usually, Dixie skipped past the front desk at HPD's Homicide Division with a wave, having picked up her ID sticker downstairs, but today an officer stopped her.

"Identification?"

Dixie showed her sticker.

"You have an appointment?"

"Sergeant Rashly's expecting me. Didn't someone call from downstairs?"

Ignoring her question, the officer picked up the desk phone and punched a button.

"Sergeant, a woman's out here. Flannigan." He replaced the receiver, his hard gaze inching over her face as if memorizing it. "Sergeant Rashly will be right out."

"Thanks." Dixie smiled at him and stepped a few paces away. A cop had been killed that morning, not in the line of duty but in his own driveway. Other cops would naturally be looking over their shoulders—and scrutinizing civilian visitors with a keener eye.

Spying an abandoned newspaper on a chair against the wall, Dixie reached over to pick it up and caught a glimpse of Police Chief Edward Wanamaker entering a room down the hall. A thick, stumpy man, mid-fifties, without a single gray hair in his black mane, Wanamaker always looked as if he could single-handedly conquer an army. If his voice had matched his looks, it'd be as rough as burnt cork. Every time Dixie thought of him issuing commands in his Irish tenor, she couldn't help smiling.

The Chief stopped to speak with a younger man who had the sort of nondescript appearance Dixie associated with FBI or Internal Affairs. She watched their lips but couldn't make out what they said. Edging closer, she found an angle that allowed her to see partially inside the room. She unfolded the newspaper and pretended to read.

Councilman Jason "Gib" Gibson, a shrewd, hardheaded businessman, stood military-stiff at the end of a conference table, talking to another FBI type. Known for his loud and dogged criticism of the HPD—before and after Wanamaker came aboard—Gib Gibson reminded Dixie of a pit bull. Once he got his teeth into a juicy, headline-making issue, only a bigger, tastier issue would entice him to let go.

"Ms. Flannigan!" The desk officer scowled at her. "Would you wait over here, please?"

She smiled. "Can't shoot me for being curious." The stupid remark was out of her mouth before she realized how deliberate it sounded.

The officer didn't miss it. His nostrils flared and he looked ready to come out of his chair.

"Sorry. Scratch that," Dixie muttered hurriedly. "Foot-in-mouth disease."

Fortunately, she spotted Rashly headed her way, tamping tobacco into his pipe bowl.

"C'mon. I gotta get outta here," he said. "D'you eat?"

Lunch, sort of. Dinner, no. What time zone was he in? "I could eat something."

She hurried alongside as he continued toward the elevators. He'd been raking his hands through his white hair. It stood on end, revealing the dollar-size bald spot that rarely showed except when he was agitated. He'd shed his gray suit jacket and rolled up his shirtsleeves. His square face looked fierce. They reached a turn just as Mayor Avery Banning approached from the other direction. Dixie and Rashly stepped back for the Mayor to pass.

"Pardon me, Ms. Flannigan, Sergeant." With a distracted nod, Banning stormed grimly by.

Dixie watched him enter the meeting room down the hall.

"Councilman Gibson and Mayor Banning together? That should be fun to watch. Robbery and two civilian fatalities—ought to be enough ammunition to make Gib a happy man. What do you suppose is going on in there?"

Rashly didn't reply until they'd reached an outdoor parking area and he'd struck a lighter to his pipe.

"Goddamn media." He puffed to coax the tobacco to burn. "They're chapping the Chief's butt about those two robbery shootings, and Gibson's egging them on. Wouldn't be so bad if our guys hadn't stepped over into Webster territory for one of the squeals. Banning called the meeting here to throw the reporters off. He's probably in there now trying to talk some sense into Gibson."

Dixie hadn't realized that HPD officers were involved in the Webster shooting. Jurisdiction between HPD and Webster had always been a little slippery.

"Rotten timing for Banning," she mused. "Puts an ugly blemish on his Memorial Day commendation to Wanamaker for taking down that drug ring." A particularly nasty gang-related drug ring. HPD Narcotics had gained points with the public and earned some favorable press afterward. But how did that balance against nine officers gunning down one elderly woman?

Despite his remark about eating, Rashly didn't appear to be headed anywhere in particular. Just needed a smoke break, Dixie figured. And to walk off some steam. He stopped beside Councilman Gibson's Lexus and scowled at the familiar personalized license plate: VIGILANT.

"Do politicians ever stop politicking and do the goddamn job they're hired for?"

"Not if they have an eye on a better job." Dixie realized she'd carried the newspaper out. She tucked it under her arm.

"Everybody in that room back there's trying to scrape off shit and fling it on someone else. You ask me, it's Gibson running his mouth got that officer killed today."

"You think the sniper was retaliating for the robbery shootings?"

"What the hell else? Nothing unusual in Art Harris' record or personal life. When was the last time we had a cop killer in this town? We got men ready to round up the whole Ames family, line 'em up for a firing squad."

"Rash, you're not serious."

"I've never seen this department so stirred up. Me, I don't see the Ameses in it. You were there today. They look like a family hepped up on revenge?"

"Just the opposite. Carrie Severn blames her mother for bringing disgrace on the family." She studied Rashly's weathered face. "Was Arthur Harris one of the cops who shot Lucy Ames?"

He stared back at her. "Names of officers involved in the Ames and Pine shootings were not released to the public."

"So his murder may have nothing to do with the robbery shootings." When Rashly didn't say anything, she took the hint and moved on. "Any leads on the missing money?"

He shook his head. "Like it dropped into a pit."

"What about the woman who started it all, the one robber last week who got away?"

"I'm not buying that third robber crap."

"Her description doesn't fit either Lucy Ames or Edna Pine."

"Put a dark wig and sunglasses on either of 'em, it could fit."

Dixie didn't want to hear that. "Does that mean you're not looking for her?"

"It means we got refocused this morning after an officer caught a bullet." He knocked his pipe against the building and dumped the ash under Gib's Lexus. "I didn't call you up here, Flannigan, to answer your damn questions. I'm being up front with you because I want you to know exactly what you're getting into messing with this case."

"And I'm trying to understand the reason a friend was killed. I knew Edna Pine, knew her husband, and grew up with her son. Unlike Carrie Severn, Marty doesn't believe his mother went batty since he last saw her. The man's hurting, Rash. And there are too many unanswered questions for you guys to drop —"

"I never said we were dropping anything."

"No, but you'd sure like it to go away. Two aging widows decide to pull a Butch-Cassidy-and-Sundance-Kid, including the part where they go out in a blaze of bullets. Do you *really* believe that's what happened?"

"People change, Flannigan. Some get old and doddering, some old and crazy, some old and mean. I know people who believe growing old is a fate worse than death." He scowled at his reflection in the Lexus window. With a harsh sigh, he turned away from it. "So, what answers have you come up with?"

"No answers. Only more questions." She told him briefly about the changes in Edna's lifestyle leading up to the robbery. "Marty feels responsible. He needs to know what happened to make his mother do something so alien to everything she believed in. She was an old-fashioned woman. Never worked outside the home. Never got involved with causes. Never took an interest in politics."

"You're saying you struck out at the funeral?" Rashly glared at her. "What're you holding back?"

Dixie hesitated. She hadn't consciously held back anything but her hunches. Yet dealing with Rashly meant dealing the whole deck.

"I learned one thing: Lucy Ames didn't have much support from her family after her divorce. Her daughter's bitter. Her son didn't care enough to show up. Lucy must've been a very lonely woman."

"So?"

"Edna was lonely, too. And somehow they became acquainted. Which means they started hanging out wherever lonely senior women go for company."

"Sounds like some blue-haired singles club."

"Exactly. I know Edna went to a club called Fortyniners. And I've a hunch that if I backtrack her movements for the past few months, I'll run across Lucy's name."

"Stay out of it, Flannigan. We'll do all that."

"I'm a single woman. I'll do it better." Seeing Rashly's scowl darken, Dixie rushed on. "What I'll look for is that third name."

He heaved another harsh sigh. "You're convinced there was another Granny Bandit."

"The press only started using that term after Edna was killed. Take another gander at the mystery woman's description —"

"Hell, Flannigan, give me ten eyewitnesses and I'll show you ten totally different sworn descriptions."

"True, but some points were agreed upon." Dixie was guessing here, based on what the press had reported, and hoping Rashly would confirm. "The first woman—brown hair, medium build, big sunglasses, pegged between thirty-five and fifty-five—was *not* the image of a grandmother."

But Rashly shook his head. "You're stretching. *Three* women pulling off near-perfect holdups? What's true is Edna Pine and Lucy Ames maybe didn't know each other at all. Ames does the first heist, gets away clean, and goes for the second. Pine picks up the idea after seeing the news reports."

Dixie mentally added the part he hadn't said, *as a way to commit the perfect suicide.*

"You're suggesting two middle-aged women *independently* acquired hand-guns and successfully executed bank robberies. I might buy that idea, except for the missing cash. That money didn't disappear into *The Twilight Zone.*"

Rashly gave Dixie one of his penetrating mean-cop looks. "You'll be doing your friend a favor, Flannigan, if you convince him to let this go. Bury his mother, put a FOR SALE sign on her house, and head back to his business in Dallas. Whatever you uncover isn't going to make him any happier."

"You think I'll get in the way of finding your cop killer."

He looked out at the city street, filled now with late-afternoon traffic.

"So Ames and Pine hook up together somehow and cry on each other's shoulder about the rotten deal God handed them. About how miserable it is to make a good home, raise a family, only to have them all leave—move away, die, whatever reason. And this pair of sob-sisters decide to stir up some attention for themselves. Only it backfires. Or they have that part figured in, too, convinced they'd rather be remembered as a real-life Thelma-and-Louise act than written off as a couple of old bags who'd outlived their usefulness." Rashly turned his hard stare back at Dixie. "Figure that'll make your friend feel better?"

"I figure there's another female out there smart enough to mastermind three heists, use suicidal women for the risky part, and end up with all the loot in her own pocket." Until talking to Rashly, Dixie hadn't realized the strength of her conviction.

His eyes got that faraway look that meant he was considering it. "I saw you studying the women at the funeral. Think one of them is your first Granny Bandit?"

"Or is planning to be the next one."

Chapter Twenty-seven

Rose Yenik cupped the revolver in her left hand, impatience quickening her movements. Practice had not gone as well as she had hoped. The Shepherd had asked her to stop before all the chambers were empty.

"I can do what needs to be done," she told him.

Afternoon light filtering through narrow slits in the window blinds cast stripes on the wall and across his gentle presence. Tall plants and the soft-pillowed chair she sat on made her feel cozy. Rose loved the fragrance of this room, spicy and romantic. Drinking tea with him in his most private office let her know he considered her special.

"I know you can do it, Rose. I saw your strength the moment I gazed into those incredible blue eyes. That strength now must be converted to patience."

She opened the loading gate with her thumb. "I can have patience."

"I'm sure you can." Standing, he moved behind her and kneaded her shoulders, his hands soothing her. "So where's all this tension coming from?"

"I want to do my part." She pulled the hammer back two clicks. "To get on with it."

"You aren't worried."

"No, no." When his hands abruptly stopped moving, she admitted, "Certainly, I'm somewhat concerned. That's to be expected." She knew about worry. *God will punish you, Rose.* Her mother's precious lobster plate shattered, porcelain shards and red clawed creatures flying everywhere. *Do you know what that platter cost? God will punish you,* Mother promised. Spilled juice on the piano keys. *God will punish you, Rose Yenik!*

His magical fingers continued their massage. "Everything has been rehearsed. What's to worry about?"

Grasping the pistol grip, she rotated the cylinder and pushed a cartridge out of the chamber. "Lucy, Edna—"

"Lucy and Edna went on to the next life. Their courage and commitment ensured perfection of the soul. *Nobody* was hurt. You know that." His fingers paused. "Have you been watching newscasts?"

God will punish you, Rose.

Her hand shook. "Only one."

"Rose, we talked about that."

"It's worse not knowing. I don't mind if I . . . follow Lucy and Edna. You know I don't. It's—" As she removed another cartridge, her gaze fell on a copy of an architectural rendering, more beautiful than usual in the filtered sun rays: THE CHURCH OF THE LIGHT. "I was selected, and it's what I want . . . to do my part. Only, I need to get on with it."

"Patience, Rose."

All the chambers empty now, she closed the loading gate, placed her thumb on the hammer spur, and pulled the trigger to release the hammer, guiding it gently in place with her thumb.

"I can have patience," she repeated.

His fingers encircled her throat, lightly brushing her jaw, sending a tiny electrical shiver down her spine. "I want you to stay here tonight, Rose. Forget money, forget the newscasts. Let the serenity of the Church settle your worries."

Chapter Twenty-eight

Climbing into the Mustang, Dixie pitched the newspaper she had carried from Homicide Division onto the passenger seat. She eased into bumper-to-bumper rush-hour traffic leaving downtown and finally turned onto the expressway feeder.

As she gained speed, a driver ahead slammed on his brakes. Dixie braked behind him, and the newspaper flopped open. Officer E. Arthur Harris stared up at her—the same officer she'd yelled at after Edna was killed. Dixie hadn't realized it was the same man.

Harris dead, after she'd singled him out. At random?

No, something had drawn her to him. Something in his eyes that differed from the other officers'. The realization sent a worm of uncertainty into her thoughts.

She snatched up the paper.

According to Rashly, the names of the officers involved in the shootings had not been made public. She scanned the article—

Damn. *Now* traffic moved.

Tossing the paper aside, she shifted gears and accelerated into the stream. From what she'd read, Dixie didn't think the reporters had made the connection. Had it been merely a fluke that the sniper picked Arthur Harris? Not very damn likely—not with some five thousand HPD officers to choose from.

Recalling the citizens who'd stopped to rubberneck—some with cameras—Dixie couldn't help wondering if her verbal attack on Harris had led to his being targeted. Too much coincidence, otherwise.

Don't squat on your spurs, lass, Barney would say. Dixie needed another patch of guilt like a tomcat needs a trousseau.

Yet, as she broke free of traffic and sped toward home, stealing glances at Art Harris' photo, the guilt phantom curled into the back of her mind and settled. Either her impulsive attack had tagged the officer to be killed, or the same unknown quality that caused her to single out Harris had also drawn the sniper.

An hour later, her black funeral suit exchanged for jeans, boots, and a pale yellow camp shirt, Dixie headed back to town, armed with a thin leather folder containing Edna's photo, the November newspaper article on the group Meanstreak, and the ticket Edna had saved from Club Cato. The article represented the earliest date in Edna's records that suggested a change in behavior. After that date, she had made purchases at Unique Boutique, Artistry Spa, and Fit After Fifty.

The address on Washington Avenue near Heights Boulevard placed the club about thirty miles from Edna's house. Dixie located Club Cato in a narrow building, originally a cartographer's shop, according to the bronze plaque beside the door. For a ten-dollar cover fee, she received a ticket exactly like Edna's but stamped with today's date.

Even with the air conditioning cranked to chill and three enormous fans whirring near the high ceilings, the long room smelled faintly of smoke, beer, and sweat. Maps, old and new, covered every surface. A framed five-by-seven-foot aerial of the Texas Gulf Coast hung behind the bar. On closer inspection, she discovered the photograph was compiled from overlapping eight-by-ten prints, pieced together and hand-colored. Dixie liked the effect, and wondered about getting one for Parker's bare walls. Brokering yachts, he spent a lot of time up and down that coast.

A map of a different Texas town, signed by Calvin Cato and protected by layers of clear varnish, embellished each tabletop. Nautical tin candle holders lighted table cards that announced the band currently belting out "Wheel of Fortune." Dixie vaguely recognized the song from Kathleen and Barney's audiotape collection.

Grabbing a stool at the bar, she ordered a Shiner Bock.

"Is that Meanstreak playing?" she yelled above the music to the bartender.

He nodded. A silver feather dangled from his left ear. "Wouldn't think a group that young could do such fine retro. Forties, fifties, sixties—wail it like they were born to it."

She followed his appreciative gaze to the players. The woman at the microphone wore a metal-studded leather corset, fishnet hose, and knee boots—a teenage dominatrix. She sat draped over a dentist's chair. Jet-black hair, fringed in scarlet as if the tip of each strand had been dipped in red paint, swung away from her angular face as she appeared to battle a runaway dentist's drill in her other hand. Her antics with the drill seemed totally unconnected to the song's plaintive words or to her sultry voice.

Two guitar players flanked her. The bald man playing lead stood naked to the waist, unless you counted the tattoos covering every inch of skin below his ears. LIFE IS PAIN in four-inch letters snaked across his muscular back through a tapestry of flowers, birds, and zoo animals. He gaped at the woman fighting the drill as if he'd never seen her act.

The bass man ignored her as he concentrated on the strings at his fingertips. His black pearl-buttoned shirt, tight black jeans, and black felt hat came straight out of every old western Dixie'd ever seen. She hoped the shiny revolver, holstered low and tied to his thigh with a leather thong, was as fake as it looked.

Almost ordinary in comparison, the young woman on keyboard flashed a friendly smile at the audience, revealing half-inch fangs. The drummer, hidden behind his cymbals, might've been a ghost. Or just exceptionally pale-skinned and bashful.

Dixie envisioned Edna at one of the tables, watching this strange band with their weird antics. Closing her eyes, listening to the fabulous music, the vision became clearer. The mid-1950s would've marked the beginning of Edna's life with Bill Pine—a much happier time for her.

The bartender returned with Dixie's Shiner and a dish of bar crackers. As Dixie paid him, they watched the singer bring the dentist's whirling drill dangerously close to her breast.

"That girl's like a wildcat in heat," he said.

"Do they play here nightly?"

"Yep. Own the place. Or most of it, anyway."

Dixie jotted *Join me during the next break?* on a business card, folded a twenty-dollar bill around it, and threaded her way among the tables to the bandstand. She handed the card to the tattooed guitarist.

He glanced at the twenty, then leaned close. "What would you like to hear, babe?"

"Surprise me."

Deftly sliding the bill aside, he read the message. Nodded. Slipped the card in his jeans pocket. Before he could make the money disappear the same way, Dominatrix snatched it and, grinning devilishly, pushed it down her ample, leather-encased cleavage.

Near the bandstand, Dixie claimed a table big enough to seat the entire group. The Shiner hit her stomach with a chilly explosion, a reminder that she'd skipped dinner.

Finally winning the battle against the drill, the woman turned a knob on a tank labeled "nitrous oxide" and took a campy, mind-numbing whiff. The band segued into "Java Jive," with Tattoo singing lead, Dominatrix and Tex singing harmony. Out of time, out of place—yet the Ink Spots themselves had never sounded better. And their vintage audience appeared to enjoy the show.

At the break, the three leads joined Dixie at her table. Tattoo made introductions. He turned out to be Rick, Dominatrix was Corinne, and Tex was Walt. Dixie liked her own tags better.

"What're you drinking?" she asked them.

With a whirl of his finger, Tattoo signaled the bartender to bring their usual. Then he whipped a chair around and straddled it.

"Now, D. A. Dixie Flannigan, to what do we owe your generosity?"

"DA?" Corinne blinked. "We're having drinks with suit fuzz?"

"Not 'District Attorney,' " Dixie assured her, though at other times she allowed the confusion to stand. "My initials."

"Don't tell me." Tattoo placed her business card on his forehead and focused in the distance. "Debbie Ann."

"Rick," Corinne admonished, slapping his shoulder. "C'mon, does this woman look like a Debbie Ann?"

They both studied Dixie. Tex—Walt—had been staring at her since he sat down, but Dixie wasn't certain he actually saw anything. His hazel eyes had a blank glaze that the room's bad lighting couldn't quite account for.

"I prefer Dixie," she said.

But Tattoo wouldn't give up. "Daphne Alison."

Dixie shook her head.

"Delia Amelia?"

"Here, dodo." Corinne, with long, crimson-nailed fingers, pulled the twenty from between her breasts and pitched it at him. "Give the money back, maybe she'll *tell* you her name."

A waitress appeared before he could answer. She passed bottles of Heineken for Rick and Corinne, another Shiner for Dixie, and a double Scotch rocks for Walt—whose glazed gaze remained stuck on Dixie even as he drank.

Dixie unzipped the thin leather folder she'd brought and took out Edna's recent glamour photo.

"Do you recall seeing this woman in the club?"

Corinne pulled the photograph closer to her side of the table. "Lots of old folks come in here." She passed the picture to Rick.

He shook his head and pushed it toward Walt, who took a full two seconds to swivel his eyes downward.

"Maybe this one's better." Dixie replaced the photo with an older one, taken before Bill Pine died.

"Maybe." Corinne wrinkled her forehead and tapped the photograph with a red talon. "Was the man with her?"

Dixie started to say no, then stopped. Who was to say Bill and Edna hadn't discovered this place together, then she returned in November to rekindle the memory?

"Not in the past year," Dixie replied. "But the woman may have come in alone last fall."

Rick positioned the photograph for a better view, shook his head, and then tossed the photo across the table for Walt's slow scrutiny.

"Uh-huh, she was here," Walt drawled. "Sat here through all four sets. Alone."

Maybe the alcohol had lubricated his jaw.

"What made you remember her?" Dixie asked.

"Spittin' image of my aunt. Bought her a drink. Wine, I think. White. She looked sad."

"Did you talk to her?" From the corner of her eye, Dixie saw Tattoo start to slip the twenty into his pocket. Corinne snatched it as fast as a wink, and it disappeared again into her cleavage.

"She weren't into talking," Walt said. "Requested ballads, though. 'Smoke Gets in Your Eyes,' 'Tennessee Waltz.' "

"I remember her now!" Corinne squealed. "She kept staring at you, Rick. At one of the breaks, she asked me if your tattoos were real. When I said yeah, she asked if you rode a motorcycle or if you'd been in the navy. Like one or the other had to account for you painting yourself up like that."

"Hey, she don't like my body art, she can take her trade elsewhere."

"She came back, too! When, Walt? The next week or so?"

"Uh-huh, came back a buncha times. Quiet lady."

"Did she ever talk to anyone else?" Dixie asked. "Another woman, maybe?"

"Not at first." Walt's eighty-proof breath wafted across the table. "Sat right there alone until closing. When she left, I'd walk her out, make sure she got in her car all right."

"What make of car?"

"Little blue Subaru."

That was Edna. Bill's last major purchase, about nine months before he died, had been the new car. "You said, 'Not at first.' "

"Round Thanksgiving she got to talking with this other old bird. Little bitty thing."

Dixie wished she had a photograph of Lucy Ames, but the only chance she'd had to get one was at the funeral. The *Chronicle* hadn't run a photo. She knew only one person crass enough to photograph a corpse in a casket—

And come to think of it, Casey James, stringer for the sort of tabloids people pretend to ignore at grocery store checkout counters, might be a damn good contact. The mystery of the Granny Bandits wouldn't set Casey's heart to pounding, but she'd find it amusing.

"Do you recall if the two women left together?" Dixie asked. "Or sat together after that night?"

Walt took a long drink of his Scotch, then stared down at the naked ice, with Dixie, Tattoo, and Dominatrix hanging on his next words.

"Nope," he said finally. "Never saw either of 'em after that night. Shame. Seemed like nice old birds."

• • •

Seventeen minutes after Dixie's phone call, Casey James settled her squatty body in the chair Rick had vacated. The reporter's piggish black eyes locked on the lead guitar player.

"Truth, Dixie, if you'd told me I could ogle such a colorful hunk of masculine muscle, I'd've been here sooner." Casey grinned and fanned herself with the tent card advertising the band. "Wonder what artistry is hidden under the pants. Think he's got little snake eyes on the end of his tool?"

"Ask nice, maybe he'll show you."

"You think?" Casey widened her eyes and grinned salaciously.

Dixie brought the conversation back to business. "Did you consider my question?"

"Honey, there's not a sane and sober mind in this city that isn't ruminating over what happened to the stolen bank loot. Treasure hunters have combed the terrain from both branch locations to the sites where the women were blown away. And you *know* the cops tossed both houses, searching for the dough from the first robbery."

"Yes, Casey, but what I want is your own needle-fine take on it. You have a mind that slides around corners."

"I heard the description of the woman who got away, honey. Straight from the man who soiled his pants when she threatened to shoot off an important part of his anatomy. Her description wouldn't fit Lucy Ames or Edna Pine, even after the world's best makeup job."

"That's exactly how I heard it, but the cops don't seem to be spending much energy finding her."

Casey hooted. "Don't ask me to figure cops. Here's that picture you wanted." She dropped a close-up of Lucy Ames onto the table.

Dixie strode to the bandstand, showed it to Walt, and waited for his nod that Edna and Lucy had indeed sat together once. Back at the table, she studied the thin-boned face. "Where do women of a certain age go in this town to dispel loneliness?"

"Same places they've always gone—church, nightclubs, or sewing circles."

"You mean that literally?" Dixie figured Edna had come to Club Cato for the music.

"If they want the company of men, they go to bars. If they want to be around other women, they take up a craft—pottery, jewelry, quilting. If they've had it with mortals and want to fill that emptiness with a higher light, they go to church."

Dixie thought about that. Edna's visits here and to Fortyniners suggested searching for a man. Yet she'd apparently struck up an acquaintance with Lucy Ames. And she'd made a sizable bequest to the Church of The Light. Maybe she had no idea what she was searching for. Dixie could relate, having drifted out of law into whatever came along.

"Thanks," she told Casey. "What do I owe you for the photograph?"

"A date with Mr. Wonderful up there."

"I think he might be spoken for by Ms. Tits-and-Ass."

Casey's grin turned her gnomelike face comical. "If she makes it a threesome, honey, I won't object."

Chapter Twenty-nine

At The People's shooting gallery, Philip Laskey emptied his Sig Sauer into a life-size target of Chief Wanamaker.

Left eye—*pop!* Right eye—*pop!* No point in drilling body armor.

Nelson Dodge and Rudy Martinez fired at Mayor Banning. Cronin, the fifteen-year-old rookie, watched eagerly, yet flinched at every shot. Along with his new khaki uniform and lapel pin, Cronin wore ear protectors to filter out the din.

It was Dodge's job to show his recruit around, but the big guy had been in a state all night after an argument with his father. Reluctantly, Philip had offered to take over. He didn't like Cronin. And his sympathy with Dodge ran shallow. Philip's own father had died the same year Philip was born. His only knowledge of the man whose seed he carried sat on his mother's bureau—a yellowed snapshot.

"A fine, good man," Anna Marie had told Philip. "A trifle heavy with the rod at times, but your pa was always there for us."

Not for Philip. Ever. At times, a voice in his head asked, *If the man was so fine and good, Anna Marie, why did all his sons move away as fast as they were old enough?*

Philip's closest brother in age was twenty-two years older and lived somewhere in California.

"A son each year, until there were five, Philip. And then so many years passed, my womb drying up, my baby off to join the navy—what was God thinking, sending me another little one? When your father died, I knew. God sent me a son so that I would not die alone."

Cranking the target to arm's reach, Philip yanked the Chief off his hook. The firing pattern needed improvement. He retrieved his shell casings, removed his ear guards, and motioned the rookie outside, away from the noise. Cronin lingered, watching Dodge's rapid, tight shots, then followed.

"Come back to the locker room," Philip instructed. "I'll show you where to stow your gear."

A wasp buzzed past Philip's head. He eyed it as he continued walking. When the wasp zoomed in for another pass, Philip smacked it out of the air and into the wall, so fast he barely felt the weight of it on his hand. It fell to the floor, stunned, and Philip crushed it under his shoe.

"Clean it up," he told Cronin.

"Why me?"

"Because you're the rookie, and the rookie polices the camp."

Cronin glared for a full ten seconds before he finally picked up the wasp by a wing from the otherwise immaculate floor, and tossed it into a waste can.

As they approached the training room, Philip heard voices of the men warming up.

"Martial-arts practice, every night, two hours," he told Cronin. "You'll train seven nights a week the first three months, then have one night a week free."

The kid nodded. "What about shooting practice?"

"Starting next month, an hour each night."

"Some men have handguns, some rifles."

"You'll train with both but won't be issued a piece until you qualify. Colonel Jay decides where your strength lies." He handed Cronin a sheet of paper.

"What's this?"

"Training diet." The same diet Philip followed, twenty-four ounces of meat, three glasses of vegetable juice, two quarts of distilled water. Fruit juice allowed after the third week. "Random saliva and urine tests show whether you're following it."

Cronin looked up from the list. "You're kidding, right?"

"To build a perfect world, first build a perfect body."

Philip strode to his own locker and suited up, already preparing his mind for the training room. As they crossed the hall, he glanced back toward the gallery, where Dodge and Martinez continued shooting. The Colonel would choose one man to take down the enemy. Rudy Martinez couldn't be beat on long-range shooting, no argument. But long range might not be practical this time, and Philip intended to show Colonel Jay he could do more than organizational detail work. If the opportunity arose, he intended to qualify as number-one backup.

Chapter Thirty

Friday

Edna Pine met Lucy Ames in November at Club Cato.

Dixie rolled that fact around in her brain, willing it to stick to something. It remained the only connection she'd found linking Aunt Edna to the other robberies.

Robbery, actually. Still no link to the first one, which occurred a full week before Lucy Ames held up the Webster branch. Then Edna ripped off the Richmond bank the next day.

Did Lucy and Edna cook up their heists *after* hearing about the successful robbery in Houston? There'd been no headlines on it. Since no shooting occurred, the *Chronicle* had buried the item on an inside page, and the bank's public-relations department had issued only the barest details. Holdups scared away customers. But Lucy, an employee of Texas Citizens, would've known. She also could've supplied insider knowledge about when the branches would be cash heavy.

Comparing the info picked up at Club Cato with what she'd learned from Terrence Jackson, Dixie saw a pattern emerging: a recently widowed country woman determined to seek out new experiences. Not much, but a thread more than she'd known fifty-eight hours ago, when she agreed to help Marty. Maybe she could follow this thread to a "new experience" that included both Lucy and Edna.

The first checks written to Unique Boutique and Artistry Spa appeared in late December, after Edna met Lucy. Lucy may have introduced Edna to the spa and boutique, or the two friends may have discovered the places together. Or not.

Dixie flipped a coin and headed toward Artistry Spa. When she peeled the

Mustang off Loop 610 onto Westheimer, the heart of the Galleria area retail and office complex, she hit the speed-dial button on her cell phone.

"What do people do at singles clubs?" she asked when Parker answered.

"You pulled me out of the shower to ask about singles clubs?"

Dixie's gaze flickered to the stained-glass bauble dangling from her rearview mirror. *My day begins with your smile, your scent, your touch . . .*

"Must be nice, lie in bed till nine, stroll into work at ten." Her own body clock started at dawn, except on weekends.

"Boat buyers keep the same hours."

"Do you want to get back in the shower or tell me about singles clubs?"

"You've never been to one?"

"Parker! Do all salespeople answer a question with a question? If I'd been to one, I'd know what people do there."

His gruff chuckle nudged a sleeping memory of them snuggled together in front of the fireplace, watching a late-night comedy.

"You caught me," he said. "Most buyers are so flattered to talk about themselves, they don't notice the salesman's evading their questions."

"I wouldn't buy anything from someone who did that."

"No?"

"I'm telling you, those 'persuade and close' gimmicks don't work on me." Yet listening to Terrence Jackson, hadn't she felt an incredible urge to find some "languishing" dollars for him to invest?

She maneuvered a left turn, nearly throwing her neck out of joint trying to balance the phone.

"People who believe they can't be hooked are the easiest," Parker teased. "Did you drop a wad on a new toy and get buyer's remorse?"

She told him about Jackson, leaving out the part about finding him handsome.

"I think Jackson might've conned Edna out of some dough, and I'm wondering if he's the man you saw at her house after New Year's. How would you like to attend a singles fiesta with me tonight and have a look at him?" It *was* Friday, after all.

"Bringing a date to a singles function is like wearing a sign that says 'hate me.' "

"Okay, we'll go separately. In addition to your taking a gander at Jackson, I thought we'd play detective."

"Hmmm, sounds kinky." They agreed on a time to meet. "By the way," Parker added, "I can give you a sales resistance trick that works every time."

"Really?" Not that she needed one. "So give."

"Create a picture in your mind of Jackson being his most persuasive."

She conjured Jackson's espresso-brown eyes as they'd locked with hers, and felt again that shiver of interest she'd experienced in his office. "Okay."

"Hear what he's saying?"

She tried to concentrate on the words, but Jackson's hypnotic voice made that impossible. "Yeah," she lied.

"Now, change his suit to a purple tutu."

Dixie grinned, imagining it. "Okay."

"Add a long, pointy nose and floppy ears."

Jackson became the donkey boy in *Pinocchio*. "Got it."

"And a squeaky, silly voice."

"Hey, it works!"

"Every time — did I hear brakes squeal?"

"Some idiot ahead of me using his cell phone."

Dixie disconnected and slid into a parking space in front of Artistry Spa. A funky sculpture of colored shapes boldly illustrating the spa's name marked the entrance. Turning a spoon-shaped knob in a polished steel door, Dixie heard the string sounds of Pachelbel's "Canon," and caught a quick whiff of what heaven must smell like. Flowers? Yes, but also vanilla, spice, something musky . . .

Aromatherapy. Dixie wondered if they sold the scent in a bottle, and if so, how much her credit card would allow her to take home.

Artistry Spa: the ultimate sensual experience, the Yellow Pages ad had promised. *All-natural glacial facials, seaweed body wraps, therapeutic massage, pressure water massage, aromatic mud baths . . .*

Dixie shuddered. Why would anyone put herself through such embarrassment? The list in the ad had measured over an inch deep in ten-point type, and the woman who greeted Dixie must've had the works. Chocolate-brown hair, alabaster skin, and cherry-red nails all glistened as if they'd been turned out by a pastry chef and glazed with sugar. Her clothes fit like a banana skin.

When Dixie asked for Lonnie Gray, the woman smiled with perfect teeth. "If you're willing to see someone else, we could take you right now."

"I just had a few questions—"

"Then I can help you." She slipped a brochure from a drawer in a silver-leafed table.

So far the woman hadn't said enough to fill a sound bite, and she didn't appear to be the person who'd have the most revealing information on clients.

"I really need to see the owner." Dixie offered the business card she'd taken from Edna's dresser: LONNIE GRAY, PROPRIETOR.

"Lonnie does reserve Mondays for consultation appointments, but at the moment he's unavailable."

No way to get out of this without a treatment, Dixie realized. Perhaps following Edna's experiences might in itself be revealing. If she had to endure a "seaweed body wrap," it damned well better be useful.

She tried a little Southern aggression.

"I heard so much about Lonnie from my friend Edna," she gushed. "I don't

believe I could trust anyone else to do me—and I *did* make an appointment."
Fortunately.

"Well . . . Lonnie's here, but . . . he's having an emergency."

"How long will I have to wait?"

The woman moved with fashion-model slinkiness to a phone on a tiny silver desk beside a teal chair far too delicate to invite sitting. Except for the dollar signs Dixie saw stacking up rapidly, the decor gave away nothing concerning the transformations taking place beyond a pair of satin-finished lavender doors. Neither did the one-sided conversation she overheard.

"Half an hour," the woman said, cradling the phone. "You can wait in the steam room, if you like. Open those pores."

Eight minutes later, stripped, showered, and wrapped in a towel as big as a bedsheet, with a smaller one around her vigorously shampooed head, Dixie lay on a teakwood bench within a dense cloud of eucalyptus steam. In no time at all, her skin felt so relaxed it might slide right off her bones. If pampering oneself felt this terrific, she could be sold, after all.

Before she became a complete puddle, the door opened, and a ribbon of cool air invaded the delicious heat.

"Ms. Flannigan. Lonnie can evaluate you now . . . if you'll come with me."

Dixie swam up from her near slumber and followed the cool air out the door. A different woman, as perfectly polished as the receptionist but dressed in lounging pajamas, led her through another lavender door. The spacious room— mirrors at all angles—held a massage table, a beautician's adjustable swivel chair, a teal sofa, and a silver coffee table, where a carafe of orange juice chilled in a bowl of ice. The woman gave her a lavender satin robe that glided like oil over Dixie's lobster-pink skin.

"Would you care for a mimosa?"

Champagne and orange juice. With no food in her stomach, she'd be dizzy in two sips, but what the hell, why not get the full effect of shameless hedonism? Maybe the alcohol would make the torture bearable.

"A small one," she said, and then before she could stop herself, tossed back a third of the delicious liquid in one swallow.

"Make yourself comfortable. Lonnie will be in shortly." The woman indicated the beautician's chair.

Dixie sat. "Any chance of a bagel to go with this drink?"

The shadow that crossed the woman's features couldn't be called a frown. Such a perfect face wouldn't dare.

"We have fruit. Will that do?"

"Anything."

"I'll bring it right in. Oh . . . and here's Lonnie!" Her smile said Dixie should feel honored by the noble attention.

She left the door ajar, and Dixie heard the man speak before she saw him.

"This color is *extraordinary* on you, sweetheart. *Gorgeous.* And I can't get over how *slim* you're becoming. Look at you. Who is this slender young thing?"

Dixie caught a glimpse of the woman whose shoulders his arm encircled. Six-tyish, in her strawberry-pink suit, carefully styled hair, and flawless makeup, she reminded Dixie of Edna. Not her old neighbor, but the Edna who'd smiled amiably over a gun barrel. Dixie's antenna homed in.

Lonnie, a youthful forty-five or so—thinning hair, a trim beard, and a wiry body—entered the room wearing designer jeans and a knit shirt that hugged him in all the right places.

"Don't be a stranger, sweetheart," Lonnie called outside the door. The woman with Dixie's fruit followed him into the room.

"Who is *this* lovely?" Lonnie demanded.

"Dixie Flannigan, a new client." The woman set a beautiful, if skimpy, fruit salad on the counter beside Dixie and handed her a gold fork wrapped in a pink cloth napkin. "Referred by a friend."

"That lady in the hall looked familiar," Dixie lied. "What was her name?"

"Opal drives all the way from Victoria to visit us, and we've worked a minor miracle, let me tell you." Lonnie approached Dixie's chair, whipped the towel from her head, and thrust his hand into her thick, damp hair. "Sweetheart, this is *marvelous.* The angels are smiling on me today, sending this luscious bit of clay to sculpture. We'll create a *masterpiece.*"

Sculpture? "I believe I know an Opal in Victoria. What was her last name?"

"Shack, Shattuck? I don't do last names, sweetheart." He swiveled Dixie's chair toward the mirror, opened a drawer, and plucked out a pair of scissors.

"Shouldn't we talk first?" Dixie asked.

"You talk, while I work. Kitchi! We need you in here."

"You'll *love* Kitchi," the fruit woman promised, refilling Dixie's glass.

The scissors snipped.

"You won't use color, will you?" Dixie moved her salad bowl away from the falling hair.

"Darling, you're *years* from needing color. A little shaping, a *tiny* bit of curl . . ."

The fruit woman slid open a drawer, set jars and bottles on the counter, pinned a fresh towel around Dixie's shoulders, and left the room. *Hair grows back,* Dixie reminded herself. She lowered her eyes from the mirror and finished the fruit before the door opened again.

"Kitchi, sweetheart, come look at how the gods have blessed us." Lonnie's scissors paused while he ran his fingers into Dixie's hair again, lifted it, let it fall.

He had strong hands and, despite the gushing flattery, a genuine gleam of interest in his eyes that made Dixie glad she'd "blessed" him with her presence. That gleam told her no one else could've made such a difference in his otherwise miserable day. With her wet hair and steamed pores, she felt totally gorgeous in his hands, even while the mirror told her otherwise.

Kitchi, horse-faced and dwarfish—certainly not one of the spa's beautiful people but with her own colorful style—pinched gently at Dixie's cheek.

"You have good skin, love. Clear and tight, but you neglect it, don't you?"

"I wash it," Dixie said. "I use lotion."

Kitchi patted Lonnie's arm, still snipping, and plucked one of the jars from the counter. "You go ahead and work, Lonnie, while Dixie and I chat."

"Do you know Opal's last name?"

"Can't say that I do." Using a small wooden paddle, she scooped a glob of green from the jar and plopped it on a small square tray.

Snip, snip, snip. Dixie prayed she hadn't made a huge mistake coming here.

"Skin needs nurturing, love. It isn't age that ruins us, it's living in polluted times." Kitchi measured a tiny spoonful of white powder into the green paste and stirred. "We'll send you home with everything you need. Retinol lotion for night care, a fruit-acid moisturizer, and a good sun block—those are the essentials."

Lonnie worked a conditioner into Dixie's hair, then wrapped it in a plastic cap. As soon as he stepped aside, a dollop of Kitchi's green goo landed on Dixie's face, cool and smelling of cucumbers. Kitchi spread it around with the paddle.

"My friend Edna—" Dixie began, then snapped her mouth shut to avoid the goop. When the paddle passed on toward her hairline, she said, "My friend Edna Pine sang your praises."

In the mirror, Lonnie's face went comically sad. "Poor Edna. That poor, poor darling."

"Did we miss the funeral?" Kitchi looked dismayed.

"Appointments," Lonnie explained. "Back to back."

What? Edna hadn't been buried yet.

"You must mean Lucy Ames' funeral." Dixie watched the pair exchange a glance.

"Ames, yes," Kitchi clucked. "She came here that one time with Edna, Lonnie. Remember?"

"A shock, both of them dying like that." Lonnie's strong hands massaged Dixie's scalp through the plastic bag. "But didn't they exit in style!"

"Lucy's funeral was yesterday afternoon," Dixie said, closing her eyes as Kitchi came at her with another concoction.

"Yes, that's the one I read about—but you had that seminar, Lonnie."

"Too late to cancel."

"And we mustn't both be away at the same time."

"Did Lucy or Edna ever bring another woman here? Or meet someone here?"

Kitchi shook her head. "Edna visited us weekly. How long, Lonnie?"

Dixie eased her eyes open.

"Awhile." Lonnie's hands slowed their gentle massage. "I remember she mentioned her son was taking her to the ballet, and she wanted to look smashing. It *was* the ballet, Kitchi?"

"*The Nutcracker.*" Kitchi examined Dixie's hand. "*Nobody* wears nails cut at the quick anymore, sweetie, not with solar gels, silk wraps, linen wraps. You have strong nails, but you must feed them . . . vitamins, calcium, a good protein—"

"*The Nutcracker,*" Dixie prompted. "Around Christmas, Edna's looks improved remarkably."

"Sweetheart, for Edna Pine, it took more than a snip and a curl. A lovely woman in her time, I'm sure, but she *had* let herself go, hadn't she, Kitchi?"

The facial technician pursed her lips and nodded dourly.

"We gave Edna a full makeover for a New Year's party," Lonnie added. "She longed to be a *new* woman for the *new year.*"

"Don't we all?" Kitchi dabbed brown oil on Dixie's nails.

"And, sweetheart, Edna didn't *renege* on her New Year's resolution like . . . *some* of us do." Lonnie shot a disdainful glance at Kitchi.

"I saw pictures, before and after," Dixie gushed. "What a difference you made!"

"Oh, *I'll* take credit where credit's due. We created a minor *miracle.* But, sweetheart, that woman worked like a *demon* on herself—sweating with the oldies, I suppose. Lost a *ton* of *weight.*"

"Was something special happening after the new year—? *Ow!*"

Kitchi's nail file had slipped under a cuticle.

"Sorry, dear. Now, don't talk . . . your face will crack."

Dixie studied the woman's solemn demeanor, imagined a brown wig covering her gray hair, and wondered if the slip of her file had really been an accident. Had the new year promised an event more exciting than *The Nutcracker*? Armed robbery, for instance?

And how much of Lonnie's act was just that—an act?

He clicked on a hair dryer and aimed its heat at Dixie's plastic-wrapped head. Over the roar, she couldn't hear their conversation. Had the pair exchanged another furtive glance? She watched them, wondering how many friends Edna had made here and whether any had come into money in the past week. Tomorrow would be too soon to return for another treatment.

She consoled herself that at least she wouldn't have to worry about gussying up for the singles party tonight. New hair, new face. With a different blouse, her black funeral suit would look fine for cocktails. Or maybe she'd spring for a sexy new dress to go with her new image. Shock city.

Minutes later, she found herself on the massage table, the lavender robe down around her middle and a strong-fingered woman working on her back muscles while Lonnie massaged her feet. He had discreetly turned away when the robe came down, although Dixie felt no embarrassment. Alcohol *did* lower one's inhibitions.

Or maybe she actually enjoyed the way Lonnie complimented every inch she exposed. "Look at these, Kitchi. Have you ever seen such feet? *These* toes have not been pinched into shoes too tight or too high. She could *model* these feet. Carmine—he's our reflexologist, Dixie—Carmine will *lust* for these feet, Kitchi."

Dixie closed her eyes and imagined being twenty-five years older, widowed a year ago, and starved for human companionship. Though she believed only one out of every five words Lonnie uttered, the barrage of appreciation worked like a tonic. She felt prettier, sexier, happier. She felt loved. People who hadn't known she existed a few hours ago knew more about her aging body than her own husband had after years of intimacy. And through their eyes, she was not a worn-out sixty-six-year-old; she radiated potential.

Dixie opened her eyes. Except for the age distinction, was she really so different from Edna? Not widowed, of course, never even married. But alone. By choice—she'd always considered "I do" the world's longest sentence. Now the one man in her life she could imagine marrying had recast her as a good buddy. A pal with a lovable dog.

"*Cellulite*, Kitchi. *None, nada.* Can't find a single lump of cottage cheese. But too much dead skin. This body needs a dry brush massage before the mud. Use the spicy mud, sweetheart, I want this skin to glow like *moonlight* on Maui."

Covered in mud to her chin, green goo on her face, Dixie dozed in a shallow tub, sipping mimosas and feeling like royalty. *Gorgeous* royalty—otherwise, why would anyone treat her so swell? Had Edna felt seduced by the attention? Never mind that she paid for it. Dixie couldn't recall anyone quoting a price—and at the moment, could think of no reason not to max out her credit card.

She'd worry later about whether she'd bought any worthwhile information.

Chapter Thirty-one

Officer Ted Tally shoved aside his empty coffee cup and picked up the tab. His turn to pay.

"Nine days fishing and camping," Dietz coaxed. "So deep in the Thicket you need a compass to find your way out."

Sounded tempting. First thing Ted Tally did every morning, after pouring his caffeine hit, was tie a new fishing lure. He'd practiced tying them all, bay bugs, chuggers, paddle-tails, deciding which was fastest, neatest. Which could be tied in the brush with materials at hand. Had a boxful going unused. Fishing sure sounded better than three days of desk duty while IA finished their report.

"Don't have nine days' vacation coming," he told Dietz. "And no comp time."

"I hear there's a big bad flu going around, friend." Dietz pushed his two hundred-plus pounds out of his chair. "Takes about nine days to shake it. Don't you feel sick?"

"Sick of listening to your bullshit." Dietz wouldn't lay out sick anymore than he would, not with a cop killer to be found. Ted stood and dropped tip money on the table. "Besides, you saw that new pickup I'm driving. Think I want to scratch it up on those backwoods trails?"

Dietz angled toward the door, but hung back. "Tally, think about it." His voice had gone serious. "Being a cop in this town right now might not be healthy, forget the flu."

Talking about Art Harris now. Harris, who'd sat right here, drinking his watered-down joe—claimed the chemicals in decaf would kill you—ten minutes before Ted caught the Pine squeal. Harris, too keyed up from the first shooting to sit still, never mind this wasn't his beat, never mind he was thirty miles west of where he oughta be. Harris wanting to make it right, take this actor down with no killing. Harris, who should've stayed out of it. Maybe the Pine shooting had nothing to do with Art catching a bullet, but what a rotten day to remember as you're sucking in that final breath.

"I'll think about it," Ted lied. "Maybe join you in a couple days."

"We'll notch the trees, so you can find us," Dietz called.

Also lying. Dietz might be worried, might even seriously consider taking the trip he'd been planning for weeks, but Ted knew he wouldn't go. Like every other officer in town, Dietz would hang in—fishing trip be damned—until they nailed this motherfucking cop killer.

Chapter Thirty-two

At Fit After Fifty, instead of lavender doors, Pachelbel, and heavenly scents, Dixie stood at a check-in desk furnished in chrome and leather, listening to Elvis Presley's "Jailhouse Rock," and studying before-and-after pictures of prized clients. Pages and pages of flab-turned-fit.

She'd stopped first at the Unique Boutique, which turned out to be right next door. A sign in the window had said, BACK IN TEN MINUTES, and Dixie decided to use that time efficiently.

"I remember Edna Pine," the FAF attendant told her. "One of our 'believe it' cases."

The FIT AFTER FIFTY emblem embroidered on his shirt didn't convince Dixie this man was half a century old. Twenty percent body fat, a hundred sixty pounds, all sinewy strength. Graying at the temples, but no wrinkles showing. Thirty-eight, maybe.

"Believe what?" she asked.

"Most of these people come because their doctors tell them to take off weight or expect to drop dead tomorrow. Others wake up one day feeling old and want to turn back the clock—"

"I'd say Edna wanted to turn back the clock," Dixie agreed.

"And she did it! Came here overweight, tired, depressed. You should see her now—" The realization that Edna's *now* was over froze his smile. "I mean, you know, before . . ."

"I saw the pictures." Dixie nodded toward the album. "Impressive. But you said she came here depressed?"

"Yeah, well . . . like most people . . . unhappy about being fat."

"Then she lost the weight. How, some special program?"

"Every program is custom. We can design one that'll put you in top condition, working out only forty minutes, three times—"

"Were you Edna's trainer?"

He shook his head. "Wish I could take that credit. She enrolled in a self-monitored program, and then she must've invested in home equipment. Started coming only once a week—"

Dixie'd seen no exercise equipment at Edna's house.

"—mostly for the sauna. Which is excellent." He pushed a brochure across the counter. "Even if you work out at home, you'd want to enroll for the sauna."

Instead of buying equipment, Edna had taken aerobics with Mike. A supply of his flyers, posted on FAF's bulletin board, had caught Dixie's eye on the way in. Had she taken classes with any other instructors? "Do you have a record of Edna's progress?"

The man shook his head. "We only keep records when you sign with a personal trainer. In fact, if you sign up today—"

"You must have some sort of records. You put Edna's photograph in your album."

He stared at Dixie, as if weighing her pain-in-the-ass factor against a possible sale. "All right, I'll check the computer." He sat down at the keyboard, and after a few passes with the mouse, reported, "Edna Pine never used a staff trainer, but she did enroll in exercise classes—"

"When?"

"December first. We have a list of classes, if you're interested—dancercize, yoga—"

"Which ones did Edna take?" Dixie persisted.

He looked back at the monitor. "No list, but the instructor's noted here. One of our outside consultants, Mike Tesche."

Which she already knew. "Only one?"

He nodded.

"What about other students in her class?"

"I can't give you that information. *Must* be some sort of privacy invasion."

A customer arrived, and the attendant started to rise.

"Wait! Just tell me if Lucy Ames was ever enrolled here."

With an annoyed huff, he scrolled hastily. "No. No record."

The elusive Lucy. Which reminded Dixie of someone else she hadn't heard from in a while. She moved away from the counter and used her cell phone.

Amy picked up on the first ring. "Marty flew back to Dallas."

"That jerk! He could've phoned instead of leaving me hanging." After receiving his mysterious letter from Edna, Marty'd apparently lost interest in why his mother robbed a bank.

"He seemed upset, Dixie. You'd think the gallery could manage without him for a while. Anyway, he'll be back tonight."

A television positioned for easy viewing during workouts started a news update. Dixie watched it as she finished her conversation with Amy. No news on the Harris assassination. Still no sign of the stolen bank money. And blessedly, no more robberies. *Yet.*

Perhaps the spree had ended.

Dixie realized she'd been practically holding her breath, imagining the third robber as a brown-haired witch who duped suicidal women into stealing for her and who now sat cackling over her clever plan, counting her quarter million while Aunt Edna lay on a mortician's slab. Perhaps Lucy and Edna really had cooked up the idea between them.

Nevertheless, Dixie strode into the sunshine, with "Jailhouse Rock" playing a loop in her head, and stopped next door at Unique Boutique. Marty might've given up on following his mother's path from gardening to gunslinging, but Dixie hadn't.

Eyeing the stunning outfits featured in the display window, she decided a clerk might be more talkative to a potential customer than to a nosy stranger. Yesterday's black suit was definitely too somber for a happy-hour fiesta—and too drab for the newly made-over Dixie Flannigan. Sleek new hair, glowing skin, nails magically lengthened and polished.

Had Edna gazed in the same window, having similar thoughts after sweating off those extra pounds?

The store looked new and expensively chic. A brilliant space designer had laid out the interior. Dresses, blouses, skirts, pants—all bearing the store's private label—occupied every usable inch of the minuscule area, without appearing crowded. As much as Dixie despised shopping, she felt the tug of each rack leading her to the next.

A sign above every section stated COTTON, WOOL, SILK—NATURAL FIBERS BREATHE. A space beneath those words bore the size designation for that rack, then, LIMITED RELEASE DESIGNS FOR THE UNIQUE YOU.

What did that mean, exactly? Ready-made clothes at custom prices? The styles certainly had a timeless quality and seemed appropriate for a wide age span; the old Edna would've laughed, shaken her head, and headed for the wash-and-wear at JCPenney. Yet nearly all the items in her closet now bore the boutique's pricey label.

Six months ago, in November, Edna had broken out of her mold to visit Club Cato, where she met Lucy Aaron Ames. On December first, she'd started working off the fat at Fit After Fifty. A couple weeks later she'd written her first checks to Artistry Spa and Unique Boutique. Remaking herself.

Shopping for a new life? A new mate? She'd met Terrence Jackson and allowed him to assume control of her investments, a role that Bill Pine had always filled. Interesting.

Also interesting was the proprietor of Unique Boutique—JESSICA LOVE, according to the card Dixie'd plucked from a holder near the register. Between thirty-five and fifty-five, closer to the high end, Dixie judged, Jessica had a medium build and radiant brown hair. Dixie envisioned big sunglasses covering her eyes, a .38 in her hand. Canvas bags stuffed with stolen cash over her shoulder.

The first bank robber's vague description fit thousands of women in the greater Houston area, but the image had plunked into Dixie's head when Jessica approached wearing a blue dress identical to the one Edna wore during the robbery.

"That must be a popular design," Dixie commented.

"A classic. Would you like to see one in your size?"

Dixie recalled the blue silk splotched with blood. *Absolutely not.*

"I need something for evening . . . comfortable . . . not too slinky."

"I have a beautiful black suit with a beaded jacket."

No. She'd spent yesterday in funeral black. But Dixie followed the woman to a rack of clothing with as much sparkle as a Christmas tree. Without asking her size, Jessica extracted the black suit, then sorted through the rack and selected a red dress, a cream-white jumpsuit, and a bronze metallic tunic with matching pants.

"A friend recommended this place." Dixie waited for Jessica to face her before continuing. "Edna Pine."

The proprietor's professional smile turned plaster-stiff. She regarded Dixie with cool gray eyes.

"Mrs. Pine was a good customer." Jessica led the way toward the dressing room.

Dixie followed. "Edna loved this boutique. And she couldn't say enough about you . . . the way you helped her."

"I showed her some flattering colors."

Jessica opened the dressing-room door and hung the clothes on a wall hook, without once glancing at Dixie. Upset that a former customer had turned bank robber? Or nervous about being identified as Edna's accomplice? A leap, but why not go with it?

"She said you two shared more than just shopping." Fumbling . . . a good fumble often drew unexpected information.

"We both worked out at the gym next door. Is that what you mean?"

"Edna considered you a friend, Jessica. Someone she confided in."

The woman nodded slowly. "Nice lady, if a little dreamy. We did talk a few times."

"Dreamy?"

"Like when you plan a big event in your head, and you know it'll be wonderful? When I saw on TV about the robbery, I wondered if she'd dreamed up the whole thing while trying on clothes. In a morbid sort of way, it's like knowing a celebrity—this nice lady who got right in their face. Really awful, those damned cops!"

"Didn't Lucy Ames shop here, too?"

"The other *robber?*" Jessica's face remained poker-smooth. "No. Listen, give a holler if you need help."

The door clicked shut, closing Dixie in the dressing room with four choice outfits and a vague notion that she might've just learned something useful. So far, she'd placed Lucy Ames and Aunt Edna together only at Club Cato and Artistry Spa. At neither place had they hooked up with a third woman—unless Jessica was lying about Lucy not being a customer.

Once again, Dixie imagined the brown-haired proprietor wearing face-hiding sunglasses and, this time, shouldering a huge concrete dollar sign. The cost of keeping the doors open on a chic boutique must be incredibly heavy. Dixie was the only customer in the store this afternoon. Businesses failed most often within the first one to three years; this one was new enough that the carpet hadn't yet lost its surface fuzz. And the store opened each day at eleven A.M., allowing plenty of time to pull off an early-morning heist.

Chapter Thirty-three

As he watched Dietz exit the coffee shop, Ted Tally slipped a ten out of his wallet. He'd forgotten to mention the pin he saw yesterday on a kid's jacket. Certainly not a local gang symbol, and the kid struck Ted as too clean to be gang-connected. Pulled him over for no brake lights. Wrote out a warning.

The driver had been cool. Too cool. Uptight cool. And way too polite. For grins Ted asked what the pin represented.

"Perseverance." The boy smiled, big freckles covering his face.

The Cherokee's plates turned up clean. No reason to rag the driver. No hint of drugs. Nothing visible inside the car—spotless, in fact. Yet, he was definitely uptight.

And Ted had seen that triangular design somewhere before. It would eat at him until he remembered. He'd sketched it, thinking Dietz might recognize it, having been on gang detail up north. They could've fed the design into the computer—if Ted hadn't left the damn sketch at home this morning.

He checked the lunch tab against his ten and shot a glance at Sarah, the green-eyed goddess behind the counter. For three weeks he'd been hinting for a date with her. He dropped the money beside the cash register.

"How about tomorrow night, Sarah?"

Her eyes sparkled, flirting, but she shook her head, ringing up the total.

"Come on, nobody works *all* the time. Even cops take a day off now and then."

"If I were a cop, maybe I'd get a day off, too. Maybe we'd get the *same* day off and spend it together. But I work every Saturday night. Sorry."

Was that a nibble?

"Saturday's only a suggestion. I'm on day shift, so my time's yours after three o'clock. How about let's take out my wave runner, catch some sun before sundown?"

"My shift isn't over until six."

Tally felt his grin broaden. More than a nibble, a big-mouthed bite.

"Where do I pick you up?" He handed her a pen and slid a napkin over to write on.

She hesitated. "Maybe we should meet somewhere."

Then they'd have two cars. Couldn't take her home. "Hey, if you can't trust a cop, who can you trust?"

She smiled, shrugged, then wrote down her address.

"Six o'clock?"

"Seven. I have to change clothes."

"Seven it is." Outside, he whistled as he strolled to his squad car. Three weeks, about ten days longer than he'd ever dangled a hook. Was he dreaming, or was she worth the extra wait?

Better than nine days with Dietz in the woods, for sure—

Then it hit him, where he'd seen that red-blue-and-gold symbol. The day Chief Wanamaker took office, Ted had been fishing and almost missed the big deal at Wortham Center, an auditorium full of cops, plus City Council, Mayor Banning—and a couple of kids wearing that same pin. Hell, maybe it did stand for "perseverance." Took plenty to become Chief.

Ted reached for the door handle—

The force of the bullet slammed him against the car, lifting his feet off the asphalt, and sprayed bits of bone and tissue over blue-and-white paint. For the space of a millisecond, Ted saw his world explode in brilliant color.

Chapter Thirty-four

Sunset played a color symphony in the western sky as Dixie raised a sleeve of her new tunic to glance at her watch. Diaphanous bronze silk, virtually weightless, the fabric sparkled in the light and moved against her skin like a feather.

"That pantsuit is *you*," Jessica Love had assured her. "You look fabulous." And there, in the cozy boutique, just the two of them, Dixie believed her. The sheer silk had felt sexy and exotic and fun. Now it felt brazen. She'd never worn a thing that so clearly shouted "Look at me!" Three months of Parker's "Let's just be pals" had turned her into a hormone harlot.

FIESTA NIGHT
$10
HAPPY-HOUR PRICES

Punctual Parker would be inside the club already.

Dixie fluffed her hair and commanded her galloping pulse to slow down. The party atmosphere—certainly more intimate than their usual Friday-night restaurant—along with her new duds, new face, new hair . . . did she expect these to jolt Parker out of his stubborn hands-off attitude? Well, *yes*, dammit.

But she also had a job to do here. According to Terrence Jackson, members of Fortyniners formed relationships. What better place for Edna to've hooked up with Ms. Mysterious Moneybags, who, so far, remained the only successful Granny Bandit?

"One happy hour a week," Jackson'd said. And this was it. Dixie had three, maybe four hours to gather all the information to be gained from this bunch, or wait for their next event.

She swept past the sign and entered.

City Streets, a property manager, had taken over a number of small defunct retail stores in a shopping mall. Wide doorways connected the spaces, encouraged mingling, yet divided the huge area into cozy sections. Fortyniners occupied one section; similar organizations met in the other rooms. And farther back, the on-site nightclub beckoned loners to drop in.

What had brought Aunt Edna here? Lucy Ames? Another friend? Or had she stopped for a drink after shopping in a still vital part of the retail mall? At the fringe of the Galleria area, City Streets sat twenty-seven miles from Edna's home in Richmond, but only blocks from Terrence Jackson's office, Artistry Spa, Fit After Fifty, and Unique Boutique.

At the registration table, a man who must've turned forty-nine three decades ago took Dixie's ten bucks in exchange for a cheerful, leering grin, a drink ticket, and a name tag. His orange jacket would've been loud even without the melon-pink tie. He plastered the name tag to her right shoulder.

"Save me a dance later," he urged, handing her a business card from his jacket pocket. "I'm Crawford Garston. Club treasurer."

Dixie read the card. "Esquire" appeared beneath his name. "I'd be happy to save a dance for you, *Judge* Garston."

His eyes crinkled at the corners. "Do I know you?"

"You threw out one of my cases, eleven years, two months, and twenty-six days ago." *Approximately.* "Told me to march right back to law school."

Garston chuckled, studying her as if trying to recall the case. "Hope your dancing's as good as your memory."

"I hope retirement has mellowed your disposition." It certainly hadn't improved his color sense.

Inside the meeting room, a five-piece band played a popular tune in a style reminiscent of the forties. Three couples swayed on the dance floor. Dixie spied Parker, rakishly handsome, as always, chatting with a blue-haired woman in a green polka-dot party dress. The woman waved Dixie over.

"My, how nice to see new people here." Nora, according to her name tag, looked to be a good age match for Judge Garston. Apparently, forty-nine lasted a very long time with this group.

"Terrence Jackson invited me," Dixie said.

Parker's gaze had lodged in her cleavage. Dixie felt a rush of heat in precisely the same spot.

"That devil Terrence hasn't arrived yet!" Nora's smile suggested Jackson was the best tonic since Geritol. "He'll show up later. Always does. I'm Nora Raye, tonight's hostess. You see, Parker, we do have a few young folks who attend. Now, let me show you both to the free buffet."

Nora seemed the type to know everybody who'd ever attended, but the word "buffet" turned Dixie's stomach into a growling beast. Her skimpy fruit salad had disappeared hours ago. While she fed the beast she could catch up on what Parker had learned, then question Nora later.

Past mounds of cheese, crackers, and raw vegetables, she spotted a platter of finger-roll sandwiches. Parker beat her to the tongs and placed three on her plate. His blue blazer and the lighter streaks in his dark hair gave him the appearance of having stepped right off a yacht—which he probably had. He carried the clean, fresh scent of sun and sea.

"How long have you been here?" Dixie licked a drop of red sauce off her finger.

"Long enough to figure out why you asked about sales techniques this morning."

Actually, she'd inquired about singles clubs, and their conversation had taken a turn. "What gave it away?"

"At least a third of this bunch use the club as a sales network."

Dixie scanned the crowd milling around the buffet and seated at tables. "Are they wearing signs? Or is this a case of 'it takes one to know one'?"

"Fortyniners is an evolved networking club," Parker insisted as they made their way to a tall table with two stools.

Dixie sat across from him—not as close as she'd like to be. A waitress took their drink orders.

"I know about networks—with six phone calls you can reach anyone in the world." Dixie'd developed her own eccentric but highly effective network for locating skips in most of the fifty states and Mexico. "But why bother with regular meetings?"

"Sales, Dixie. Walk up to anybody here. Say 'hello,' and if you get a business card shoved at you, you've just met a seller."

"Like Judge Garston?"

"The colorful old guy at the door? Didn't make him for a judge, but it figures. Read the back of his business card."

Dixie slipped it from her new bronze handbag and read the reverse side. "Aromatherapy Products."

"Network marketing. An entire industry developed from groups like this. Retired professionals selling products to avoid turning into couch potatoes."

Terrence Jackson was not retired.

"Okay, so . . . ?" She was too hungry to ask intelligent questions, but she wanted Parker to keep talking.

"Back in the eighties—country deep in recession, people out of work—groups like this cropped up all over. Buffet breakfasts. Luncheon meetings. Cocktail happy hours. All for cramming salespeople together with marks."

"You're telling me these salespeople are con artists?" Dixie shot another glance around the room.

"Only difference between a scam and a sale is the value of the product."

"Good point." She'd prosecuted a few cons in her day, but the best managed to bilk the public and skate free.

"The eighties economy destroyed marriages. Networking groups became singles social clubs—until AIDS. The clubs that hung in developed stringent rules."

Dixie'd been in her twenties, dating cautiously. She hadn't attended any singles clubs, but she remembered them. "A test slip verifying your 'AIDS free' status was your ticket to join. Dorks with documents finally got laid."

Parker chuckled. "Guess that's why those clubs didn't last long."

Appetite appeased, Dixie pushed her plate away and caught him stealing a glance at her.

"What?" she demanded.

"You look different."

"Different good or different bad?" Dixie resisted tugging the bronze silk higher over her breasts.

"Before the night's over, you'll have every male in the room drooling like a lovesick hound."

Dixie looked away from him. She knew he meant the remark as a compliment, but as a child, watching her birth mother spend forever "doing her face," then seeing the lecherous men her face brought home, Dixie'd decided her own mug could do without. She didn't want men *drooling* over her—not even the one sitting on the opposite stool.

"What'd I say wrong?" Parker asked.

"Nothing. Only, let's not talk about me. Tell me what Edna would've found interesting about a networking club."

"*Evolved* networking club. Serves a variety of needs. Singles meet, match up. Others enjoy the social events with no personal entanglement. A couple of ace salespeople here are making real money. Others would like to be—"

"Terrence Jackson appeared to be plenty successful already. Why would he need to shop for clients?"

Parker shrugged. "A smart salesman never stops selling."

Dixie considered the number of senior women in the room, probably widowed or divorced, which could mean healthy bank accounts after insurance or property settlements.

"The flock of prospects changes continuously," Parker explained. "Let a new mark arrive and the swarm strikes, each drawing a little blood. But not too much—parasites never kill their host. Best prospects are passed around. 'Need a widget? Good ol' Charlie can get it for you.' "

"Kickbacks?"

"For some. One or two percent of the sale. More important, when good ol' Charlie runs across a hot prospect, he returns the favor. In a good business network, everybody wins. Including the customer."

Which could be said of any such system, Dixie figured. She'd built her own by doing favors, exchanging information, chalking up credits.

"Recently widowed and comfortably fixed, I suppose Edna would've been the center of attention until all the salespeople had a chance to bite," Dixie mused.

Parker's gaze drifted back to Dixie's cleavage. "Like you'll be when you circulate in that dress."

"What about you?" she snapped. "Or do they only hit on females?"

"Oh, no." He drew a handful of business cards from his pocket. "I've already committed to buying . . ." He sorted through the cards. "Magnetic shoe inserts. A full-body massage. An electronic pocket calendar—"

"What happened to your own sales resistance trick?"

He shrugged. "Buying a few things breaks the ice, makes people easier about talking."

"Okay. What did you learn?"

"Besides the fact that our friend Nora"—he dropped one of the business cards on the table—"has been in the club since it was founded sixteen years ago? And that Edna bought therapeutic magnets for a pain in her shoulder?" He dropped another card. "And my Taurus-Cancer nature causes me to be overly nurturing—"

"What?" Dixie snatched the card from his hand.

VERNICE URICH, PH.D., M.S.W., A.C.P.

Another name from Edna's appointment calendar.

"Vernice"—Parker nodded at a woman standing alone near the buffet table and gazing intently toward the entrance—"is a psychotherapist."

Dixie recognized the woman, the well-dressed prune at Lucy Ames' funeral, standing at the edge of the crowd. Tonight, a peach-colored tube dress enhanced her willowy shape. In the nightclub's soft lighting, she looked years younger than the man in an orange jacket and melon-pink tie approaching behind her.

Judge Garston and Vernice Urich. Interesting match.

The judge slipped both hands over her shoulders and seemed to be massaging them, but the woman's attention remained riveted in the distance.

Dixie followed her gaze to a group of females greeting the silver-haired "devil" who'd just arrived.

"Parker, is that the man you saw at Edna's?"

"Bingo!"

"Great. Then we should split up. Ask more questions. We didn't come here to hang out together."

"Is he your super-salesman?"

She nodded. "Terrence Jackson."

"Just keep picturing him in a purple tutu." Parker dutifully zeroed in on a woman who looked eager to dance.

Watching Jackson, Dixie's thoughts flashed on an old Disney film: A friendly animated bear enters a forest and instantly attracts a following of butterflies and big-eyed singing squirrels. With one unfriendly swipe, the bear could knock them all senseless, but danger never enters their adoring minds.

Like the bear, Jackson smiled and chatted his way to a corner table, shaking hands, pressing an arm, a shoulder. By the time he sat down, he'd touched each of his admirers—not all of them women. A waitress removed a RESERVED sign from the table and set a drink in its place. A plate, already filled from the buffet, landed in front of him. In this pocket of the city, Jackson was Prince.

Dixie sidled close enough to hear snatches of conversations.

". . . you look stunning in green, Nora."

". . . Judge, that investment is already on the up-curve . . ."

". . . come to my office tomorrow . . ."

One by one, the Fortyniners warmed themselves by Jackson's flame, then moved on.

"Thank you for inviting me," Dixie said when she finally occupied a chair at his table.

Unlike every other man in the room, Jackson kept his eyes above her neckline. That gained him points.

"I'm glad you came tonight, Ms. Flannigan. The club also visits art galleries, theater, sports events, ballet—yet these weekly mixers are where we get acquainted."

"Wouldn't you have more fun in a younger crowd?"

"Depends on what you consider fun."

"What do *you* consider fun?"

"Dancing with a beautiful woman in an absolutely striking ensemble." Standing, he reached for her hand.

"I haven't danced much since high school."

He smiled, and his handsome face arranged itself into those phenomenal planes that could've been chiseled by an Italian sculptor.

"Then relax and follow my lead."

Not easy. She hated relinquishing control to anyone. But she allowed herself to be guided and dipped and twirled.

"Was Edna a good dancer?" she asked him.

"Not bad. She was a fast learner."

"How about Lucy Ames?"

"Why would you ask that? I told you I didn't know the woman."

"You said she wasn't a client. But she might've attended a happy-hour function. You might even have danced with her."

"I looked you up, Ms. D. A. Flannigan, attorney at law. You no longer practice law. In fact, you don't do much of anything, except get your name in headlines occasionally. Now you're trying to outguess the authorities on these Granny Bandit robberies. What are you really seeking?"

"I need to find out what *Edna* was seeking. What drove her into that bank with a gun?"

"Maybe you should talk with Vernice. All these women tell her their secrets."

Dixie absolutely intended to question Vernice Urich. Although the psychotherapist hadn't rushed to greet Terrence Jackson, she'd never taken her eyes off him. Even now she watched as he and Dixie danced.

The music stopped, and Jackson led Dixie back to the table.

"You could be a fine dancer, with a few lessons," he said.

A prince of flattery. "I'll bet you could teach me."

"I paid my way through college giving dance lessons," he admitted. "Now I dance for fun, but you'd be an engaging pupil. Once a week, right here. What do you say?"

"Sounds like you're soliciting members for Fortyniners."

His smile dimmed a watt or two. "With the country's population gracefully aging, Ms. Flannigan, we never have a shortage of members. People who spent their youth hammering out a career or nurturing a family find they crave the social pleasures missed when they were younger."

The average age on the dance floor, Dixie calculated, was closer to sixty-five than forty-nine.

"Either you're older than you look, Terrence, or you love dancing even more than you let on. Aren't there any clubs with members more your own age?"

He raised his glass to her. "You never let up, do you?"

"Curiosity. My curse."

"Fortyniners is an opportunity to combine business with pleasure. Many of the members are my clients. People will trust their investments to someone they know socially."

Parker had once said the same about selling yachts. It made sense.

"Do you ever make house calls?"

"When business demands. Speaking of business—" Jackson stood, his gaze sliding past Dixie. "Thank you for providing the most pleasurable part of my evening."

Perhaps his visit to Edna *was* sales-related, as Parker had suggested. Dixie turned to see what had grabbed his attention.

Jessica Love, wearing the beaded black suit from Unique Boutique, flashed Jackson a dazzling smile. The crowd actually parted as he crossed the room to join her. They made an attractive couple.

"Isn't that Terrence a fine dancer?" Nora said, sitting down at Dixie's table. "Not a lady here doesn't perk up when Terrence arrives."

"The woman he's with now, is she a Fortyniner?"

"Jessica? Oh, yes, a regular."

Interesting that the boutique owner never mentioned seeing Edna here. "Was Edna Pine a regular?"

"Oh . . ." Nora made a tsk-tsk sound with her tongue. "Edna came here for a while . . . during the holidays, I believe."

"Not more recently?" . . . *only one happy hour a week. Edna never missed it.* Why would Jackson lie? Or had he simply failed to notice?

"Edna got the gospel, if I remember right. Lots of them do, you know, when they've lost someone close."

"Gospel?"

"You know—this belief or that. Some dial up the television psychics. Others join self-improvement groups. Some turn to God. Edna struck me as needing a force to believe in."

"Like the Church of The Light?"

"I don't recall . . . but then, my brain isn't what it used to be."

"Do you know a woman named Opal Shack, or Shattuck, from Victoria, Texas?"

Nora shook her head. "Doesn't ring a bell."

"Lucy Ames was a member, wasn't she?"

"My, my, now you *are* taxing my memory. Oh, look. Here's that nice young man again. Such a fine dancer, Dixie. Why don't you two take a little spin around the floor?"

"Actually," Parker said, "I'd like to dance with you, Nora."

"Oh, well . . . the spirit is willing, but my poor old feet can't take any more tonight. You young people go ahead." She shooed Dixie out of her chair.

Dixie could think of nothing she'd enjoy more than Parker's arms around her for a while, but first she intended to talk with Vernice Urich. She scanned the bar, where the woman had sat earlier, then the dance floor, where Terrence Jackson and Jessica Love dazzled onlookers with a fancy Latin step, and then the other tables. Maybe Vernice had gone to the ladies' room.

"I'll be back," she told Parker.

But Vernice wasn't in the ladies' room. Dixie peeked into the part of City Streets occupied by other organizations. A sign outside one room identified the group as the Senior Singles Network. On the stage, a speaker explained the reasons a national sales tax should replace the federal income tax. Vernice was not among the audience. Nor was she in the nightclub or in the next room, where a mini-trade show was in progress. About the same time Jessica Love arrived, Vernice Urich had disappeared.

As Dixie retraced her steps to the Fortyniners gathering, a light clicked on in her brain and she recalled why the name Fortyniners had sounded familiar the first time Terrence Jackson mentioned it. As a volunteer for Avery Banning's election campaign, Dixie'd helped arrange speaking engagements at business and professional meetings—including the Senior Singles Network. The chairman had mentioned that members of other organizations often popped in. One of those groups was Fortyniners.

Did this mean something? Or was it just another indication that it's a small world?

Chapter Thirty-five

At The People's training center, Philip Laskey sat before a personal computer typing letters from Colonel Jay's notes. From another part of the center came the energetic sounds of men training. When The People inherited this nation, they'd be strong and worthy of it.

Before touching the PRINT key, Philip slid his hands into a pair of thin rubber gloves. Then he loaded paper from a fresh package and opened a new box of envelopes. He studied the envelopes in their box, thin white edges, faultlessly aligned. Precision pleased him.

Once the letters and envelopes printed out, he placed them side by side on the desk. Selecting a ballpoint pen from a cluster of writing implements in a drawer, he scribbled on a paper scrap to check the ink flow, then signed each letter in clean, clear script: *The People.*

He admired the letterhead's insignia, blue, red, and gold, no bigger than a nickel.

"How do you respond when asked what that emblem stands for?" the Colonel often inquired.

"Freedom, sir!" thirty voices replied.

Except when the wrong person asked. Then the "P" stood for perseverance, preservation, prism, peace—anything but The People.

Philip noted a message on the printer: TONER LOW. He opened the cover, removed the toner cartridge, and shook it a few times before reinserting it. Then he folded the letters—only one of the three was significant—placed each in its matching envelope, sealed, stamped, and slid it into a brown paper bag.

By dropping them at the downtown post office, he could assure they'd arrive tomorrow with The People's dual message.

No officer-turned-killer would be tolerated.

Any commander who excused murder had ordered his own execution.

Chapter Thirty-six

Enjoying Parker's arm around her waist as they left City Streets, Dixie slowed her steps to extend their walk in the parking lot as long as possible. The night was clear and cool and endless with stars. With all the city's tall buildings behind them, the western skyline seemed to stretch forever.

"Did you pick up any clues tonight?" Parker asked.

"I don't know yet. No one admitted knowing Lucy Ames, and Edna stopped attending long before the robberies." Dixie related her conversations with Nora Raye, Terrence Jackson, others she'd questioned, and her notion that Jessica Love might be the third Granny Bandit.

"My eyes must be failing me. Did she look like a granny?"

"Okay, then how about Nora Raye?"

"I didn't peg her as a mastermind."

Dixie hadn't, either.

Parker guided her around an oil slick on the asphalt. "What if Lucy Ames, with her insider knowledge, caught the first Granny Bandit's act and decided to pull off the same trick. Only she doesn't know about guns. Talks to her new friend, Edna Pine, who *does* know about buying guns—after all, her husband had a cabinetful. Lucy confides her idea, and together they plan 'The Great Bank Robbery.' A lark. A nose-thumb at the world. If they pull it off, fine. Life gets more interesting—action, money, a moment in the limelight. If not, what a rousing final curtain. They 'lie here enjoying the timeless fame.' "

"Shakespeare again?"

"Simonides. Think about it, what did they have to lose?"

Dixie'd forgotten how much she enjoyed tossing around ideas with Parker. His scenario sounded much like the one she'd heard from Rashly, and it still didn't account for the missing cash.

"You sound as if you knew Lucy and Edna," she remarked.

"Loneliness isn't limited to middle-aged females."

She glanced up at him, wondering if the comment was more personal than general. In the near darkness, she couldn't read his hooded eyes and vague smile.

"What did you learn about the psychotherapist, Vernice Urich, who left before I could talk to her? Her name was penciled on Edna's calendar, and Terrence Jackson said she introduced him to Edna."

They'd reached the Mustang. Dixie unlocked it, then turned, leaned against the door. Parker looked down at her, and Dixie sensed his desire to close the short distance between them was as strong as her own.

"Vernice specializes in weight loss and marriage counseling," he said. "Having been wed six times, she considers herself an expert—"

"Six men proposed to her? With that face?" Dixie slapped a hand over her mouth. "Sorry. Cat jumped out."

Parker grinned. "I'm sure she wasn't born with wrinkles as thick as broom straws."

"Bet she's tagged Terrence Jackson for number seven." Even while enjoying Judge Garston's impromptu massage, Vernice had seemed entranced by the Millennium Midas.

Parker kicked at a soda can someone had left on the pavement. "*You* obviously enjoyed the company of your super-salesman tonight. Didn't know you were such a fancy stepper."

"Neither did I." She couldn't deny the dance with Jackson had been fun, even though he'd struck her as a controlling SOB. "Parker, the Fortyniners trust Terrence Jackson. Is he conning them?"

"Sure, he is—to some extent. Remember, the only difference between a con and a sale—"

"Yeah, yeah—is the value of the product." The *Financial Times* article had given Jackson high points for delivering value to his clients.

"Dixie, if I couldn't convince buyers to trust me, I'd never make a sale. Jackson's no different in that respect."

"He tried to recruit me to Fortyniners." *Then denied it.*

"Can't blame him." Parker ran a finger across her bare shoulder. He slipped his other hand around her waist and whirled her in a tricky dance step.

Dixie moved close, savoring the moment. "Think I should ask for a follow-up lesson?"

"The 'devil' must be special, the way women's eyes light up when he's around."

"Personally, I wouldn't trade one Parker Dann for ten Terrence Jacksons,"

Dixie murmured. "Want to see *my* eyes light up?" She tugged his head down and whispered in his ear.

"Woman, you make me blush." Parker gently disengaged from her, then kissed her cheek and winked. "Call you tomorrow."

When he opened the car door, Dixie slowly slid behind the wheel, a rush of embarrassment heating her face. Feeling a complete fool, she watched him stroll across the parking lot.

The brief firmness against her leg attested that Parker Dann had not become sexually immune to her. Didn't he feel the miserable ache—as she did—of these three celibate months? Did he have more willpower? Or was he gratifying his desires elsewhere?

With every man in her life, Dixie had been the one to break off the relationship. Maybe her own ego kept her from seeing that Parker had *already* broken it off—and moved on.

Blinking fast to keep the dampness in her eyes from smearing the goddamn layers of mascara, she couldn't decide whether she felt anger, sadness, humiliation—or a frustrating, gut-wrenching mixture of all three.

Her pager chirped. She'd left it in the car on purpose, and now it showed five messages from Amy. Thrusting the key into the ignition, she watched Parker's Cadillac turn toward Galveston, putting miles between them.

She started the Mustang's engine, then glanced back at her pager. *Jeez, Amy, what is it now?* Reluctantly, wanting nothing more to think about, preferring to wallow in the misery of rejection, she punched the quick-dial button on her cell phone as she eased out of the parking space.

"Where have you been?" her sister demanded.

"Amy, just tell me what's wrong."

"They arrested Marty! The cops came and made him go down to the police station. I told them he'd already answered all their questions—he wasn't even here when Edna . . . well, he wasn't! But they wouldn't listen, Dixie. They took him."

"I'm sure it's only to clarify a few things. I'll call—"

"These were *not* the nice cops. I know all about how they gang up, one all buddy-buddy, the other angry and cruel—like on *NYPD Blue*. How could they think Marty helped Edna?"

"I'm sure they simply need some answers, Amy. Did they take him in the police car or let him drive his rental?"

"He drove, but with two cop cars in front and two behind."

Heavy police escort—an intimidation technique Dixie knew well. It meant they planned to sweat Marty once they got him downtown.

"Stop worrying, Amy. If they let him take his car, he wasn't arrested. I'll call you as soon as I know anything."

Allowing Marty to drive his own vehicle would bolster his confidence, lead him to believe he had nothing to worry about, while the conspicuous show of power kept him nervous. Then they'd put him in a depressing little room — no arrest, so no lawyer — and intimidate him into giving up everything he knew.

What the hell did they think he knew?

Dixie phoned Ben Rashly — a long shot, since he rarely worked so late. Amazingly, he answered, but cut her off when she tried to explain the problem.

"Stay out of this, Flannigan. I don't care how well you think you know this guy. When cops get killed — "

"Cops? As in plural?"

"What'd you do, take a shuttle to Mars for the afternoon? Another sniper shooting — Officer Ted Tally. Exactly like Harris. And the Pine robbery was the only squeal those two men ever caught together."

"But, Rash, Marty Pine wasn't in Houston when Harris was shot. He flew back to Dallas the night before." Right after they'd finished looking through Edna's house.

"Shows how much you know about your buddy."

As the line went dead, Dixie reflected on the four messages Marty had left when he asked her to meet him at Edna's. Marty was supposed to be in Dallas that night, too, and he'd given a Dallas number for her to call back, but the number showing in her Caller ID window had a 713 area code. Houston.

Making a U-turn toward downtown, Dixie tuned the radio to a news station, then phoned Belle Richards — only to learn that Marty had already called.

Chapter Thirty-seven

"Charge my client now, Sergeant, or release him," Belle demanded.

"If he has nothing to hide—"

"Let's go." Belle grasped Marty's arm and ushered him past the scowling officer.

Dixie followed as they moved toward the elevators. Still in her party clothes, she'd watched heads turn earlier as she hurried through Homicide Division, and had recognized some of the smiles. This time, every officer they passed returned an angry stare.

In the elevator, empty except for the three of them, Dixie learned that the interview had scarcely started before Marty asked for his lawyer. The fact that the officers hadn't charged him meant their evidence was flimsy. For now.

Taking separate cars, they drove to the Richards, Blackmon & Drake offices. Belle stopped Dixie at the door to her conference room, gesturing Marty inside.

"Flannigan, I'm not convinced it's a good idea for you to be present during this interview, but Marty insisted. Your part is to listen, mouth zipped, unless I specifically ask for your input. Got it?"

Dixie nodded. They both sat down opposite Marty. With a yellow wooden pencil not yet showing teeth marks, Belle made one small dot on a white legal pad.

"You were smart," she told him, "to keep quiet. But that stops here. I'm the one you don't lie to. Ever. The police know you never returned to Dallas Wednesday night. Where did you go?"

His mouth twitched. "To see a friend. An old friend. I needed some . . . I was upset, spending all that time in the house . . . seeing a side of my mother I didn't know existed. I needed someone I could . . . talk to." His gaze wavered guiltily toward Dixie.

"You stayed with this friend overnight?"

"At a hotel."

"And you were together Thursday morning, when Officer Harris was shot?"

"Yes."

Belle made another dot on her tablet. "Then you have an alibi."

"Not one I can make public."

The lawyer sighed and flicked a glance at Dixie. "I'm assuming you don't want this—friend—to be contacted, but trust me, Marty, chivalry is overrated. Nothing is worth spending your life in jail. Eventually, you'll have to reveal her name."

He stared mutely down at his fingers tapping on the table. "That's not an option. You have to find a better solution."

Wearily, Belle shook her head. "What about the second shooting? Where were you this afternoon?"

"Same friend. And don't ask. Just don't. This is one part of my life I will not muck up."

"Same hotel?"

"We met at a park to . . . talk."

"Which park?"

"Near Montrose."

"That's only a few miles from the crime scene. Did anyone see you?"

"I don't think so."

Belle stood and crossed the room to stare through the plate glass toward downtown.

Dixie cleared her throat. "Marty, why don't you just tell it, all of it? Everything withheld will only sabotage you later, and Belle can't fight this without the facts."

He slid his gaze to meet hers, eyes filled with confused anguish. Then he dropped his forehead against the heels of his hands and clutched handfuls of his carefully styled hair. Dixie had the urge to reach over and pat his arm, tell him this would all go away if he told the truth. But would it?

Finally, still staring down at the table, he tugged his tie loose and nodded.

"You asked me once why I moved away, Dixie. I had . . . something to hide, at least I thought so at the time. Now . . . I don't know. Everything came apart anyway. After I met Ashton, we opened the gallery, and business mushroomed. I thought, okay, it's time. I can't go on living one life in Dallas, another when I visit Houston—or my family visits me—a lie that's getting harder and harder to hold together. Remember our senior prom?"

The night her rhinestones kept popping. Dixie nodded.

"You asked why I insisted on dancing right up close to the bandstand," he said. "You even commented that the lead guitar player looked like Sean Cassidy.

What you never realized is . . . I had a panting, lovesick crush on the guy. My first real crush—although I always watched *The Brady Bunch* to see Greg, not Marcia."

Marty's revelation didn't come as quite the shock he obviously expected. Dixie *had* noticed the way he looked at that lead guitar player.

"I told Mom and Dad two Christmases ago," he continued. "The year I brought Ashton down to visit. After Christmas dinner, he flew back, and I told them—we were lovers, Ashton and I."

Marty cleared his throat and took a sip of water.

"Dad—he was never much of a talker, as you know—he just stared at me for two or three minutes, not saying a word. Then he rose from that damn chair he always sat in and walked into his bedroom and shut the door. Still hadn't come out when I left the next day. And Mom—can you believe this?—Mom begged me to see a doctor. Said there had to be something we could do. Like I had a sickness. Like her brain was stuck in the fifties. Where had they lived the past forty years?"

He stopped abruptly. Then he swiveled his chair toward the same view of downtown that Belle continued to stare at. Dixie knew the attorney was giving Marty a measure of privacy, her way of encouraging communication.

Dixie preferred observing Marty's face as he talked.

"When Dad died, Mom blamed *me*. Oh, she never came right out and said, 'You killed him, Marty.' She'd say, 'He never got over it, Marty. He never did.' But Mom tried to accept my life after that. She came to our big show last fall and stayed three days. That's when I invited her to move to Dallas—not to sell the old homestead, but . . . to spend time with us. I'd rent her a town house. 'No,' she told me. 'I don't fit here. I don't fit much of anywhere anymore, but certainly not here.' Not long after that I noticed the changes. Small things at first—her voice on the phone, firmer, more exact, then her clothes. When I flew down for Christmas, she wore a silk jogging suit. Silk. You ever know Mom to spring for silk, Dixie? 'Dacron's fine,' she'd say. 'Washable. Where would I wear silk? To weed the flower beds?' There she stood in this silk periwinkle jogging suit. And she'd been exercising, dieting. She'd lost ten pounds."

He whirled his chair to face Dixie, his features more animated.

"I *liked* seeing the changes—a positive sign, I thought. Hah! That's when she asked me not to bring Ashton home again. Said she understood and wanted me to be happy, but she couldn't bear it if her friends knew."

He finished the water and stared blankly into the glass.

"This spring, Ashton and I started having . . . problems. He's such a damn scrooge, at times. Especially about money. It was his money—and *my* brilliant talent, if I may brag a little—that started Essence Gallery. Ever notice how easily money falls into neat rows of figures you can add up and subtract and roll into one big green stick to brandish over someone? Talent simply . . . *is*. Talent flows into your soul. Talent sparkles. But it takes Ashton's money to keep the doors open until we attract the deep pockets. We were in the middle of a stinko argument when this whole crazy mess with Mom came out of nowhere. The police call, telling me she's dead. I arrive and . . . and there's speculation it was *suicide?*" He closed his eyes. "I needed someone I could talk to, someone who really knew *me.*"

Apparently relieved to have spilled his secrets, he looked squarely at Dixie. He must've found what he sought in her eyes, because he continued talking.

"I called my friend—the one who brought me out, years before I moved away. Older than me. The son of a . . . friend of Dad's. I think maybe Dad figured that part out later, after I dropped the bomb that Christmas. Anyway, he's not . . . I can't drag him into this. Ashton may be tight with money, but my friend's situation is . . . hell, it's *impossible.*"

Although Dixie believed him, believed that his mother's death had rattled Marty enough to seek the comfort of an old friend, she could also see him loading all his misery into a rifle and aiming it at the officers who'd canceled any chance of Marty ever mending the rift with his family. Marty's emotional expression had always leaned toward extreme. And the convenient "friend who doesn't deserve to be dragged down into the dirt" dramatically completed the scenario.

Dixie could hear Barney's gentle words, as if he were sitting beside her, *A foolish friend is twice the burden of your gravest enemy.*

"Did the cops identify the weapon that killed either Harris or Tally?" Dixie asked Belle.

"They're not saying." Belle returned to the table. "And since they didn't charge Marty we can't ask. But we know they found receipts for all the rifles in Bill's gun cabinet. Apparently, he kept excellent records. One additional receipt, for a . . . ." She consulted her notes. "Remington 30.06 Springfield, with a rangefinder telescopic sight, didn't match any of the rifles accounted for. A notation on the sales ticket gave them the hint they needed: Marty's birthday."

Marty frowned, hair sticking up where he'd clutched it.

"My first year at college—Dad and I went hunting during the holidays. But I sold that rifle after I moved to Dallas and needed cash. They can't be saying my rifle killed those cops."

"What they're saying is you had access to the type of weapon it takes to kill a man from five hundred yards," Dixie said, filling in the blanks.

"But I'm telling you, I *sold* that rifle."

Belle made a third dot on her legal pad. "If you keep records as good as your father's, you'll have the bill of sale to prove it."

"Listen, I needed money, and a guy offered me three hundred bucks—cash. I took it."

"You remember the guy's name?" Belle asked.

"No." Marty raked at his hair. "But there's no way it could be that gun. Sold twelve years ago in Dallas? What are the odds?"

Dixie made a mental note to find out from Rashly—provided he'd speak to her—if he had ballistics test results yet. By now the police investigators should know where the sniper holed up to shoot Tally. And they might have found some spent casings, if the shooter was in too much of a hurry to pick up his brass. Riflings on the lead, which probably flattened on impact, might not be precise enough to indicate a specific model.

"Let's get real clear, Marty," Belle said. "This is no ordinary shooting you're suspected of. In a legal system where every opinion has a counter opinion, *nobody* likes cop killers. If enough people are convinced you murdered those officers, evidence will stack up to prove it. Trust me."

The lines in Marty's face flattened out. "You mean, the police will *manufacture* the evidence they need?" For the first time, he looked more scared than miserable.

"They simply won't notice anything that doesn't point in the right direction," Dixie told him. "The direction they're convinced leads to the killer."

"Then you'll have to find evidence that proves I didn't do it."

Friendship wears a price tag, lass. "Marty, you've seen bubble-wrapped items hanging on store racks?" Dixie asked. "Toys, tools, kitchen implements—stuck to a piece of cardboard, with plastic molded over the whole thing? The cops will have this case sealed up tighter than one of those plastic bubbles."

"But they have to *prove* I did it. If I didn't do it, they can't prove it."

"Technically, yes," Belle said quietly. "But *juries* don't like cop killers, either. They'll be eager to convict."

Dixie laid a hand on Marty's arm. "If you have an alibi, now is a good time to use it. Before every police officer and some key prosecutors in this city have invested energy in proving they arrested the right man."

She could feel him tremble through his tailored jacket, but his mouth tightened and he shook his head.

"I lose either way. If Ashton finds out who I was with, I kiss everything good-bye—my home, my business. My *life*. Ashton's told me, if he ever caught me with anyone—but this friend, *especially*—we're through."

"I thought you were partners," Dixie commented. "Don't you have a partnership agreement?"

"Not on paper."

Of course not.

Leaving Marty at the conference table, Belle motioned Dixie into the next room.

"Even if he gives us the name of his friend, it may not be enough."

"Why not?" Putting herself in the prosecutor's shoes, Dixie had already mentally earmarked the problems with Marty's defense, but she wanted to hear Belle's take.

"First, the gay angle. Voir dire could take weeks and we still might not weed out the homophobes. The fact that Marty and his Houston lover have both lied about their relationship for years could taint any testimony from this mystery man. Second, supposing we get past the gay lies, can his lover convince a jury that Marty never left the hotel that night? Never went out for cigarettes or snacks or magazines? The lover never fell asleep? And third, there's all those rifles. A jury—with the prosecutor's help—will picture Marty sitting at his mother's house, mad as hell that not one but *nine* officers shot at her, and staring at his father's rifles—a tried-and-true Texas code for settling disputes. A jury—again with the prosecutor's help—will appreciate Marty's rage, may even feel some of that rage themselves. They'll forget that none of the guns in that case is the murder weapon, or that Marty's missing rifle can't be positively identified as the murder weapon. They'll see the missing rifle as 'proof' of concealment. The mere presence of those other guns, and the fact that Marty knows how to shoot them, will slant the jury's opinion. They'll feel sorry for Marty's loss. They'll speculate on how *they* might have acted in his shoes. And in the end, they'll believe he did it."

Yep. That's pretty much how Dixie'd figured it. "What now?"

"I'll try to find out exactly what the prosecution's holding. You, first and most important, keep Marty in sight at all times."

"In case another officer is killed."

"Lord, I don't want that to happen, Dixie. But we both know it would take suspicion off Marty—provided we absolutely can prove his whereabouts at the time."

A foolish friend is a heavier burden . . . "And second?"

"Find some better suspects."

Chapter Thirty-eight

Saturday, 4:30 A.M.

By habit, Dixie wasn't a runner. She preferred bending-lifting-stretching exercises, reserved running for the racquetball court, where it actually accomplished something—when a ball went high and wide—but she awoke knowing she *had* to exercise yesterday's frustrations out of her muscles.

She pulled on baggy shorts and athletic shoes, drew a comb through her hair, not even taking time to brush the sleep off her teeth, and called to Mud as she ran down the driveway, through the gate, out to the main road, and away from town. The air felt heavy with overnight moisture. Clouds in the west promised a chance of rain later.

Mud, delighted with this new game, sprinted alongside for a while, then dashed ahead to scare out a squirrel. Dixie sprinted past the Pine house without looking and continued to a gravel road that cut back into undeveloped acreage. So much had happened last night that she hadn't had time to think about. Not consciously. While she slept, her brain had whittled at the information, trying to shape it. Several times during the night she'd awakened with a half-formed idea, but as she tried to bring it closer, to *see* it, the image dissolved like wet rice paper. Once she'd grasped a picture of Parker, strikingly handsome in his white shorts on a fine sailboat, his laughter whipping in the wind like the sails. An instant later the image vanished.

Dixie had no desire to analyze that one.

The image she awoke with was of Marty on a golf course, chasing balls for Derry Hager. Derry, four years older, could get kids to do things. His family had money, but that wasn't it—Derry never *paid* for favors. He simply expected and received. Dixie hadn't liked him and had steered clear when he visited. Marty seemed to prefer that, anyway, almost picking a fight at times so Dixie wouldn't horn in on his fun with Derry Hager.

And twenty years later, it had been Derry who set Marty up with a friend in Dallas wanting to open a gallery.

Already winded from the unaccustomed pace, Dixie slowed past a weathered shack, windows long gone, shingles curling, and wondered briefly who'd lived there and if their lives had wasted away like the house. Dewberry vines covered the fence in mounds, dark ripe fruit thick among the paler leaves. Mud stopped to snuffle around the roots, but Dixie ran on.

Another image from her restless night had been sparked by a late-night newscast featuring the two slain HPD officers. Dixie recognized the photo of Theodore Tally from the circle of blue uniforms gathered around Edna's body after the shooting. Ted and a female officer had been standing nearby when Dixie yelled at Arthur Harris.

If she could see head shots of the other seven officers at the scene, Dixie thought she might recognize all of them—the terrible event had etched their faces in her memory—but how could the sniper know that both Art Harris and Ted Tally had taken part in Edna's death?

Unless the assassin was among the rubberneckers who stopped to watch. At least one camera lens had winked in the morning sunlight. With pictures and perseverance, all the officers could be identified.

On the other hand, reporters—anyone working with news media—would have access to press photos, including shots never released to the public. Who else could have snapped a shot of Dixie yelling at Art Harris? A shut-in from a neighboring house?

Reporters also had sources within the police department. Anyone in the Mayor's office or on City Council might weasel the names from an HPD employee. And at HPD? Internal Affairs, of course. Homicide. Everyone on the task force. The HPD psychiatrist, Emile Arceneaux, could poke around just about anywhere. Any of the other law enforcement agencies involved might learn the names by merely asking enough officers who knew. The list seemed endless, now that she thought about it, especially since she hadn't the time to interview them all.

As Dixie's lungs began to ache, she sorted this information into a mental file cabinet. No way would the police let her near any evidence. But after watching the late-night report on the assassinations, she'd read everything she could find in her week-old stack of newspapers, highlighting specific details . . .

HARRIS WAS SHOT COMING OUT OF HIS HOME IN SOUTHEAST HOUSTON. THE TASK FORCE, GAUGING THE BULLET'S TRAJECTORY, PLACED THE SNIPER ON THE ROOF OF A NEARBY TWO-STORY APARTMENT BUILDING.

Three hundred fifty units. People coming and going at all hours . . . a wide ethnic mix . . . nobody would've noticed the sniper slinking in the shadows.

EVIDENCE GATHERED AT THE SCENE SUGGESTED THE SHOOTER MAY HAVE CLIMBED DOWN TO THE UPPER BALCONY.

From there he could've taken the open staircase like any resident. Police had canvassed the area for witnesses. By now, investigators would be flashing Marty's photograph around.

The sky had lightened to pale gray, a wisp of coral peeking above the skyline. Soon she'd have to pick up Marty. But Dixie needed to finish filling her mental file cabinet before the frail ideas and images vaporized with the dawning light.

OFFICER TALLY WAS SHOT IN THE PARKING LOT OF A SOUTHWEST HOUSTON RESTAURANT WHERE HE HAD STOPPED FOR COFFEE.

Like Art Harris, he'd died instantly, but Ted had lain beside his patrol car until a woman noticed him as she parked — blood still fresh — probably no more than a minute, according to the medics. Plenty of time for the shooter to disappear.

BOTH HARRIS AND TALLY WORKED HPD BEAT PATROLS.

The two robberies that resulted in "shoot-outs" occurred in the towns of Webster and Richmond. HPD responded when the robbers crossed into Houston jurisdiction, which in Edna's case didn't occur until she'd passed through two other jurisdictions, picking up a patrol car in both.

Dixie had consulted a map that showed all three cities. Webster lay just southeast of Houston, Richmond southwest. The distance between the robberies spanned fifty-two miles, the distance between the shootings roughly thirty miles. Apparently, both women had been driving into Houston when police stopped them. *Where* in Houston?

The Pine robbery was the only squeal those two men ever caught together, Rashly'd told her.

Most Houston patrol officers rode solo, not in pairs, and Art Harris worked out of the Clear Lake police station. When he responded to the Richmond robbery pursuit, he was way off his beat. Off duty, maybe? If so, the newspaper hadn't mentioned it. On the other hand, he'd have been in exactly the right neighborhood to respond to the Webster robbery. Had he felt cheated, not getting in on that action, and later defied departmental policy to respond to the Edna Pine chase? Maybe he lived near the spot where Edna was forced off the road.

Feeling her second wind now, Dixie made a mental note to get Art Harris' home address—not an easy task, with most officers' phone numbers unlisted. She knew a couple who could do it, if anyone could.

Now that she had an objective, Dixie itched to take action, but it was far too early to knock on doors. The sun's orb had not yet joined the ribbon of color above the horizon. Also too early to pick up Marty. He'd slept at Amy's house, with instructions to stay put until Dixie's arrival, and the Royal household didn't rise with the sun.

Dixie regretted now that she'd agreed to tether Marty to her side—poking around in a cop killing would be tedious enough. Yet he'd need that airtight alibi should the sniper strike again.

As the gravel road came to a dead end, where brush had grown across it from lack of use, Dixie's busy thoughts locked on a blur of faces: the remaining six officers who'd shot Edna, all young and proud in their blue uniforms—but shocked and stunned. In all probability, none of them had ever before shot a weapon in the line of duty. Turning toward home, Dixie saw those faces in obituaries, one by one, victims of a sniper's bullet.

A sense of urgency quickened her pace.

On her way to Amy's house, she could stop by the restaurant where Ted Tally was killed. Investigators had already examined every inch of it, but Dixie wouldn't be looking for physical evidence.

The restaurant faced the Southwest Freeway and shared a parking lot with a three-story motel. All the rooms featured outside access, either directly from the parking area or, on floors two and three, from partially enclosed stairs and an outdoor walkway.

In line with an eight-foot square of the parking lot roped off with yellow crime-scene tape, Dixie spied a police seal on the door of a second-story room. The task force must've calculated the sniper waited in that motel room to drop Tally. Quite a shot: about four hundred yards from that angle. Other rooms offered better positioning, but perhaps they'd been occupied.

She climbed the stairs and examined the door. The card-access lock appeared to be intact. The killer either possessed the skill to disarm it or had rented the room under a false name. Or one other possibility: According to the newspaper, Ted Tally's murder occurred at approximately two-thirty in the afternoon. With checkout time at one, the rooms would be cleaned between noon and three, and wouldn't start filling up again until five o'clock, ground-floor units going first. The killer might've scoped out rooms with the best angles, then slipped in during housekeeping.

Dixie scanned the distance to the crime scene below. *Sit in the darkened room, door open a crack, rifle ready. Wait for Ted to arrive for his usual afternoon coffee stop. But no—when he arrives, you don't see a clear shot. He walks too fast, or a car blocks your target. You wait . . . take aim as he returns to his car . . . and pop! Freeway traffic disguises the shot. Afterward, slide the rifle under your shirt, down your pants leg, skip downstairs, melt into the landscape.* The killer either knew Officer Tally's habits or had followed him until the right moment presented itself.

Dixie retraced her steps down the stairs and approached the taped-off area. A brown stain marred the asphalt beside the parking space Ted's car had occupied. She sighted back toward the motel room, then along the bullet's exit path. In the restaurant's rear wall, near the ground, she found the spot where Forensics had extracted a slug of lead from the wood siding.

Inside the restaurant, Dixie took a seat at the counter. A middle-aged couple occupied a table in the smoking section, and a single male sat in a booth near the front. A waitress was filling a shelf with pies—fresh-baked, judging by the aroma. Thirty-something, with stout arms and a pinched face, the woman glanced at Dixie unenthusiastically, wiped her hands, and laid her cleaning towel aside. Another waitress moved among the tables with a tray of salt and pepper shakers.

A menu dropped onto the counter in front of Dixie.

"Coffee?" The pinched face split into a forced smile.

"Yes, thanks. Black."

When the coffee arrived, Dixie ordered an omelet in her friendliest voice.

"Quiet in here this morning," she commented.

"Finally!" The woman rolled her eyes heavenward. "Lord Almighty, you should've been here a couple hours ago. Thought the late-nighters would never leave, everybody talking about that cop got killed here yesterday."

"That was here?" Dixie looked around, feigning surprise. Damned good job of it, too, she thought. The newspaper article hadn't given an exact location, but anyone who knew the area could read between the lines. "Didn't happen on your shift, though. Unless you work longer hours than I do."

"I come on at eleven. Night shift. But Sarah was here." She nodded at the second waitress. "That poor cop was a regular."

"I guess a lot of cops eat in here."

"A few. Ted lived nearby. Stopped in almost every day, sometimes twice." She gave Dixie's order to the fry cook and went back to filling the pie shelf.

Dixie sipped her coffee, then slid off her stool, strolled casually to the ladies' room, and washed her hands. On her return, she veered toward a table where Sarah had just deposited her last pair of salt and pepper shakers. Her freshly pressed uniform suggested she'd recently come on duty. Dixie handed the woman a business card.

"I'm looking into the death of Officer Ted Tally. I understand you talked with him yesterday."

"I told the cops everything I know."

"Yes, and I'm sorry to ask you to repeat it, but we'd like to take the psycho who killed him off the street."

"I hope you just shoot him down, the way he shot Ted."

Dixie allowed her serious mouth to lift a trifle at the corners. "Believe me, that's *exactly* what I'd like to do. Did you know Ted well?"

"I've only worked here a few weeks, but I liked him."

"Did he usually come in alone?"

"Sometimes he came with another cop, like yesterday."

Tom Dietz, the news story had said. "Always the same two?"

The waitress nodded. "And that other officer who was killed. I think they were all pretty good friends."

"Arthur Harris?"

"Yeah. I feel so sorry for Art's wife, them with a new baby and all."

Officers on duty weren't allowed to eat outside their beat, so Harris must've placed a premium importance on meeting Ted. "Do you remember if Art stopped in with Ted on Tuesday morning?"

"Tuesday . . . ?" Sarah frowned. "Sorry, I don't—"

"You might recall a number of police cars going by—"

"Oh! Yes! That poor woman was shot. But Ted didn't . . . he wasn't one of *those* cops . . . was he?"

"Sarah, I'm merely following up all the loose ends, trying to find out who shot those officers. Were they in here together that morning?"

"Yeah. About nine-thirty—"

While Edna was waving her .38 at Len Bacon.

"—Ted didn't usually come in that early."

Two anomalies, then. Art off his beat, maybe—Dixie needed to check his work schedule—and Ted stopping early for coffee.

"Did you notice any customers who struck you as unusual that morning? Perhaps someone who asked about the two cops? Or watched them?"

Sarah shook her head slowly. "You think the killer could've been here?"

"Just a routine question," Dixie assured her. The killer could've seen the officers leave the restaurant and join the police pursuit. "I'd appreciate your thoughts. Did anyone follow them out?"

Sarah continued frowning and shaking her head.

"What about yesterday?" Dixie prompted. "Did you notice anything different when Ted was here?"

"You mean, did Ted look like he planned to walk out and get his head blown off? Did he say, 'Sorry I can't keep our date, Sarah. I'm wanted for target practice'? No! It was a day like any other day. He had coffee and pie. His friend had coffee and pie—"

"You dated Ted?"

"No, not—" Her voice broke. "Not yet."

"But you intended to."

"He said we'd take his wave runner out after I finished work."

"Did Ted ever talk about his job?"

"We never talked about anything, really. Just him asking me out and me saying no."

A couple entered the café and waited at the door to be seated.

"Until yesterday?"

"Yeah." She said it softly. "Listen, I have work to do, and I really don't know anything, but I hope you find the sonofabitch, 'cause Ted was a damn nice guy. And so was his friend."

Dixie's omelet awaited her at the counter. She poked at it and finished her coffee. As she fished money from her pocket to cover the tab, a familiar shape dropped down on the stool beside her.

"What the hell're you doing here, Flannigan?"

"A sharp detective like you, Rash, ought to pick up on the clues. Plate of half-eaten eggs, utensils, empty coffee cup . . ."

"Long way from home, and too damn close to a case you need to butt out of." He signaled the waitress to bring him a coffee.

"Marty didn't kill those officers, Rash. If I butt out, who's going to prove it?"

"Always the smartass. Always think you know more than a team of good police officers."

"Your boys jumped on the first convenient suspect."

"Not my boys. Goddamn task force."

"What could they have on Marty? That he was in town when he claimed to be in Dallas? That he once owned a rifle?"

"Whole gun case full of rifles."

"Only took one to do the job. Since I know it wasn't Marty's, your ballistics report isn't all you'd like it to be, is it?"

"Stop baiting me, Flannigan."

"You know it's strictly political. Make an arrest, even if it's wrong."

He glared at her. "Did you know your friend has a record?"

Dixie struggled to keep the surprise off her face. "For spitting on the sidewalk?"

"Cocaine. He and his Dallas buddy."

"Next civilian party you attend, Rash, frisk all the guests. Bet you'll find a few carrying nose candy." When she got her hands on Marty, she'd wring his scrawny neck. "Why not tell me what you have? You know Belle Richards will get disclosure on every piece of evidence the DA's planning to use."

The waitress arrived with his coffee. "Put it on my friend's tab," Rashly told her.

When Dixie nodded, the woman turned to another customer.

"The way I see it," Dixie said, "the big question is: How would Marty know which officers were involved in the shootings? Unless you think he's psychic."

"I'm warning you, Flannigan, butt out of this one. Don't expect anybody to cut you any slack." He took one sip of his coffee, shoved it aside, and walked out of the restaurant.

Watching him go, Dixie wondered what had brought the Homicide sergeant here at this hour—only to bark at her and leave. Until now, she'd maintained a mutually beneficial relationship with HPD and other law enforcement departments across the country. If that relationship soured, she could forget bounty hunting. If it soured enough, officers she'd once counted as friends could make her life damned miserable without overstepping the legal line to harassment. All the goodwill she'd racked up over the years would be as worthless as pigeon poop.

Chapter Thirty-nine

Before leaving the café parking lot to pick up Marty, Dixie phoned the only couple she knew who could get information on police officers fast and without alerting the other five thousand cops in Houston. An elderly male voice answered. In its rusty squeak Dixie heard enthusiasm and instantly pictured Smokin's trim white beard, half-size reading glasses, and orange suspenders.

"Yep, yep. It's Dixie Flannigan, Pearly," he called away from the phone. Then he came back. "Felt in my bones we were due some fun today. Told the old woman so. Long before sunup, coffee still dripping, I said, 'Today we're due some fun.' Didn't I, Pearly?"

"He says that every morning, Dixie," came a throaty female voice. Pearly White had picked up on an extension.

Snowy-haired and even smaller than her five-foot-one-inch husband, Pearly would be perched at a desk made from a wooden door slung across a pair of sawhorses. Smokin's identical desk sat nearby, on the other side of a thick black tape line that divided their home office precisely down the middle.

"Let's have it." Smokin coughed, and Dixie could almost smell the Marlboro burning steadily in his butt-crammed ashtray.

"Can you get me some general information, then follow wherever that leads?"

"Yep, yep. Lay it on us."

Dixie'd met the remarkable pair through a mutual friend. The couple's expertise with computers rivaled any teenager's, and they loved tapping into the most secure databases. But asking them to snoop in the HPD personnel files didn't sit well with Dixie—and it might feel as offensive to them.

"I suppose you've heard about the officers who were murdered," she began awkwardly.

"Sweetie, you've seen our big-screen television," came Pearly's throaty answer. "What do you imagine we do when we're not on-line?"

Right. "And we've discussed the fact that investigation starts with the victim." Despite appearances, Art Harris' and Ted Tally's deaths might have nothing to do with their involvement in the robbery shootings. The killer might've piggy-backed on the shootings to throw investigators off. In that case, the slain officers' backgrounds might provide a clue to the killer's identity. In fact, one cop might've been the true target and the other killed to make their deaths *appear* connected to the Granny Bandit shootings. "Which means looking into the officers' backgrounds."

"We understand, sweetie. Now what, exactly, do you want to know?"

Good question. "I'm not at all certain what we're looking for, Pearly. By examining everything we can find, I'm hoping to recognize a pattern."

Pearly delicately cleared her throat. "And you'll use this information to find out who killed those officers?"

"Absolutely." Dixie could already hear the click of computer keys. "A few more names I need you to look up—" She ran through the list: Lucy Ames, Terrence Jackson, Jessica Love, Vernice Urich, Lonnie Gray. Marty's focus might've changed since his arrest, but Dixie still intended to find out why an otherwise ordinary pair of senior women ended their lives in such a bizarre manner. After an instant's hesitation, she added Marty Pine, Essence Gallery, and the two churches—Uptown Interdenominational and Church of The Light—to the list.

"And Edna Pine?" Pearly added.

"Yes, but leave Edna till last. I want you to be as thorough as possible on the others."

"Sweetie, you know we like to help you any way we can, but peeking into other folks' lives is . . . well, we can't be arbitrary about it. If you see what I mean. Are all these individuals suspects?"

"They could be."

"Even the two dead women?"

"Pearly, what's going on? You've never had a problem with this before."

"No, no . . . when a person's life is at risk, that's good reason, but to invade a stranger's privacy, without suspicion of criminal activities . . . Dixie, we're not comfortable with that. Are we, Smokin?"

"Speak for yourself, old woman. I love it. This here Terrence Jackson fellow makes a hunk of money for himself. Stock market investments. Spends a bundle, too."

"Stock market?" Rebuke sharpened Pearly's voice. "That's *my* bailiwick, Smokin. Get your fingers out of there."

Smokin chuckled. "Gotcha, old woman. I wasn't even—"

"Wait," Dixie cut in. "What I need first are the two officers' home addresses. Can you get those?"

"Right here," Smokin said.

Dixie jotted down the street numbers he rattled off, then left the pair feuding over who would acquire the information she sought. But Pearly White's remarks burrowed into her thoughts as she drove to Amy's. Her own bank account had been plundered by a person who knew how to "wash" checks—and it infuriated her. How would *she* feel about computer-savvy snoops tapping into her personal records in search of anything that looked wrong? Did her records contain information that could be misinterpreted?

The questions soured her stomach. Maybe she needed a new line of work. Maybe she needed a new life.

After picking up Marty, Dixie drove to Arthur Harris' southeast neighborhood, parked at the curb across from his trim front yard, and felt the sourness in her stomach rise into her throat. Harris' bereaved young widow had a right to be alone with her grief—and no reason to answer Dixie's questions.

Marty, however, had seemed damned eager when she'd told him their destination. He hadn't been nearly so eager to answer her question about the cocaine charge in Dallas.

"The charges were dropped," he told her. "And it has nothing to do with what's happening now. I don't want to talk about it."

"You need to tell Belle. It could influence—"

"It wasn't even my coke. One of Ashton's friends brought it. Then he picked a fight with Ashton, and the cops showed up. Are you satisfied?"

"You'll talk to Belle?"

"Yeah, okay—"

Dixie's cell phone warbled.

"You're out early," Parker said.

"Early if you're a beach bum."

"This particular bum picked up a sizable lead last night."

"At Fortyniners? We were trolling for clues, not sales."

Marty climbed out of the car.

"Your colorful friend Judge Garston's in the market for a twenty-five-foot motorcraft."

"He's not my friend, Parker, in case you called me for a character reference."

"You'll never believe who called *me* this morning."

"Nope." Parker knew she despised guessing names.

"Vernice Urich." Dramatic pause. "She heard you'd asked about her last night, and since I gave her my card . . ."

"Someone must've noticed us leaving together."

"Dixie, everyone noticed us. You were extremely noticeable."

"What did you tell her?"

"That you'd heard she's a psychotherapist, and you'd considered therapy in the past but wanted someone discreet."

"Not bad. I can run with that."

"Great, because I made a provisional appointment for you."

"Provisional?"

"If you don't like the time, I call back and reschedule."

"Why don't *I* call back and reschedule?"

"Vernice likes my voice."

So do I. "I'll keep the appointment, if I can find a place to stash Marty for an hour or so." She told him about HPD's suspicions.

"My afternoon's open. I could take over Marty-watch for a while."

"You don't like him, Parker." *Without even meeting him.*

"Sure don't," he said cheerily. "Do I have to?"

Dixie's own feelings about Marty couldn't be called favorable these days. She agreed, and they made arrangements to meet for lunch.

As she powered off the phone and studied the Harris house, one of Barney's directives popped into her mind: *Tackle the tough jobs first, lass.* Today it failed to galvanize her. She simply wasn't up to speaking to Art Harris' widow, especially with Marty along. She'd tackle the neighbors first.

Chapter Forty

The Clary home, pale yellow with white shutters, sat away from the street, flower beds bursting with color, sidewalks swept spotless, oak-and-brass placard proclaiming the family name, a mint-condition twelve-year-old Volvo parked under a vine-covered portico. The Clarys lived immediately west of the Harrises. Dixie rang the doorbell.

"Sorry to bother you, Mr. Clary," she told the man who answered.

He stood about five-nine, in clean, pressed Dockers and a T-shirt boasting his participation as a blood donor. Thin, thirtyish, and suspicious as hell, he scrutinized Marty from hair to sneakers, then turned his piercing gaze at Dixie. As a pair, she and Marty might've been from different planets, the man's frown suggested.

"You're not from the church," he stated.

"No." Dixie handed him a card.

"I was expecting a couple from the church to pick up the white elephants my wife donated. Carol! It's a lawyer!" He glanced at Marty.

A plump, thirtyish woman joined him on the threshold.

"Whose lawyer?" She took the card from her husband.

"I'm looking into the death of your neighbor, Arthur Harris." Dixie's vague explanation had worked once that morning. "Sometimes friends, neighbors, know more than they realize."

"Don't see how we can help, but come in and have a seat." The man pushed the door wide.

A narrow entry opened into a pale yellow living area. The carpet appeared freshly vacuumed. Dixie examined her boot soles before walking in. A pair of matched love seats, pristine white, sat on either side of a glass coffee table. She spied a club chair with a yellow slipcover and motioned Marty toward a love seat. Instead, he perched on a straight-back chair pulled away from the dining table.

"How well did you know Arthur?" Dixie asked, when they were all seated.

"Not well at all." Carol looked at her husband. "We invited them over—remember, Joe? Before the baby came, but they didn't stay long. Ann was close to term and obviously miserable."

"Ms. Flannigan didn't ask about Ann. She asked about Art." Joe plucked a tiny leaf off his pants. "Art and I talked quite often. He'd be out with the stroller, me working in the yard."

"Not all that often," Carol argued. "We didn't know the Harrises at all, really, not at all."

"I knew Art well enough. What did you want to know?" Joe glanced at Marty again, then back to Dixie.

"Just a sense of what he was like away from the job. Did he ever talk about work?"

"Not as much as he talked about that baby," Carol replied. "You know, 'Peggy turned over.' 'Peggy smiled.' 'Peggy spat up her dinner.' "

Joe aimed his careful scrutiny at his wife. "I never realized you and Art—"

"Now, you stop with the jealousy, Joe Clary." Carol turned to Dixie. "On his days off, Art sometimes brought Peggy over and we'd have a glass of tea. I always told him, 'Bring Ann along.' But she'd be in the shower or whatever."

"Did the Harrises have many visitors? Other officers, perhaps?"

Marty stood and strolled to a media unit—TV, VCR, CD player—and appeared to study the titles of their music collection.

"No." Carol shook her head. "Never saw anybody over there."

"I did." Joe lowered his voice. "Last Saturday, a blue-and-white parked in Art's driveway. Art came out, leaned in the window, and talked for, I'd say, twenty-five minutes. Didn't have Peggy with him."

"Did you see who was in the car?" Dixie asked.

"A man. Blond." He reached behind him and grabbed a folded newspaper off the sofa table. Opening it to the front-page story on the sniper murders, he pointed to Ted Tally. "Could've been that man."

"It would help if you could be more certain."

"Sorry, no."

Carol picked up the paper. "Joe, that man is dead, too."

"Yes, I know that."

"Well, I don't believe you saw him at Art's house."

"I saw someone, and it could have been him."

"Had you ever seen Officer Tally visit Art before?" Dixie asked.

Joe shrugged. "It's not as if we kept track of their visitors."

"They never *had* visitors," Carol insisted.

As she rang a doorbell across the street from the Harrises, Dixie asked Marty, "What were you doing in there?"

"Checking out their stuff, looking for clues."

"What clues? The Clarys aren't suspects."

"Why not?"

"I grant you, it's possible, but Clary didn't strike me as a coolheaded cop killer. Your average working Joe is rarely a practiced marksman."

"I felt like a dolt, sitting, doing nothing, you asking all the questions."

"Then make like a Watson and take notes."

They tried two other houses, with no luck, then approached a brick bungalow directly east of the Harrises'.

"Nobody's home," called a voice from a neighboring yard. Partially hidden by rosebushes, a tall, rawboned woman with close-cropped blond hair and sun-weathered skin wielded a watering hose.

"Do you know where they've gone?" Dixie called back. Under her breath she told Marty, "Ring the bell anyway. Nosy neighbors can be wrong."

"Off to Vegas for the holiday weekend," the woman said as Dixie strolled closer.

She could be fifty or a well-preserved sixty, Dixie decided. "Gorgeous roses. How do you make them so prolific?"

"Pinch 'em. Soon as the first buds show up, pinch 'em off. For ever blossom pinched, three more grow in its place."

Dixie recalled Kathleen saying the same thing about mums, and the Flannigan garden always made a spectacular show, when she'd been alive to tend them.

"Gotta keep water off the leaves, or they'll spot," the woman added, garden hose directed carefully at the dirt around the bushes. "And never water 'em at night."

"Maybe you could help us." Dixie gave the rose lady her business card. "I'm sure you heard about Art Harris."

"Pretty much all we've talked about on this street since Thursday. You're not aiming to cause that young widow of his any trouble, are you?" She glanced at the card.

"Not at all. We're—"

"To my notion, that's what lawyers do, cause trouble."

Marty's bell ringing hadn't brought anyone to the door, so he stepped off the porch, taking out a pen and a palm-size tablet that looked suspiciously like the back of his checkbook.

"Mrs. Harris won't have any trouble from us," Dixie assured the woman. "We're merely looking into Art's death."

"Looking into it? What the hell does that mean?"

"We want to find out who killed him."

"A lawyer?" She looked at Dixie's card again. "Then what are the cops doing?"

"Ma'am, every law enforcement person in this city wants to find out who killed Officers Harris and Tally. If you knew Art, Ms. . . . ?"

"Easton. Janet Easton. Mrs. Divorced."

"If you knew him, Mrs. Easton, you might answer a few questions for us."

"You want to know about Art, why don't you talk to Ann?"

"We plan to, but the more we find out in advance, the less we'll have to trouble her at such a sad time."

Janet Easton redirected her watering hose to a row of hibiscus. "Fair enough, then. Ask away."

"Did you and the Harrises visit often?"

"I stopped in from time to time, when Art was at work, to see if Ann needed anything. Looked after little Peggy ever once in a while, so they could get out to dinner or a movie."

"Did Ann stop leaving the house after Peggy was born?"

"Never got out *before* that child was born. A lazy lump, if you ask me."

"Had they been married long?"

"Five years. Soon as Art finished junior college, they married, bought that house over there, he applied to the police academy, and Ann had that baby. Blip, blip, blip, blip. Couples with any sense these days put off childbearing until they're *both* ready."

Five years sounded to Dixie like a reasonable period to wait.

"I suppose children can be a burden," she said. "With Ann not working, the financial responsibility . . ." She shrugged, hoping Easton would jump in with some useful information.

"Ann might call Peggy a burden, all right, but Art never complained. Wasn't a better father on this earth than Arthur Harris. Can't imagine where that child will end up now." She shook her head gravely. "He worried about Ann not taking to motherhood, worried she might up and leave him."

"You and Art talked about this?"

"Talked about a lotta things. Sitting on the steps together, Peggy and Ann both asleep, Art and I solved the world's problems a couple times ever week."

"Did he seem worried recently? Besides his concern about Ann."

Easton moved along the hibiscus row as she considered the question.

"Art worried about not being good enough," she said finally.

"Good enough for what?"

"Anything. Grew up rough—but I guess you'd know about that, being a lawyer."

"Not really."

"Got caught up in some gang doings back in Dallas—that's where he and Ann lived before moving here. Father deserted 'em. Mother hopped from one boyfriend to another, looking for one dumb enough to adopt a ready-made family. Gangs take on a surrogate-family role to lost boys, and Art was about as lost as they get."

"But then he became a cop. So he must've left the gang before he landed in any serious trouble."

"Fights, drugs, weapons, petty theft—all juvenile, but Art said he treaded darn close to serious. A Big Brother turned all that around."

"Big Brother, as in the organization?"

The woman nodded and moved down the side of the house toward a bed of caladiums. "When Art finally started seeing things straight, he looked back on what a terror he'd been and tried to make up for it. Intended to join the gang task force."

"Had he applied?"

"Wouldn't know about that."

Harris worked out of the Clear Lake station, a high-dollar district. Gang activity might not be obvious there, but it existed. And a cop who tried to influence gang members to drop out would make enemies.

When Janet Easton turned off the water and began rolling up her garden hose, Dixie studied the Harris house: red brick, green shutters, a baby swing hanging from the lowest limb of a live oak tree.

Tackle the tough job, lass. She'd put off talking to the widow Harris long enough.

Chapter Forty-one

Hearing her husband's shower cease, Kaylynn Banning knocked on the bathroom door. She entered, and found Avery toweling his chest in front of the steamy wall mirror.

Kaylynn liked to linger in bed late on Saturdays, and usually she could convince Avery to linger alongside her, but with Memorial Day less than forty-eight hours away, the Mayor was eager to be downtown.

"Can't expect people to work enthusiastically," he'd told her, "when they know the boss is sprawled out, catching an extra forty."

Now he swiped steam off the mirror and leaned close to scrutinize his face.

"No, you cannot go to the office without shaving," she said, smiling at him in the mirror.

Fresh from her own shower, auburn hair damp around her ears, she intentionally wore a light dressing gown that hugged her slender curves. A year older than his forty-six, she knew she still looked damned good, and didn't want Avery to forget it. Kaylynn Welsh Banning came from old money, old politics, and she already had an eye on redecorating the Governor's mansion.

"How did you guess what I was thinking?"

"Avery, you never shave on Saturdays, if you can avoid it. You think nobody notices."

"My beard's so light—"

"It's not that light."

"I thought going extra casual might relax the atmosphere around the office today. You know, everybody pitching in—"

"In that case, you'll have an extra few minutes before you need to leave." She slipped the dressing gown off her shoulders and let it drop to the floor. Sliding her arms around his middle, she pressed her groin to his buttocks.

"Kaylynn, there's no time—"

"Nobody likes a boss who arrives early. It makes everyone sneaking in late look bad." Her fingers caressed his testicles; her lips trailed a string of soft kisses over his back.

In the mirror, she saw a calculating glint in his eyes: He couldn't deny her logic. And he wouldn't dare deny her what she craved. Mayor Avery Banning might have the entire city—and an impressive old-boy network nationwide—wrapped around his little finger, but Kaylynn controlled the purse strings.

Thirty-seven minutes later, she watched him sort through a rack of sports coats. When he reached for a gray bomber jacket, she pushed his hand aside and selected a navy blazer. She regarded it against his beige slacks and pale blue shirt.

"Perfect," she murmured.

"No, too dressy." He chose a tan, loose-weave silk that looked like hopsack and emphasized the faint spray of freckles across his nose.

Reluctantly, she nodded her agreement and thumbed through his tie rack.

"No tie," he said. "Today, I'm one of the guys . . . toss my jacket over a chair, roll up my sleeves, do whatever-the-hell job needs doing."

She nodded again. In some areas, Avery did know best. He could assemble a roomful of drones who'd work until their eyes rolled out of their heads. Whirling from his closet, she went to her own and dressed in her gardening clothes. Their yardman handled the heavy work, but she enjoyed digging around in the beds, coaxing the beds to greater profusion every year. In the annual "Azalea Trail" tour of Houston homes, theirs always drew oohs and ahs.

Later, in the living room, Kaylynn sorted through a handful of mail.

"A letter came for you." She held it up to the light. Anything really important usually went to his office.

"Who from?"

"Doesn't say. An invitation, maybe. Nice paper."

"Someone begging a donation. Go ahead, open it."

She slit the top with a crystal-handled letter knife and unfolded a single page. Her stomach tightened as she read.

"What is it?" he asked.

"A crank letter. Probably nothing." She handed it to him.

A shadow darkened his eyes as he scanned the message she'd already seen: *You see what poor management causes, Mayor? This will be the only warning you receive. Unless your resignation is announced within 36 hours, and unless every man responsible for killing Lucy Aaron Ames and Edna Lou Pine is relieved of duty, with no chance of reassignment to a law enforcement agency, you are all hereby sentenced to death.* It was signed, *The People.*

Avery scrutinized the emblem embossed at the top of the page. Apparently, it meant as little to him as it had to her. He turned the letter over. Nothing there.

"Let me see that envelope." He snatched it from her, passed his thumb over the address. "Typed, not laser-printed. Downtown postmark. No return."

The same emblem was embossed and foil-stamped on the heavy cream-colored paper. Not cheap.

"You don't think it's a crank letter?" she asked quietly.

He shook his head. "At the press conference last night, I never mentioned Tally was involved in the Pine shooting, or that idiot Harris—who was supposed to be on desk duty after the Ames fiasco—pulled a Rambo and somehow ended up right alongside Tally. No one outside Chief Wanamaker, the FBI task force, and the officers at the two scenes had access to that information."

"The reporters guessed," Kaylynn argued. She'd heard them ask. *Mayor Banning, could the assassination of these officers have anything to do with the recent bank robberies and the women who were killed?*

"That possibility is being investigated," Avery had told them. "The task force will follow every conceivable avenue of investigation until the killer is caught."

Now, seeing the fear on her husband's face, Kaylynn knew this letter was no prank. "Avery, you should cancel the Memorial Day celebration."

"I can't. My press secretary worked up a speech addendum specifically commemorating the two cops. The city expects it. Anyway, we can't feed this assassin's ego."

"According to the letter, you're not dealing with a lone assassin. Who are The People, Avery?"

He looked down at the letter and shook his head. But he knew—or suspected—more than he was telling. In their two years of marriage, Kaylynn had never seen her husband frightened. What she saw now was genuine terror.

Police Chief Edward Wanamaker glared at his phone. The kind of calls he'd been getting, if it rang once more he might shoot the damn thing.

Late Saturday morning, and here he was at his desk instead of lazing in the backyard, Mira yapping about the shutters needed painting. Ed did his honey-dos on Saturday mornings, but he liked working at his own pace, which drove Mira nuts, her bean-counter side coming out, wanting him to make a list, be first in line at the Home Depot, then hustle to finish the list in a day. Ed liked tackling a chore only after he'd deliberated on it a while, feet on the picnic table next to an ice chest filled with cold Coors, reading the sports pages.

His office door opened.

"Some letters to sign, Chief."

"Can't they wait till Monday?"

His assistant laid a neat stack on his desk pad.

"Not the ones you dictated yesterday. I put those on top." She took his pen from a brass holder attached to a slab of gray plastic and held it patiently until he accepted it. "Mira phoned, Chief. Told me to remind you to be home by two o'clock to dress for the funeral services."

Ed nodded, and she left the room.

Burying both officers at the same service had seemed appropriate. The men attended the police academy together, fought for the same cause, and almost certainly died by the same hand. Arthur Harris' wife and Theodore Tally's parents seemed to find comfort in holding a joint service. Ed hoped they'd feel the same afterward, not feel that either man had been slighted.

He glanced at the magazine in his top drawer, open to a piece on Oprah, tucked down low so he could read it without anyone noticing. Took his mind off the bitter phone calls. Let 'em rattle on in his ear while he read Oprah's latest inspiration. Today, however, nothing distracted him from his own thoughts.

He was a good cop, not a great detective, but one helluva good beat cop in his day. Never really wanted to be Chief—that was Banning's idea. Smooth-talking Avery Banning. From Ed's small-town Arkansas background, becoming Chief of the Houston Police Department had looked like finally grabbing the brass ring. Couldn't turn down such an offer—not and live with Mira afterward.

"Houston already has a strong police force," Banning had coaxed. "What better place to step up in your career?"

The salary sure beat what he'd earned in Arkansas, or even in the small Texas college town where he'd met Banning.

"Nothing to it," Banning had told him. "Study what the former Chief did, keep doing more of the same. Easy as fried corn bread."

Terminal lung cancer and early retirement—that's what Ed owed his big break to. Made him feel ghoulish.

He glanced down at Oprah, wondering how she'd lost all that weight. Mira would say to take a lesson.

Behind the magazine, way back in a space you had to pull the drawer all the way out to find, he'd stashed a pint of Wild Turkey. Too early yet, but Ed wouldn't mind a nip, help him turn his mind to what it ought to be churning on, what he'd avoided all morning, those two dead officers, barely as old as his own daughter. How the hell did you deal with that?

He slipped his hand into an open bag of sunflower seeds in the drawer and scooped out a few. Mira's idea, sunflower seeds. Said it'd help him quit smoking, which it had. Now he'd got the seed habit, and what would help him quit that? He cracked a shell, popped the seed in his mouth.

His friendship with Avery Banning went all the way back to those college days. Not that Ed went to college, no patience for books, but he'd been on the job in the town where Banning attended. Busted the little snotnose for a slew of traffic tickets, then helped him clear his record. After that, they played poker once a week. He liked Banning, even with his sneaky streak that kept other players on their toes. Despite some trouble in school, the boy had grown up to have a damn good head on his shoulders, knew how to make things happen, for sure.

But if Ed'd known something like this would come down his first six months as Chief, he never would've taken the offer—although Banning had a way of talking you into things.

He slid the drawer shut on Oprah. Turned his attention to the mail—opened and sorted, neatly slit envelope clipped behind each letter, interdepartmental stuff in one pile, civilian correspondence in another. He wondered if Mira had been up here giving lessons.

With a sigh, he signed all the letters he'd dictated yesterday, then started reading through the civilian stack. Most of it came from folks wanting a piece of the action at Banning's Memorial Day commemorative. Ed glanced at the clock. Still too early for a nip.

Near the bottom of the stack came a stopper.

You see what poor management causes, Chief? This will be the only warning you receive . . .

After reading those first lines, Ed reached for a sheet protector, slipped the letter inside, and finished reading it through the plastic.

Jean Gibson flipped through an assortment of bills and paused at an expensive envelope—personal executive size with an engraved three-color logo—addressed to her husband: Councilman John Jason Gibson. The title never failed to give her a satisfying thrill.

They'd married in such a rush of excitement. Before Gib's proposal, Jean had been at her lowest, certain she'd remain a spinster the rest of her natural life. Three years after Gib's first wife died in a drowning accident—drunk as a sailor, but Gib kept that part from making the tabloids—Jean had met him at a political rally. Strong, commanding, decisive, just like her father. In nine days, her life had turned around. In two weeks, she was engaged.

Gib's proposition, that he and Jean marry before he tossed his hat in the ring for the mayoral race, hadn't been very romantic, but at her age, forget candlelight and roses. Gib wanted her at his side as he ran against Avery Banning. Gib was obviously the better man for the job. And the insurance from his first wife's death would've helped finance his campaign. Then Gib decided not to run this term.

Jean glanced at his picture on the mantel. Homely, no other way to say it, but in his Marine officer's uniform Gib was the grandest man she'd ever met. Served proudly in the Gulf War, called back from reserves—that fact alone gave him an edge on Banning.

Banning's slick handsomeness and glib oratory had seduced the media, though, and the voters ate up his lies like apples from the Tree of Plenty. Jean had watched him last night on the tube, attempting to smooth over this sniper business. Even Mr. Mealymouthed Banning sweated this problem.

She slid her hand over the textured envelope. No return address, but her dressmaker's fingers recognized quality.

"Gib?" She resisted tearing the envelope open. She and her husband respected each other's privacy.

"Out here, Jean. Let's eat breakfast on the patio. We don't see days as magnificent as this too often."

She found him perched on a bench, reading *The Wall Street Journal*, finished sections stacked neatly on the brick pavers. Military neat, that was her Gib.

"Do you recognize this emblem?" She held the envelope in front of the financial pages.

"No," he said after a moment. "Should I?"

"Looks important. Should I open it?"

He started to take it, then waved it aside.

"Yes, open it."

Jean tapped the letter down to one end, tore a narrow strip off the other, and slid the page out.

"*Councilman John Jason Gibson,*" she read proudly aloud. Then her heart began to thump much too fast. "*You see what poor management causes, Gib? This will be the only warning you receive . . .*"

Chapter Forty-two

Dixie rang the Harrises' doorbell.

No answer. With her husband's funeral only a few hours away, perhaps the reluctant mother had gone to a friend's or relative's house where she'd have comfort and help with the baby.

Relief lifted Dixie's spirits. Questioning a widow at such a time — even in an effort to find her husband's killer — had seemed cold-blooded. Yet, a brief talk with Ann Harris could answer a lot of questions, especially if Art's death was unrelated to the robbery shootings. Dixie'd have to return later, maybe tomorrow. The timing wouldn't be much better, but for the moment she was glad to put it off.

Twenty-six miles down the road, she and Marty stood at the home of former HPD Officer Ted Tally. The fifties-style ranch house sat nine blocks from the restaurant where he was killed. Seeing an OUT OF ORDER note taped over the doorbell, Dixie knocked and waited, with no idea whether Ted had lived alone.

"Did your mother ever belong to a sorority?" she asked Marty.

Looking surprised at the question, he shook his head. "Mom tried three times to finish college, though."

"I remember that — she took commercial art at night school."

"Tried. Dad always found a reason Mom needed to stay at home. He told me once that wives should never be well educated, that it gave them wandering fever."

As Dixie knocked again on the door, she pictured Bill Pine in his favorite chair, watching TV, Edna bringing whatever he needed. Bill had been a regular Archie Bunker, and Dixie hadn't noticed at the time.

When they'd waited another minute with no answer, Dixie tried the doorknob, out of habit, not expecting it to open. Then she started around the house, peeking in windows, Marty close behind her. A tall hedge encircled the yard, blocking the view from neighbors. There appeared to be no one inside the house. At the back door, Dixie tried the knob again—and this time it turned freely. The door opened.

She froze. What cop left his door unlocked? But it *had* opened . . . she heard no one inside . . . and curiosity drew her forward.

"We can't go in there," Marty whispered.

"Hello?" Dixie called. No response.

The laundry room—dirty clothes piled high in an open hamper—suggested a bachelor lived here.

"Hello! Anybody here?"

No answer. Dixie waved Marty in and shut the door.

"Dix! We're trespassing here. Aren't we? I know he's dead, but—?"

"We'll only stay a minute," Dixie promised. "Keep your hands in your pockets." Unlikely that Ted's house would be dusted for prints now, but why risk it?

The kitchen had a well-used microwave, crusted with food spatters, a practically new stove and oven, and a refrigerator with nothing inside but a frozen pizza, a carton of Bluebell Double Fudge ice cream, jars of mustard, catsup, pickles, and nine bottles of Corona. Reminded Dixie of her own fridge.

In the living room, a fairly new multimedia system dominated one wall. Directly across from it sat a couch and two chairs, well used. A bed pillow and blanket suggested someone had slept on the couch. A clutter of objects covered the coffee table—newspaper, a plate and utensils, a *TV Guide*, an empty Corona bottle, a copy of *The Purloined Letter and Other Stories* by Edgar Allan Poe, and a stack of opened mail. Dixie peeked into the bedroom: an unmade bed—one pillow, no blanket—nightstand, lamp, chest of drawers.

Returning to the living room, she found Marty eyeballing a CD rack.

"Country and western," he mumbled. "Not a bad selection, if you like country. What are we looking for?"

"I won't know until I see it."

A bookshelf held items of a personal nature: a set of Funk and Wagnalls, four recent best-sellers, a battered paperback of *Catcher in the Rye*, a coffee-table volume on sports cars, a pair of gift-shop candle holders with unburned tapers, and a row of what looked to be family photographs in various frames. One photo showed a gray-haired woman flipping burgers on an oil-drum barbecue grill, two young girls playing with a tabby cat; Ted making a face at the camera; and a man and woman, mid-thirties, taking beers from a cooler. In a smaller studio close-up of the man, he wore a police uniform. Ted's brother? Close family resemblance, anyway. A pair of matched frames held studio shots of the couple and the gray-haired woman. The woman appeared in yet another snapshot, looking several years younger, with a man about her same age.

Propped behind all these sat an eight-by-ten of Ted's graduating class at the police academy. Dixie nudged the smaller frames aside for a better look at the graduates. Young Officer Tally looked impressive in his dress blues. So did Officer Harris.

Classmates assigned to beats thirty-odd miles apart respond to the same squeal. Having coffee together. Harris off his beat but caught up in the excitement?

Unframed on the same shelf, a snapshot showed Ted with an African-American teenager, his arm wrapped around the kid's shoulder. Dixie lifted it by the edges to look at the back. Someone had penned *My Little Brother Samuel* and a recent date.

Janet Easton had said the man who turned Art Harris from the Dallas gang was a Big Brother. The Tally-Harris friendship dating back at least to their academy days, coupled with their common interest in Big Brothers, made their deaths seem less and less coincidental. Even if the shooter was systematically taking out the officers responsible for killing Edna Pine, what were the odds of "accidentally" singling out two friends as the first victims? The killer had to know more details about those officers than any passerby.

"There's a bunch of notes inside this book," Marty said. "You might want to look at them."

"I told you not to touch—" She sighed. Damage done. "Anything interesting?"

"Beats me." He held out a handful of pages. "Here, you—"

A car pulled into the driveway.

Damn. They *couldn't* be caught here.

"Marty! Out the back!"

Fortunately, Dixie'd parked the Mustang at the curb across the street; it would likely go unnoticed.

Marty darted for the kitchen, Dixie on his heels. They slipped out the back door. Dixie peeked around the house as the couple from the barbecue photo stepped out of a white Chevy pickup. Ted's family.

Dixie waved Marty toward a slim gap in the hedgerow separating Ted's yard from his neighbor's. Thirty fast strides and they hit the street. Slowing, they approached the Mustang and climbed in.

Dixie looked back at the couple entering Ted's house. Maybe they'd stopped by earlier. Grieving family members might forget to thoroughly lock up a house whose only occupant wouldn't be returning.

"Where do I put these?" Marty still held the book and note pages from Ted's coffee table.

"You *took* them?"

"Not intentionally."

"Well . . . let's get out of here. Then we'll see if you stole anything useful."

•   •   •

In West University Village, where she'd arranged to meet Parker, narrow streets, crowded with shoppers and late-lunchers taking advantage of the fine weather, made for slow going. Spotting a parking place beside Parker's Cadillac—astonishing in the Village—Dixie took that as a good omen, and they entered Charlie's Hamburger Joint.

"I don't need a baby-sitter," Marty grumbled when they'd ordered their burgers at the counter and joined Parker at a table.

"Considering the trouble you provoked without one, I'm surprised to hear you say that."

After an uncomfortable silence, Parker remarked, "Guess we could think of this as a consultation. My new house has bare walls, and what I know about art wouldn't fill a clamshell. Don't even know where to start."

Marty perked up. "Parker, within five miles of this very spot, I can show you undiscovered genius and deals you won't believe. You can buy the pieces you love—under my direction, of course—then watch them appreciate on your walls."

While Parker and Marty avidly discussed art, Dixie claimed their orders, loaded the tray with condiments and utensils, and carried it back to the table.

"No, no, I don't need any help," she groused, plunking the tray down.

They both sheepishly helped unload. Marty returned the empty tray. Talking subsided while they tucked into old-fashioned burgers and crisp fries, then Parker asked about their morning.

"This woman talks about *me* getting in trouble," Marty told him. "Can you believe we broke into a *cop's* house?"

"We didn't break in. The door was open." Dixie explained what she'd discovered about Art Harris and Ted Tally. "I'm thinking Art Harris logged a coffee break, then drove into town for a chat with his friend Ted. While he's here, the squeal comes in for a seven-car pursuit from Richmond, and Art couldn't resist joining in—even knowing he'd have to grovel to his supervisor afterward."

"Especially if he missed out on the one in his own backyard," Parker pointed out.

Dixie opened an envelope that she'd stuffed with the book and papers from Ted's coffee table.

Parker leaned closer. "What's all that?"

"Maybe nothing. But considering the laws we broke to have it in our possession, let's hope it's not Ted's golf scores."

Parker slid the book across the table and opened it. The four sheets of notepaper were covered with drawings rendered in colored markers.

"Looks like graffiti," Marty said.

"That's exactly what it is." Dixie spread the pages side by side. "Only these aren't the innocent drawings of street artists. They're gang tags." Dixie recognized a crown for the Kings, a pitchfork, dice, a 187, and a lot of purple. One symbol, drawn on a page by itself, featured a gold "P" in the center of a red triangle on a blue background. Dixie'd never seen that one before.

"Great book," Parker said. "But why were those pages stuck inside it?"

"Looked like Ted slept on the couch the night before he died. He was probably reading the book and stuffed the papers in to mark his place."

"What do those drawings mean?"

"Maybe nothing. A neighbor told us Art Harris wanted to join a gang task force. Maybe he and Ted tracked some gang activity between their two beats."

"I don't see how any of that helps me," Marty grumbled. "And it sure isn't art."

Parker moved the pages around, as if they were puzzle pieces he was trying to decipher. "Is one of these different from the others?"

"This one I've never seen before." Dixie pointed to the triangle. "Why?"

"The page marked in the Poe book is where Auguste Dupin finds the purloined letter."

Dixie didn't understand his point. "So?"

Parker waved it off. "Guess it's nothing."

"What?"

"Okay. The purloined letter was hidden in plain sight in a card rack above a writing desk. Maybe Ted took a hint from Edgar and hid an important drawing among the others."

Dixie studied the triangle, with its blue and red background. "Or maybe Ted found this one painted on a building among other tags and recognized it as . . . I don't know, a new gang in the area?"

Parker grinned. "Or like you said, Sherlock, maybe he just used them as a bookmark."

With a glance at her watch, Dixie slid everything back in the envelope to think about later and pushed aside her unfinished burger. She was about to be late for her "therapy" session with Vernice Urich, the woman who reputedly knew everyone's secrets.

Chapter Forty-three

A small brass sign that read VERNICE URICH, PH.D., M.S.W., A.C.P. hung beside the psychotherapist's front door. Vernice worked out of her home, a modest 1950s bungalow in a neighborhood of newer, more pretentious two-story constructions.

Before ringing the bell, Dixie paused to clear away any hostile thoughts. She innately distrusted people who poked around in other people's minds. She was here to find out why Aunt Edna had sought psychotherapy. Although Marty no longer seemed interested in how his mother became armed and dangerous, Dixie couldn't let it go.

"Here you are, exactly on time," Vernice Urich greeted her. "I do appreciate punctuality, Dixie. Don't you?"

"Especially when I'm paying for it." *Whoops, was that a hostile thought?*

But Vernice smiled, with even white teeth too precise to be the version she was born with. In the bright afternoon light, her wrinkled face appeared sunken. Yet her eyes held the sparkle of youth. Maybe that's why Dixie believed the woman wasn't as old as she first appeared.

"Follow me, dear."

The home's modest exterior gave way to more gilt and chintz than Dixie'd seen except in magazines, as Vernice led the way to an office immediately off the entry. Originally, it would've been a formal living room, Dixie supposed.

"Would you like tea? I have Apple Spice and Earl Grey."

In the dim lighting, Dixie squinted to see an ornate cart with china cups and saucers, hot water, tea bags, sugar, cream, and packets of artificial sweetener. A massive carved desk in a style her uninformed eye decided was baroque occupied half the room. A brocade chair with delicate claw feet perched in front of it.

"Earl Grey sounds good." Dixie eyed the antique, certain it would collapse if she sat down.

Vernice gestured toward a pair of wingbacks in the corner, wearing the same classy fabric.

"A woman as attractive as you, Dixie, I'm frankly amazed you escaped matrimony all these years," she commented once they were seated, Dixie's teacup balanced on her knee.

The praise sounded false, perhaps because Dixie had heard better flatterers recently. She made no response.

Vernice opened a stenographer's tablet. "When were you born, dear?"

"I'm thirty-nine." *For a few more months.*

"You don't look a day over thirty. But let's be more specific. First, your birth date. Including the time, if you know it."

"November third. Four-twenty on a Tuesday afternoon." *Pain you wouldn't believe*, Carla Jean had told her. *Like pulling teeth out through your navel.*

"When did you reach womanhood?"

"Pardon?"

"When did you start menstruating, dear? It marks the time that boys rightly begin to occupy one's thoughts more frequently than dolls."

"I don't recall ever thinking about dolls." Not that Carla Jean hadn't supplied a few. Dixie's birth mother loved the ones with fancy dresses and curly hair, dolls that sat on a shelf or a dresser, big glassy eyes, painted cheeks, vacuous smiles. Dixie preferred books, which Carla Jean considered a waste of money. *Once you've read one, what good is it?* she'd ask.

"Just a figure of speech," Vernice amended. "Meaning childish things. At onset of menstruation we trade toys for boys. How old were you?"

"Ten. But that's not what I wanted to talk about—"

"We'll get there, dear. Let's take care of a few more questions. When did you first kiss a boy?"

None of your damn business. Dixie had never consulted a psychotherapist, but she'd taken the standard college courses, plus criminal psychology in law school. Vernice's technique struck her as offbeat and pushy. Or was that just another hostile thought?

"I was in high school. About fifteen, I guess." *If you don't count my mother's sicko boyfriends.* Dixie scanned a bookcase near the desk: *Astrology for Everyone, What's Your Number, A Guide to Numerology, Sex Signs, The Modern Woman's Book of Wicca.* Vernice's choice of reading material lent a different slant to her questions.

"A special night? A holiday, perhaps? I'd prefer the exact date, if we can burrow down and find it."

"May first." Until that moment, Dixie hadn't remembered. The PTA had sponsored a fund-raising bazaar to buy uniforms for her high school baseball team. She and Marty slipped away early to see an afternoon showing of *Elmer Gantry*. He'd kissed her in the dark.

"And the first time you fornicated."

"*What?*"

"Sex, dear. When was your first unmarried encounter?"

"Did you ask Edna Pine these questions?"

"Edna Pine?" Vernice's toothy smile vanished.

"What sort of questions did you ask her?"

"I can't imagine why you'd want to know that. You're no bigger than a minute—you can't possibly want to lose weight." When Dixie remained silent, Vernice continued. "But I *can* tell you we create very successful programs for weight loss, through hypnotic suggestion. Was Edna a close friend, dear?"

Hypnotic suggestion? Interesting. "A neighbor. I grew up with her son."

"Ah-ha! And was he the first boy in your young life? The one who broke your heart?"

How did she know that? Dixie loathed having her thoughts read as if every line were written on her face.

"Was he the one who broke your cherry, dear?"

"No!" What was this woman, a verbal voyeur?

"I can see this was a painful experience, but once we get those old tapes played out, we can help you assume a more satisfying alliance with your sexuality."

Oh, really? Hocus-pocus pop psychology, with numbers and star signs and witchcraft? Dixie scanned the walls for a diploma.

"My friend Edna—"

"I can't talk about another client. Surely you realize that would be most un-ethical. You wouldn't want me revealing *your* deepest secrets, would you?"

"But Edna's dead." Dixie decided to cut to her real reason for this meeting. "What you discussed could have some bearing on . . . events that led to her death."

"I don't see how."

"She robbed a bank at gunpoint. She shot a police officer. The Edna Pine I knew growing up couldn't harm a gopher. She used herbs to discourage pests from eating her plants. Something happened within the past few months to change that gentle chubby woman into a trim, sleek, very ungentle thief. And you're the person who poked around in her mind. What did you do in there?"

"My goodness, you have a distorted view of psychotherapy. Even if I could ef-fect such a change, why *would* I?"

But Vernice's hand had started moving over the tablet page—making meaningless doodles, from what Dixie could see.

"Money, for starters. Edna paid you a healthy fee." Actually, Dixie had no idea what Edna paid, if anything. She'd found no checks issued to Vernice Urich. "But your fee's nothing compared to the unrecovered money stolen from Texas Citizens Bank."

Vernice smiled. "Me, a female Svengali? Too much film and television, dear. Hypnosis doesn't turn people into helpless drones."

But her hand kept moving, drawing circles and stars and arrows, with Vernice never glancing at the page.

Chapter Forty-four

"Keep your incompetent hands off of this, Wanamaker. Let the FBI handle it."

As he spit the words, Gib Gibson's hawkish nose hovered beside Ed's cheek. Ed itched to reach up and twist it.

"If we sit back and do nothing," Banning argued, "the media will crucify us all." Banning had summoned Ed to his office after Gib dropped by with his usual meddling demands.

Ed didn't care about the media. But he thought the FBI might be headed in the wrong direction. Third-world terrorists? Those letters had looked home-grown to Ed.

Gib turned his pointy nose at Banning.

"I say we provide *any* support requested, but otherwise stay out of their way. What we don't need is a bunch of bumbling locals muddying the trail." The greenish-brown suit he wore had been tailored to fit his trim, muscular body and, the way Gib stood, stiff as a general issuing orders, Ed could imagine brass stars on the Councilman's shoulders.

"What trail?" Ed asked mildly.

"If you understood professionalism, Wanamaker, perhaps the FBI would take you into their confidence."

"I suppose you think they'll confide in you?" Ed hoped The People turned up in an FBI database, but he wouldn't put money on it. And he didn't want his own men sitting on their thumbs while a bunch of wrongheaded punk assassins snuck around in the shadows with rifles.

"What about protection?" Banning suggested. "Ed, can you put a couple of officers at each house? The feds didn't say—"

"Are you scared, Avery?" Gib grinned, even more snidely than usual. "Must be soiling your britches if you think a bodyguard could stop a sniper's bullet. Be a waste of taxpayers' money."

Ed had to agree. The Mayor's twenty-four-hour guard came with the job, but it wouldn't be enough. No way could the department spare enough men to sweep three neighborhoods around the clock. And the FBI boys were too busy punching their keyboards.

"Unlike you, Councilman," Banning replied evenly, "I can't hide inside my house for thirty-six hours. The Memorial Day Commemorative—"

"Another monumental waste!" Gib turned his nose back toward Ed. "I'm telling you, Wanamaker, stay out of the way on this, or I'll see that your every stupid move makes headlines!"

He snatched the door open and stalked out.

As an army noncom, Ed had taken plenty of bullshit orders from officers, but this was civilian life. Gib could cram his demands up his Marine-tight ass.

But when the latch snapped shut, Ed said, "Gib does have a sympathetic ear on all the local news teams. Loud and irritating gets lots of attention."

Banning tugged at his trouser knee to keep the stretch out before crossing his legs. He always looked like someone had rolled him off an inspection line, cleaned, clipped, pressed, and Scotchgarded.

"What *are* you planning to do, Ed?"

"When you think about it, thirty-six hours isn't a helluva lot of time. Maybe you and Gib should lay low. Let the feds dig." Ed raked a hand through his wiry hair. "We'll roust all the usual gangs, give 'em a chance to tell what they know."

Banning turned his deliberate politician's gaze at Ed.

"Chief, 'laying low' is not what I want to hear from you. I have a job to do. And so do you."

Ed found a sunflower seed in his pocket and cracked it. Banning was an okay guy until he pulled this control crap. But Ed wasn't buying his tough act this time. The Mayor was more concerned than he wanted to let on.

Chapter Forty-five

In the subdued lighting of Vernice's office, Dixie watched the psychotherapist's hand move across the page, making circles, squares, triangles, and wondered if the marks were more than mere doodles. Dixie's gaze flickered to a mahogany cabinet she had first thought to be a buffet; now she recognized it as an executive file cabinet. Somehow, she needed to arrange five minutes alone with those files.

"My dear, you are unfailingly loyal, aren't you?" Vernice asked, still scribbling. "Even to your mother—who doesn't deserve it, you know. She didn't provide a decent childhood."

How could she even guess that? Dixie's natural mother, Carla Jean, lay in a long-term care facility, an invalid who no longer recognized her only daughter. As a mother, Carla Jean had struck out miserably. Never married. Entertained a string of lovers and never acknowledged that some of them found their way into Dixie's bedroom before the Flannigans adopted her. But after decades of separation, Dixie rarely missed a Sunday visit. Maybe that was loyalty. Dixie didn't always know why she did things that seemed to need doing.

She cleared her throat. "Did Edna ever mention her son?"

"My dear, eating habits are so complicated, and family situations always figure in, don't they?"

Was that a yes?

"Like your situation," Vernice continued. "You shouldn't be alone so much. It isn't healthy, and you haven't missed the childbearing years completely. There's still time. A son or daughter would bring so much joy to your life. Scorpios are sexual creatures. I'm sure you've had your share of fornication, Dixie, but let a man get close enough to make nesting noises and you scramble away like a frightened crab. Why do you suppose that happens?"

"I don't scramble." At least, not from Parker. *He* created the distance.

"Color it with your own crayons, but you can't abide any infringement on your privacy. That's Scorpio. Yet your Taurus moon craves intimacy and, my dear, this aspect pulls you in opposite directions at times, doesn't it? You desire that closeness, that deep understanding and familiarity and tenderness that you've brushed against. But it's frightening to let someone get near enough to really know you."

Terrifying.

"Cows," Vernice said.

"Pardon me?"

"Cows walking to their death. Peacefully. Because a woman, a scientist, discovered the magic of hugging. Hugging the cows calmed them as they neared the slaughterhouse. We all need hugging, dear. Even a privacy-loving Scorpio."

"Did you and Edna talk about astrology?"

"Astrology is a tool, Dixie, merely a tool, but an extremely useful tool that digs deep with sharp little teeth. Edna, with her Pisces conjunction, was a sponge that had been squeezed dry by her family and tossed aside to desiccate. She found astrology fascinating. You do, too, don't you? Secretive Scorpio can't stand anyone else having secrets. When we know a person's planetary signature, their secrets are like stamens on a morning glory, exposed in the sunlight."

"Edna's husband *died*. He didn't toss her aside."

"Didn't he? What is death but the ultimate abandonment for those of us who remain behind? You've experienced it, Dixie."

Kathleen and Barney. In the space of eighteen months she'd lost them both. Kathleen battled the cancer right to the end, but Barney practically packed his bags and waited for the Grim Reaper to beckon. She'd watched him disappear a little each day, fading like an old snapshot.

Was that what happened to Edna? Had she missed Bill so much she found her own way to follow him?

"Vernice, was Edna on a suicide mission? Do you counsel your patients to seek death?" *Hypnotic suggestion, maybe?*

"What else is death but deliverance? I counsel my patients to explore the destiny they've been dealt. You've drawn a difficult star path, Dixie, filled with obstacles and disappointments. Every time you knock one of those Scorpio boulders out of your way, every time you smile in the face of your Pisces disillusionment, don't you feel stronger for it?"

"Pisces? You said Edna was Pisces."

"Sun *and* moon, double the compassion, double the illusion, born to view the world through rose-colored glasses. But you, Dixie, have Pisces rising, softening your Scorpio-Taurus crust. When you want to be oh-so-tough, Pisces draws a curtain aside and forces you to see human frailty. When you want to be oh-so-perceptive, Pisces fogs your vision. Neptune, the Piscean ruler, loves to expose your vulnerability. A dastardly bastard, isn't he, dear?"

"Are you saying Edna's loss—and her planets—left her vulnerable to illusionists?" Terrence Jackson. Lonnie Gray. *Vernice Urich.* "And to misjudgments?"

"Were we talking about Edna, dear? I thought we were discussing you."

Chapter Forty-six

Dixie sat in her Mustang, fingering Vernice's appointment card and trying to decide whether to toss it into her plastic trash bag. No matter how she approached the question, the woman had refused to admit *or* deny having Lucy Ames as a patient. If she'd never counseled Lucy, why not say so? She'd owned up to hypnotizing Edna into weight loss—more or less. How many other Fortyniners had the woman seduced with her pseudo-psychology?

A good word, "seduced." Lonely people attracted charlatans of all types. Telephone scam artists made fortunes, promising riches from a "small" investment, or soliciting donations to the "Police Officers' Widows Fund," or threatening arrest for some imaginary offense unless the person put up a cash "security" bond. A silver tongue and a stone conscience were all the tools a good con needed.

And the only difference between a con and a sale is the value of the product.

Had Dixie received value for the consultation fee she paid Vernice? The woman's insights had hit damned close to home. *Let a man get close and you scramble like a frightened crab.* Eerie.

Dixie's insistence on clinging to a lifestyle that kept distance between her and Parker *might* be considered scrambling. Parker *had* tried to get close. When the danger he saw in Dixie's work made him back off, she'd refused to consider setting the work aside. Bounty hunting wasn't even a true career choice—she'd merely landed there after turning away from her real profession. With her income from the pecan farm, she certainly didn't need the big fees she earned. She *could* choose to practice law again. Not as a prosecutor—she'd lost her stomach for it. And she'd never jump to Belle's side of criminal law—a guilty client had a right to a decent defense, but not from Dixie. That left plenty of options in civil law. Why had she dismissed those without a passing consideration?

Two o'clock Monday. Keeping the appointment would mean another chance to look in the psychotherapist's files. The hour had passed so fast today that Dixie was out the door before realizing she'd never come close to snooping in the files for Lucy's name.

The appointment card's raised lettering announced: VERNICE URICH, PH.D., M.S.W., A.C.P. PSYCHOTHERAPY—HYPNOTHERAPY. No mention of astrology, numerology, witchcraft, the topics of the books on Vernice's shelves. She probably hadn't listed those on her license application, either. For fun, Dixie read her daily horoscope, and the vague generalities could apply to anyone. But Vernice's observations hadn't been so general.

Did she really believe the psychotherapist could answer her relationship problems? Did the woman *really* have a license to practice psychotherapy?

Dixie crammed the appointment card into her trash bag. Vernice's creepy insights hit too close to home. She'd rather get at those files through an open window.

A quick phone call told her Marty and Parker were still gallery hopping, which gave her time to drop in on Smokin and Pearly White. They'd been hacking out information for her since early morning.

When she reached the Heights, a near-town community, genteel Victorian mansions shoulder to shoulder with crumbling apartment complexes, Dixie turned down a dead-end street, passed through a gate posted with bogus HIGH VOLTAGE signs, and entered an alley behind a shipping company. A set of stairs opened into a narrow, musty-smelling hallway that turned twice before arriving at a plain wooden door, identical to others along the hall.

Dixie heard voices raised in argument as she started to knock.

"You *have* to tell her." Smokin's voice.

"No, I don't, old man. I don't. We made no promises to tell her anything."

Dixie frowned, listening, but heard nothing more. She rapped on the door. Seconds later, Smokin's voice asked, "Who is it?"

"Dixie."

He opened the door a crack, seemed reluctant, but finally drew the door wide enough for Dixie to enter. A delicious coffee aroma overpowered the cigarette odor Dixie expected.

"Got a mess of stuff to show you, Dixie. Yep, yep." Smokin's enthusiasm sounded forced. "Pearly, where are those printouts?"

Pearly White sat at her keyboard, rigid as a mannequin. "Get 'em yourself, old man."

Smokin shook his head, exasperated, and waved a hand toward his wife. "Pearly's got a bone in her craw. Don't pay her no mind. Take a gander at these while I pour the coffee."

He patted the recliner on his own side of the black tape line, which extended the length of the room, computers at one end, television and recliners at the other. Everything on one side of the tape was duplicated on the other, except the big-screen TV-VCR, which straddled the line. As much as they squabbled, Dixie wondered how the couple ever agreed on a program to watch. When she sat down, Smokin handed her a stack of paper from the laser printer.

Uptown Interdenominational Church, she discovered, was thirty-seven years in business and had recently acquired a new pastor. Church of The Light had been founded only four years ago. None of the board names was familiar.

Considering the volume of information represented in the stack of printouts, Dixie merely scanned for names, laying aside the pages that referred to Marty and his Dallas gallery, Edna, Lucy Ames, Vernice Urich, Terrence Jackson, Lonnie Gray, and Jessica Love. She itched to look into those, but first she needed the information on Art Harris and Ted Tally.

The printouts showed the standard graduation announcement for their police academy class, a wedding announcement for Art Harris, Peggy's birth announcement, and a short piece about Ted Tally catching a bullet in the leg while capturing a burglary suspect. Nothing suspicious in the mix. Dixie noticed that Ted, twenty-six, was three years younger than Art. Both were too young to be dead. Ted had a bachelor's degree in psychology.

Smokin returned carrying a bright green tray with mugs of coffee, cream, and sugar. Legs unfolded under the tray, turning it into a snack table that he placed beside Dixie's chair. The aroma drew her attention from her stack of papers.

"Smells delicious. Vanilla?"

Smokin beamed. "A teaspoon in every pot."

She sipped it, burning her tongue. "Did you give up cigarettes?" she asked him.

"Hah!" Pearly hooted.

"Nah, the old woman bought me one of those ashtrays that sucks up the smoke. Find what you wanted?" He indicated the pages Dixie held.

"Not yet. What about financial records? DMV records? Military service?"

"No military time for either of 'em. Clean driving records—you should have the printout there."

Dixie shuffled through the pages and found it. Neither officer had any traffic tickets during the past three years—no big surprise. Ted drove a new Chevy pickup and Art owned a four-year-old Cougar.

"Nothing exciting here," she told him.

"Pearly's the one can get the financials for you." Smokin rose abruptly and headed back toward the kitchen. "If she's not too peevish."

"I have the bank records up," Pearly said primly. "No printout, but you can pull that stool over and read them on-screen."

Dixie moved the wooden stool and perched on it, a good ten inches too high to comfortably see the monitor. Scanning the meager sum in the Harris account gave her an ache in that place around her heart she reserved for tear-jerk movies. Art Harris provided for his entire family for a month on less than smooth-talking wizards like Terrence Jackson spent on private club fees.

"If the Mayor's new budget includes an HPD pay increase, it'll get my support," she told Pearly.

The hacker glanced at her, then as stiff as ever, looked back at the monitor.

Dixie scrolled through Ted's bank records. He spent more freely than Art, saved less, and suffered an occasional overdraft. Nothing the least bit suspicious.

When Pearly keyed up financials for Jackson, Urich, Gray, and Love, Dixie whistled and jotted notes on the respective printouts to review later. Edna's records held no surprises. Lucy Ames had made a modest salary, spent everything she earned, and paid her bills promptly.

"Go back to Urich's file," Dixie said. When Pearly brought it up, she asked, "What does ACH mean?"

"Automatic checking. Electronic debits and credits—no paper."

Dixie understood the concept—marginally. She paid toll fees and property maintenance fees by automatic transfer.

"Those all look like credits." Columns of transfer amounts in one-hour-fee increments marched across the screen.

"That's correct," Pearly snapped.

Apparently, Vernice had set up her clients on direct-transfer payments. Her total monthly income was startling. "Can we see how far back these go?"

Pearly scrolled backward four years; the same account numbers appeared over and over. Recent months showed payments for more hours than a psychologist could physically handle. Either Vernice had an associate, or she worked twenty-four hours a day.

"Can you find out who these payees are?"

Pearly patiently accessed each account. One that began in December and continued to the present belonged to Edna. Lucy's name didn't show up. Dixie jotted down a few names whose accounts had been paying consistently for the full four years—LeRoy Haines, Beatrice French, Dolly Mae Aichison, Rose Yenik. Dixie recognized none of them.

Terrence Jackson's numerous bank accounts ran into the millions, but because he invested the sums, Dixie didn't find that surprising. With her meager financial skill, she noticed nothing unusual. Jessica Love's business account at the Unique Boutique had acquired a sixty-thousand-dollar ACH transfer during the past month, just in time to avoid overdrafting her account.

"Can we see where this amount came from?" Dixie asked.

Pearly cross-referenced to an investment account managed by Terrence Jackson. No surprise that Jessica trusted her investments to the Millennium Midas. So far, Dixie had seen nothing suspicious in Jackson's business.

Lonnie Gray operated Artistry Spa at barely above break-even, while his personal account supported three sizable mortgages and two sizable monthly automobile payments.

"Is that it?" Pearly asked sharply when Dixie looked away from the monitor.

Despite an ache across her shoulders, Dixie leaned down again to meet Pearly's gaze.

"You know I'm not out to damage the reputation of these dead officers, don't you?" What else could account for the hacker's surly attitude?

A muscle in Pearly's jaw knotted.

"All I want," Dixie continued softly, "is to prove that the HPD's chief suspect didn't kill them—which he didn't. If I found proof that convinced me otherwise, I would never protect a murderer."

The woman's rigid posture relaxed a fraction.

"What did you discover, Pearly, that you're not telling me?"

"Nothing . . . in the financials." She looked down at her hands.

"Then what?"

Pearly shook her head. "You have everything I can give you."

From what Dixie'd already seen, Art Harris grew up in Dallas. Smokin and Pearly White had lived in Dallas. And Art's neighbor, Janet Easton, indicated that he might've been in some trouble back then. Had Pearly uncovered a skeleton in that Dallas closet? Clearly, she didn't intend to say, and Dixie respected their relationship too much to insist.

As Smokin returned with a slice of homemade chocolate cake and a refill on the coffee, one more question occurred to Dixie.

"How easily could I access pornography on the Internet?"

Smokin's face fell, and he shot a glance at Pearly.

"Ask Mr. Smut-lover himself," she hooted over her shoulder.

"Not true!" He turned innocent eyes at Dixie. "The question should be, how to avoid the stuff once you're tagged as a looker."

"What do you mean?"

"Suppliers trick you into hitting their Web site, then you're bombarded with dirty mail."

"I still don't understand. How do they trick you?"

"Key your search engine with an ordinary word—smooth, three, cabriolet—"

"He knows them all!" Pearly said.

"You'll end up at Lovin' Threesomes or Smooth Moves. And there you are, staring at more flesh than you've seen in sixty years."

"And this is free?"

"Yep. Plenty of free stuff floating around. Unless you click on a button that won't open without an access code, you can look all you want, never pay a dime."

"But to access the heavy . . . pornography . . . you need a credit card?"

"Yep."

"Unless you have Smokin fingers," Pearly amended.

"Not true," Smokin declared. "Looking's one thing, stealing's another." Yet the guilty gleam in his eyes suggested he might've stolen a peek or two.

Dixie couldn't decide whether this knowledge made her feel better or worse about Ryan's secret pastime. Hacking into protected pornographic files could land her nephew in big-time legal trouble. The alternative worried her even more.

Leaving the hackers' apartment with her stack of computer printouts, Dixie worried Pearly's strange behavior around in her mind. The couple worked from a self-determined code of ethics that Dixie had never questioned. They would either tackle a job or not, but never before had they refused to part with the information obtained. Only one reason made sense to Dixie: Pearly had learned something that might damage the reputation of one of the officers—and thus bring disgrace, ridicule, or possibly danger to his family.

Fortunately, Dixie's network included other sources. The one she phoned now knew dirt on law enforcement officers in every backwater town in the state. Anything Slim Jim McGrue didn't know, he could find out in an eye blink. Jim was scary in other ways, too. As she punched in his cellular phone number, Dixie pictured Jim's six-foot-eight, sticklike body folded behind the wheel of his State Trooper patrol car. McGrue's grim good looks—leathery skin stretched tight over a keenly chiseled skull—had frightened many a highway speed-demon into becoming a born-again safety advocate. At least once a year McGrue tossed out a hint that he'd like to be more than a network resource in Dixie's life, and at least once a year Dixie gave the idea a passing consideration. McGrue fascinated her. He was an interesting friend; he'd be terrifying as an enemy.

"Jim," she said when he answered. "This is Dixie Flannigan."

"Always a pleasure. What's the occasion?"

She related briefly her situation with Marty.

"He's no killer, Jim. But if we accept the scenario that Ted Tally and Art Harris were assassinated in retaliation for the Granny Bandit shootings, he appears to be the best candidate. I'm thinking there's something deeper going on. Maybe digging around in the officers' backgrounds won't unearth any bones that connect with the body of information I'm assembling, but the coincidences can't be ignored."

She explained the officers' friendship, dating at least back to the police academy, then admitted her verbal attack on Art after Edna's death.

"If the shooter was on the scene, perhaps he homed in on Art because he thought I singled him out for a reason, then took out Ted Tally because he saw them together at some point."

"Dixie, I'll do this for you." Slim Jim allowed a long breath of silence before he continued. "But if your friend crawls out of the facts as the doer, I'll smash him."

"Yeah, Jim. I wouldn't have it any other way."

Chapter Forty-seven

Chief Ed Wanamaker lifted his dress uniform from the closet, hung it on the back of the door, and examined it through the cleaning bag. He'd worn it last at Christmas. A happy occasion. Not like today. This was the saddest damn day he could remember. Not enough that two good men died, the whole town had to take up sides over it.

He ripped the plastic off and unbuttoned the shirt.

"Aren't you going to shower?" Mira sat on the bed behind him pulling on panty hose.

"I showered this morning." He sniffed his armpit.

"You're wearing that beautiful, fresh, clean uniform without a shower?"

"Woman, aren't you listening?" He watched her in the dresser mirror as he buttoned the shirt. His wife was a graceful woman, even at a task as ungraceful as stuffing herself into panty hose. "I showered this morning. It's not like I've been mowing the grass."

She popped the elastic on his jockey shorts. "What did you eat for lunch?"

"Stopped at a Greek place."

"I didn't say where, I said what."

"Greek salad." Better not to mention the fried seafood platter.

She draped the towel over her shoulders. Damned if she didn't look sexy standing there.

"Ed, do you ever think about . . . moving back to Arkansas?" She said it softly, without the ever-present barb in her voice.

He glanced at the photos on the dresser, their daughter—as a newborn, a six-year-old, a graduate, and finally an Arkansas police officer. "Sometimes. You?"

"Never more than I've thought about it this week."

He put an arm around Mira's shoulders. She was tall, something he appreciated most on the dance floor and in the sack.

"Even a small-town police force can have a bad week," he reminded her. He nibbled her earlobe. "You like this new house, don't you?"

"Oh, absolutely."

"You joined a bridge club, the Ballet Guild—"

"I can unjoin anytime you say the word."

He turned her so he could see her face.

"Mira, are you saying you want to leave?"

She met his gaze squarely. "I'm saying you're a good man, Ed Wanamaker. And you don't have a thing to prove. I heard those newscasters taking their shots at you."

"Do you believe I'm ashamed of the job I've done here?"

"You're the best damn Chief this city's ever had. If they don't see it, that's their problem. Your friend Banning didn't warn you the Houston academy turned out officers without enough judgment training."

"What's that supposed to mean?"

She blinked. "With better judgment, don't you think they might've found another way—"

"Mira, don't listen to that crap. When an officer says, 'Put down your gun,' and instead an actor aims and fires, it's the officer's duty to shoot."

"What if it had been a child?"

"A child with a gun?"

"It's happening, kids carrying guns to school, shooting each other."

Ed grabbed a photograph from the dresser.

"Our *daughter*, Officer Wanamaker, faces down a twelve-year-old kid with a gun. She says, 'Put the gun down,' and he cocks it. Mira, is she *supposed* to take the bullet?"

She stared at him a second, her face twisted with the pain he'd caused. Then she pulled away and stalked toward the bathroom, turning to fling her towel at him.

"I *hate* this!"

Ed watched her slam the bathroom door behind her, then he looked down at the picture he held. That gal looked so damn proud, fresh out of the academy. Setting the frame back on the dresser, he noticed the folded photocopy of The People's letter, where he'd tossed it when he started changing clothes. He tucked it in his wallet. He hadn't shown the letter to Mira.

In the bathroom, Mira's hair dryer was going. He pulled on his pants. Then he opened a dresser drawer and felt around in back for the bottle he knew would be there.

It'd been a lot of years since a shot of Wild Turkey was all that kept him going.

Chapter Forty-eight

Jean Gibson dropped her husband's folded shirt into a suitcase as she heard him open the door behind her.

"What are you doing, Jean? You're not packing?"

"We're leaving." She tossed a handful of his dress socks on top of the shirts.

"Leaving to go where, precisely?"

"I read that letter, Gib. We're not staying here for that crackpot to make good on his threat."

"Jean, put that away. We have a funeral to attend."

"Fine." She could feel him standing behind her, rigid as a post. "We'll load the bags in the trunk and leave straight from the funeral."

"Jean . . ." He caught her hands, filled with a stack of his boxer shorts. "Listen to me." He tried to take the shorts, but she held on. "Think about how it would look if I turned tail now. If I leave town, I'm finished. I lose everything. Mayor? Forget it. Governor? Senate? Never happen. People have long memories for leaders who weaken at a time of crisis."

"Then blame it on me. Say I've had a nervous breakdown. A death in the family. Any damn thing. The letter said *thirty-six* hours, Gib. Thirty-six hours from *when*? It's already been seven hours since the letter arrived. That leaves twenty-nine. You expect Ed Wanamaker to find this lunatic before tomorrow night? That idiot can't find his pecker with both hands and a flashlight."

For once, she would not be afraid of annoying him. She tossed his shorts in the suitcase and avoided his grasp to gather up her own things.

"Jean, you're hysterical. We are not depending on Wanamaker. I called

Washington and made a racket they won't quickly forget. FBI, Secret Service—an entire task force is on the case. Once the feds clear this up, Wanamaker's out of here, and Banning along with him."

She looked at his homely face, and her heart thumped. She loved him so goddamn much. But maybe he was right. He knew about offensive objectives and tactical maneuvers and such—a chestful of military medals proved it. He could talk on such subjects for hours.

"But what if they're too late, Gib?" She forced her voice to sound calm and strong. "What if they catch this man *after* he kills you? Then what is it all for?"

"That won't happen."

"How can you be so composed? So certain? Didn't he kill those officers without anyone even suspecting? Both men just getting into their cars, and *blam!* They're dead. Nobody even saw it . . . until they lay bleeding on the ground."

She turned from him, covering her face to block out the images. She felt the dampness on her cheeks and realized she was crying, and *goddammit* she hadn't wanted to cry. Gib hated any display of weakness.

"Jean, that will not happen to me." His voice was cold, factual.

She couldn't talk without blubbering, so she kept her back to him, shutting him out, saying nothing, which Gib hated almost as much as he hated weakness. Did he really know something he wasn't telling? Or was he just being his normal, stubborn self?

"It will *not* happen, Jean. Now pile those clothes back in the bureau. Get dressed. We have an appearance to make." He encircled her shoulders with his arm and lifted her chin. "The puffiness around your eyes will look natural, under the circumstances. Quite understandable."

Turning to the mirror, he gazed at his own face. "In fact, I'll shed a few tears myself."

Chapter Forty-nine

Leaving the Heights, Dixie telephoned Amy to find out if Parker had dropped Marty off. Amy put Parker on the line.

"How'd the shopping go?" Dixie asked.

Marty answered on an extension. "Fabulous! You won't believe the pieces we found. I convinced Parker to commission a sexy Sue Lorenz mural for the bedroom, and, Dixie, we found a J. W. Sharp original to *die* for. You've seen the barns—"

"We didn't buy the barn painting," Parker amended. "We bought—"

"Mardi Gras! Dixie, Mardi Gras like you've never—"

"Old Mardi Gras floats." Parker, in his own laid-back style, seemed as excited as Marty. "Paintings of faded, broken-down floats. They're—"

"Fabulous! That's all we can say, love. You'll have to see for yourself. I've been dying to show both artists at Essence." Marty broke off abruptly. "Listen, I'm through horning in. I need to help Amy with dinner." The extension clicked.

"Marty seemed entirely too excited after your gallery binge. Parker, are you sure you didn't overspend?"

"Nah, we did fine. And Marty promised to help me hang everything next week. How did your snooping go?"

"Well enough, but I know I didn't have as much fun as you guys. Are you staying at Amy's for dinner?"

"I have a boat to show. Want to come along?"

What? Since when did they see each other on Saturday nights? "You're asking me to help you sell a boat? Parker, what's up?"

"Nice couple, nice boat. Thought it might be fun."

"Thanks for the invitation, but Ryan and I have a movie date tonight. Maybe another time."

"Okay. I need to get a move on. Here's Amy."

Dixie's mind ran with the idea of the boat ride. Safe, with the other couple, "just pals" stuff. But what had Parker planned for later? Anything? Or was this more of his mixed messages?

"Did you and Marty discuss the arrangements for Edna's cremation?" Amy asked.

"We're not doing that yet," Marty piped in the background, his words muffled as if he had aimed them at the receiver next to Amy's ear.

"Dixie! See what he's like? Talk to him!"

"Put him on."

"No, he's in the kitchen now. It's useless, anyway."

"Can't you handle the . . . cremation and everything, Amy?" Dixie asked.

"I don't see how. He's her son. He has to sign—"

"Then do whatever's necessary and I'll make him sign."

"What about the party? Oh, that sounds so crass. But Marty said Edna made it clear—a party. She did, didn't she? A party, not a memorial service? Maybe just a gathering, a few friends telling what they remember about her—"

"She said a party."

"Well, it won't be cheerful." She lowered her voice. "I worry about him, Dixie. The way he's acting. I know he has to grieve in his own way, but refusing to bury her, or whatever, is that normal? Should I call a doctor? I don't know a psychiatrist. Carl might, he knows everybody with money."

"Don't call a psychiatrist. Go ahead and do what you're good at. Arrange the viewing—"

"Dixie, do they have a viewing for a cremation?"

Hell, she didn't know. "Find out, Amy. Would you? Think about what Edna would want and just do it. As soon as possible. Invite everyone Edna knew to the party. I'll give you a list of her new friends." That might be interesting. "Marty will come to his senses. Is my nephew around?"

"Ryan's off with a friend. Such a beautiful day, and they wanted to spend it at that arcade, all those dim lights and that noise. I told him to go to the park."

"Did he say which friend?"

"Blake, I think. Or Ernie. Why, Dixie? He'll be home in time for your movie. Is something wrong?"

"No." Amy must've heard the tension in her voice. "I miss the little fart, that's all. He used to call me every day. Now I'm lucky to hear from him once a week. How about Carl?"

"You want to talk to Carl?"

"Don't make it sound so ominous. I talk to Carl occasionally."

"Not on purpose."

"You're saying he's not there?"

"In perfect golf weather?"

"Right. I have to go, Amy. Are you okay now, with Edna's last wishes?"

"I'm inviting Parker to the party," she said emphatically.

"Of course. Parker liked Edna."

"I hope you two are making up. I miss him."

"Amy, Parker's a friend. Yours, mine, Carl's—you can invite him over anytime."

"You sound so cool about it."

I don't feel cool. But what am I supposed to do, knock him down and brand him?

"Amy, Parker and I are fine. For a few weeks last winter, I guess it looked like we might be headed for something more . . . special . . . than friendship, but that's past. That doesn't mean we won't all see each other occasionally."

When Dixie disconnected, she had a page from Rashly at Homicide. Hoping he'd cooled off since that morning, when he told her to get lost, she dialed Rashly's number, got his voice mail, and left a message.

She'd reached the Southwest Freeway, but instead of taking it, she pointed the Mustang toward one of the only two parks in bicycling distance from Ryan's house. At the nearest park, scarcely half a block square and filled with playground toys, Dixie saw in one glance that Ryan wasn't there. A young mother sat reading while her two children played on the slide. Bell Park, about two miles away, had more trees and benches and no playground. Dixie spotted Ryan and three other boys gathered under a tree, four bikes nearby.

Sliding into a parking space, she watched for a few minutes. Ryan, clearly the smallest and youngest of the boys, was also clearly the center of attention. The others encircled him and seemed to be comparing sheets of paper, passing them back and forth, pointing, punching each other, laughing. Ryan made an occasional comment.

Dixie felt uncomfortable spying on the kid, but she also felt relief. As disgusting as she might find this rendezvous—they were obviously passing around Ryan's dirty pictures—she saw no danger in it. No creepy old man lurked in the shadows. After another minute or so, the older boys dug in their pockets and handed Ryan money. The imp had a dirty little peep-show business going. Didn't say much for his ambitions in life.

She dialed the Homicide Division's main number, recognized the voice that answered but couldn't put a name to it.

"This is Dixie Flannigan, returning a call to Sergeant Rashly. I left a message on his voice mail, but do you know if he's in the building?"

"Rashly's at the funeral, Dixie."

The Harris and Tally service. Dixie should be there, but the thought of another dreary memorial speech made her want to crawl into a hole. What she longed for was another of Lonnie Gray's massages. A facial. A mimosa. But she had one more stop to squeeze into the day. Glancing at her watch, she compromised on drive-through iced tea and a drive-by funeral.

Chapter Fifty

Philip Laskey finished typing and photocopying Mayor Banning's letters and placed them on his desk. Only a few people came into the office on Saturdays. They'd all gone. He set one stack of the photocopies in the Mayor's correspondence file; the other stack he slipped into a large envelope for Colonel Jay.

During the Mayor's electoral campaign, Philip had worked hard enough as a volunteer that making the transition to paid staff became a snap. At times he even like the job and considered Banning a decent guy, for a politician.

But the Colonel had known Banning longer and knew the corruption he was capable of.

Outside, Philip walked to a nearby florist shop. He bought three pink roses and a spray of baby's breath. Anna Marie liked fresh flowers on the dinner table. He rode the bus home and found her napping, a prime rib roasting in the oven.

He cut and arranged the flowers in a clear vase with cold water and sugar crystals. Placed them on the table. It was already set for dinner, but he'd let Anna Marie sleep awhile.

In his bedroom, he locked the Sig Sauer away, slipped out of his khaki jacket, and hung it in the precise space allotted in his closet.

He paused at the bureau. Above it in six identical five-by-seven silver frames, his brothers and father stared back at him. Not one had been in this house in fifteen years. Father was dead, of course. The others made excuses—families, jobs, responsibilities. Philip knew about responsibility. Some own it, some ignore it, others abuse it. Philip had grown up owning his. He brushed a thumb across his lapel pin in its wooden box. Couldn't wear it at the Mayor's office.

In a larger frame beside the six, a newspaper headline shouted: ANNA MARIE LASKEY ACQUITTED. The subhead: JURY RULES JUSTIFIABLE HOMICIDE. The two-column story began: *Laskey held her two-year-old son Philip today after a jury returned a verdict of not guilty. Accused of killing her husband with a concrete block for beating their son . . .*

Philip scooped the change from his pocket and lined it up on the bureau: quarters, nickels, dimes, pennies, in four neat rows. He placed his wallet in a wooden tray, glanced at the six photographs again, and left the room.

Entering Anna Marie's bedroom with the stealth of a midnight lover, he sat in an armchair near her bed. For twenty-four minutes, he watched the gentle rise and fall of her matronly breasts beneath the light bedcover and the plaid dress she wore. Then he rose and kissed her left cheek.

"Dinnertime," he said.

Chapter Fifty-one

After the funeral, Chief Ed Wanamaker accompanied Mayor Avery Banning through Tranquility Park as the Mayor inspected the stage setup for his Memorial Day Commemorative. Ed noted that some of the task force were on the job, making damn sure nobody planted a bomb. So Avery wasn't fooling anybody; he was checking out the photo ops, seeing if the sun would be shining in his eyes, all that shit.

A few steps behind them, the Mayor's bodyguard kept pace. Avery seemed at ease with him, but the man's presence bothered the hell out of Ed. Creeping around, just out of earshot, like a specter in his gray suit.

Earlier, leaving the cemetery, Ed had sent Mira on home. He'd needed some time alone with his thoughts after burying two officers. And those letters from The People had churned up in his mind some of the trouble Avery'd had in college. Not the traffic tickets—as a young man, Ed collected a fistful himself—but other stuff. Trouble seemed to happen *around* Avery Banning, never quite touching him. Happened on campus, mostly, not drawing attention from the local law. But there'd been one kid . . . a suicide . . . that Ed never quite got out of his head. Only reason for coming to the park today was to talk to the Mayor in private. And now, there's this gray specter dogging their footsteps.

"That stage needs to be rotated ten degrees to the right," Avery directed. As workmen carried out the order, the Mayor joined Ed under the shade of a live oak. "I planned this celebration to highlight positive results of changes I've made since my election," he said. "But after the problems of the past week, I'm reconsidering my entire approach."

The Chief cracked a sunflower seed between his fingers.

"I saw the petition for that group staging the demonstration against 'police brutality.' Same mouthy bunch pickets after every major arrest. March, shout, wave signs—never any rough stuff."

"No connection with The People?"

"The task force says no. So far, they haven't turned up any terrorist group or local gang calling themselves simply 'The People.' Seems to be no connection with Chicago."

"Why would there be?"

Avery hadn't been interested in law enforcement back in the eighties. No reason he should remember.

"Two gang nations out of Chicago—People and Folks. Took a while to work down this far, but most gang sets now align with one nation or the other. Loosely align. Fight amongst themselves, then regroup. They use the symbols—six-pointed star for Folks, five-pointed for People, sometimes a pyramid and crescent—to show their alignment. That emblem on the letters we got doesn't match up."

"People and *The* People, there's a difference?"

"Read your own law enforcement Web page. The red and blue are common gang colors, but usually one or the other, not both. And the letters didn't use any standard gang language."

The supervisor had gotten the stage repositioned now. Avery gave him a nod and turned to the rest of the park. Fifty feet away, pipe fitters erected the big stage where various bands and dance troops would perform. Technicians strung cable for speakers and microphones.

"Ed, not one of the reporters I've talked with has mentioned The People's letters. Isn't it usual for such groups to copy the press?"

"Terrorists would, yeah. Especially if they jumped on a moving tank. Gangs crave a different kind of attention, communicate with signs and graffiti. Not the U.S. mail."

"By 'a moving tank,' you mean claiming responsibility for assassinations committed by another group?"

Ed nodded. "It takes only one finger to send a bullet into a man's head."

"Then we don't know for sure that The People committed those murders."

"You're not listening, Avery. What I'm telling you is the task force has *nothing* on this bunch." Ed cleared his throat. "Given any thought to calling off your party? The day could go as planned, another spring festival, without all the awards and speeches."

"I've thought about it. But how would it look not to honor those two dead officers? You can see everyone's gone all out for this event." He gestured toward a young man wrapping a tall platform with red and blue bunting. A balloon statue of Uncle Sam stood waiting to be lifted aboard. "Even the weather's cooperating."

"It's your call." Spying a cardinal, Ed tossed a handful of seeds on the ground. "But shorten your speech. Fill it with those fancy words you like to use, but make it fast. Once we're on that stage, we're sitting ducks."

Avery searched the trees, like he might be looking for places an assassin could hide. "The FBI sent over a bulletproof vest."

Ed nodded. "Wear it. I'll be wearing mine." He tossed the rest of the sunflower seeds and dusted his hands. "I wouldn't say this to anyone else, Avery, but Mira's almost convinced me this job isn't worth hanging on to. Not that I'm scared to die, but I'd like to see my killer's face when I go. This sniper gives me the damn shakes." He glanced casually behind at Avery's bodyguard. "The list that each of us gave the task force—enemies, adversaries, anyone who might bear a grudge—did you include your old college buddies?"

The Mayor went squint-eyed and glanced around for ears within range. "Why would I? We broke up over twenty years ago."

"Called your little gang . . . what? The Right Wave, The Right to Win? What was it?"

"I did not belong to a *gang*, Ed."

"Naw, more like a clique, you said . . . or a cult—"

"It was not a cult."

"Lot of females in the group, if I remember right. You always had a way with the women, and didn't one of your girls accuse a professor of feeling her up? Was that how it started?"

Avery shrugged.

"The professor might be damned old now to be acting out a grudge. But his children wouldn't be."

"Ed, digging up ancient history won't gain anything—except mud for my opponents to sling at me."

"Your *clique* got a man canned, probably ruined his chance of being hired by any other school. And I'll bet you didn't stop with ruining one man—not to mention the other incident. And here you are climbing the golden ladder. Your old friends, Avery, are they doing as well?"

"The group broke up after . . ."

"After that boy's suicide."

The Mayor grimaced and stole a glance at his bodyguard. "All right, I'll give you the names. They won't do any good."

Ed nodded, satisfied. He could've dug up the information on his own. Mostly he wanted to see if the Mayor would cooperate. He fished a pad and pencil from his inside pocket and handed them over.

Hesitantly, Avery opened the notebook. "Promise me the task force will investigate discreetly."

"As if I could tell the task force anything."

"I know you're not happy working with them—"

"Avery, I'm happy as a clam working with anybody can get the job done."

"But you don't trust their instincts."

"*They* don't trust instinct. They don't trust cops. They trust numbers and statistics and profiles. They're betting on The People staging the big hoopla on Memorial Day. Big media presence."

"Do you think they're wrong?"

"Probably they're right. But if this group wanted media attention, why didn't they copy the TV stations with their letters?"

"Okay, what do *you* think they want?"

"Remember that old-fashioned word 'clout'? Your college club-mates would've understood it. If we do as the letters say—resign—The People get off on strutting their power, and nobody gets hurt."

"They must realize we won't do that."

"Sure. So they follow through on their threat—take out our officers from the shadows exactly as they've done so far. Each one that goes down, public fear goes up. More pressure on us to comply with The People's orders."

"We cannot surrender to terrorists."

"I know that, and you know that. But citizens seeing Houston's finest picked off like ducks on a pond are going to panic. The families of those officers will demand to know what's being done." He stared grimly at the notebook in Avery's hands, still blank. "Finding the missing money and making an arrest in the robberies might help."

Avery's eyebrows crawled up his forehead, like this was a whole new thought. "You believe The People would back down then?"

"Not back down. But their cause would be tarnished some." He nodded at the notebook. "You going to write anything in that?"

The Mayor reluctantly jotted a name, then another.

"To tell the truth," Ed admitted, "I'm not too worried about being on that stage. The task force will throw up a barrier around this park. It'll look like part of the festive doodads but force everyone to enter at one of four points. With your stage draped on three sides, a marksman outside the park would need to be stationed on the open side to get a clear shot. They'll stake out parking garages and buildings with visibility. Monday morning, we'll station men with scanners at the entrances. A shooter will have a tough time getting close, but those metal detectors aren't foolproof—"

"Can't we use the kind they have at airports?"

"Not if you want to clear anybody through in time to hear your speech. Somebody comes in with a big silver belt buckle, the thing goes off. A pocketful of change, the thing goes off. Woman with big metal earrings—"

"Okay, I get it."

The Mayor hadn't met Ed's eyes since he'd started writing. And he'd still put only two names in the notebook. Was his memory failing? Or was he holding out after all?

With a bleak sigh, Ed continued. "What I'm more worried about than stepping up on that stage Monday is stepping out my front door. The People's thirty-six-hour deadline runs out tomorrow night."

Chapter Fifty-two

Ryan emerged from behind the HAZARDOUS WASTE sign on his door wearing his best summer duds, socks with sneakers, precisely parted hair, and a weak facsimile of his usual infectious grin.

"Hey, slick. Who stole my nephew?"

He ducked his head, the grin sliding to a grimace. "Mom said to dress up."

Yeah, and you just happened *to pick the shirt I bought. Nice try, kid.* But Dixie hooked an arm around his neck and ruffled his hair.

"Maybe we should stop in the garage, see if your dad's got a big stick I can use to keep the girls away."

Ryan turned a satisfying shade of pink and squeezed out of her hold to lope ahead. "I told Mom we'd eat at the movie. Is that okay?"

"Depends on whether I decide to torture you."

His shoulders rolled forward, head ducked low.

"No, Ryan, I didn't forget why we called this movie meeting," Dixie muttered. Earlier, she had driven past the cemetery just as the burial ceremony finished. A sea of blue uniforms surrounded the grave and clustered around a lithe blonde with a baby. Had to be Ann Harris. It was not a good time to catch the young widow alone, so once again Dixie squeaked out of a difficult Q&A. Now here she was about to start one that promised to be equally difficult. As Ryan held the door for her, she yelled toward the TV sounds, "Amy, Carl—we're gone."

Back behind the Mustang's wheel and a string of taillights, she realized how much she loathed getting into a conversation with Ryan about smut. Was she being a priggish old-maid aunt? She lowered the volume on the radio, which he had promptly tuned to his favorite rap station. Get it over with now and maybe they could enjoy the film.

"Where did you hide those pictures so your mother won't stumble across them, as I did?" she asked.

"In my lockbox. She wouldn't open it."

No. Amy and Carl both believed a child needed privacy. Dixie had, too, until now. Now she wasn't sure whether walking into his room when she did had been an invasion of his space or a nudge from the Child God that kids need a watchful eye around to keep them out of trouble.

"Why do you want those pictures?" *Duh! Great start.* "You're curious — okay, I get that part. What they show in school about sex, the female body, it's all clinical and dull and . . . and you're growing up . . . but, Ryan, what I saw in your room wasn't a *Playboy* centerfold. Those photos were as raw as they get."

"I trade them," he mumbled.

"Trade for what? Money?"

"Sometimes. Or for others, better ones. To get a whole set . . . or . . . you know." He fiddled with the door handle. "A different position." He sounded as miserable as she felt.

"Like baseball cards?"

"Sort of. Only you can't buy them, like, at a store." He kept his eyes on the handle as he clicked it back and forth.

Dixie checked the door lock.

"Not everyone can get the good ones," he mumbled.

"Don't other kids have an Internet setup?"

"Yeah, most. Some are restricted."

"And those are the kids you trade with?"

"Some. Others don't hang on the net."

"You mean some kids don't spend sixteen hours a day behind a computer?"

"I don't—"

"Never mind. Tell me why *you* can get the good dirty pictures. That *is* what you're saying, isn't it? Not everyone can, but *you* can?" Ryan was smarter than the average kid, but no genius.

He hesitated, rubbing at a spot on the window. "I have better connections."

"Connections like in . . ." She knew enough about computers to call a technician when hers jammed. "Like in how your hardware's hooked up?"

"Connections on the net. The best places."

"You mean some vendors sell better smut than others."

"Yeah . . ." He shrugged.

"Yeah, *what?* Help me here, kid, or we'll turn around and talk to you-know-who."

"Some sites are harder to get to. Restrictions and stuff."

"But you figured out how to get past the restrictions?"

Another hesitation. Holding back? Or simply embarrassed to talk about this with a grown-up?

"I . . . you need a credit card."

"You said you weren't using your parents' cards. Ryan, you're not using a stolen card number, are you?"

"No!"

"Then dammit, how?" Great. Yell at the kid, that'll make him talk.

He stared at his knees. "I have a . . . friend."

A chill lodged at the base of Dixie's spine: *Some mofo out there sold my kid shit.* A gang connection? Was porno replacing drugs?

With the cineplex only two blocks away, Dixie turned in the wrong direction to keep the conversation going.

"Where did you meet this friend?" she asked casually.

"A chat room. On-line."

"So . . . then what? You *chat*? Tell him the pictures you want. He finds them, sends them to you?"

Ryan nodded, shooting a quick glance at the dash clock.

"What are you not telling me? And don't think I'll cut your inquisition short because the movie's about to start, I haven't pounded any toothpicks under your fingernails yet."

He heaved a big disgruntled sigh.

"Cut the crap. Talk to me."

"He doesn't have to *find* the pictures. I can do that. He *buys* them."

"So your friend is the one using his parents' credit. Or a stolen card number."

"I don't know. I don't think so."

The chill crawled a little higher up Dixie's back.

"How old is your friend?"

"I don't know."

"Is he an adult?"

"We never talked about that."

"What do you talk about?"

"Just what's going on . . . and stuff."

"Girl stuff?"

"Sometimes. Not too much."

"Does he know a lot about girls?"

"I guess."

"What else do you talk about?"

"Doing stuff. What I'm doing, what he's doing. Mostly he goes places on his dirt bike."

"Where?" Dixie was ready to choke the answers out of him.

"Parks . . . fishing, camping out . . . sometimes towns."

So this "friend" was a lot older than twelve. "Are these towns nearby?"

"Austin, Roundtop. Around there."

A three-hour drive. Take the kid for a ride on your nifty dirt bike. Head out of town—what's the little imp to do about it? Scream over the engine roar? Jump off?

"Has he ever suggested you meet in person?"

"He said maybe he'd be in Houston sometime. What's wrong with that?" Ryan seemed genuinely puzzled at the turn her questions had taken.

Nearing the cineplex again, she veered down a side street.

"Ryan, if this guy's old enough to ride a motorbike and go wherever he wants, why would he hang out with someone your age instead of other adults?"

"He doesn't know how old I am."

Sure, kid. "Doesn't he wonder why you don't buy your own dirty pictures?"

"He never asked."

"Has he ever asked you to pay him back, or does he just give you this stuff?"

"He said we'd work it out someday."

Oh, shit! "How?"

"He might need something, and maybe I could help him out."

Right, a child helping an adult. "I want you to give me this man's name and E-mail address."

"What for?"

"So I can talk to him."

Ryan stared at his knees. He shook his head. "You'll get him in trouble."

"If he hasn't done anything wrong, how could he be in trouble?"

"Then why do you need to talk to him?"

"I need to know why he's so generous."

"That's not fair. He's a friend, and you just want to hassle him."

Dixie pulled into the parking lot and slid into a space. Ryan's stubborn streak always reminded her of Barney, unmovable when he dug in his heels. Except for checking out his on-line buddy, she might as well let the kid off the hook. He'd reached that age between childhood and adulthood where all the forbidden knowledge would be explored. And who was she to know what sort of smut a twelve-year-old boy could view without brain warp?

"I think you should show those photographs to your father."

He finally looked at her, his face tight with stubborn defeat. "Awwww . . . Aunt Dix! Can't we keep this between us?"

"You think Carl's never seen pictures like that?" *Maybe not recently. And not so graphically enhanced by electronics.*

"I don't know, but . . ."

"Are you embarrassed to show him?"

"Yeah . . ."

"But not too embarrassed to show your friends?"

"That's different."

"What's different about it? You're both guys. Your father was twelve once." *Probably not until he was chronologically fifteen or sixteen. Or maybe thirty.*

"Okay, what if I tear up the stuff and throw it away?"

"Your whole collection?"

He gave a halfhearted nod.

"You can always get more where those came from," Dixie said. "No, I think your father needs to know what's replaced baseball cards. You decide how to break it to him. All I want is the name of your friend with the credit card and dirt bike."

Ryan shook his head.

"Ryan, this man could be dangerous. You're smart enough to know that. You've heard about chicken hawks. We've talked about it—men who like kids for sex. They used to lure kids like you into back alleys. Now they hang out on the Internet."

"He's not like that."

"How do you know?"

"He's just a guy. A great guy."

"If he's so great, he'll realize you're being smart. If he's so great, he won't mind talking to your worried aunt."

Ryan remained hunkered into himself, silent.

"An E-mail address, what does that tell me, anyway? It's not like I can drive to it."

"You'd find a way."

Chapter Fifty-three

Dixie dropped off Ryan and dialed Belle's home number. The lawyer had been in court and unreachable all day.

"I feel sleazy checking out cops, Ric. They were the *victims*, and their families don't deserve to be harassed."

"Is this your way of telling me you haven't turned up any new suspects?"

"Unless you consider a juvenile gang-related shooting accident in Officer Harris' past."

"What happened to all your DA and HPD connections?"

"They think I've switched sides. Even so, in any ordinary case I could find someone willing to chat. Emotions are high on this one—and this time we are the enemy."

Belle was silent. Dixie could hear voices in the background. Real voices, not TV. Saturday night at home. In Belle's case, it meant a husband and whichever of their three teenage children had stayed in. Frequently, the Richardses entertained friends and associates. Occasionally, they invited Dixie. Headed toward an empty house, Dixie almost wished she'd been invited tonight.

"Marty may not be HPD's only suspect any longer," Belle said. "I don't have anything concrete, but there's a buzz going around about some letters, threats— a terrorist group claiming assassination responsibility."

"Well, hallelujah. I think." *Could that fit with the gang symbol drawings Marty grabbed from Ted Tally's house?* "Who started this buzz?"

"Blackmon heard it at the Mayor's office. The task force checked out the site today for the Memorial Day bash, and Blackmon heard them talking afterward."

"Having a senior partner on the Mayor's committee seems to be more useful than hiring yours truly. Maybe you should crown Blackmon your chief investigator."

"I'm not letting you off that easy. You keep Marty buttoned down tight. In case the sniper does strike again, I want our boy smelling as innocent as a newborn babe."

"Why did this become my responsibility, Ric?"

"Because you begged me to take his case."

"Begged? Your firm didn't mind taking Marty's money for civil work."

"Okay. How about, you and Marty Pine go way back, and when it comes to friendship you couldn't be more loyal if you had four legs and a cold nose."

"Am I hearing things or did you just call me a dog?"

"Maybe I need to work on that metaphor a bit."

"Next time I want to feel really shitty about myself, I'll know who to ring up." Dixie powered the cell phone off. She didn't want to hear any more party sounds. Maybe she should drive over to Club Cato for a few drinks. Meanstreak's music might cheer her up.

Almost instantly her cell phone rang.

"Flannigan," she snapped.

"What lonely road are you traveling tonight, lady?"

"Slim Jim?" Dixie grinned. McGrue had such a solemn disposition, Dixie usually felt cheery by contrast. "Got something for me?"

"Got some answers. Don't know what use they'll be."

"You just moved to the top of my Christmas list."

"This is May. Could be dead by Christmas. Let's think of a way to pay off your debt sooner. I phoned a retired officer in Dallas who knew the Harris family, an old gossip, but a reliable gossip. Harris served some juvie time for drugs."

"Using or dealing?"

"Both, if my friend's memory serves. You know those records are sealed. Seems Harris ran with a nasty gang as a youngster."

Pearly must've thought this information would discredit Art's law enforcement record and jeopardize any benefits the widow had coming.

"He cleaned up his act, though," Dixie said. "Couldn't've been the first young offender to discover the safer side of law provided the danger he craved without the consequences."

"There's more." Jim's voice rasped over static—must be moving out of cell range. "An accident involving a handgun. One of the gang members died."

"Was Harris charged?"

"No. But the gun came from his mother's closet."

"Did another gang member go to jail for the crime? If so, he might be paroled now."

"Can't say. Could be I'll find a bailiff who remembers the case. Might even find him before Christmas."

Either he signed off or the static totally swallowed McGrue's signal. The notion of Art Harris being killed to settle an old score had merit. Maybe the Granny Bandit connection was coincidental, at first, and once the idea caught fire, the shooter killed Ted to stoke the coals. The idea needed following up, but no judge would open sealed juvie records and allow Dixie to snoop.

She drove home, flipped on every light in the house, turned on rock music, and poured a glass of jug wine. *White zinfandel, whoopee.* Scanning the cable stations for a good movie, she found a rerun of *Lethal Weapon*, which had already started. *Enchanted April* she wouldn't mind seeing again. An hour till start time. She tossed the guide aside, looked up Ben Rashly's home number in her pocket directory, and sipping her wine, punched it in one-handed.

"What's this I hear about a terrorist group, Rash? And threat letters?"

"What the hell do you know about any letters?"

"I know that a terrorist group taking responsibility lets my friend Marty off the hook for two murders."

"Like hell. He's as deep in it as ever." But a note in Rashly's voice said he wasn't convinced.

"He can't be, Rash. Marty didn't kill those cops."

He huffed in her ear. "You say you knew Pine growing up?"

"Through high school. Then we saw each other on most holidays."

"What about college?"

Dixie's call button lit up. She let it roll to voice mail, and noticed messages already stored.

"We didn't attend the same school, if that's what you mean."

"He ever mention a gang or social club he belonged to?"

"You mean a fraternity?"

"Any kind of club, might've called themselves The People."

Rashly was fishing. The letter "P" on the symbol Ted had sketched flashed in her mind.

"I don't remember any group like that, but Marty and I didn't see each other often during college. And that's nearly twenty years ago—what's the connection?"

"Hell, Flannigan. Guess we'll have to ask your friend." He banged the phone down.

Dixie retrieved her messages. Terrence Jackson had phoned, inviting her to join the Fortyniners tonight at a theater. Still trolling for members, she figured. The play sounded vastly more interesting than spending the night alone, but Dixie could never shower, dress, and drive to downtown Houston before curtain.

Kitchi, the facial technician at Artistry Spa, had also extended an invitation. "Lonnie wants you to have a complimentary seaweed body wrap and herbal bath on your next visit." She left a "preferred customer" phone number. Dixie jotted it down as Kitchi's voice continued. "Sorry I can't attend Edna's send-off party tomorrow, dear. But Lonnie will be there."

The last message, the one that rolled while Dixie was talking to Rash, came from Amy.

"The funeral director complained about the short notice, but I convinced him to have a viewing tomorrow. Two o'clock." She gave the address. "Marty won't speak to me, Dixie. The party's at three, our house. I invited all those strange names on the phone list you gave me."

Dixie returned Jackson's call, got his machine, and told it, "I arrived home too late to accept your invitation. Sorry I missed you." She really *was* sorry. B.P.— before Parker—she'd never been a party animal, but neither did she spend Saturday nights moping around home. "I hope to see you at Edna Pine's party tomorrow," she finished. The other two calls didn't require a response, so she peeled off her clothes, poured a second glass of white zinfandel, and stood under a hot shower—wishing it were a "herbal bath"—until her toes wrinkled.

The phone rang again. *One visit to a singles club and my voice mail goes into overtime.* With her hair full of shampoo, she let it ring. Only after the recommended three-minute rinse did she step out, pad to the kitchen, and retrieve the message.

Parker sounded cheery. "Guess it's too early for the great detective to be at home. Thought I'd bring over a pizza. Instead, I'll catch some late waves, find a hamburger shack down the beach, and see you tomorrow at Amy's."

Shit. She returned the call, but Parker had already gone, and she hung up without leaving a message. If she wasn't depressed before, she was damned depressed now.

She picked up the envelope of gang symbol drawings she'd left on the counter and carried them with her to the bedroom. In the closet, she found the lavender tote bag from Artistry Spa filled with creams and lotions. She'd bought everything Lonnie and Kitchi recommended that day. When she opened the tote, a terrific scent enveloped her. Maybe aromatherapy would lift her out of the doldrums. She shoved a padded bench up to the dresser, and sat down with her goodie bag.

The first bottle was labeled "Ylang-Ylang," the scent that permeated Terrence Jackson's office. Exotic, sexy, but not especially uplifting. She set the bottle aside. Cucumber masque. Dixie opened the jar and spread a layer across her cheek. Immediately, the scent of fresh cucumbers carried her back to the spa, where horse-faced Kitchi slathered her face while Lonnie Gray snipped her hair. That had been fun, and she'd emerged feeling exquisitely feminine. Maybe a bit of pampering at times wasn't too terribly self-indulgent. Or maybe self-indulgence wasn't as loathsome as she'd always thought.

With her face covered in the fragrant green goop, she studied Ted's gang symbols. She recognized the pitchfork pointed downward, a symbol of disrespect to gangs with allegiance to the Folks Nation, and 187, the California penal code for murder. The three-pointed crown, for the Folks Nation, had "B.G.D." under it for Black Gangster Disciples. The five-pointed star, for the People Nation, and also the Latin Kings, was rendered in their colors, black and gold. "KINGS" lettered backward, a sign of disrespect, drawn beneath a five-pointed star being blown up, could mean conflict between the gangs.

Janet Easton had said Art Harris wanted to join the gang task force in his area. Ted had been sketching gang graffiti. His sketches included a triangle in red and blue drawn around a gold "P." And Rashly had asked whether Marty was involved with a group called The People. Interesting.

Rummaging an emery board from her Artistry Spa bag, she used it to smooth the ends of her nails. She didn't know a lot about gangs, but she thought spray-painting "187" on cop cars would be more their style than sending a threat letter.

Examining her nails, she decided they had lost a bit of their shine. She found a bottle of clear polish and spread a coat over her thumbnail. Much better.

Now she needed a calendar.

She found one in her desk, brought it back, and made some notes. On Wednesday of the previous week, an unknown female robbed the Houston branch of Texas Citizens and got away clean. Then on Monday afternoon Lucy Ames robbed the Webster branch and was killed. On Tuesday morning, after robbing the Richmond branch, Edna was also killed. Since then, no more robberies.

Thursday morning—Art Harris, murdered. Friday afternoon—Ted Tally, murdered. Two for two.

If the shooter's rationale was "an eye for an eye," the spree might be ended. Also, if the shooter actually murdered Art or Ted for personal reasons, and killed the other to make the murders appear linked to the robberies, the spree might be ended. In either case, Marty remained a suspect. But as disloyal as it might be, Dixie would rather have that than another dead officer.

How much did she truly know about the adult Marty Pine? His confession to being gay hadn't shocked her. It fit with her vague feelings about his association with Derry Hager. Yet Marty had kept his secret for all this time, and he wasn't being totally forthcoming even now.

When she'd covered all but one nail with clear polish, the phone rang. *Naturally.* Parker's number appeared in the caller ID window. She snatched up the receiver carefully, with two fingers.

"Hi. How were the waves?"

"Flat. How's the snoop business?"

"Frustrating. But I'm learning how Edna managed her amazing transformation, and maybe some of the reasons for it. I wish I'd spent more time with her after Bill died."

"To make up for the loss of her husband? You're not equipped."

"I could've knocked on her door occasionally."

"Did she ever knock on *your* door and say, 'Dixie, let's talk'?"

"Okay, I get the point, Parker. What are you doing after the party tomorrow?"

"Showing a forty-six-footer to a couple of NASA engineers. Did you need me to help?"

"No." *I need you, but not for snooping.* "With HPD and two federal agencies involved, what made me think I could do better?"

"Madam, there are more pleasant things to do than beat yourself up."

"Sounds like a quote. Shakespeare?"

"Muhammad Ali. Paraphrased."

"A true poet."

"Are you bringing Mud to the party tomorrow?"

"You're kidding, right?"

"He liked Edna. And he'd enjoy going with me to show this boat. My good buddy's a seasoned sailor now."

Mud had spent a week with Parker while Dixie chased a skip over half of Texas. Was this Parker's way of admitting he led a goddamn lonely life, too?

"Okay, I'll ask Mud if he wants to go to the party."

They hung up a few moments later. Dixie returned to the bedroom and tried to recapture her interest in pampering herself. The masque had hardened past its setting time. She soaked it off with a wet washcloth. Seemed better than a chisel. Then she oozed lotion over her skin and sprayed a fragrance designed to "quiet your chattering inner critic and instill a sense of well-being." She rubbed peppermint foot lotion around her toes, over her rough heels. The fragrances and creams were nice, but they'd sure felt more elegant when another person's hands smoothed them on. Maybe that's why Edna's jars and bottles remained nearly full.

With nothing more she could rub or spray on her body, Dixie applied conditioners to her hair and turned on the dryer. Using an Artistry Spa brush, she recaptured her new hairstyle almost as Lonnie'd done it. No one around to notice, but it looked pretty damn fine, she thought.

It'd be dumb to apply the other items in the bag—foundation, lipstick, eye shadow—then go to bed. Alone.

Tossing the jars back in the tote bag, she found the receipt from her purchases. Ouch! She'd spent enough on this junk to feed a third-world family for a year. Two years.

Why hadn't the cost of those products registered when she bought them? She remembered the day as a credit card blowout, but had felt no qualms about buying every item Lonnie recommended—and usually she resented any money squandered on unnecessary girlie gizmos. Of course, she'd imbibed several mimosas and felt deliciously decadent before checkout time. No wonder Lonnie Gray could afford three mortgages and two luxury automobiles.

Terrence Jackson wouldn't go broke anytime soon, either. Nor would Vernice Urich.

Dixie glanced at the clock, then at the four names she'd jotted down from Vernice's records: LeRoy Haines, Beatrice French, Dolly Mae Aichison, Rose Yenik. She found all of them in the phone directory. When she dialed LeRoy, his sister answered.

"My brother is in a nursing home. May I help you?"

"I'm so sorry about LeRoy. How long has he been ill?"

"Oh, awhile, now. More than a year."

Yet Vernice Urich received weekly ACH payments from his account. Dixie dialed Beatrice French, listed at the address noted in her financials. The number had been disconnected.

Only five Aichisons listed. Dixie started at the top. On the third, a male voice informed her, "My mother's bedridden. Tell me your name again."

"Flannigan, but I don't know Dolly Mae. I'm calling for Vernice Urich, a psychologist who treated your mother before her infirmity."

"I remember Mother speaking of her." All suspicion fell from the man's voice. "I'm afraid I wasn't in town during those days, but Dr. Urich helped Mother through a bad patch after Dad died."

"Do you receive a periodic accounting for the balance owed?"

"I wasn't aware of any balance."

By the time Dixie ended the conversation, Dolly Mae's son intended to request a full audit of his mother's accounts. Dixie tried the final number.

"Hello?" A woman's voice.

"Rose Yenik?"

"Yes, this is Rose."

Dixie gave her name. "Ms. Yenik, I consulted with Vernice Urich this week. I believe you're also her patient."

"Oh, yes. I enjoyed Vernice very much. I hope she's well."

"How long since you saw her?"

"Why, my goodness. Six months, I suppose. Time moves like a snail, doesn't it?"

For some, perhaps. "Did you feel you received adequate service for the large balance still owed?"

Silence, and then, "Vernice and I explored many interesting ideas, and I received full value for my dollar. But you're mistaken about any balance due. I paid every week, regular as clockwork."

"By check?"

"Oh, no. My bank handled the payments directly. By computer."

. . . those damn computers. Once they start messing with your money, watch out. Carl had hit it on the nose that time. How many more of Vernice's patients continued paying long after treatment ended? For the financially uninformed, like

Dixie, who loathed balancing a checkbook, this sort of fraud could go unde-
tected for years. And Dixie hadn't any idea how to untangle this sort of crime.
She urged Rose Yenik to contact her bank about the ACH transfers.

At least Vernice's patients considered their money well spent—the part they
knew about, anyway. What had Parker said? *The only difference between a good
salesperson and a con artist is the value of the product.* Paraphrased.

Looking back on her day at Artistry Spa, Dixie didn't begrudge the expense.
She'd enjoyed being pampered for four hours—the sauna, the massage, Kitchi's
soothing hands and motherly suggestions to "nurture her skin as well as her soul."
Lonnie's endless flattery.

They hadn't seemed false at the time, but rather funny and sweet. Perhaps
Dixie didn't have the daintiest nose in the world, or the longest legs, or the sexiest
mouth. Her eyebrows were too straight and her fingers too short. But she *did* have
good skin. And her hair *was* rather luxurious. Lonnie had focused on her positive
attributes and ignored or downplayed the negatives. He didn't need to lie to his
clients to make them feel good and keep them returning.

And what the hell, Dixie'd earned the damn money. Better to blow it on a good
time than leave it in a bank for someone to swipe.

Instead of pulling on her usual T-shirt and cotton underwear, she found a pair
of yellow silk pajamas, a birthday present from Amy. Settled in front of the television with milk and Oreos, she tuned in *Enchanted April.*

The phone rang. This time the caller ID window remained blank.

"Hello?"

"Dixie Flannigan?" The male voice sounded familiar.

"Yes."

"Mike Tesche. Your number's on the volunteer list at the women's center.
Hope you don't mind."

"No. What's up, Mike?"

"At the moment, nothing. In fact, I'm enjoying the first free evening I've had
in a while . . ."

Why did "free" sound so much better than "alone"?

". . . but tomorrow's a full day for me—starting two new YMCA classes. I expressed my regrets to your sister when she called, and I wanted to tell you personally how sorry I am to miss Edna's party. I think it's a terrific idea."

Dixie agreed. "Thoughtful of you to call."

"After you kick up your heels at the party, remember our invitation to join the
Sundown Ceremony tomorrow."

*While Parker was showing his boat . . . inviting Mud along, but not her. A sun-
down whatever-the-hell sounded great.* She scanned the counter for the invitation. "Was that *this* Sunday?"

"Yes, and don't worry if you've lost the directions. I'll fax you the map."

"Tell me again, what's a Sundown Ceremony?"

"Not as mysterious as it may sound. My advanced students get together for fellowship, conversation, modest refreshments, and to renew their commitments."

"Commitments to what?"

"Whatever they're committed to — exercise, diet, health, emotional well-being. My commitment is to stay in touch. You know how sometimes we think about making a call, and we don't, and months later we wish we had but it's too late? I don't want that to happen with you. You'll meet some interesting people. And the food's good."

"How many people?" Dixie didn't enjoy crowds.

"Twelve, counting you."

Enough to find at least one common interest, and not so many she'd feel claustrophobic. "What do I wear?"

"Anything casual and comfortable. We start with a few stretches and some meditation."

"Is this going to be a workout?"

He chuckled. "Nothing strenuous, I promise. Twenty minutes of easy movement to release the day's tension."

Actually, it sounded good. She could use a few squats and kicks right now. Or twenty minutes of hard sex.

"Do I have to answer tonight?"

His hesitation stretched until she wondered if he was still there, then he replied, "A 'yes' now would be terrific. And if you find later that you can't make it, we'll only need an hour's notice to find another twelfth."

The mellow tones of Mike's voice bounced against her ribs like the soft beat of bongo drums. Why not be a "twelfth"? She gave Mike her fax number, a qualified "yes," and listened to his voice some more as he described the difference between his men's and women's workouts.

When she finally cradled the phone, Dixie felt better than she had all evening. Watching the movie, she painted that final nail, reviewed Ted Tally's drawings, and decided for once not to follow her instincts.

Keep your nose out of this, said the cautionary voice in her head — which sounded a whole lot like Rashly's, at the moment. *You'll piss off the entire cop community.*

Nevertheless, she intended to finish the job she'd started that day. She might squirm at questioning the bereaved families of police officers, but if the murders were related to Art Harris or Ted Tally, rather than the Granny Bandit robberies, then somebody had to do it.

Chapter Fifty-four

Sunday

Officer Theodore Tally is survived by his mother Barbara and his brother Raymond.
The obituary didn't provide an address, but the B. Tally listed in the phone book
lived close enough to young Ted that Dixie took a chance. After her usual brief
Sunday visit to Carla Jean in the nursing home, she'd already struck out again
with Ann Harris. No answer to her knock. No car visible through the garage
window.

A Cyclone fence surrounded a rather plain white shingle house at the Tally address. In the yard, an enormous live oak tree prevented grass from growing, and
the St. Augustine that did grow could use a mowing, but none of that mattered
with such a rich tapestry of greens to enjoy—ivy, monkey grass, and other ground
cover.

When Dixie knocked, a woman with gray hair and steady gray eyes answered
the door. She looked twig-brittle and much smaller than in the photo on Ted's
bookshelf.

"Mrs. Tally?" Behind the woman, Dixie recognized the couple who had surprised her and Marty at Ted's house. "I'm Dixie Flannigan. I apologize for
calling at a difficult time, but I—"

"She's a bounty hunter," said the man. Officer Raymond Tally had his brother's
good looks, with or without the uniform. He moved to stand behind his mother.
"I've heard your name around the station. You turned in Jimmy Voller last week."

From his face and tone of voice, Dixie figured a bounty hunter was a step up
from a two-headed toad, but he'd like to take a good look at the toad before he
squashed it.

"Would you mind if I came in for a few minutes?"

"What for?"

"Ray! Mind your manners." Tiny Barbara Tally gave her towering son a look that sent him back a step. "Come on in, Ms. Flannigan."

"Thank you. I promise not to take much of your time." Amy expected her at Edna's viewing in less than an hour.

"That's all right," Barbara assured her. "Ray, move that sweater so the lady can sit down. Ms. Flannigan, this is my daughter-in-law Catherine, and my son Raymond."

In her panic to escape the previous day, Dixie hadn't noticed the woman at Ted's house was pregnant—several months along and as clear-skinned gorgeous as pregnant women are expected to be. Beneath a smooth cap of dark auburn hair, narrow brown eyes gazed at Dixie with interest. She sat at a bar that separated the compact living area from the kitchen. Dixie nodded a greeting as Barbara continued speaking.

"Bounty hunters find people, if I'm not mistaken. Criminals. Do you intend to find my son's murderer?"

"Not without a bounty," Ray said. "And I haven't heard of any reward being offered." He smiled at Dixie without a trace of humor. "Or is that why you're here?"

"No." Dixie returned his hard smile. "This is one killer we all want to take off the streets."

"Then keep out of the way. Let people who know what they're doing get the job done."

"Ray Tally! You will not speak impolitely to a guest in my home. I want to hear what the lady has to say."

"Actually, all I have are questions, Mrs. Tally. Ted and Art Harris were both interested in local gang activity. I'm wondering if their killer might have used the robberies as a blind, to draw suspicion away from personal motivation."

"The task force will investigate that possibility," Ray insisted.

"And if so," Dixie continued, ignoring him, "could the motive be related to a gang or a gang member they'd singled out?"

Ray's hard gaze turned thoughtful.

Barbara focused a challenging stare at her son. "Will you tell her, or will I?"

He threw out his hands. "Go ahead, Ma. You've got the floor."

"Then make yourself useful. Bring us a cold drink. Ms. Flannigan, we have Dr Pepper, orange soda, and iced tea, all sugar-free. Which would you like?"

"Whichever you're having will be fine."

"We didn't always live in this lovely neighborhood," Barbara said. "My sons grew up in my husband's family home. When their grandparents built the house, they were surrounded by good people. But things changed. The good people moved away, or died, and trash moved in. Don't take that as an economic slur, or a racial, or religious, or any other kind of slur. When I say trash, I mean trash.

Nasty, hateful, wicked trash. My husband worked long hours, but he always had time for his sons. That wasn't true of other fathers. Single mothers lived all around us, most of them on drugs."

Ray returned with their drinks, diet orange.

"Thanks, Ray." His mother smiled up at him.

"You bet."

Dixie liked the look that passed between them, full of humor and love and respect. "Thank you," she told him.

Barbara took a long pull on the soda before continuing her story.

"Ted's best friend was being harassed by a bunch of young bucks who thought the world ought to bow down and lick their sneakers. I don't know exactly what happened—something to do with money the boy refused to give up. Ted and Peter—that was the boy's name—walked home from school after staying late for Peter's band practice. Seven boys grabbed them, pulled them back behind a fence. Ted got bruised up good for fighting them, but it wasn't him they were after. They took Peter's saxophone for the money they said he owed, but that wasn't enough. They kicked and punched the boy until he couldn't move. Spray-painted his face red. And then they stabbed him. All the while, they're holding Ted and forcing him to watch it. When they finally ran off, Ted was afraid to leave his friend and find help, so he picked the boy up and *carried* him the three blocks home. Peter was dead before they got there."

Barbara had told the whole story with those steady gray eyes aimed straight at Dixie.

"I suppose you could say Ted was strong on bringing down gangs and terrorists," Ray added.

"Strong, yeah," his wife put in. "I saw him stop a kid once for wearing a blue bandanna around his ankle. Ted drove him home, ripped the bandanna in half, gave it to the kid's father, and explained for nearly an hour what the gang colors and hand signs mean."

"Do you know of any specific groups Ted tightened down on?" Dixie asked. "Groups who had the means to retaliate with a high-powered rifle at nearly five hundred yards?"

"Not something we talked about," Ray said.

"When I spend time with my sons," Barbara added, "it's family time. I tell them, leave work outside the door."

"I suppose that's all I have, then." Dixie rose. "I appreciate your time and . . . your willingness to talk."

"We're the ones to thank you," Barbara told her. "Maybe you'll find my son's killer, maybe you won't. But the more good people like you who're looking, the harder for that demon to hide."

As Dixie said her good-byes, she thought of one more question, but hesitated. She saw Ray notice the hesitation.

"I need to stretch my legs," he told his wife. "Think I'll walk Ms. Flannigan to her car."

Outside, Dixie said, "I'm familiar with most of the gang symbols. But one I haven't seen before. A red triangle on a blue background, with a gold letter 'P' in the center."

Ray shook his head. "Ted had some sketches. Probably the same ones you stole from his house."

Dixie could've lied, but Ray's eyes said he wasn't guessing. He knew. She kept silent.

"I don't know what you're up to," Ray told her. "What I've heard about you is you're fair and you're good. So I'm taking a chance on you. But don't come here again. Don't go to my brother's house again. And if you step in the middle and screw up the official investigation, I'll fuck you over until you won't see another bounty contract in this town."

Chapter Fifty-five

"I didn't tell the newspapers," Amy wailed when Dixie met her inside the funeral home. "No guests, just as Edna requested. The funeral director *swears* he didn't tell them. Nothing's working out!"

Seeing the desperate look in her sister's eyes as she glanced at Marty, Dixie knew the strangers trailing past the casket weren't the worst of her problems. She firmly closed the viewing-room door and stood alongside to open it for strays to leave until only her family remained.

"Our turn," she told them.

Marty hung back. "You all go ahead. I'll be along . . . after a minute."

"He won't," Amy whispered. "I've had to kick him here all the way."

"It's all right." Dixie waved her sister toward the dais and put a hand on Marty's arm.

He jerked it away.

"What good have you been?" he demanded. "I thought you'd help. Did you find out why she did this? Did you find her journal? Here we are, about to turn her into ashes. Stuff her in a jar. Did you find *anything*? What *good* were you?"

Oh. So now your mother's important again?

"Marty, I've learned plenty about how your mother spent her time these last few months, but it doesn't tell us why this happened." She glanced at Ryan, looking all grown-up in his blue suit, nearly as tall as his dad, but maybe not grown-up enough to hear this. Then again, if he'd decided to be adult enough to trade in cyberporn, how could a dose of hard, honest facts hurt him?

"Your mother was grieving," Dixie continued. "As you're grieving now. And she was trying to deal with it."

"By killing herself?"

"We don't know—"

"Give me a break. I read the papers. Mom and that Ames woman—now *that's* who you ought to be investigating—cooked up this whole charade to trick the cops into blowing them away. Suicide in a blaze of headlines. The insurance pays off—"

"Did it occur to you that maybe the insurance company dreamed up that story? They haven't sent a check, have they?"

"Why else would she pull such a harebrained stunt? She *couldn't* believe she'd escape with the money. A bank isn't dumb enough to let an old woman hold them up and ride off a winner. They have alarms. They have marked bills and . . . and . . . and . . . all kinds of tricks. How could she think they wouldn't catch her? Was this some kind of . . . of . . . of last-ditch thrill? Or was she . . . punishing me . . . for *disappointing* her?" His face twisted.

Dixie put her arms around him.

"She *hated* me, Dixie. She hated me for . . . being who I am and . . . for killing Dad—"

"She didn't hate you, Marty. She was confused, maybe, and incredibly lonely. But nothing I've learned leads me to believe she blamed you for the way her life turned out."

"She called me. The night before she . . ."

"*Monday* night?" Dixie pulled away to look at him. "The day before the robbery?"

He nodded.

"What did she say?"

"I . . . wasn't there. I came home late. And the next day I kept planning to call her back later. And then the . . . the cops phoned, said she—" He jerked a handkerchief from his pocket and blew into it.

Was this the guilt he'd been dragging around all week? "Marty, what did her message say?"

"Nothing, I mean . . . nothing that helps. She said—" He tightened his lips. "She said, 'I understand now, son. And I love you.' Then she said, 'Marty, your father loved you, too.' "

Dixie patted his arm. She'd been damned pissed off at Marty Pine the past two days while his life fell apart around him.

"Come on," she told him. "We need to do this."

He walked beside her to the dais.

The viewing casket presented itself well, with vases of flowers at each end, spring flowers, the kind Edna grew in her own garden.

Dixie gently pushed Marty ahead of her. Carl and Amy had already moved on, but Ryan still lingered. He plucked a bearded iris from one of the vases and placed it at Edna's shoulder on the white satin quilting. A collage of images raced through Dixie's head—campfires, pecan trees, peanut-butter cookies—but the one that stuck was Aunt Edna's proud smile the night of the senior prom, as her handsome son pinned a pink rose from her own garden around Dixie's wrist.

After a brief hesitation, Marty placed his hand over his mother's.

"If my mom died," Ryan said softly, "I'd miss her a lot. And we'd both miss Dad if he died, but I think maybe they'd miss each other most. Mom and Dad don't know how to be without each other."

"Yes," Marty said after a moment. "I guess that's right."

When he moved on and Dixie took his place, she couldn't help comparing this woman to the one she'd seen under similar circumstances only days earlier. Both had clear, translucent skin and a firmness to their flesh that even death hadn't stolen.

"Sleep well, Edna," Dixie whispered.

When she touched the still hand, a coin rolled from beneath it. She picked it up. Not a coin. A brass disk, engraved with three words:

WE THE PEOPLE.

Chapter Fifty-six

Jean Gibson served her husband a perfect martini in the Waterford crystal, with two olives, chilled precisely the way he liked it. Her own glass contained olives, a touch of vermouth, and Evian water.

"Gib, there will be plenty of time before the next election to smooth over any doubts the voters may have." She spoke carefully, logically. "You attended the officers' funerals. You made a moving statement. Why stay here now?"

"I believe Wanamaker may resign."

That stopped her. "Because of the letters?" The Chief of Police had always struck her as something of a coward. But Ed would never get another important position *anywhere* if he quit now. "What makes you think he'll resign?"

"Banning and Wanamaker spent an hour with the task force today. Afterward, work slowed down on preparations for Banning's Memorial Day presentation."

"You think he'll call it off?" Then there'd be no reason she and Gib couldn't leave town for a while.

Jean stared distractedly at the olives in her glass. After the Mayor's commemoration to Wanamaker and the dead cops tomorrow, Gib planned to set the press straight, to enumerate the stupid mistakes the police department had made since the Chief's appointment and explain the sorry state their city government was really in. But with the commemoration canceled . . .

Gib chuckled. "You can bet Wanamaker's shaking in his shoes about climbing on that platform. By tomorrow the sniper's thirty-six hours will have long run out."

Jean didn't exactly blame the Chief for being fearful. She feared for Gib. Her Gib was determined to call the sniper's bluff, but she wouldn't let him.

"Thirty-six hours from the time the letter came is just before the ten o'clock news tonight. What makes you think they'll wait until tomorrow?"

"They'll wait."

Jean touched the long, faint surgical scar on her husband's cheek that marked a skin graft. He had escaped death when a land mine exploded, seeing the trip wire and diving to cover just in time, he'd said. But he hadn't escaped the bits of flying metal. Was he seeing the trip wire now . . . aware of something no one else noticed? He seemed to believe so emphatically that he was not the target. She wished she shared his conviction.

"Chief Wanamaker's resignation makes leaving here even easier." She set her glass down and stroked his arm. "Everyone will agree Banning made a bad decision appointing him in the first place. Who'll even notice you're gone?"

From his instant flush, Jean knew she'd said the wrong thing. "I didn't mean it like—"

"You think nobody notices me? That I'm a blowhard? That I couldn't have beat Banning in that last election? If I *had* won by a narrow margin, *I'd* be the one having to prove myself over and over. I made a wise business decision—to pull out and let Banning screw himself."

"You did!" Jean said desperately. "And it's working. Granny Bandits. Killer cops, cop killers! The voters are seeing their mistake, Gib, just as you said they would."

"If I leave now, I miss a window of opportunity. That's a business term, Jean. Something you don't understand."

No, she didn't understand business. Or politics. She should, then maybe her husband would respect her more. But she believed in her heart that The People would deliver on their threat. And she couldn't bear to lose Gib.

An inspiration struck her. "What if I had a heart attack? Remember how sympathetic the press was last year when I went in with that tremor? I can fake a heart attack, then you could—"

"Jean, don't be stupid. Nothing is going to happen to me. It's not me The People want."

"How can you be so sure? You received the same letter as Banning and Wanamaker. And nobody else on the Council got one."

"Guess that shows I'm not as *unimportant* as my loving wife seems to believe." He pulled her into his lap and kissed her. "Come on. Let's pick out a stunning suit for you to wear. Stunning, but suitable for a solemn occasion. One way or another, I expect Banning's future to die on that platform tomorrow."

Chapter Fifty-seven

Kaylynn Banning sat across the table from her husband, after a late lunch at The Courtyard, and despaired that life could be so unpredictable. Six months ago they'd sat at this same table and toasted Avery's political success.

"I don't see how anyone could blame you for not mounting that stage tomorrow," she said, too quietly for diners at neighboring tables to hear. "Sweetheart, people don't expect you to become the bait to catch this assassin."

Slowly, he shook his head as he pushed strawberries around his dessert plate with a silver spoon.

"Unless we allow the radical who wrote those letters an opportunity to strike tomorrow morning, we'll be looking over our shoulders constantly until we're picked off one by one walking down the street. This way, we stand a chance of catching the killer cold. We'll stop it right there."

"You make it sound so reasonable. Until I picture you behind the microphone, people all around, giving the Chief his much-deserved commendation. Then I hear this sound, Avery—like a truck going down Walker Street, beside the park, and having a blowout . . . or a backfire. Only it's not a truck. All the people hush as the Chief's knees buckle under him, and I'm staring at Mira, praying, 'Thank God it wasn't Avery.' Then *another* backfire. A red stain spreads on your chest—"

"Jesus Christ, Kaylynn!"

"When I see *that* in my head, Avery, your words don't sound so reasonable anymore."

"Do you think I should resign because the letter demands it? Is that what you want?"

"You've never been a quitter. I don't expect you to bail out now. But there must be another answer."

He polished off his wine. Kaylynn hated the fear and deceit she had seen in her husband's eyes since the day that hateful letter had arrived. Frankly, she didn't give a damn about his plebeian past. She never pried when he disappeared for hours—thinking, he claimed. Yet, she was no fool, and now she regretted not taking a firmer hand. In today's world, a woman couldn't depend on a man to protect her interests.

"You talked in your sleep last night," she said. "You must have had a nightmare."

He looked at her warily. "What did I say?"

"Not much. You shouted 'beetles, beetles,' and mumbled some words about control."

"That was all?"

"What did it mean?"

He shrugged. "I walked around the park last evening with Ed. Saw bugs everywhere."

Kaylynn could always tell when Avery was outright lying.

She'd married for love, but not without a plan for a prominent future. Her husband had the combination of charm and intelligence that could take him anywhere, and Kaylynn had recognized instantly that they made a magnificent couple. She enjoyed the envy she saw in other women's eyes, and the admiration she detected in men. But she knew Avery had secrets. He had a lust for life and a lust for power. He might not be strong enough to handle both, and couldn't an admiring public turn vicious when a leader failed to live up to their expectations?

At every step of his success, Kaylynn had praised her husband's accomplishments. Now she prayed that whatever he was hiding wouldn't destroy both of them.

Chapter Fifty-eight

"J. Claude!" Amy exclaimed. "Dixie, you remember Bill and Edna's friend, J. Claude Hager."

"I chased too many of your golf balls to ever forget," Dixie agreed, shaking J. Claude's hand. It felt cool and dry.

In his well-preserved seventies, wearing an exquisitely tailored black suit and a military spit-shine on his shoes, J. Claude Hager had a commanding presence. Guests had noticed his entrance. A few who remembered him from Bill and Edna's backyard barbecues stepped forward to greet their distinguished old friend personally.

Amy's house rocked with Meanstreak's version of "Blue Moon." The group had brought only their two guitars and keyboard to the party and had toned down their costumes considerably. Rick wore a shirt over his body art. Corinne wore tight black leather pants and a white silk blouse, her mouth and nails adding splashes of coral. Walt looked less stoned. Their retro music made a big hit with the guests, mostly Edna's contemporaries, who were old enough to remember the original recordings.

Carl had pushed the furniture aside, rolled back the rug for dancing, and set up a temporary bar in the dining room. Amy defrosted all her therapy-baked goodies. Only the draped piano held any indication that this party celebrated Edna's death: Between a pair of glowing candles in crystal holders sat a photograph of Edna and Bill.

When J. Claude turned away to speak to another old friend, Marty gripped Dixie's shoulder.

"Who invited him?" he demanded.

"J. Claude attended Bill's funeral—I knew he'd want to be here for Edna's." Dixie turned to study Marty's face. "It didn't take long to figure out that Derry Hager was the friend you went to see those times you supposedly flew back to Dallas."

He reddened belligerently. "You didn't invite Derry, too. Tell me you didn't!"

"It would've been rude not to, Marty." As she spoke, Dixie saw Amy at the front door admitting Derry and Felicia Hager.

Despite his anger, Marty's entire body seemed to relax as he watched Derry. Dixie had seen that same response in him when they were both teenagers and Derry Hager was a young adult. A sexy young adult. Dixie'd had a brief crush on Derry herself. Very brief. She'd never liked the way he manipulated people. Now she wondered if half the world's population was manipulating the other half in some manner.

"You can see why he'd never agree to be my alibi." Marty's gaze was on Felicia Hager now.

Hager-Cross Preschool owned six child-care centers in Houston, Dallas, and San Antonio. J. Claude had founded the business. Derry Hager and Felicia Cross, the couple who operated it, were married, childless, and thought to be the best news for preschoolers since *Sesame Street*. Even a whisper of homosexuality could destroy the school's reputation.

"I can see why Derry would *hesitate* to be your alibi. But if you two are as close as I believe you are—"

Marty shook his head. "You're wrong about inviting them here. After I dropped the bomb that Christmas, Dad avoided J. Claude, blamed him for 'letting it happen.' I tried to tell Dad that Derry's father didn't know—and still doesn't know. But I don't believe Dad and J. Claude ever spoke again."

"They would have, if your father had lived past his anger." Dixie'd never seen two better friends so different in personality. Bill Pine had left his military regimentation far behind when he left the army, but not J. Claude. His demand for rigid discipline had alienated his son and sent his wife to divorce court.

Even now, Derry Hager merely nodded stiffly at his father. No trace of closeness. J. Claude's manner with Felicia was friendly but formal, barely softening when his daughter-in-law kissed his cheek.

"Does Derry's wife know?" Dixie asked.

"No. Felicia assumes he has an occasional affair, but she'd leave him in an instant if she knew the truth."

"And he's willing to let you go to jail to protect his lie?"

Marty sighed. "You just don't understand."

"I'm trying. And while we're on the subject of truth—" From her pocket she tugged a small thin box that she'd pilfered from Amy's gift-wrap supply, figuring a bag would smudge any fingerprints on the brass disk. She removed the lid. "How did this get into your mother's casket?"

"What is it?"

"You don't know?"

"Why should I?" He reached for the box.

Dixie lifted the coin by its edges to show him the engraving.

Marty shook his head, and seemed sincerely puzzled. She reminded herself he'd had plenty of experience with deception.

"Maybe it's nothing." Closing the box, she slid it back into her pocket as Amy approached.

"Marty, you won't believe who's here!" Amy scooped him away to greet the Hagers.

J. Claude had collected a circle of attentive listeners. He could always command an audience, Dixie recalled.

She meandered toward the bar. Parker's Cadillac hadn't been among the cars when she arrived, and she hadn't seen him come in before she went to help Carl with drinks. It wasn't like Parker to be late. Helping herself to a glass of chardonnay, she found herself standing near Terrence Jackson, who was carrying on a spirited conversation with Carl. Dixie overheard such words as "on-line investing" and "maximize your leverage."

Jessica Love had been a no-show, with no apology. But Lonnie Gray and his flawlessly decorated receptionist huddled in an obviously intimate conversation that suggested Lonnie wasn't the fey gay he pretended to be.

Picturing the brown-haired woman wearing big sunglasses and carrying money bags, Dixie ambled casually within eavesdropping distance.

"You have to do this for me, Lonnie," the woman crooned in a voice as smooth as the fabric stretched over her ripe curves. "Look at me, I'm a walking advertisement for Artistry. And we'll meet women on this cruise with tubs of money. All you have to do is—"

"I know what to do," Lonnie replied, without a hint of the drama he conveyed at the spa. "But do you *appreciate* what I do for you, sweetheart?"

"Maybe we should stop off at the spa, and I'll show you my appreciation." Her red mouth shaped an "O" as her fingers trailed down his leg.

Dixie spotted Vernice Urich conversing intently with Amy. Discussing what? Fornication, weight loss, direct transfer payments? Fortunately, Carl kept a sharp eye on the Royal family accounts. And Carl considered himself too wise an investor to be seduced by Terrence Jackson's sales techniques—although a little of the Midas touch might push the Royal investments into new growth areas. While Jackson's aggressive methods for acquiring clients might raise an eyebrow or two among more conservative financial planners, nothing Dixie had found on Jackson suggested he mishandled his clients' money. And his success certainly spoke well for his persuasive sales techniques.

Persuasion. Seduction. Manipulation. Dixie glanced at Derry Hager and Vernice Urich and felt surrounded by it. Lonnie Gray and his receptionist moved toward the door. Lonnie's hand rested on the upper curve of her voluptuous hip.

Dixie saw other guests beginning to leave and decided this might be a perfect time for her to get the hell out, too. Obviously, Parker had decided not to come. Another boat sale?

Marty bumped against her, carrying a glass of what smelled like straight Scotch. The gleam of its effect showed in his eyes.

"Are we planning to work on my case tomorrow?" he asked. "Or do snoops take holidays off?"

"I'm not sure how much more I can do." She could have the brass disk dusted for fingerprints, and then find someone to run a comparison . . . but against whose? Marty's? No better suspect had surfaced yet. HPD could match them against millions of prints on file. "We The People" would cause a few brows to furrow. The right thing was to hand over the disk and Tally's sketch to Rashly. She'd find herself in trouble for withholding evidence, but she could only die once.

"If you weren't going to help," Marty blurted, "then why did you take my case?"

"I agreed to find out about your mother's lifestyle changes these past months. That's all. If the entire FBI task force, with their unlimited resources, can't find this cop killer, what do you expect me to do, Marty? Magic?"

Marty sipped his Scotch. "Maybe I should hire a *real* investigator."

"A damn good idea. Maybe a willing friend is not what you need." Dixie pushed past him toward the door, but found herself face-to-face with Parker as Meanstreak started a rendition of "Tennessee Waltz," one of Edna's favorites. When had he arrived?

"Perfect timing." Parker gathered Dixie into a waltz step. "Am I showing my age," he asked, "when I say I like this music?"

"It's easier to dance to than rap," she agreed.

He drew her closer, his mouth brushing the hair at her temple. That spot inside her that always turned to liquid when he came near did its melting routine. She relaxed against his broad chest. The heat from his body and the clean sea-air scent of him triggered provocative memories.

Then he spun her away, and when he drew her back again, left space between them. She looked up into his familiar blue eyes.

"Parker, what's happening with us?" she asked impulsively.

He raised an eyebrow. "Dancing, aren't we? And doing a good job of it, I thought."

She suppressed the urge to stomp on his foot.

He whirled her, then drew her firmly close again. "Have you ever considered traveling around the world?"

"On a boat?"

"Partially. I may have a yacht to deliver down the coast to the Yucatán. Usually, we hire someone to make delivery. But I'm working on another deal in the Caribbean. We could go together."

"The Caribbean is not exactly 'around the world.' "

He maneuvered her even closer and murmured in her ear. "Spend a few romantic weeks hopping from island to island, then fly to wherever sounds like fun."

Anywhere that didn't include a bail jumper to bring in or a defense attorney who needs a bit of off-the-record investigation. Parker was never happy staying in one spot for long. And his body language made it clear that this "round the world" excursion would revive the intimacy they'd shared before he became so distant. She loved him so much it was damned tempting. But she couldn't shake the uneasy feeling he'd been withholding sex as a sort of punishment. Or a carrot.

Now he was telling her, *Come play with me. Forget responsibility and career and family and roots.*

Maybe the smidgen of Apache blood that ran through her veins caused the suspicion to infuriate her. She didn't jump to anyone's whistle, not even Parker's. Enticing her one moment with his words and gestures, those soft murmurs in her ear, the sensuous brush of his lips. Then keeping her at a distance. Society had a name for *women* who used such tactics.

The waltz ended. Dixie murmured something about "mingling" and moved away from him. She'd had enough manipulation for one day. She paused near the piano to tell Amy what a fine job she'd done with a difficult project.

J. Claude Hager also appeared to be leaving. He stopped at the picture of Edna and Bill Pine that perched between candles on the draped piano. Straightening to military attention, he gave a brief salute to the photograph of his old friend. Then he strode briskly out the door.

Twenty years past retirement but always the commander, Dixie marveled. *Did people ever really change?*

Chapter Fifty-nine

Change. The stained-glass bauble Parker had given her reflected late-afternoon sunlight into the Mustang. Dixie untied it from the rearview mirror, wiped a drop of moisture from the corner of her eye, and rubbed it over the glass, deepening the colors. She never embraced change easily. Parker had moved out of her house, out of her life, the night before Valentine's Day, after giving her the card containing this sentiment but before she'd had a chance to open it. *My day begins with your smile, your scent, your touch. Without those I would be cold and dark inside.* Obviously, his sentiment had changed

She opened her glove box and tossed the sunburst inside. Then she tuned the radio to hard, mind-numbing rock music and drove with no particular destination.

The prospect of another solitary evening sat in her stomach like cold split-pea soup. Reaching across to the passenger seat, she retrieved the copy of Mike's invitation to the May Sundown Ceremony.

ARRIVE BY SEVEN-THIRTY P.M. CASUAL ATTIRE.

ASK FOR ANGELA.

"We'll start with some easy stretches to release the day's tension," Mike had said. To arrive before seven-thirty, she wouldn't have time to change. Her jeans and camp shirt were casual enough, if not what she'd generally choose for stretching.

At the moment, a "Sundown Ceremony"—whatever the hell that was—

sounded perfect. Forget cop killers and gang symbols. Forget an engraved brass disk materializing in the hand of a corpse. Tomorrow, she would decide what to hand over to Rashly. But tonight she would relax, nudge herself out of the damn lovesick rut she'd been wallowing in, and enjoy a totally new experience.

Mike's expressive face eased into her mind. Dixie smiled. Mike Tesche was personable, thoughtful, amusing—and about twelve percent body fat. Handsome was considerably overrated.

When Parker's big, gorgeous face imposed itself over Mike's, Dixie's center did its quick melt again, and for an agonizing instant she felt like a puppy left out in the cold. But the instant passed. Parker's grin faded, replaced by Mike's intelligent green eyes. Tonight, she would take each moment as it came. No expectations. No judgment. No regrets.

On the interstate, she zipped through heavy traffic for Sunday evening, then turned east, into a densely wooded area. Beneath tall Texas pines, scrub oaks, and basswood trees, yaupon grew thick. The two-lane asphalt road wound gently northeast. She watched her odometer until she'd traveled six-point-four miles. A few yards farther along, she spied a gravel side road, the entrance flanked by a pair of stone markers. Each bore a PRIVATE PROPERTY sign.

Two miles later she reached a locked iron gate and another sign: THE WINNING STRETCH HEALTH RETREAT. Beneath that, in smaller letters: NO ACCESS AFTER SUNDOWN. She pushed a white button and spoke into the intercom.

"Dixie Flannigan to see Angela."

"Hello, Dixie! We're expecting you!" came a tinny reply.

After a moment, the gate opened and Dixie drove on. Here, the scrub brush had been cleared away and flowering shrubs planted. Finally, she came to a garden wall made of river stone, and behind it, a parking area.

A slate walkway meandered through a lavish garden bursting with color and fragrance and ended at a sprawling multilevel house of river stone and cedar. The place looked so natural it could've been carved out of the landscape. When the front door opened, Dixie recognized the assistant who'd helped Mike lead his class at the women's center.

"Hi, Dixie. I'm Angela. We're so glad you could join us." Wearing a simple white ankle-length jumpsuit, blond hair pulled back with a soft white scarf, she held out her arms in a greeting that was charmingly childlike.

Her effusive welcome reminded Dixie of Amy, who possessed the gift of making the most unwanted stranger feel like an honored guest.

Angela clasped Dixie's hand in both of her own. "Oh, dear, you've had quite a day, haven't you? I hope you didn't mind that long drive. Did you have trouble finding us?"

Only the faint laugh lines around her wide brown eyes gave away Angela's age as over fifty. From her clear, sweet voice and youthful mannerisms Dixie had pegged her at about eighteen. Maybe younger. The contrast was odd.

"No trouble at all. Mike's directions were perfect."

"You're stressed, but we'll fix that," Angela said. "Come on in."

She wound an arm around Dixie's and guided her through an atrium filled with exotic plants into a spacious lounge. Minimal furnishings. Nubby cotton throw pillows in shades of white, with a touch of green and pale rose. Skylights and numerous windows brought the woods and gardens into the interior, with honeycomb blinds filtering out the brightest sunlight.

Plump cushions dotted the white floor. A cloud-white sculpture featuring four life masks hung above a plaster fireplace mantel. It was titled "Matriarch Goddess." Candles glowed beneath it.

Past a kitchen-dining area, where a group of women engaged in food preparation smiled up at them, Angela opened the door to a dressing room. The lighting here was subdued. A glass-enclosed shower, with another huge window, looked out on a pocket garden walled in with stone for privacy.

Angela turned on the brass spigots, and the enclosure began to fill with steam.

"You have a few minutes before the program begins. A hot shower will help soak away the city's frustrations and impurities. You won't have time to wash and dry your hair, but there's a brush on the vanity." Smiling ingenuously, Angela lowered her voice to a confidential whisper. "We don't want to carry worldly contaminants into the ceremonial space."

Her naive enthusiasm reminded Dixie of a head-wound victim she'd once known. An innocent bystander at a holdup, the woman had survived a head shot, but had lost most of her adult memory. Retraining had taken months, and the woman had eventually learned to function normally, but she'd never fully regained her life, nor had she lost that childlike quality to her voice and mannerisms.

Selecting a slender bottle from a colorful array on a shelf, Angela sprayed a fragrant mist into the shower.

"Lilac, for relaxation. Would you prefer a one-piece?" She held out the sides of her soft cotton jumpsuit and curtsied. "Or pants and shirt?"

"Two pieces." Dixie supposed her own clothes would carry "worldly contaminants."

"I'll be right back with your clothes. Enjoy your bath." She started to leave, then abruptly turned back and gave Dixie a brief, enthusiastic hug. "I'm so glad you're here." She closed the door gently behind her.

The shower did look inviting. Mike had never totally answered Dixie's question about what to expect here. But she'd once taken part in an Indian smoke ceremony, surprised to discover she wasn't required to smoke a peace pipe, and had enjoyed sharing the spiritual experience from a different culture. Perhaps this evening would be similar.

She hung her clothes on the hooks provided, stepped into the steaming water, and snapped the glass door shut. Maybe she'd skip the ceremony and stare out at this garden for about a month. As she soaped, she heard music playing softly and recognized the same soothing background Mike used in the meditation portion of his exercise class. She wondered lazily how it would be to live in a secluded spot like this, venturing into town only when you ran out of food or books.

She heard the outer door open.

"Fresh-squeezed juice and filtered water," Angela called. "You have about five minutes."

"All right." *Now go away and let me daydream.*

Dixie emerged a minute later, fresh and clearheaded. As she toweled off and dressed in the loose-fitting white cotton pajama outfit Angela had brought, she sipped the juice. Cranberry? With lime, honey, and some sort of herb. It tasted clean and light, not too sweet.

Her own clothes and boots had vanished. A pair of terry-cloth slippers lay beneath her pajamas. Angela had been barefoot, and the white floors had looked immaculate. When Angela knocked again, Dixie abandoned the slippers.

They entered a room with only one wall of windows, covered with opaque honeycomb blinds. A small table stood in one corner. Otherwise, the room had no furnishings.

Ten women lay on white mats arranged in a circle. Some of these women hadn't seen fifty for a long time, but like Aunt Edna they appeared to be in great shape, with clear skin and gleaming white, blond, or silver hair. Expensive hair. Manicured hands and toes. These women were upper middle class, not at all the mix Mike taught at the women's center. Despite the identical white cotton exercise garments, their higher economic status showed in their professionally tended bodies.

The music played slightly louder in here. Angela introduced Dixie as "our honored guest this evening," motioned her to one of two vacant mats, then took the last for herself.

"Assume the lotus. Inhale, slowly, slowly, distend the abdomen, and hold . . . three . . . four . . . five . . . exhale, squeeze it in, ladies, three . . . four . . ." Angela followed her own directive.

The stretches, similar to those Dixie had experienced in Mike's class at the center, felt wonderful. Finally, Angela led them through the cool-down postures, ending with deep breathing.

"Clear your mind," she recited. "Lie back. Enjoy a brief period of guided meditation."

The light dimmed as they stretched out on the mats, and the ceiling overhead began to change and move. Clouds. It was a giant movie screen, Dixie realized, as the clouds turned to oceans, to mountain streams, to sandy beaches, all with the warm orange and pink tones of an afternoon sky. The images ended with an incredible sunset. Dixie followed her cue as the other women slowly stretched and rose, although she wouldn't have minded languishing awhile longer in the serenity. The blinds covering the window wall slid silently toward the ceiling, revealing the true sunset outside.

Angela and one of the other women brought the small table from the corner and placed it in the center of the circle. Twelve white candles surrounded a silver bowl, twelve pencils, paper, matches, and an incense burner emitting a spicy fragrance.

As her helper passed a pencil and a paper circle to each woman, Angela recited in her clear, melodious voice.

"As the sun sets on the old world, and we look toward a brighter future, we each have valuables to carry with us and baggage to leave behind." She struck a match. "I commit to Love in the new world. I light this candle for Love."

She lit the nearest candle and sat down. Her assistant stepped to the table and struck a match.

"I commit to Enlightenment in the new world. I light this candle for Enlightenment."

As each woman in turn committed to some higher awareness, Dixie considered what to say when her turn came. The eleventh woman lit the next-to-last candle.

"I commit to Acceptance in the new world. I light this candle for Acceptance."

Rising, Dixie moved to the table. This new-age, touchy-feely stuff usually turned her off completely, but at the moment she couldn't imagine why. Saying out loud, or telling a friend, the changes you intended to make in your life seemed an ideal way to reinforce your commitment. It focused attention, like a karate shout.

"I commit to . . . Togetherness in the new world," she murmured. "I light this candle for Togetherness."

Now, where had that come from? Wasn't she the person who'd actively embraced solitude all her life?

When she sat down, Angela took the floor again, holding a paper circle that she folded in quarters.

"Write down what you want to leave behind. Then let the fire consume it."

She held the paper in the candle flame until it caught fire, then dropped the flaming circle into the silver bowl. One by one, the other women followed suit.

Dixie scribbled on her paper, LONELINESS, folded it quickly, and held it over the candle. When the paper began to burn, she found herself wondering what Edna's word had been. If you attended this ceremony often enough, you could toss all sorts of unwanted crap into that bowl and let it burn its way out of your life. Heartbreak. Jealousy. Sadness.

Longing.

Before Parker's face could fully materialize in her mind, Dixie felt the flame reach her fingers. She held on another instant, then tossed the burning remnant into the bowl.

Chapter Sixty

In the glow of candlelight, the eleven older women, in their pale flowing garments, looked as ethereal as angels. Although Dixie had little in common with any of them, she felt a deep sense of belonging and acceptance. Was this what Casey James had meant when she said to enjoy the presence of other women you "take up a craft"? Must that craft be quilting, jewelry-making? Or might it be simply lighting candles together? Experiencing psychic harmony?

The women rose, almost as a unit.

"What happens now?" Dixie asked Angela.

"Dinner, fellowship. Then private meditation. Sound all right?"

Dixie nodded, vaguely disappointed. "I suppose I expected to see Mike."

"Oh, Michael rarely joins us during the ceremony, but he wouldn't miss greeting our honored guest. Right now, he's counseling a client."

No matter. Dixie suddenly felt ravenous.

At dinner, seated at a long table, passing around bowls of beans, pasta, and vegetables "picked fresh from our garden," Dixie encouraged her newfound friends to contribute to the Aunt Edna puzzle she was piecing together. She learned that Edna had been a frequent visitor, had contributed her wisdom by coaxing the beautiful blooms in the gardens and atrium into profusion, and had transformed here from a lost, unhappy soul to a "bright, strong light."

For every question they answered, the women asked three of Dixie. "What do you do? Are you a native Texan? Would I know your parents?" Not prying but interested. Dixie couldn't recall ever feeling more truly welcome anywhere.

She also learned that only one woman knew Terrence Jackson, another had counseled with Vernice Urich, several had visited Fortyniners, Artistry Spa, or bought clothes at Unique Boutique, but no one was familiar with all of them, and no one remembered Lucy Ames, except from the newspaper reports of her violent death. Apparently, Edna had kept this sanctuary for herself, not sharing it with her other new friends. And her visits to The Winning Stretch had ceased in April, weeks before the robberies. What had prevented her neighbor from finding the contentment here that these eleven so obviously appreciated?

Dixie finished her meal pleased that she'd come, and even more pleased that she wouldn't see the women at this table in a Granny Bandit headline. After helping to clear the plates away, Dixie drew Angela aside.

"I've had a terrific evening. I hope you'll tell Mike I'm sorry I missed him. I need to leave now, if you'll take me to where you put my clothes—"

"Oh, Dixie! I thought you knew." Angela's lovely mouth compressed in a frown. "We never open the house or gate after sundown on Commitment Night. It disperses the energy."

"We'll only have them open a minute. I'll be gone in a flash."

"I'm so sorry, Dixie. Please understand. We have plenty of room. You'll have a wonderful night's rest."

"You said Mike was coming later. If you won't open the door, how will *he* get in?"

A step sounded behind Dixie.

"I'm already here," Mike told them. "Is there a problem?"

"False imprisonment." Dixie smiled to soften the comment, although she only partially joked. She hated being confined. Nevertheless, the sound of his voice revived her real desire for coming here.

Mike wore his usual tweed blazer over a Dallas Cowboys sweatshirt. No baseball cap today. His disorderly hair curled around his ears. He returned her smile with an amused grin.

"Dixie, I apologize for the misunderstanding. Most of our guests pay outrageous sums to stay here overnight. We haven't resorted to imprisonment yet. Have we, Angela?"

"I thought she knew." Angela's gaze slid from Dixie to Mike. "I should have—"

"No, it's my mistake." Mike spoke gently, as if to a child. "You know how I overlook details." Then he reached for Dixie's hand and held it in both of his. "I only this moment freed up some time, and there's no one I want to spend it with but you. Don't rush off."

What did she have to rush home to? After the Sundown Ceremony and that delicious meal, she felt much too energized to spend the remainder of the evening in front of the tube. And she certainly deserved one night off from worrying over the mess Marty'd landed in.

"I have some time," she agreed.

"Excellent. Angela, would you bring hot water for tea? Unless you'd prefer decaf—" He coughed, tried to finish his sentence but coughed again, repeatedly.

"Mike, are you okay?"

He nodded, drew a small tin from his pocket, and slipped a tablet from it into his mouth. "Sorry," he gasped, finally getting his breath.

"Tea is perfect," Dixie assured him. This past week she'd tasted more varieties than she knew existed, but the one served at dinner, fragrant and deliciously tangy, could easily become habit-forming.

"Then let's get comfortable." Extending an arm, he invited her toward a wing of the vast house Dixie hadn't yet seen.

Sconces at intervals down the long hallway cast an incandescent glow that chased away the darkness. Mike's companionable presence—like a cat's purr, unnoticed in a busy room, but soothing when you drew the furry rumble against your body—could become as habit-forming as the tea. He continued to hold her hand as they passed two closed doors, increasing the distance from Angela and the others. Dixie's anticipation sharpened.

At the third door, she asked, "What's in there?"

Her voice seemed too loud in the snug space.

"Expansion areas." Mike swung the door open. "Long-term living quarters. Once completed, The Winning Stretch will be available to hundreds of residents." He flipped on a light to reveal bare concrete floors, exposed joists, pipes, wiring, and pink insulation enclosing an area easily large enough to encompass Dixie's house twice over. "We're entirely self-contained. You saw the garden. We also have our own water well and a generator to supply electricity."

"Long-term? Does that mean permanent? Like a retirement community?"

"It could be, I suppose. I prefer 'indefinite.' Separation from external stress encourages healing," he explained. "A woman will make enormous progress while she's here, yet slip into poor eating and exercise habits after a few days' absence. Give me three intensive months and the good habits are permanently fixed."

Having watched her students lose coordination and speed after only a few weeks' absence, Dixie could see the potential. In a place like this, perhaps Joan would heal enough to leave her abusive husband.

"At the age of most of your clients, I suppose free time is plentiful."

"More than that, time is the enemy. Consider: Your spouse is gone, your friends scattered, you've never worked. Your children are busy and you don't fit in their lives except on occasional holidays. What compels you to rise each day? You cook. Who's to eat it? You clean, you decorate, you garden. Who notices? You spend your days between the bed, the television, the shopping malls, and church. Even your church is filled with young people engaged in youthful activities, who consider you an antique biding time on your way to the grave."

"You don't paint a happy picture, Mike."

"Did you meet anyone tonight who didn't appear happy?"

"They obviously enjoyed the ceremony and one another's company. And they all look so healthy. Whatever you do here, it clearly works."

"It's what they do for themselves and each other. Rebirth. Commitment to a new self. Intense focus accomplishes miracles."

They'd reached another door, which he held wide, allowing her to enter first. The spaciousness of the outer rooms hadn't prepared her for the cozy intimacy here. Lush green plants in huge pots divided a span of seating area, casual dining, and an office cove, where a computer bounced colored images against the rose-beige walls.

"Mike, with all this, why do you teach anywhere else?" Dixie didn't see a bed, but assumed he also slept here, since the gate didn't open after sundown. On Commitment Night, anyway.

"Money." He grinned. "Like you, I volunteer my time at the women's health center, but teaching at Y's and commercial gyms provides income and the occasional advanced student we invite to join us here."

"Advanced and affluent, to judge from the women I met tonight."

Mike nodded. "Donations are always appreciated. The Winning Stretch is a self-funded, nonprofit organization. I own only a tiny percentage of what you see."

He guided Dixie toward a circular leather sofa and a round coffee table, padded at the edges to invite propping your feet up. A low ceiling, sculptures, art, and the soft furnishings contributed to the cloistered feeling. Easy to imagine the rest of the spacious house existed in another dimension. As in the bathroom, one entire wall opened to an enclosed garden, glowing with low, unobtrusive spotlights against the surrounding darkness.

"This is where I allow my mind to unbend and consider new possibilities," he told her.

With a retreat like this to "unbend" in, who would ever need a vacation? No wonder Mike's patrons wanted to stay "indefinitely." Dixie curled up on the couch, facing the garden.

"Angela mentioned you were counseling a client. Did she mean psychological counseling?"

He brought a teapot, two mugs, saucers, and a tin of biscotti from a buffet in the dining alcove and placed them on the table. In a silver vase, a stick of incense burned, the fragrance faintly sweet and exotic.

Mike sat near her on the couch.

"Like everyone these days, I've studied basic psychology," he admitted, "but I leave head-shrinking to people who like to peer into dark places. We discuss the benefits of diet, exercise —"

Dixie yawned.

"—and a good night's sleep." He smiled as she guiltily clapped a hand over her mouth. Then he adjusted a button on a remote control pad, slightly increasing the volume of the music that had become such a part of the atmosphere Dixie'd scarcely realized the soothing sounds were piped all over the house.

"You designed all this yourself?" Near the incense burner an unusual piece of art gleamed in the subdued light. She lifted the object to study it—an irregular slab of onyx imbedded with twelve crystals circling a single garnet—like the twelve women encircling the flames in the silver bowl this evening. Silver threads laced the crystals and garnet in a concentric design. The piece was simple but exquisite, like everything she'd seen at The Winning Stretch. The artwork seemed familiar, unsigned, yet obviously custom-crafted. Dixie glanced at the ring on Mike's hand: a garnet encircled with diamonds. Same designer.

"I merely told the architects what I wanted to achieve," Mike was saying. "Serenity."

"They sure got it right."

A knock sounded, and he hopped up to accept a tray from Angela.

"We have a bed ready." Angela's clear, sweet voice carried across the room. "If Dixie wants to stay with us."

"That's fine. We'll let you know what Dixie decides."

He brought the tray, filled the teapot from a carafe of hot water, and set a plate of sectioned oranges on the table. At home, Dixie reflected, dessert would be Bluebell Ice Cream straight from the carton. She carefully replaced the onyx sculpture.

"My friend Edna was a regular visitor until several weeks ago. I wonder why she stopped coming here. Did she ever hint at what she'd planned?"

"You mean knocking off a bank?" Mike's green eyes glittered with merriment. "We do encourage innovation, but that idea would have sparked a conversation I'd surely remember."

He poured the fragrant tea into pottery mugs and handed her one. Not the exact tea she'd had before, this tasted sweeter, smelled more pungent.

"Edna's behavior certainly sparked a conversation at dinner tonight."

"Did it?" He looked interested.

"Many of the women admired her spunk."

"You must admit she took command of her own destiny."

"Mike, surely you don't—"

"Support her actions? Dixie, I knew Edna as a woman determined to experience life. Her death . . . ?" He shook his head and breathed a long, disheartened sigh.

"What sort of *commitments* did Edna discuss?"

He shrugged. "Commitments are private. But in general, students commit to perfecting the body, the spirit, and eventually their entire world."

"Sounds overwhelming."

"Not when taken one step at a time. Build strength. Defeat fear. Erase pain. With one small, bold step after another, we can do anything."

Wasn't that exactly what she taught in her own self-defense classes? Why did it sound so much *bigger* when he said it? His words carried such conviction.

"What causes *you* so much pain, Dixie Flannigan?"

"What do you mean?" He couldn't know how miserable she'd been these past months since Parker became so distant.

Mike moved closer, took the empty cup—*her cup was empty . . . when had she . . . ?*—and set it on the table. Then he opened her hand. His fingers floated tenderly over her palm.

"Pain leaves its trace, long after the wound has healed." Her fingers tried to close over his, to stop the tingling that pulsed from her palm through her arm and sent tiny flickers of sensitivity throughout her body. But he coaxed them open and continued the butterfly touch on her palm. "A soul that knows pain develops wisdom. A soul that knows strength develops skill. You have a beautiful soul, Dixie Flannigan—scarred with wisdom, solid with strength. I've seen you shepherd the lost spirits at the women's center. You would make a valued partner, a commendable leader."

His voice enveloped her. His expressive face, so close, so filled with understanding, made her long for his arms to enfold her as well. "Leader? Mike, I have trouble coping with crowds of two."

"Two is a difficult number, either static or combative. Three, five, nine, twelve— these numbers have synergy and strength, the power to move mountains."

"That's true. I saw that at dinner tonight . . . your students . . ." Dixie's tongue felt lazy. But her mind—she knew exactly what he meant. Each of those women had been alone and disoriented before finding one another. The group leadership brought them focus. Dixie glanced at her empty cup. Her limbs felt heavy, her mouth dry.

Selecting an orange slice, she rose with effort, moved to the window, and gazed out at the garden.

"Beautiful, isn't it?" Mike stood behind her, his hands lightly on her shoulders. "This is a magical place, Dixie Flannigan."

Yes. She believed that. She'd sensed the magic from the moment she stepped into the spaciousness, the light. All evening, she'd scarcely thought about the robberies . . . Marty's impending arrest . . . or Parker.

She bit into the orange slice, and as the sweet juice flooded her mouth, a memory surfaced: a teenage birthday party. Chocolate, Dixie's favorite flavor, had been nixed by the dermatologist. Kathleen made Dreamsicle Surprise— vanilla ice cream layered with delicate sponge cake and orange filling—and Dixie discovered a treat she might otherwise never have tried.

The weight . . . and warmth . . . of Mike's hands instilled peace, contentment. Like the Dreamsicle Surprise, an unexpected pleasure. He had an amazing charm and magnetism in the lyrical roll of his voice, the comfort of his touch. Another image came into her mind. *Cows.* Contented cows.

"Your aura is so strong, Dixie, I can feel it in my hands."

"Aura?"

"Your body's energy field. We use our auras to repel or attract. Yours is a shield, but it doesn't have to be. I'll show you how to lower the shield and let people in, without fear of losing yourself."

She did fear letting people in.

His mouth felt warm against her ear.

"Align with me, Dixie. With your rare combination of strength and compassion, wisdom and skill, you would make me whole. Together, we can create a world—"

A tap at the door, then Angela's hopeful voice sounded. "Time for lights out. Is Dixie staying?"

Mike touched Dixie's arm, turned her from the window.

"I want you to stay here tonight," he murmured. "Enjoy the retreat's serenity for a few more hours."

"All right." She glanced at the teapot and the incense still burning in its holder. Why leave?

Mike's fingers lightly caressed her neck as she moved to follow Angela out the door.

In yet another wing of the house, they entered a dorm with twelve beds. Angela gave Dixie a white cotton gown and robe, exactly like the set she herself wore. The women she'd met—Dixie hadn't managed to keep their names straight—bustled in and out of the bathroom. Rows of lidded baskets on shelves provided locker space, where they stored or retrieved personal items.

While Dixie waited her turn, she explored her new sleeping quarters—a single bed, plump and inviting, with a feather mattress and two fat pillows. On a side table sat a pitcher of water, a glass, a lamp.

Unlike other rooms in the house, this one had no windows. A circular skylight over the beds invited the stars in. A heavenly fragrance permeated the air, and the ever-present music played softly.

A painting dominated the longest wall. Dixie stepped closer to examine it. She recognized the slate walkway that approached The Winning Stretch, the gardens, the atrium. But the house in the painting went on and on, with expansions yet to be built—an architectural projection. In a space at the bottom of the canvas, the architect had lettered the words:

THE CHURCH OF THE LIGHT

The name seemed familiar, yet Dixie couldn't recall why. She needed to get her thoughts together about it—that seemed imperative . . . something about Edna and the Church . . . but it wouldn't come.

Lovely gardens . . . spacious rooms . . . friendships . . . enlightenment. *Rebirth,* Mike had said. Completion of the Church would mean a haven for hundreds of women. Such a vision deserved to become a reality, didn't it? Dixie could help . . . certainly, no question. For now, she was content staring at the painting as she waited her turn in the bathroom . . . the Church of The Light.

Disturbing images intruded. A pool of blood on asphalt. Edna's sprawled body. A ring of blue uniforms. Marty's face twisted in grief. Mike's face . . . his hands. Dixie's thoughts skittered on as she inhaled the spicy air . . . listened to the music . . . the *shoosh* of feet on the vinyl floor . . . blood on asphalt—

With a shudder, Dixie glanced down at the nightgown and robe draped over her arm, then at the inviting bed a few paces away. She longed to ignore the terrible images, to slide beneath the scented covers, sleep beneath the stars.

Sleep . . . Edna sleeping . . . an iris on white quilted satin . . . a cold hand . . . Marty's sobs against her shoulder . . .

Dixie sat on the bed and gazed at the Church of The Light, her eyelids like weighted curtains.

Chapter Sixty-one

At The People's training center, Philip Laskey cleaned his Sig Sauer Pistole 75. He had shot well tonight, his pattern tighter than ever before, and the gun had finally felt right in his hands, an extension of his own energy. When he squeezed the trigger, every cell in his body seemed projected into the explosive bullet, his hand, arm, his every breath a nucleus of power.

"How does it feel to kill a cop?" Cronin asked him.

"I don't know." The rookie irritated Philip.

"Who killed those cops, then? Dodge? Martinez?"

"That's not a question to ask. *Who* doesn't matter. The People work as a team."

"Who's the target tomorrow?"

Young Cronin had too many questions.

"If all goes well, *no one,*" Philip replied. "To build a perfect world, seeds of imperfection must be eliminated, but if the civic leaders proceed as our letter directed, no blood will be spilled."

"Are you kidding? That asshole Banning—"

Philip hit him, a backfist, controlled.

"We don't use coarse language," he explained calmly, noting the angry flare in Cronin's eyes after the blow. To serve The People, that anger had to be contained and focused. Perhaps the Colonel's message tomorrow would address the positive use of rage.

Dodge and Martinez emerged from the shooting gallery. Dodge immediately began breaking down his gun. But Martinez radiated nervous energy like Saint Elmo's fire.

"Laskey! You heard anything, man?"

"Nothing on the early news."

"Being so tight with Banning, you'd get the message before any reporters," Dodge said.

"Maybe." Philip usually typed the Mayor's handwritten speech edits. Tomorrow, they'd meet at seven A.M. for final revisions.

"You practice the code, dude?" Martinez feigned a punch at Dodge's arm.

The Colonel had issued cell phones to keep in touch tomorrow, and a simple code to defeat eavesdropping.

Dodge grunted. "Seven words—what's to practice?"

Straddling a bench, Martinez reached for a cleaning rag. Cronin sat down near him.

"Is that clock right?" Martinez asked. "*Can't* be right. It's stopped, man."

"It's exactly on time," Philip told him. The thirty-six-hour deadline would end in one hour and twenty-seven minutes. Unless The People's demands were met before then, a deadly new clock would start ticking. By the time the Mayor's commemoration speech began tomorrow morning, The People would be in position, awaiting the Colonel's order.

Philip found himself praying that Mayor Banning made the right decision. Philip would do whatever was required. Corrupt units had to be eliminated. But killing was ultimately wasteful. One life affected so many.

"What d'ya think, kid?" Martinez punched Cronin's arm. "Tomorrow we'll see some action!" Then he aimed a stage whisper toward Philip. "And tomorrow night, a different kind of action. Eh, dude?"

Philip's groin tensed at a memory as fresh as the smell of gun oil on his hands—full red lips, soft cheeks, eyes like pools of ink. Those eyes locked with his own as he rocked above them, sweat dripping from his bare skin, every nerve in his body focused on a sensation he'd never before experienced.

The Colonel believed in reward for work well done. After Martinez eliminated the first murdering police officer, the Colonel's reward for his top three men had been a woman each.

Lizzie . . .

After the second officer was eliminated, Philip had asked for her by name. Last night, her face had taunted him in his sleep, her red lips whispering his name. He could still taste the salty sweetness of her skin, feel the fragrant roughness of her nipple against his tongue.

Tomorrow night . . . after a job well done, Lizzie would again be his reward.

Chapter Sixty-two

Dixie shuddered awake, cramped and groggy. She blinked at the clothing clutched in her arms. What was it? Why had she fallen asleep leaning against the headboard, legs dangling off the bed?

Not her own bed. Peering around the starlit room, she saw eleven beds, all occupied. Women she'd met at dinner. At The Winning Stretch . . . the Church—

She glanced at the painting. Mike's church. *Edna bequeathed nine hundred thousand dollars to the Church of The Light.*

Dixie tossed the clothes on the bed. In the bathroom, she fumbled at the spigots. Plugged the sink. Ran it full of cold water. Taking a deep breath, she plunged her face into the chilly liquid. After a full minute, she rose for another breath, then pushed her head deeper, allowing the water to wet her hair and seep over the back of her neck. When she emerged the second time, shaking, her thoughts slid into better focus.

She'd experienced drugs before, marijuana in college, nitrous oxide and codeine at the dentist's office, cocaine once to understand its effects. Had Mike drugged her on purpose? He drank from the same pot of tea. Perhaps her system had reacted strangely to one of the ingredients. Euphoria, but without an edge. Contentment, in fact, an exhilaration of total acceptance. The music, the incense, the atmosphere of the entire house had seduced her to relax.

As her thoughts tumbled into a semblance of order, Dixie knew she needed to go . . . yet a deep, anxious sadness overwhelmed her at the thought of leaving. She wanted to protect this sanctuary. Mike's dream, his ability to understand the emptiness in a woman's psyche, and to fill that emptiness with purpose, deserved safeguarding. She could be a part of that dream —

Abruptly, Dixie inhaled and bobbed beneath the water's surface. She envisioned Mike Tesche wearing a purple tutu. In a squeaky voice, he told her, *You have a beautiful soul, Dixie Flannigan.*

Rising, Dixie gasped, coughed, and squinted at her face in an oval mirror. *Woman, get out of here.*

She grabbed a towel, dried her sodden hair as she snapped off the light, and allowed her eyes to adjust to total darkness. Then she stepped into the starlit bedroom.

In a quick study of the shelves of baskets, she found one labeled "Dixie." Sliding it out, she found her clothes inside — *yes!* — slipped out of the workout pajamas — into her jeans, shirt. Her watch told her she'd slept a few hours; it was now three thirty-seven A.M. As she pulled on her socks, Dixie continued scanning the baskets — Alice, Angela, Charlotte, Dolores, *Edna.*

She tugged the basket off the shelf and removed the lid. Nothing inside.

Following a vague hunch, she opened Angela's basket. Under a neat stack of clothing, she found a small bag containing lipstick, moisturizer . . . and a bottle of brown hair rinse. The temporary kind that shampoos out. With her blond hair dyed brown, Angela could easily be the first Granny Bandit.

She could never have *masterminded* the robberies — Angela didn't have the mentality. But with her sweet, childlike desire to accommodate, she could've followed directions precisely, as she did at The Winning Stretch.

Whose directions? Mike's? Did he conspire with Lucy and Edna to rob Texas Citizens' branches? Or had the pair become so enamored of the Church vision that they dreamed up the scheme on their own as a way to hasten the project?

Mike claimed he hadn't known Lucy Ames. And the women Dixie'd met tonight — last night? — how long had she slept? — only remembered Lucy from the news.

Shoving the baskets back in place, dressed but carrying her boots, Dixie stopped for one last look at the architectural rendering. How far would the robbery money go toward completing the Church of The Light? Not nearly as far as Edna's nine-hundred-thousand-dollar bequest.

She eased the door open and slipped into the empty hall. After the brighter dorm room, the intense blackness rendered her blind. But in her mind's eye, she retraced her steps as Angela had led her from Mike's suite. *Left turn, right turn, right, left . . .*

Mike wouldn't be the first charismatic leader to encourage the transfer of all worldly goods to the Church and to expect sacrifice or even theft from his followers. Breaking man's laws to do God's will was considered necessary and respectable by many fringe religious groups.

Silent in her cotton socks, Dixie followed her instincts. By the time she reached the second left, her night vision had returned. At the room she believed to be Mike's, she checked around the door for light seepage.

Even with proof that Mike encouraged the bank robberies, the law might not be able to touch him. All religious organizations were protected by constitutional rights. But Dixie wanted desperately to believe Mike was the healer, the nurturer she'd seen in his classroom and whose inspiration she'd witnessed through the eleven vibrant women at dinner.

No light under his door. So far, Dixie'd encountered no locks anywhere inside the house. She slowly turned the knob. The latch *click*ed. She froze, listening.

Hearing only the pervasive music, she eased the door open and slipped inside the room. Ahead, the glow from the lighted garden softened the darkness. To the right, a screen saver on Mike's PC played a patch of colored images on the corner wall.

Dixie padded silently to the desk. She hadn't determined earlier which direction Mike's sleeping quarters might be, but the wall directly behind the office seemed most likely. She swiveled the monitor forward and searched for a sound button on the speakers that flanked it. Locating the button, she turned it all the way left, praying this would mute the usual *beep*s and *pong*s.

A *click* of the mouse brought up a dialog box requesting a password. Dixie had no techno-snoop experience, but she typed the first word that came to mind: LIGHT. After a moment, a new message appeared: UNABLE TO LOG IN. The cursor blinked beside the request for a password. Dixie typed: CHURCH. No dice. Then: STRETCH. This time the hourglass symbol stayed on the screen an instant longer, followed by the dual message: UNABLE TO LOG IN and PLEASE ENTER YOUR ID.

Stumped, and worried that Mike would see this new dialog screen and realize someone had tried to access his files, Dixie keyed the START button to reboot. Maybe he'd think a power surge caused a glitch.

Turning her attention to the desk, she noted a scanner and microphone connected to the PC, a cup filled with pens and pencils, a simulated leather surface protector, and a telephone. Nowhere else in the house had she seen a phone, nor had she heard one ring since she'd arrived.

As the computer screen blinked through its start-up sequence, she opened drawers. In shadowy light, she saw a stapler, letter opener, rubber bands, paper clips, notepads—nothing more ominous. Invitations to The Winning Stretch. In a lower drawer, she found a lockbox. Dixie lifted it to the desk and examined the simple lock. No problem opening it. She bent a paper clip to the right shape, and seconds later the latch snapped open. Light from the computer monitor glinted off an array of glass vials. Some held dark, coarse powder. Others were empty. The box also contained a plastic bag filled with a pale leafy mixture, a laboratory flask and condenser, and a supply of sterile hypodermic needles. Drugs? If so, they didn't resemble anything Dixie'd seen. She sniffed the finely ground leaves in the plastic bag—not pot.

She returned the relocked box to its drawer, then opened the next drawer up. It contained two thin smooth-edged notebooks, the pages still blank. Her searching hand brushed another volume that must've slid behind the first two. Dixie pulled it into the screen-saver light.

A spray of tropical flowers embellished the satiny cover. *Edna's missing journal!* Dixie tilted the pages toward the meager light and recognized her neighbor's rounded, almost girlish penmanship.

Hearing a creak somewhere in the house, she slid the book under her shirt and wedged it in the waistband of her jeans. When no other sounds issued, she searched the final drawer, found nothing of interest, and decided she'd pressed her luck far enough—

A step sounded nearby.

Dixie slid off the chair and scanned frantically for a place to hide. A broad-leaf philodendron in a fat pot offered the only cover. She scooted backward, keeping low, as she saw a door open in the wall behind the desk. Mike stepped from the shadows.

He circled the desk and snapped on a small lamp. Dixie huddled lower behind the pot. After a moment, she heard the *clickety-click* of computer keys, then the *rip* of paper being torn from a notebook. She ventured a peek through the philodendron. Seated, Mike guided a page into the scanner. A few passes with the mouse, then he fed the page into what Dixie had thought was a wastebasket. A shredder *whirr*ed into action. Three pages later, he laid the notebook on the desk, snapped off the lamp, and rose.

Dixie shrank as small as possible.

When Mike's footsteps receded toward the living area, she darted a look. He must be in the dining alcove.

Dixie glanced at the outer door, mentally measuring the distance. Six long strides. No cover. She recalled the noisy latch . . . glanced back at the alcove . . . he would surely hear if she opened the door.

His silhouette glided in front of the window to the lighted garden. Dixie held her breath and peered between the wide philodendron leaves as he walked toward her.

He passed her. The noisy door latch clicked open . . . and a moment later clicked shut.

Dixie ventured a look. Mike was gone.

Now go! Get out!

No . . . not yet. She might bump into him in the hall.

Waiting, counting the seconds, her legs going numb beneath her . . . she noticed the light from the monitor was motionless. Mike hadn't exited from his program. That meant he'd return shortly . . . or . . . that his password-protected screen saver would start up automatically after a brief period of non-use.

Dixie craved another chance at that computer.

She glanced back at the door . . . and decided to risk it.

Chapter Sixty-three

When Dixie touched the mouse, the monitor remained lighted, the program active. *Okay, good.* She pointed the cursor at the OPEN FILE icon and scanned the list.

AMES	FORMULAS	MK-ULTRA	WALLACE
DELGADO	FREY	PINE	YENIK
EDWARDS	MARCHETT	TECHNIC	

Ames. A coincidence? Not very damn likely.

When Dixie clicked on the file, a dialogue box appeared requesting her password. She clicked on the PINE file and got the same request. Well, shit!

Clicked on DELGADO: The file opened.

> JOSÉ DELGADO, NEUROPHYSIOLOGIST, YALE UNIVERSITY. ELECTRONIC STIMULATION. BY IMPLANTING A SMALL PROBE INTO THE BRAIN, DELGADO WIELDED ENORMOUS POWER OVER HIS SUBJECTS. USING A DEVICE HE CALLED THE STIMOCEIVER, OPERATED BY FM RADIO WAVES, HE ELECTRICALLY ORCHESTRATED A RANGE OF HUMAN EMOTIONS, INCLUDING RAGE, LUST, AND FATIGUE.

The file, which seemed to be notes from a research paper, went on for pages. *Electronic implants?* Sounded like a plot for *Alien Invasion.* Dixie clicked it closed and opened FORMULAS.

702010AW-INJ	405010LA	405010EP	405010RY
603010AW-INJ	304030LA	304030EP	304030RY
502030AW-INJ	203050LA	203050EP	203050RY

What sort of formulas? The third column of progressive numbers ended in the letters EP. *Edna Pine?* The second column contained identical numbers ending in the letters LA—for Lucy Ames. *Damn your lies, Mike Tesche.*

In the first row, the numbers were all larger and ended with AW, plus an extension, INJ. Dixie didn't know Angela's last name, or Alice's—the other A at dinner—but she'd bet one of them began with W. Back at the menu, she clicked on WALLACE.

PLEASE ENTER YOUR PASSWORD:

Mike had password-protected his client files. Ames, Pine, and Wallace—all locked. Then who was RY? Scrolling down the menu to YENIK, Dixie realized she'd heard the name somewhere. She clicked on the file.

PLEASE ENTER YOUR PASSWORD:

Mentally reviewing the names of the women she'd met at dinner—Laura, Charlotte, Dolores—Dixie remembered none beginning with R.

If the numbers were formulas, as the file name suggested, then formulas for what? The string 203050 added together equaled ten, or 20+30+50 equaled one hundred. The same was true of all the other numbers. Percentages? Twenty parts X, plus thirty parts Y, plus 50 parts Z equals the magic formula?

The formula for the drugged tea, possibly?

Dixie didn't believe that tea would've made her rush out to rob a bank. But it had induced a sense of euphoria and a desire to be . . . *helpful,* was that the right word? She'd felt an intense desire to see the Church of The Light completed. *Suggestible.* Mike had suggested she'd make a "valued partner."

Why did the first row—Angela's? Alice's?—differ from the other three rows? Perhaps Mike changed his formula after the first trial. The INJ extension could mean . . . ? Not many words began with INJ . . . injury . . . injustice . . . injunction . . . injection—

The hypodermic needles in Mike's lockbox. Most drugs were more powerful when injected. Too powerful? Enough to advocate decreasing the dosage for LA, EP, and RY?

Speculation, Flannigan. Mind-control drugs had proved ineffective, hadn't they? Even sodium pentothal, the so-called truth serum, was unreliable.

Scanning the remainder of the menu, Dixie recalled reading of a mind-control project conducted by the CIA in the 1950s—MK-ULTRA. Supposedly abandoned after a public outrage, the project had spawned a slew of espionage and sci-fi films. She opened the file.

> MK-ULTRA, CIA SUPER-SECRET PROJECT TO COUNTER SOVIET AD-VANCES IN BRAINWASHING. TRUE CIA OBJECTIVE: STUDY METHODS BY WHICH CONTROL OF AN INDIVIDUAL MAY BE ATTAINED THROUGH "NARCOHYPNOSIS," THE BLENDING OF MIND-ALTERING DRUGS WITH CAREFUL HYPNOTIC PROGRAMMING.

The following text described interrogation techniques using all manner of narcotics, from marijuana to LSD, heroin, and sodium pentothal, to ensure that subjects would not remember being interrogated and programmed. The document described MK-ULTRA as an "umbrella project" with 149 "sub-projects," and ended with a disturbing passage.

> NEW YORK, NOVEMBER 28, 1953. DR. FRANK OLSON, SCIENTIST FOR THE U.S. ARMY'S CHEMICAL CORPS SPECIAL OPERATIONS DI-VISION, THREW HIMSELF OUT OF A TENTH-FLOOR HOTEL WINDOW AFTER CONSUMING A TEST AMOUNT OF LSD. THE CIA INITIATED A 20-YEAR COVER-UP OF THE CIRCUMSTANCES SURROUNDING OLSON'S DEATH.

In the MARCHETT file, Victor Marchetti, CIA, 1977, revealed that mind-manipulation programs had not ceased as claimed.

> SUCCESSES ACHIEVED IN MK-ULTRA NARCOHYPNOSIS PROJECT COV-ERED UP BY CONGRESSIONAL SUBCOMMITTEE. CIA EFFORTS NOW FOCUSED ON PSYCHOELECTRONICS.

The FREY file reported that Allen Frey, scientist, remotely induced sleep with electromagnetic waves and transmitted acoustic noises—booming, buzzing, hissing—directly inside a subject's head. A major breakthrough for the deaf.

Mike Tesche wasn't old enough to have participated in any of these projects but had likely studied the notes for his own experiments. Dixie refused to believe he had succeeded in finding a mind-control drug that escaped discovery by the U.S. government.

Then she read the EDWARDS file.

> JONATHON EDWARDS, EVANGELIST. INDUCED GUILT AND ACUTE AP-PREHENSION TO INCREASE TENSION. "SINNERS" ATTENDING RE-VIVAL MEETINGS WOULD BREAK DOWN AND COMPLETELY SUBMIT.

TECHNICALLY, EDWARDS CREATED CONDITIONS THAT WIPE THE
BRAIN SLATE CLEAN; THE MIND THEN ACCEPTS NEW PROGRAMMING.
SUBJECTS ARE WIDE OPEN TO SUGGESTION.

The text explained Pavlov's progressive states of transmarginal inhibition,
through which conditioned responses and behavior patterns turn from positive to
negative or negative to positive.

FIRST STEP: WORK ON THE SUBJECT'S EMOTIONS UNTIL THEY
REACH AN ABNORMAL LEVEL OF ANGER, FEAR, EXCITEMENT, OR
NERVOUS TENSION. THE PROGRESSIVE RESULT IS IMPAIRED JUDG-
MENT AND INCREASED SUGGESTIBILITY. THE MORE THE CONDITION
CAN BE MAINTAINED OR INTENSIFIED, THE MORE IT COMPOUNDS.
SECOND STEP: ONCE CATHARSIS, OR THE FIRST BRAIN PHASE, IS
REACHED, EXISTING MENTAL PROGRAMMING IS REPLACED WITH
NEW PATTERNS OF THINKING AND BEHAVIOR.

Dixie had never prosecuted a cult member, but she'd studied occurrences in
Texas during her term on the DA's staff. In one case, tried in both Texas and
Florida, a self-proclaimed minister, Ron Larrinaga, had insinuated himself into a
family, winning over first the woman, then her husband, and keeping them psychological prisoners for two decades. Despite association with the outside world,
despite periods of separation, Larrinaga retained a powerful hold over the parents
and their children, who spurned their extended family and friends, submitted to
physical, psychological, and sexual abuse, and devoted every moment to ful-
filling the vision of a clever, charismatic leader.

Described by the adult children who had grown up under Larrinaga's influence, his techniques sounded exactly like Jonathon Edwards'. This was the sort of
"mind control" Dixie *knew* existed—though it seemed impossible until you
encountered it. With growing concern, she clicked on the last menu item,
TECHNIC.

USEFUL TOOLS AND TECHNIQUES: FASTING, RADICAL
DIETS, PHYSICAL DISCOMFORT, REGULATION OF BREATHING,
MANTRA CHANTING IN MEDITATION, SPECIAL LIGHTING AND SOUND
EFFECTS, PROGRAMMED RESPONSE TO INCENSE, INTOXICATING
DRUGS, PHYSICAL DISCIPLINE, ISOLATION, RITUAL PUNISHMENT.
IMPORTANT NOTE: HYPNOSIS AND CONVERSION TACTICS ARE
DISTINCTLY DIFFERENT. CONVERSION IS FAR MORE POWERFUL.
MIXING THE TWO PRODUCES OPTIMUM RESULTS.
REPETITIVE MUSIC: RANGING FROM 45 TO 72 BEATS PER

MINUTE (CLOSE TO THE BEAT OF THE HUMAN HEART). GENERATES
AN EYES-OPEN ALTERED STATE OF CONSCIOUSNESS IN A VERY HIGH
PERCENTAGE OF SUBJECTS. SUBJECT IS HIGHLY SUSCEPTIBLE TO
SUGGESTION.
VOICE-ROLL TECHNIQUE: PATTERNED, PACED STYLE USED
BY HYPNOTISTS WHEN INDUCING A TRANCE; WORDS DELIVERED AT
THE RATE OF 45 TO 60 BEATS PER MINUTE MAXIMIZE THE HYPNOTIC
EFFECT.

Dixie knew lawyers who used the voice-roll technique to entrench a point firmly in the minds of jurors. The lawyers practiced talking to the beat of a metronome, emphasizing every word in a monotonous, patterned style. She'd also seen it work in church, the pastor generating excitement and expectation through repetition of key phrases.

Drugged tea. Hypnotic relaxation music. If she'd correctly interpreted Mike's notes, he began indoctrinating his subjects during aerobics classes—repetitive music, motion that induced relaxation. Then he tested them with a simple command. *Your given name, the name on your birth certificate. Tell me. You won't forget the Sundown Ceremony this weekend.* Taken in context, such statements seemed entirely harmless. But the response enabled him to select promising subjects.

In the Sundown Ceremony, they'd used the repetitive phrase, "I commit to . . ." And in Mike's private quarters, encouraged by compliments and personal attention—along with the drugged tea and whatever-the-hell incense he used— Dixie had totally lost her intention to leave. Why entice her to stay the night, if not to be subjected to the music for a longer period? *Leave now, woman!*

The computer's digital clock read four forty-six A.M. She could return to her room, pretend sleep, and depart when the other women awakened. No reason to believe she'd be restrained from leaving after sunrise. Mike's "programming" apparently worked in stages, the first stage enticing you to return for more. Yet she was already dressed, and while she truly didn't expect to be susceptible now that she'd analyzed the techniques, why risk it?

Out in the hall, she released the latch gently against the striker. Mike could be anywhere in the building, and if he caught her sneaking away from his private wing, he'd realize she was onto him. She hurried to the first turn, slowed to get her bearings, then continued through the maze of hallways. Turning away from the dorm, she found herself in another long hall and remembered being there with Mike. One of the doors ahead led to the spacious lounge area off the atrium, and then outdoors. But which? She'd have to try them all.

The first door opened into an unfinished area, with bare rafters. Soon to be "long-term living quarters," Mike had said. Another unfinished area lay behind the next, with additional doors leading in two directions. A ribbon of light seeped beneath one of them. Could that be where Mike had gone?

To do what at this hour?

Dixie itched to know what was in that room. Despite what she'd learned from his computer files, she had no proof that he'd instigated the robberies. Entering the unfinished area, she moved toward the lighted strip . . . *Hey, Mike, I'm lost . . . where do you find an early cup of coffee in this place?* While he's talking, steal a glance in the room, see what he's working on at this hour.

What if he was with Angela, engaged in nothing more clandestine than a tumble in the sheets? Dixie listened at the door. Were those voices? She tapped lightly.

"Yes?" A woman. Almost a whisper.

"Ummm, hi. Guess I'm sort of lost here. Could you help me out?"

"Go away." Not Angela.

"Yeah, well, that's the problem. I can't seem to find my way, all these halls doubling back and forth. Could you maybe give me some direction?"

"Go away. You aren't supposed to be here."

"Oh, that part's okay, I was invited. Didn't we meet last evening, at the ceremony? I'm Dixie . . . you know, 'I commit to Togetherness'? Are you Laura? Or Dolores?" *What were the other names?*

"Go away! We'll be punished."

Punishment, the last entry under "useful tools" in Mike's notes. Larrinaga's flock had been beaten, ridiculed, forced to stand for hours in dark closets. Dixie didn't want to get anybody punished. She could no longer hear other voices in the room. Had they come from a television or radio? Or was Mike in there?

Dixie was certain all eleven women had retired to the dorm. Had this woman been summoned here for some sort of training? Or *discipline*, another item in Mike's list? Was she the client Mike was "counseling"?

"You don't have to stay here and be punished," Dixie said softly. "Come with me."

"No, no! Go away. The Shepherd will hear."

The Shepherd? Was that Mike? "Are you locked in? Can you open the door?"

"I won't open the door. Go away."

"Okay, I'm going." Dixie hesitated. She didn't want to cause any more problems for this woman than she already had. She couldn't force her to leave; cult members—and what else could you call these people?—were notoriously loyal to their beliefs and to their leader, even in abusive situations. If she burst into the room and Mike was in there, she'd have both of them against her—along with the entire household, once they heard the commotion.

But Dixie had a hunch, and she *had* to ask.

"I'm going right now, but could you just please tell me your name?"

After a moment's silence, the woman replied, "Rose."

Bingo! R for Rose, Y for Yenik. The letters in the fourth column of Mike's FOR-MULAS files.

Rose Yenik was also one of Vernice Urich's clients who continued to pay long after the counseling stopped. Coincidence? Possibly. But maybe not.

Chapter Sixty-four

Prisoner or willing guest, Rose Yenik was likely slated to be the next Granny Bandit. And possibly the next body lying in a pool of blood. Dixie couldn't let that happen.

She listened at Rose's door for another few seconds. When the voices didn't resume, she reentered the hallway. The next door she tried opened into the expansive common area, gray light of early dawn visible beyond the glassed-in atrium.

Above the mantel, the life masks in the "Matriarch Goddess" sculpture watched as Dixie crossed the room. Some cults believed that God, in the Second Coming, would appear as a woman. Did that make Mike a prophet—single male among twelve women? On the onyx slab in his sitting room, and in his ring, a single garnet was surrounded by twelve crystals. If Dixie hadn't come tonight, would Rose have been the twelfth?

A simple thumb bolt secured the outside door. Dixie turned it, stepped into a cool spring mist, slipped her boots on, and ran lightly to the Mustang. She drove the winding path toward the gate, glancing back only once for a final view of the beautiful sprawling building so exquisitely integrated with the landscape. The gate opened automatically, and Dixie headed for the city. Over an hour's drive, if she went home. She didn't want to wait an hour to read Aunt Edna's journal. She needed the answers it might provide.

As she drove, hands fixed hard to the wheel, listening to the hum of tires on pavement, noticing the familiar green-and-white highway signs, a sense of solidity returned and with it a pinch of dejection. How had she misjudged Mike Tesche so completely? Or had she? Anyone browsing through her own research books—volumes on guns, lock picking, serial killers—could label her as sinister and lawless.

The women she'd met last night hadn't seemed to be in a drugged state. At dinner, they'd been chatty, interesting, alert, amusing at times. Perhaps her reaction to the tea had been some fluke of her own body chemistry. Mike poured it in front of her, drank from the same pot, inhaled the same incense . . . why hadn't it affected him?

Dixie groaned. *The tablet Mike had swallowed to stop his coughing, shortly before they entered his quarters.* Apparently it worked instantly, because he hadn't coughed again the entire evening. *An antidote.* It seemed so obvious now.

But what did it prove? Nothing she'd learned at The Winning Stretch could be taken to a judge to obtain a search warrant for the bank's money bags—provided they hadn't already been destroyed. She needed more than suspicion. A lot more.

Edna had been a regular at The Winning Stretch aka the Church of The Light. Mike never denied that. But even if Edna's diary spelled out exactly how Mike induced her to commit armed robbery, she was not alive to testify.

At Waco, suspicion that the Branch Davidians were stockpiling illegal weapons had allowed the ATF to gain a warrant to search. But Dixie had seen no evidence of weapons at The Winning Stretch. If the handguns Edna and Lucy used had been licensed to Mike Tesche, the task force would already be knocking on his door. Dixie didn't believe he was that dumb.

In the Larrinaga case, the cult leader's demands for "constitutional rights" and "religious freedom" kept police from intervening. The Church of The Light would fall under that same constitutional protection. Only after the older children broke away from the family, complained of suffering physical and sexual abuse, and swore that their younger brothers and sisters still suffered such abuse were authorities able to obtain a warrant for Larrinaga's arrest. It had taken months.

Dixie had seen no children at the Church, and no indication that the women suffered abuse, despite Rose's statement that she would be punished. Punishment might be merely losing certain privileges. If Rose was the same Rose Yenik from Vernice Urich's ACH scam, Dixie had phoned her, spoken to her, a couple nights ago. Either she had telephone privileges in that room, or she hadn't been locked in for long.

Coming to a commercial area on the highway near Kingwood, Dixie scanned for a coffee shop open at this hour. Hot black coffee and thirty minutes with Edna's journal might be all she'd need. Only Stop & Go stores appeared. Dixie could drive and drink, but not read. There'd be something open nearer Houston. She stepped on the gas.

Was the AW in Mike's directory the only surviving bank robber? Angela? Or Alice, whom Dixie could not separate from the other nine faces?

One small fact gave Dixie hope that she might prevent another Granny Bandit robbery—and shooting. Today was Memorial Day. The banks would be closed. In the next twenty-four hours, she'd make someone listen, hog-tied, if necessary. Someone who wouldn't think her a babbling idiot. Someone who might grumble and sneer but would ultimately pay attention. Ben Rashly.

The morning mist had drifted away and the sun peeked through the clouds as a road sign announced the Houston city limits. A billboard advertising a talk radio station reminded Dixie she hadn't heard any news since Sunday morning. She punched the ON button.

"... *no further development in the assassination deaths of Officers Arthur Harris and Theodore Tally* ..."

The previous night's events had completely eclipsed her thoughts of the assassinations—and Marty's danger of arrest. Despite HPD's precautions, another Granny Bandit robbery could mean another slain woman. And if the cop killer's reasoning was "an eye for an eye," another officer would be assassinated. Three for three.

With citizens in Webster, Richmond, and Houston taking sides, Dixie wouldn't be surprised to see protest groups or even rioting. Suddenly, she felt overwhelmed by the impending presence of death.

Chapter Sixty-five

Monday, Memorial Day, 5:00 A.M.

Philip Laskey arrived at the training center after a restless night. He arranged the meeting-room chairs in tight semicircular rows, within a designated distance from the stage. Hearing the office door open behind him, he rose to salute the Colonel.

"Philip. You're eager to begin, I see."

"Yes, sir."

"Something's troubling you, Philip. What is it?"

Colonel Jay always knew. "Probably nothing, sir . . . but I heard Mayor Banning talking. He seems genuinely concerned about those officers and the women—"

"Of course he is." The Colonel looked directly into Philip's eyes. "But the Mayor's concern is not for those poor women they shot down, both of them mothers, one a *grandmother*, for God's sake." He laid a hand on Philip's shoulder. "Banning's concern, Philip, is only for the impact those deaths will have on his job. Why did he hire a man like Edward Wanamaker, a man incapable of inspiring his people with compassion, a man who teaches only to respond with force? Those officers would move a horse carriage with a bulldozer. But Avery Banning's no fool. He hired Wanamaker because he wants his own hand on the balance of order—"

"Sir, the Mayor didn't command those officers to shoot—"

"Philip, you've been reading Banning's press releases." The Colonel smiled, his gaze steady. He grasped both Philip's shoulders firmly. "Wisdom is knowing when to use a hammer and when to use a feather. Evil is having that wisdom and not using it. Avery Banning is as wise as he is evil. Don't feel bad or confused about being taken in, however briefly."

After a second's hesitation, Philip nodded. "Thank you, sir." He heard the faint noises of men entering the training center.

"I'll join you and the others in fourteen minutes," the Colonel told him.

"Yes, sir."

In the meeting room, Philip watched Rudy Martinez mount the few steps to the stage. His black hair looked wet from the gunk he applied to slick it back. *When I shoot,* Martinez had once told Philip, *I see my father's face in the crosshairs, red and swollen from drinking. And I never miss.*

"This is our big day, man," he told Philip now.

The marksman would be taking risks. "Are you ready for it?"

Martinez flashed a relaxed, confident smile that Philip had rarely seen. "You bet your sweet . . . *pistole* . . . I'm ready."

Philip nodded. The room buzzed with energy as The People continued to arrive. Nelson Dodge moved lazily to the edge of the stage. Cronin, his recruit, followed closely. Unlike many of the others, Nelson came from a successful, well-educated family. His father was a professor at Texas Southern University, his mother a gynecologist at Memorial Women's Hospital. Both aggressively sought career advancement; parenting had been an accident of faulty birth-control methods.

Dodge shook Philip's hand. Then to Cronin, he said, "Excuse us for a moment, would you?"

A shadow of resentment flitted across the rookie's face. "Sure." He clomped down the steps and strode to the water cooler.

"Philip, I need you to look out for him today," Dodge said.

"Should he even be out there?"

"If you're with him, he'll make out okay."

"No problem then."

As the time neared for Colonel Jay's address, chairs filled, the room quieted. The group force felt strong this morning, everyone eager to see the weeks and months of commitment result in change. Any kind of change would satisfy most of them.

Colonel Jay entered. The men rose, saluted. Then the Colonel made his way through, greeting one after another with words, handshakes—connecting in a way that, Philip knew, their families never had connected.

On the stage, Martinez and Dodge stood at attention.

The Colonel faced them, a hand on each man's shoulder.

"You have an important job today."

"Yes, sir," they replied in unison.

"Your actions will make history. You will eliminate an enemy of The People and put our name on the lips of every American."

"Yes, sir."

"When the instant arrives," the Colonel said, "I expect you to make the right decision. I trust your judgment."

Philip's breath caught. Dodge's judgment he'd trust anytime, but Martinez . . . ?

The lights dimmed and a photograph of the Rocky Mountains filled the presentation wall. The Colonel, standing in front of the screen, became a silhouette among the commanding peaks.

As the scene changed to wheat fields . . . to a deer in the wild, an otter beside a lake, sunrise on a Midwest farmhouse, the gnarled hands of a fisherman at his nets, a beautiful, pregnant young woman, the shadow of a cross on desert sand, and other images so beautiful they could make you ache . . . a poignant rendition of "An American Trilogy" played quietly.

"This country had strong leaders," the Colonel told them.

Mount Rushmore, now on the screen behind him, was followed by a bronze of Ben Franklin, then the Lincoln Memorial.

"Escaping from British tyranny, a handful of dedicated rebels carved out of raw land the greatest nation in the world. They sought a simple life of freedom, purity, justice, equality—and they achieved that dream."

The music swelled as images of American life filled the wall—country fairs, families on picnics, families at worship, children at play, working steel mills, cotton bales, cattle ranches, baseball games, triumphant athletes, great musicians, mountain hoedowns . . .

"But when good men relax their vigilance, even for an instant, tyranny reasserts itself."

The trilogy segued into "The Battle Hymn of the Republic," accompanied by violent images—not of great wars, but of national blemishes such as Watts, Viet Nam veterans returning home crippled, national heroes assassinated, terrorist bombings.

"Gentlemen, do you see justice here? Purity? Equality?"

"No, sir."

Photos of poverty and desolation—street people, ghettos, illegal aliens, job lines, face after face of the hopeless, the helpless, the unfortunates of society— flashed behind the Colonel.

Then the video changed abruptly to scenes of ostentatious wealth—tuxedoed men at lavish parties, pretty throats heavy with jewels, furs, limousines, yachts, mansions.

"Is there any wonder good people are driven to desperate deeds?"

"No, sir."

Photographs of Lucy Ames and Edna Pine—the sweet, sad faces of America's mothers—were followed by grainy, telephoto prints of both women gunned down, bleeding in the street.

Despite an intense desire to look away, Philip kept his eyes on the screen.

"Corruption starts at the top," the Colonel told them.

Snapshots: Mayor Banning and Chief Wanamaker wearing sly grins, engaged in secretive conversations, eating and drinking at extravagant gatherings.

"As always, it's the people who must rise up and seize control of an out-of-control situation."

Images of the men in the room filled the wall, strong, young, clean-cut faces set in determination, young bodies training for battle. Philip had taken most of this footage himself, thousands of frames as his friends laughed, talked, and trained together.

A final montage, some of the earlier images, ended with a close-up of the American flag and the Statue of Liberty. The video faded to black. Colonel Jay stood under a single light on the otherwise darkened stage.

"We are The People," the Colonel said.

As the room lights slowly rose to full intensity, Philip Laskey saluted.

"We are The People," Philip repeated.

In a rustle of movement the others stood and saluted.

"We are The People."

The Colonel returned their salute.

Five minutes later, Philip drove to his meeting with Mayor Banning, while others headed for Tranquility Park.

Chapter Sixty-six

The downtown area near City Hall had sprouted vendor booths selling T-shirts, toys, paintings, barbecued turkey legs, cold drinks, and a slew of unnecessary items that nevertheless always turned a dollar. With perfect spring weather and a hum in the air that said something important was happening, the masses had responded, jamming the streets and sidewalks and packing Tranquility Park.

Protesters carrying signs against police brutality clustered near the busiest entrance. No surprise.

What did surprise Dixie was the number of HPD officers in attendance and the number of FBI and Secret Service agents trying to pass as ordinary citizens. Perhaps the rumor about threat letters had been true. She scanned the already crowded park for Ben Rashly.

On the way here, she'd stopped to photocopy the pages in Edna's journal. Marty would find some of the entries upsetting, but others might assuage his guilt over his mother's death. His revelation had indeed angered her. After Bill's death Edna's world had narrowed to deciding which flowers needed watering each day, but an entry on January sixth spoke of the Fortyniners, where she met Vernice Urich and Terrence Jackson.

In a later installment, Edna and Lucy Ames had joined Mike Tesche's aerobics class after seeing his flyer at Fit After Fifty. Mike invited Edna to a Sundown Ceremony, where, among others, she met Rose. Shortly after that ceremony, Edna's bitterness toward her family seemed to mellow. *Marty is a fine son*, she'd written in February. *I've let go of all the hurt and anger. I wish Bill could've done the same before he died.*

But later entries were more disturbing. Edna learned that Lucy was tutoring privately with Mike. *I don't begrudge her; I only pray someday I'll ascend to that level.* And of course, she had. *Mike and Lucy have something special planned. I've been chosen to be a part of it. The Church needs so much more funding, yet Congress wastes our tax dollars. I offered to transfer half my investments now — rather than in my will — but Mike wouldn't hear of it. Lucy's plan is better, he says.*

Why would Mike turn down a donation? Unfortunately, Edna hadn't spelled out Lucy's plan specifically, and Rashly would balk at investigating a church on such vague ramblings from an old woman's pen — but the journal contained more information than the task force had at present.

From his aerobics classes, Mike chose his subjects — lonely women, abandoned by their families, hungry for the love and attention they'd lost, wealthy enough to contribute heavily to the Church of The Light. Where did Angela fit in? Fifty-plus, but mentally still a child, had she been the only one who succeeded at robbery? Or the only one who failed . . . to die?

Dixie spied Rashly at the western edge of the park, near a stage where a band played Mexican music while Folklorico dancers twirled their multicolored skirts. Among the trees, a giant candy-striped Uncle Sam balloon waved from a tall cylindrical platform. The main platform, larger and noisier than all the others, billowed with red, white, and blue flags. According to the news report Dixie'd heard driving in, the Mayor's commemoration speech was scheduled for nine-thirty. It was already nine twenty-five. Traffic had been a mess.

Making her way toward Rashly, Dixie jostled past a booth selling commemorative buttons. She dropped the journal. A young man scooped it up and handed it back to her.

"Thanks. My feet get tangled in crowds." As Dixie started to move on, a triangular metal insignia on the boy's lapel caught her eye. She gripped his arm. "What does your pin symbolize?"

He glanced down at the enameled emblem. "Preservation Society."

"Preservation of what?"

"American traditions. Hot dogs, marching bands." He smiled. "Memorial Day."

"A school group?" He looked barely high school age. Polite kid. Neatly dressed — unusual in the age of wash, dry, and go.

"Just a local club. Excuse me, I need to meet someone." He jogged toward the Uncle Sam booth.

"Preservation Society" didn't sound like an organization that would paint graffiti on buildings, and the kid looked too preppy for a gang member. But the gold "P" in a red triangle on a blue field matched the symbol in Ted Tally's sketches.

She considered mentioning the boy to Rashly . . . *nice kid, but he's wearing this pin.* Then she'd have to explain Ted's drawing, which would lead to explaining how she happened to *have* the drawings. Marty had been along during her B&E,

which wouldn't gain him any points. Besides, she needed Rashly's full concentration when she told him about the Church of The Light.

She hated turning everything over to the task force, knowing they'd move like snails. Any investigation into a church would be frustratingly slow and cautious. Perhaps she could figure a way to stay involved. No reason her early departure this morning should tip off Mike that she was on to his odious scheme. Maybe Rashly could convince the task force that Dixie was their best bet at gaining enough evidence to hang Mike Tesche. While Edna's notes hadn't specifically incriminated him, they'd back up what Dixie'd seen in Mike's files.

It was the final entry in Aunt Edna's journal, penned the night before she held up the Richmond bank, that had chilled Dixie: *Lucy's dead! Oh, I know she's moved on to a happier place, but we planned so carefully. How could this happen? I'll miss her. I'll do well for us both tomorrow.*

Not suicide but a desperate attempt to champion a cause she earnestly believed in. Reading those pages, Dixie'd grasped the depth of Edna's need for validation of her own worth. That validation should have come from lifelong friends who knew and loved her, not from a faction of zealots. Dixie, caught up in her own life, had failed to see Aunt Edna's downward spiral into desolation, just as she'd failed to see Kathleen's advancing frailty as the cancer claimed her. But Rose Yenik—*somebody's* friend and mother—could still damn well be saved.

On the main stage, the band signaled the start of the commemoration ceremony by playing louder and more vigorously. Other bands ended their numbers and people began to congregate near the big event. As Dixie called out to Rashly, dozens of moving bodies squeezed in front of her, cutting her off. Rashly vanished.

She spied Chief Wanamaker and his wife, Mira, near the main stage, surrounded by Secret Service types. Rashly might join them. Then she saw the Mayor talking with the young man from the "Preservation Society." He must be part of the program.

Drawing nearer, Dixie realized her mistake. The kid with the Mayor was freckle-faced Philip Laskey. He wore similar clothes, crisp khaki pants and jacket, light blue shirt. Certainly not a uniform—the jacket was longer than the one the other boy wore, but the *impression* of a uniform, as if they both attended the same private school.

Nearer the main platform, the crowd thickened. Dixie squeezed through, murmuring apologies. The master of ceremonies finished his welcoming comments. The band started a Sousa strain. Mayor Banning approached the stage, his wife Kaylynn applauding nearby.

As Dixie eeled through the crowd, the Mayor praised Houstonians for their support over the past six months and voters who turned out at the polls during the recent bond election. Then he praised the HPD officers, two slain and one wounded, for valor in the line of duty. He commended Chief Wanamaker for squashing an insidious drug ring that had preyed specifically on elementary schools. The Chief joined the Mayor at the lectern—

Crack!

The sound came from behind her.

Banning fell.

Shrieks. Shouts. A swell of movement toward the stage.

Dixie muscled through for a better view.

Crack! The Chief went down.

Screams and motion erupted as people realized what had happened. Paramedics scrambled into action. FBI agents swarmed the main stage, ordering everyone back.

More shots behind her.

"They got him!" A cheer among the clamor.

Dixie pushed through a dense wall of shrieking, shoving bodies headed toward the nearest exit, forcing her way in the direction of the gunshots. As she neared the Uncle Sam display, a female voice on a loudspeaker identified herself as FBI and commanded everyone away. Two men lay sprawled on the grass, khaki-clad legs splayed awkwardly.

A woman clutched Dixie's arm and shook her, babbling. Dixie jerked free and the screaming woman grabbed a man ahead of her. At the edge of the crowd encircling the slain assassins, a small boy stood crying and pointing. A young girl tried to tug him away.

Dixie pushed closer. One slain man was black, the other Hispanic. Both wore light blue shirts, khaki jackets. No triangular pins, but both looked as all-American as the "Preservation Society" member. And Philip Laskey.

A strange notion popped into Dixie's head. What if a gang didn't look like a gang? What if the members dressed against type, adopted a wholesome, all-American facade, appeared as harmless as the proverbial boy next door? Like Poe's purloined letter, such a gang could mingle in a crowd like this one with little notice, while a young man in baggies—shaved head, tattoos, skin piercings, gang colors—wouldn't get two feet inside the park without a cavity search.

She scanned the mob. No way she could get to Rashly now. And the FBI would never listen to such a wacky tale. Not when they already had the shooters.

Dixie angled toward a park entrance and worked her sharp elbows, stretching to see over shoulders and heads as she windmilled through the throng. If her hunch was right, other gang members would be making their escape.

Out on the sidewalk, the crowd divided around a news truck from a local TV station parked at the curb. A newscaster shouted into a microphone, a camera trained on her face.

"*Two suspects have been shot and apprehended!*" The newswoman wore an earphone that probably connected her to another team inside. "*Officers are now securing the area around a kiosk where the snipers apparently concealed themselves to carry out the assassinations. Camouflaged with blue and white bunting, the tower-shaped . . ."*

Dixie headed toward her Mustang, parked a block away. As she jogged, she scanned for khaki clothing—and finally saw them: two clean-cut young men striding toward a green Jeep Cherokee.

Chapter Sixty-seven

"You were told not to wear the pin, Cronin." Philip barely contained his rage as they left Tranquility Park.

"Never mind the damn pin. What happened?" the rookie demanded. "How did they screw up?"

"Order and consistency guarantee predictable outcomes." Philip clicked the doors open to his Cherokee and they climbed in. "One neglected detail undermines predictability. You were *told* not to wear the pin."

"C'mon, Laskey, forget the fuck—"

Philip's fist shot out, a hard right jab at Cronin's mouth. Teeth scraped his knuckles. Thin drops of blood sprayed the dash.

Cronin yelped.

"You don't have what it takes to be one with The People, Wynn Cronin."

The rookie lashed back with a fist. Philip clamped a hand over his wrist and twisted, stopping just short of breaking it.

"Hey! All right!" Cronin squealed.

"One weak strut topples the tower. If you can't follow simple orders, how can you be trusted to follow important ones?"

"You're nuts, yammering about a pin when men are dead back there."

Philip applied more thumb pressure on the wrist, compressing the nerves. The rookie gasped, tears sliding from his eyes.

"Soldiers die in battle," Philip whispered roughly. "Did you think this was playtime?" *But Martinez, dead? Dodge, dead? Nothing right about that. They should've had time to blend with the crowd.* "One neglected detail can get men killed." He released Cronin's wrist. "Now, go home."

"Home? My parents will know something's wrong. I'm too jumpy."

He did look ready to crawl out of his skin. Philip reached across the rookie and pushed open the passenger door. "The People don't allow nerves to rule their actions. *Walk* home."

"Walk? It's six god—" Cronin bit off the blasphemy. "Walk six miles? It'll take an hour."

"By then you'll no longer be jumpy."

"Why can't I hang around the park, see what happens next?"

"Colonel Jay issued an order: When Chief Wanamaker is dead, everyone goes home. We meet at the training center at noon."

"You always do exactly what the Colonel says?"

Philip itched to wipe the petulant smirk off the rookie's face, but not here. Not now.

"The Colonel doesn't issue orders lightly. Everything's been thought out, discussed, and decided upon. Colonel Jay commands the will of The People. Each of us took a vow to honor that will. Are you already backing down on your vow?"

"I didn't say—"

"Go home, Cronin."

The boy hesitated. "The Colonel didn't say anything about walking six miles."

"Then do what your heart tells you." Philip made his face as expressionless as he'd seen the Colonel's on such occasions. Then he placed his foot against Cronin's side and pushed him out of the Jeep.

The rookie grappled for balance and managed to land on his feet, then glared for a count of five.

"You're nuts, Laskey." But he started walking.

Satisfied at providing a lesson in patience and obedience, Philip maneuvered the Cherokee into impossible traffic. He, too, had been included in the order to return home after the mission was finished . . . only the Colonel hadn't expected Dodge and Martinez to go down. Certainly, he would require a report. He would need Philip's help now more than ever. Philip entered the freeway toward The People's training center.

Chapter Sixty-eight

Avoiding pedestrians Dixie inched the Mustang forward as she searched for the green Jeep. She spotted it in a snarl of traffic entering the freeway ramp.

But headed wrong in the tightly packed muddle, she could not make a U-turn. Recalling a little-known road that dead-ended into a vacant lot, she whipped the wheel right, drove across the lot, picked up another road, and joined the freeway at the next ramp.

Dixie had a theory about Texas drivers. If all the cars in the state were lined up bumper to bumper, some damn fool would try to pass them—and it would probably be her. Bullying her way into the traffic stream, she found an open lane and stepped on the gas.

A mile and a half later, she spotted the Jeep again. She memorized the license number, noticing there was only one person in the vehicle. Changing lanes, she eased alongside, recognized the Mayor's junior assistant, then slowed, leaving a double car length between them.

The Cherokee remained in the center lane, driving precisely to the speed limit. Finally, it eased over to exit and turned east into a wooded area.

As the county road wound among Texas pines and thick underbrush, Dixie's Mustang and the green Jeep were the only cars on it. Impossible to keep the other vehicle constantly in sight without being spotted. She dropped far enough behind to avoid alerting the driver. The road wound northeast, then a sharp curve opened into a long, straight stretch of road. The Jeep should be right ahead. It was gone.

Dixie braked, U-turned, and backtracked to a gravel side road marked PRIVATE near the spot where she'd lost sight of the Jeep. Taking the turn, she headed east into a dense thicket. Her tires kicked up brown road dust as she snaked among the trees. Ahead, traces of dust already floated on the air, showing a vehicle had passed through in the past few minutes.

The undergrowth gradually thinned out. In the distance, Dixie heard the roar of an eighteen-wheeler as the private road dead-ended into a narrow blacktop.

She scanned briefly in both directions before turning north, away from the diesel's diminishing growl. A mile down the road, she spied another turnoff, the air thick with dust. Nearly two miles after the turn, she spied the Cherokee in the driveway of a boarded-up one-story building. Dixie slowed.

A heavy-gauge chain stretched across the drive, blocking the entrance to a parking area filled with potholes. Laskey must've put up the chain after driving through. The Jeep disappeared around back.

Cruising past, Dixie made another U-turn a quarter mile down and parked the Mustang off the road near a growth of yaupon. She cut the engine and considered what to do. Whatever was inside the building might be none of her business. She might be mistaken about the young man's relationship to the sniper. Her odometer had registered thirty-six miles, which meant she could be in one of three police jurisdictions. What would she say if she called for help? "Chased the Mayor's assistant because he was wearing suspicious clothes? Saw him stop at a deserted building?"

Climbing out of the car, she circled to the trunk and grabbed a penlight, then considered the battered case containing two handguns and a combat shotgun. If Laskey was part of a gang that had engineered the assassinations, she'd be a fool to be caught in that building unarmed. She removed a .38 Smith & Wesson Airweight, loaded it, snapped it into a belt holster at her waist, then untucked her shirttail to cover it.

Slipping a pair of handcuffs into her pocket, she sprinted down the road, staying in the shadows of the yaupon. The underbrush cleared. The building came in sight.

Shit! The Cherokee was driving away!

What now? Jump back in the Mustang and follow?

No . . . she had the license number. And that building intrigued her.

Laskey had left the chain down—meaning he would likely return. Still, she might have a few minutes to explore. Ten minutes—it would take at least that long to drive anywhere from here, wouldn't it? Anywhere with grocery stores, strip centers, eateries. Ten there, ten back, twenty minutes total.

Why would anyone drive to this remote spot in the first place—unless that structure contained secrets?

Dixie jogged back to the Mustang, opened the trunk, and removed a Lock-Aid tool, a gun-shaped device capable of opening just about any lock with a keyhole. If the building was occupied, the four-by-eight sheets of plywood covering every door and window would prevent anyone seeing her approach.

Easing down one side of the building, Dixie looked for peepholes, loose boards, any way to see inside. She found nothing. She scanned the parking area, and finally peeked around the rear. No vehicles. A wide shed with overhead doors suggested enclosed parking for at least ten cars. Dixie lifted one of the doors and looked in. Empty. But it smelled like a garage, stale oil and exhaust fumes.

Directly behind the building stood a wooden stand facing open pasture, then wooded acreage. A single-station shooting range?

She circled back and turned her attention to a plywood panel that covered the rear door. It appeared solidly nailed to the building, like the others she'd tested, but closer examination showed that it was merely nailed to lath strips. When she shoved, the whole panel glided sideways on suspension rollers to reveal a padlocked door. She inserted the Lock-Aid tool into the padlock and pulled the trigger, emitting a series of clicks. The lock fell open. She slipped it out of its hasp, flipped the latch back, and rehung the padlock.

Anyone arriving would know instantly someone was inside—and Texas property owners had been known to shoot trespassers. Dixie glanced behind her at the empty parking area and the land beyond it, then turned the knob and pushed. The dead bolt was also locked, but a few clicks of the Lock-Aid snapped it open. The door swung inward with a creak that made her swallow a curse, even though the padlock suggested the building was empty.

Stepping inside, she sensed she was in a large open space. Only the thinnest rays of sunlight seeped through the boarded windows. She smelled cordite. Heard no voices, and no other sounds.

She slid the plywood panel back in place. At least no one would spot the intrusion from a distance, and the noise of the panel sliding back might give her time to take cover.

Flicking on the penlight, she saw a polished hardwood floor. Folded chairs leaned against one wall. Above the chairs, a poster read: WE ARE THE PEOPLE, WE ARE THE POWER, WE ARE PROTECTORS. Another poster showed a famous battle scene from the Civil War.

Her penlight picked out white letters on a blue background. She played the light over the writing. *We, the People of the United States . . .* the Preamble to the Constitution.

Preservation Society, the kid had said. The Civil War poster, the Preamble, both would certainly fit such a group.

She moved forward ten yards to a raised carpeted platform, with steps leading from one side. Mounting the steps, she looked down at the open floor space. She stood on the stage of an old ballroom. Judging by the lectern, with dials and buttons marked for audiovisual presentation, meetings were held here. The wall behind the stage was painted with a large graphic. She aimed her light around the edges and after a few sweeps recognized a letter "P" enclosed in a triangle. *Preservation Society.*

A videotape protruded from the VCR play slot. Locating the volume control, Dixie slid it all the way left, toward mute. She pushed the video in. Instantly, the PLAY indicator lit up, and a twelve-foot movie screen descended from the ceiling, covering the logo wall.

After a short lead, a mountain scene appeared on the screen, snowcapped peaks, then a waterfall, a hiking trail, cotton fields, lakes, streams—preservation of natural resources? The collage might've been taken from a travelogue, with a bit of the History Channel edited in.

As Dixie reached for the REWIND button, the scene changed abruptly to fires, explosions, street fights. News coverage of the Kennedy assassinations. Then a swift series of party photos, wealthy homes, men in tuxedos, women in furs and diamonds.

With a rough splice, the video jumped to still shots, and this time Dixie felt a thump of apprehension.

A smiling photo of Lucy Ames appeared, a close-up, with corner tabs to hold it in an album. The image remained on-screen longer than others had, then a similar one of Edna Pine took its place. The photo was obviously recent; Edna wore the calm, determined expression Dixie had noticed during the bank robbery.

Another abrupt cut brought a grainy black and white video segment: a police car in the foreground. Rapid movement. A figure falling. The camera zoomed in on Lucy Ames, dead.

Cut to a highway scene: police cars racing to a halt, lights blazing. A cluster of cops. It took another instant for Dixie to realize she was viewing Edna's death—footage more graphic than any she'd seen on TV news.

The camera's eye lingered on the pooled blood, the blood-spattered car, the body, until Dixie longed to rip the images off the screen. Why would anyone want to watch these women die over and over again?

Then the screen flooded with color—a head-and-shoulders snapshot of Avery Banning, another of Chief Wanamaker standing beside the Mayor, the two men laughing. A rush of gray snow signaled the tape's end.

The footage of the shooting appeared to be the work of an amateur, but with a good eye, Dixie thought, and a good camera. A private citizen brazening along behind the cops? A photographer who stumbled on the scene by accident?

Dixie punched the EJECT button and stepped down from the stage. She swept the side wall with her penlight. Posters showed young men in competition and combat. Interspersed among the images, captions proclaimed: HONOR THY COUNTRY, HONOR THY CONVICTIONS, and UNITED WE ARE ONE FORCE, THOUSANDS STRONG. Another cautioned: WATCH BIG BROTHER.

Had she stumbled on a paramilitary counterculture? No swastikas or hate slogans. No obvious racial separatism. But the message clearly celebrated a readiness to do battle.

Following the sharp odor of cordite, she found a door. It opened easily, and she peered down a long hallway flanked by closed doors on either side.

She glanced back at the entrance, at a sliver of outside light seeping through a crack. Here she was creeping around in dark forbidden places for the second time in less than twelve hours. Maybe Parker was right, teasing her about being a snoop. These people were seriously into concealment, and she was poking into their secrets. Once she entered that hallway, there'd be no chance of hearing Laskey return behind her.

He'd been gone . . . what, fourteen minutes?

Moving quickly to the first door, she put her ear to it, tried the knob. Inside a narrow room, her beam fell on metal lockers. No padlocks. She opened a few at random . . . men's gym shoes, pieces of clothing. Continuing, she found a shower space, a one-stall rest room with lavatories, urinals, and another closed door that opened into a gymnasium. About forty feet square, it looked as modern as any commercial gym, with free weights and punching bags at the far end—nice stuff—and a door that led back into the hall.

Only two doors left. Dixie checked her watch. Laskey'd been gone sixteen minutes. Staying longer increased the odds of discovery. If this group turned out to be involved in the assassinations, being discovered could taint any evidence she found. Under Texas law, evidence obtained by cops *or* civilians during the commission of a crime—such as breaking and entering—could be ruled inadmissible.

But if she could locate the office, a letterhead or business card might tell her who owned this place—and why they possessed a video of the Granny Bandit shootings.

She turned the next doorknob and peeked into shadows stinking of cordite. Three stations, ear protectors hanging on wall hooks.

Meeting room, gymnasium, shooting gallery . . . a training facility? Located far away from any neighbors who might take offense, soundproofed—Dixie hadn't heard any road noise since she entered. And a rifle range out back. *For sighting in an assassin's high-powered scope?*

She could be wrong. The videos of Lucy Ames and Aunt Edna might be as innocent as the shoot/don't-shoot films used for training police officers. *This is what can happen . . . here's how to avoid it.*

As Dixie turned to leave, her beam streaked across a face. She stifled a yelp. Then, slowly, she played the light over a life-size poster of Avery Banning. Another of Chief Wanamaker. Not one copy of each but several, hanging from clips.

Suitable for target practice.

Jazzed with sudden conviction, she swooped her light around the room. In a trash can lay a discarded poster riddled with holes. A tight firing pattern centered on the Chief's face. Any of the shots would've been a kill.

She'd found the sniper's lair.

The puzzle pieces chinked into place. A gang of middle- to upper-class boys, with enough money to outfit this building as a training center, an education that included plenty of video war games, and a notion of superiority. Wasn't it always the educated youth who protested the sorry mess the older generation had made of their world?

Dixie'd been only a child during the turbulent sixties and seventies, but she recalled the college campus riots. Today's youth took violence a giant step further—manufacturing bombs, shooting up schools.

Whatever else they might be, the "Preservation Society" boys were cop killers.

She had to get out of here. She could use the cell phone in the Mustang to call . . . who? With no legal right to be here, how could she report what she'd found without compromising the evidence?

Out in the hallway, she stared at that final door. What more might she learn in there? Did she really believe a few young men had planned and carried out the assassinations alone? The setup here—the gym, the AV equipment, all of it—was too sophisticated, too well thought out. Not to mention costly. If she had a *name*, a face . . . if she could link Laskey to a known terrorist or criminal . . .

Two minutes. I could be in and out of that room in two minutes.

Chapter Sixty-nine

The small office contained a battered metal desk with a wood chair and computer, a butt-sprung sofa, a bookcase, a four-drawer file cabinet with a thirteen-inch portable television on top of it, a water dispenser, a guest chair, and another damn door. That one opened into a bathroom, complete with shower. Dixie went straight to the computer.

While she waited for it to boot up, she searched the desk drawers. She found stationery with the triangular "P" emblem, but no name or address. No business cards. She found pencils, pens, rubber bands, computer disks. A cell phone. She looked behind the CPU for a cable connection to a wall jack . . . none. The building probably had no telephone service. Everything was remarkably neat, no stray Post-it Notes, loose paper clips, or other clutter. In a bottom drawer, she found three letters, identical except for the names at the top: Chief Edward Wanamaker, Councilman John Jason Gibson, Mayor Avery Banning.

This is the only warning you will receive . . .

Each letter was signed in a careful script, "The People."

More proof linking the building occupants with the assassinations. But where were the names she needed? Maybe she could choke them out of Philip Laskey.

Dixie wondered why Gib had been targeted along with the others. Anyone who paid attention to local politics knew that Gib Gibson opposed everything Banning and the Chief stood for. Unless all the City Council members received a similar letter, it made no sense. Had they? If so, why keep only these three copies?

A message on the computer asked for her password. Dixie didn't even try. Her two minutes were up. She rose from the chair to tackle the file cabinet.

But as she scanned the bookcase, her gaze fell on an object that totally surprised her, and a chilling new puzzle piece slid home. She reached for the sculptured onyx paperweight.

"Ms. Flannigan? What are you doing here?"

Dixie froze.

Philip Laskey tossed a plastic bag from an office supply store onto the sofa. A printer cartridge slid out. Despite the astonishment she read in Laskey's face, his hand pointing a Sig Sauer at her chest remained steady.

"I was . . . waiting." Dixie prayed the vague lie and Laskey's confusion would buy her some time to think. *She couldn't risk going for the .38 holstered at her waist.*

"Waiting for the Colonel?"

"Yes. He . . . had to run an errand. Said he'd be right back." Her thumb on the onyx sculpture traced a circle of stones surrounding a single garnet.

Laskey moved closer. "Colonel Jay doesn't run errands. That's my job."

Damn. Should've stopped with "yes," kept the lie simple.

"We were hungry." Dixie edged toward him. *Keep him talking, get within reach, aim at his kneecap . . .* "I asked him to pick up some burgers."

Laskey shook his head. "No, ma'am. No way."

Wrong again. "Philip—"

"Ma'am, would you sit down?" He circled away from her.

"Do you know who the Colonel really is, Philip? What he does?" The sculpture contained more stones than a similar model she'd seen at The Winning Stretch.

"Drop the paperweight. And sit down. Please."

"No." Once seated, she'd lose any advantage. "If you plan to shoot me, go ahead."

"I don't want to shoot you, ma'am. But I need to page the Colonel. You'll be more comfortable seated."

"Philip, this man you call Colonel Jay ordered the assassination of Mayor Banning and Chief Wanamaker, didn't he? And those two officers who were murdered—"

"Eliminated."

"—to avenge the deaths of Lucy Ames and Edna Pine?" The videos had been used to stoke the men's anger. Dixie recalled the photograph on Laskey's desk, of a woman old enough to be his mother. "Philip, Colonel Jay also sent those two mothers into the banks to steal. He knew they couldn't succeed."

"You're wrong. The Colonel had nothing to do with the bank robberies." But for an instant, his eyes had gone flat, as if he were thinking about it.

"Where did you meet the Colonel, Philip? At a YMCA fitness class?" What better place to recruit young men? "He attracts women the same way, at aerobics classes. Conditions them for service in a sort of cult he calls the Church of The Light." Dixie's thumb traced the silver filigree lacing the stones together, forming a web. "How did he get film from the shootings? He had to've been there—"

"He bought it from a TV cameraman, a friend—"

"The same friend happened to be on-site for *both* shootings? How logical is that?" How logical that *anyone* could've been at both sites? If he waited near the banks for Lucy or Edna to hand off the money, why would he then follow them? The horrible truth struck like stone. "Philip, the Colonel knew they wouldn't escape because *he* made the anonymous call to the cops."

"No, ma'am!"

"Yes, Philip. And I can show you right now where another woman, locked away in seclusion, is being conditioned for another robbery . . . and another police shooting."

The gun wavered as Philip's gaze once again flattened.

Dixie hurled the paperweight and moved in for a kick—

A bullet tore past and slammed into the wall.

Philip spun sideways. He slumped to the floor, blood running down his neck. *Surely not from the paperweight—*

A shape in the doorway. Another gun muzzle aimed at her.

He looked different in The People's khaki-and-blue uniform. He looked harder. His unruly mop was combed neatly in place and he wore no trace of his usual boyish grin: Mike Tesche.

Chapter Seventy

"I can see that you're armed, Dixie, and unlike Mr. Laskey, I know your capabilities. So lift the tail of your shirt and remove the gun with your left hand." When she complied, Mike said, "Slowly now, move to the desk and put it down."

Dixie's gaze flickered to Philip Laskey. The boy's head was a solid red cap, oozing blood. Just a kid, really, misguided by a master.

"He needs an ambulance."

"Not for long. I shot to kill."

"*Why?* Why shoot him?"

"You planted a seed of doubt. Mr. Laskey was fertile ground for growing it."

"It's becoming a habit, isn't it? Killing your own man. Or woman." Dixie seethed at the horror: He'd sent Lucy Ames and Aunt Edna to certain death, then ordered the murder of Art Harris and Ted Tally for killing them. Why?

"Like disease, Dixie, doubt must be eradicated before it spreads. Put the gun down and empty your pockets. Please use your left hand."

She placed the .38 Airweight on the desk and followed it with the Lock-Aid, her Kubaton key ring, wallet, handcuffs, penlight.

Mike wedged the Airweight under his belt. He scooped up everything but the handcuffs.

"Snap one of those around your wrist and sit down in the chair."

Reluctantly, Dixie did as he instructed. He'd already proved he'd shoot.

Mike circled Philip's body, keeping his .25 semiautomatic aimed at Dixie's chest. He slipped the Airweight from his belt, dropped it and her other things into the bottom drawer of the file cabinet. He located Philip's Sig Sauer near the boy's hand and put that in. Then he removed a metal lockbox from the drawer, and set it on the bookshelf, before locking the file cabinet.

"I know your tricks, Dixie, and you know I won't hesitate to kill you. But if you cooperate, that may not be necessary."

Oh, really? She glanced at Philip.

"Mr. Laskey's disappearance will not raise any eyebrows except his mother's, and she can be handled," Mike said. "But you, Dixie Flannigan, have too many friends in high places."

"And if I cooperate?"

He smiled, but without the boyish good humor she'd seen so often. "Then you'll leave here with no great loss, except a bit of your memory."

"How—?"

"Never mind that now. First, your cooperation." When she nodded, he said, "Put your hands behind you and push them through the chair slats. Then snap the handcuff on your free hand."

Again, Dixie complied, as her thoughts raced through her mental file for what she knew about Mike. He liked to talk, to lecture on his philosophies. *You have a beautiful soul . . .*

"What happened to, 'You would make a tremendous leader, Dixie. Align with me'?"

He moved behind her and pressed the gun to the back of her head as he checked the handcuffs.

"I do regret we never had a chance to discover our compatibilities. You're the first person I've considered bringing fully into my confidence."

"And now you've changed your mind?"

"You changed it for me by coming here, learning too soon what I would have revealed slowly." After assuring she was manacled, he lowered his gun.

"I didn't know you were part of these assassinations, Mike. Did you think I was too dense to understand your work in one pass?"

Without answering, he cast an appraising eye over Philip's body, then used his foot to push the boy's spraddled legs out of his way.

They could've passed for father and son, Dixie noticed—not their features, but in similar build and coloring. The reddish hair. The freckles.

Mike turned his steady green eyes on Dixie.

"In less than half an hour, twenty-seven men will arrive here. I will congratulate them for their part in forwarding our mission and offer reassurance that their comrades died valiantly this morning." He snapped the television on.

"*. . . Chief Wanamaker was pronounced dead at the scene. Mayor Banning was life-flighted to Hermann Hospital . . .*"

"Twenty-six minutes is not much time for you to convince me of your allegiance."

If she had a week, she'd never convince him.

Or could she? It might be her only way out. *If I couldn't convince people to trust me,* Parker'd said, *I'd never make a sale.* Was it possible to convince Mike she admired his work and desired to be a part of it? Dixie resisted a shudder.

"Mike, I know so little about the Church of The Light and almost nothing about what you've put together here. Yet I was impressed with what I saw last night. Somehow, you brought out Edna's strengths, and I believe that's true of the other women at The Winning Stretch."

"Not bad. You expressed interest and appreciation without turning sappy." He lifted the metal box from the bookshelf and carried it to the desk. "And almost managed a nice tone of sincerity."

Dixie swallowed a curse and worked on that sincerity part.

"What I don't understand," she said truthfully, "is why Lucy and Edna had to die."

"Death is inevitable. 'How' and 'when' are the only variables. Wouldn't you rather go out with excitement and drama?" He unlocked the box and from its depths extracted three amber jars. "Isn't that why you chose a dangerous profession?"

"By profession, I'm a nonpracticing lawyer. The other is just something I do." She watched him measure liquid from one of the jars into a flask, and caught a whiff of the same fragrance as the incense he'd used in his sitting room. "Mike, are you saying that Lucy and Edna *chose* to die in those shoot-outs?"

"Not intentionally. They participated knowing the chance of death existed. Effective knowledge is that which includes knowledge of the *limitations* of one's knowledge, wouldn't you agree?" He looked up from adding a measure of a second liquid to the flask. "My information in certain areas of control was limited until Lucy and Edna demonstrated that a person can be induced to willingly die."

"Were they drugged?" Dixie had a sick feeling about the concoction he was mixing.

"Not at all. Of course your suspicion derives from your own experience with your tea last night. I assure you, while we do burn a rare and extremely relaxing type of incense, the herbal tea blend, also rare, is only necessary to heighten suggestibility in the early stages."

He measured a third liquid into the flask. The "formulas" in Mike's computer file had three ingredients.

"The tea," Dixie said. "You blend it from three plants. The same plants that are reduced to extracts in those vials."

Mike's eyebrows rose. "I'm impressed."

He wouldn't be if he knew she'd seen his computer files—and the lockbox in his desk at The Winning Stretch, identical to this one.

"So am I." Dixie fought to keep fear from her voice as she watched him remove a hypodermic needle from the box. "You identify women who are emotionally distressed, obtain their trust, use mild sedatives to induce relaxation and suggestibility, then what?" She knew, but she wanted him to tell her, to trust her enough to tell.

He plunged the needle into the mixture; the syringe filled. Dixie thought of Angela, sweet, childlike. Had she always been so dim? Or only after an injection of Mike's herbal drug, a substantially higher concentration than the other women received orally?

"Everyone needs something to believe in, Dixie, a focal point for the soul, for the mind, for the enthusiasm of life. When we lose our way, life becomes a struggle."

Yes. Hadn't Dixie been struggling for a "focal point" since she abandoned law? "Your Church gave Edna and Lucy something to believe in again."

But Mike was turning up the TV sound.

"Councilman John Jason Gibson also received a letter threatening reprisal for the Granny Bandit deaths . . ."

"That was no accident, was it, leaving Gib alive?"

"A good guess. The Councilman will be useful when he replaces Banning as Mayor."

Gib would be a shoo-in if Banning died. "But Mayor Banning might recover."

Mike smiled. "I fully expect he will. He and the Chief both wore bulletproof vests, and only Wanamaker received a head shot."

"You *wanted* Banning to survive?"

"Death is only an illusion, Dixie, as we transcend this life to another. *Humiliation* is a far greater punishment. Wouldn't you agree?"

"Humiliation . . . for his failure to handle the Granny Bandit robberies without bloodshed?" The public wouldn't remember that only one robbery occurred in HPD jurisdiction—*both shootings* occurred there. And with Wanamaker dead, the only one left to shoulder the blame was Avery Banning. The media, egged on by Gib, had already questioned Banning's discretion in hiring Ed Wanamaker. "Then you believe Banning will be forced to resign."

"If not now, eventually. I'm well acquainted with the virtue of patience." Mike laid the syringe on the desk.

Dixie's gaze felt welded to it. "Why Banning?"

"Do you really want to spend your remaining six minutes talking about Avery Banning?"

Damn, he wasn't buying it. She hadn't sold many Girl Scout cookies, either.

"Surely young men respond very differently from postmenopausal women."

Mike smiled. "Again, you surprise me. A rush of hormones is all that's needed to send adolescent males raging into battle. I merely channel their natural aggression. The human mind is a powerful tool, Dixie. Imagine having the power to direct twelve or thirty minds—or an entire community—toward a single accomplishment—"

Like Jim Jones? David Koresh?

"Everyone has a personal point of vulnerability. Find it, pursue it, and you have them right here." Mike closed his hand into a fist. "It's like being connected by a strong silk strand. Direct the subject into position, thrum the strand, and vibrations occur in far-off places."

Dixie injected as much conviction into her own voice as she could manage. "I wish we'd had a chance to work together, Mike."

"Do you?"

She held his eyes, resisted glancing down at the needle. Despite the chill that had crept deep into her bones, Dixie envisioned a sunny day at the beach, a romp on the sand with Mud and Parker. Then she aimed that joy at Mike Tesche. She had to convince him.

" 'A soul that knows strength develops skill.' Mike, that's what you meant, wasn't it?" Dixie allowed her eyes to widen a fraction, as if in surprise. "The strength to pursue the mission, even when a subject must be sacrificed. Lucy, Edna— their job was to draw fire. By forcing the officers to shoot, they stirred up public hostility toward the HPD and, by extension, Chief Wanamaker and Mayor Banning." Dixie exhaled the last word in a whisper of admiration. "Brilliant."

Mike gave a single nod and glanced at his watch. "It's time to make an appearance. Can I trust you for five minutes?"

Dixie shrugged, rattling the cuffs. "Can't get in much trouble like this."

He studied her eyes for another moment, then he checked her handcuffs, tossed a glance at Laskey, and closed the door behind him.

Dixie waited a full minute. She couldn't hear his footsteps receding down the hall. That bothered her. Could he be waiting outside the door, planning to step back in and catch her trying to escape?

Swiveling the chair around on its rollers, she backed up to the desk. The cell phone was in the top drawer. Her hands wouldn't reach that high.

She struggled to her feet, dragging the heavy chair up with her. Handcuffs gouged into her wrists. She stretched her fingers . . . and finally tugged the drawer open. Shuffling around again, she saw the cell phone and dropped back into the chair. She stabbed at the POWER button with her tongue. Hard to see when she was close enough to hit it. She backed off to look—no lighted numerals. Tried again, could feel buttons move beneath her tongue, but the power refused to come on. Maybe the battery was dead.

Pencil, pen . . . she needed something to punch the buttons. *Shit.* The pencils were in the other top drawer.

Reversing, she rocked up on her feet again, the chair's weight scraping the handcuffs painfully down her chafed wrists, and opened the other drawer. Then seated, she pushed her face into the drawer, caught a pencil between her teeth. Rolled back to the cell phone. She punched the POWER button . . . and heard a satisfying *chirp*.

The NO SERVICE light came on, then the ROAM light. It winked off, then on again. When it winked out the second time, Dixie hurriedly punched 911 and SEND. Leaning far enough into the drawer to speak *and* hear sufficiently was impossible.

"Texas Department of Public Safety, Officer Bergerron."

Dixie spit out the pencil.

"This is Dixie Flannigan. I don't know the address." Unlike a standard phone, a cellular would not instantly flash her location on the dispatcher's monitor—unless their technology was more advanced than Dixie imagined. She spoke low but distinctly, conveying her situation, describing as best she could the route she'd driven to the training center. *How far to that private road? The next turn?* She estimated, remembering for certain only the final two miles after she'd turned away from the sound of an eighteen-wheeler. "My car is parked off the road, a quarter mile past the building." She described her Mustang, adding the license number.

The dispatcher asked a question. Dixie couldn't quite make the words out, but she knew the gist.

"Weapons, at least three guns," she said. "No alcohol, no drugs." She thought about the meeting Mike had referred to earlier. "Could be as many as twenty-eight men." Then she glanced at Laskey and winced. "One man's been shot. He's unconscious."

Maybe dead.

"I can't stay on the phone," she told the dispatcher. "He's coming back. But I'll leave the line open."

She nudged the drawer almost closed, praying Mike wouldn't notice the half-inch gap. When she started to close the other drawer, Dixie saw a ballpoint pen, recalled seeing a handcuff key made from an ink cylinder . . . but that was in a film. Would it work? *Jeez, she was stealing escape ideas from a movie?*

To make it work, she needed the pen in her hands, not her mouth. The chair would prevent her from reaching into the drawer. Dixie grabbed the pen between her teeth and nudged the drawer shut.

The doorknob turned.

Dipping her chin low, she poked the pen into the neck of her shirt. It slid down her side, between fabric and skin.

He instantly seemed to sense something was wrong. He glanced at the lockbox apparatus, then around the room—not a flicker of remorse as his gaze passed over Philip. Then he circled the desk and examined Dixie's cuffed wrists.

"Trying to wriggle free?" He sounded unconcerned.

"The cuffs are too tight. You didn't double-lock them. Unless you use a key, they tighten down with every movement."

He searched her eyes, as if testing the truth of what she was saying.

"We'll leave soon. I suggest you remain still until then."

"Are we going to The Winning Stretch?" She spoke as loud as she dared and tried to sound excited about the idea. *Where were those cops?*

Mike nodded, returning the items to the lockbox.

Dixie had clamped the ballpoint between her arm and side to prevent it falling out while Mike examined her wrists. Now she let it slide down to the chair seat, talking to cover any sound.

"What about Philip? We can't leave him here. If he's dead—"

"I'll take care of Mr. Laskey."

"The men who came for your meeting—are they still here?"

"Why all the questions, Dixie?"

"I'm . . . fascinated. Two completely separate groups, yet neither knows the other exists." *Talking too fast.* "Both regard you as a . . . leader? Commander? Minister?"

"You'll learn everything soon enough, if I decide I can trust you." Leaving the syringe on the desk, he carried the flask into the bathroom.

"All the time you were gone," Dixie called after him, unable to take her eyes off the needle, "I thought about the . . . symmetry of it, the robberies, which triggered the assassinations. And these boys, marksmen, from what I saw in the shooting gallery, they're avenging the slain Granny Bandits with no idea that you directed the robberies."

Running water drowned out the last of her praise.

Dixie caught the ballpoint between her fingers to unscrew the barrel. After fumbling with it for ten seconds, she realized it wasn't a screw type. She tried to wedge a fingernail between the point and the shaft, but it wouldn't pull free.

When he turned off the water, she palmed the ballpoint—as a weapon, if he got close enough. If he removed the damn handcuffs.

Where were those cops? How long had it been? Five minutes? Fifteen?

Mike returned with the clean flask, set it into the box, and locked it. Dixie leveled her most admiring gaze at him, but knew it wasn't working. She almost wished the incense *would* relax her. That needle made her damned nervous.

Mike smiled as he returned her gaze. "I knew you would be an apt pupil, Dixie."

"I like the way you think," she lied. "You're a father figure to the boys. To the women, too?" Adding a desperate flirtatious lilt to that last phrase.

"Actually, yes, you might say that." He carried the lockbox to the file cabinet. "Either the father they worshiped as a child, or a celibate lover. Isn't that what so many women want, especially in later years?"

The age-old symbiosis, men mate for sex, women for intimacy; women provide sex to enjoy intimacy, men provide intimacy to enjoy sex. Marriage counselors built careers working it out for couples. Mike had done his homework.

"I suppose that's true of some women," she agreed.

He came up behind her, placed his hands on her neck.

Dixie's gaze shifted to the spot on the desk where the hypodermic had been: *gone*. Was it in the box?

"Mike—" *Keep him talking, bragging.* "Tell me about Angela. She seems . . . special."

He stroked her neck and shoulders, as he'd done briefly at The Winning Stretch. His fingers delicately traced her jaw, her cheek, the curve of her ear.

"The tea you drank, it's wonderful for toning the skin and strengthening bone mass, but one unfortunate side effect is significantly increased levels of oxytocin and free cortisol. In higher dosage, it produces an effect akin to amnesia, causing neuronal loss." Mike's fingers slowed. "I love the way you smell, Dixie Flannigan. And the silken firmness of your flesh." One hand slid from her shoulder.

Into his pocket? *Did he have that goddamn syringe in his pocket? Had he revealed his secrets because he knew she wouldn't retain enough brain cells to remember them?* That possibility chilled her more than death.

Dixie tensed, her thoughts racing. *Whirl the chair around, knock the needle from his hand . . . he had the .25, but she'd rather be shot than brain-dead.*

Or tell him she'd called the cops. They could be surrounding the building right now. *Should* be.

"It's time you got some rest, Dixie." The jingle of keys. "At The Winning Stretch, you'll have a room of your own—"

Like Rose?

His hands at her wrists. Where was the gun?

"—I've already moved your car into the shed out back."

Shit! No wonder the cops hadn't found her. She'd told them to look for the Mustang.

The handcuffs fell, clicked open.

Dixie shoved the chair back *hard*, knocking Mike into the wall. She sprang to her feet—hands numb—and jabbed an elbow into his side, another into his throat.

He gagged. Dropped her keys. Fumbled for his pocket.

Dixie snap-kicked her boot heel into his hip, crunching the hand reaching for the gun. Retracted her foot for another kick—

An explosion deafened her. Fire tore at her arm.

He'd shot her!

Still on her feet, she aimed another kick at his wrist—

The gun thudded to the floor.

—jammed her boot into his groin.

He grunted. Folded.

She slammed her clasped hands on the back of his neck and raised her knee into his face.

He went down. Blood spurted from his nose.

She nudged the .25 out of reach.

Boot heel aimed at his face, she asked: "Are you going to stay down?"

He nodded.

Dixie ached to deliver a killing blow. Thanks to his religious immunity and her mishandling of the search, Mike Tesche would not likely serve any prison time.

"The syringe, hand it over."

He tugged it from his pocket, needle tip still encased in its plastic shield. He'd planned to get her into the car first. Inject her. Dump her. Or maybe he'd take her to The Winning Stretch, where he could monitor her response to the drug. *You have too many friends in high places.*

Blood ran down her arm and slicked her palms as she handcuffed Mike's hands behind his back. Then she grabbed the cell phone.

"Are you there? Where the hell is that patrol car?"

Chapter Seventy-one

Philip Laskey floated in red mist, counting pull-ups. ONE.

Philip, can you hear me? Someone had called his name from far away. Anna Marie? No . . . a younger voice. Ms. Flannigan. *I'll get help. You'll be all right, Philip.*

TWO. He thought it strange that he didn't feel the tug on his arms . . . but his head pounded, as if from a long workout.

. . . fine, good man, Philip . . . trifle heavy with the rod . . .

THREE . . . *killed those women . . . as surely as if he'd placed his own gun to their heads . . .*

FOUR . . .

Philip opened his eyes.

Drifting in and out, he'd heard voices. *Lucy Ames . . . Edna Pine . . . induced to willingly die.*

Philip sat up shakily.

"Philip!"

Across the room, Colonel Jay attempted to get to his feet.

"Come here, Philip. Help me up. We have to leave."

"Yes, sir." Philip rose. His head throbbed. . . . *pursue the mission . . .*

"Can you take these cuffs off, Philip?"

"I think so, sir."

"Good, but hurry. Police are coming."

Philip unbuckled his belt and slid a thin wire from its narrow placket. . . . *no idea that you directed the whole thing . . .* He looped the garrote around the Colonel's neck and yanked it tight.

. . . as surely as if he'd placed his own gun . . .

The Colonel gasped, struggled.

. . . casket's pink satin lining . . . touched the cold hand . . .

The Colonel clawed at the wire.

. . . his own gun to their heads . . .

The door opened.

"Stand down, son. Let him go."

An officer snapped a gun from its holster. Ms. Flannigan stood behind him.

Philip smiled. . . . *could melt the heart of a hangman.* His arms quivered as he tightened the garrote against the Colonel's final struggles. "It's okay." His voice echoed in his head. His cheeks felt damp. "You can shoot."

"Mister, drop your weapon!" The officer braced and aimed.

"Don't shoot him!" Ms. Flannigan said.

"Drop your weapon, mister!"

"No, McGrue!"

As the Colonel sagged lifelessly beneath Philip's noose, Ms. Flannigan stepped in front of the officer's gun, but he batted her aside and pulled the trigger.

"The People," Philip whispered, "have avenged . . ."

Chapter Seventy-two

Dixie sat in a far corner of a makeshift conference room set up for the task force. This floor of the new HPD building was already undergoing a remodeling. Behind her, a thick sheet of polyethylene masked a construction area. Paint fumes floated on every gust of air from the vent.

She'd spent part of the afternoon getting her arm bandaged, then more time explaining the hunch that prompted her to follow Philip Laskey, and the subsequent events leading to the murder of Michael Jay Tesche. Finding Philip still alive—a deep gouge creasing his skull—she'd rushed outside to meet the DPS officers and direct the medics. The familiar sight of Slim Jim McGrue unfolding his six-foot-eight body from his black-and-white patrol car had looked damn fine. And his presence had helped her cut through the tedious explanations. What Dixie longed for now was a cold beer and a month of solitude to sort through the "whys" that bounced around in her brain.

But a nod from Avery Banning—merely bruised from the blow to his bulletproof vest—had helped her weasel a fly-on-the-wall seat in the task force room. Emile Arceneaux, the HPD psychiatrist, had asked to sit in while Banning discussed his college experiences with Tesche. The meeting was closed to media.

"What Jay sought, and what he demanded from us," Banning said quietly, "was perfection. We had to be the best, the smartest, the strongest—and with Jay's encouragement, we did it. Jay Tesche had the ability to electrify a man, point him toward a cause, and make things happen."

Women, too. Dixie had experienced Mike's charisma firsthand. She still hadn't reconciled her attraction to him.

"We'd have these motivational rallies," Banning said. "Afterward we were right up there with the gods."

One of the FBI agents smirked. "Sounds like every politician's wet dream."

Sally Carter, the senior agent conducting the interview, silenced him with a look. "Mayor Banning, did Tesche engineer the commission of crimes within your—what was it, a gang? A fraternity?"

"Neither," Banning corrected. "More of a . . . an elite clique. And it never seemed that we were committing crimes, but I suppose we skirted the edges. When one of the professors—Spangler—made it clear he didn't like our elitist attitude, Jay convinced female students to write out complaints against him—for sexual harassment, although of course that term hadn't been coined yet. Professor Spangler was so demoralized he would've resigned on the spot, only the dean talked him out of it. A month later, a guard found the professor's car in the parking lot. He was drunk in the backseat with a female student bruised and crying. Next day, Spangler left the school. Quietly."

"But it was your gang who roughed up the girl?" Carter asked pointedly.

"Nothing could be proved, but the dean blamed us. A few weeks later, an associate professor—a woman with a 'rumored' drug addiction—was found passed out naked by the swimming pool with a quantity of LSD tabs. After the Spangler situation, she'd have been asked to leave, too, but somehow Jay hushed it up—without anyone ever discovering that *we* were instrumental in the woman ending up by the pool. From that day on, she was in Jay's pocket, providing everything from confidential files to"—Banning cleared his throat—"group sex."

According to The People's computer files, Tesche had utilized a similar combination of blackmail and control tactics to construct a network that now stretched across the nation. Black lines crisscrossed a map connecting a Texas senator, several state representatives, a New York City bank president, an immigration agent, key personnel in the Environmental Protection Agency, the Securities and Exchange Commission, the U.S. Treasury, and, in Los Angeles, a legendary Hollywood producer.

Some of these people were of no real consequence politically, but they could obtain information, deliver messages, accidentally *lose* important papers. Councilman Gib Gibson, without even knowing it, had nearly become Mike's latest token.

What Tesche planned to do with this network no one had yet figured out. If he could create the havoc of this past week in one city, Dixie shuddered to think what he might have done in others.

"I'm still unclear why Tesche, after all these years, conducted such an elaborate scam to even an old score with you, Mayor."

"Because he could, *cher.*" Doc Arceneaux interrupted, "All the reason he needed." Thirty-two years in Houston and Doc still talked like a Cajun TV chef, but his folksiness made him popular among the ranks. "Tesche, he's a narcissist. Relates to people only as they can satisfy his own desires. Those who won't? Or can't? Disposable, like used Kleenex. We're seeing this narcissist type more and more. Don't like your teacher? Go get Daddy's rifle, shoot up the school. Blow all the suckers away. Experts like me hate to admit it, but these kids don't fit the profile of parental abuse, neglect, no. Like Ted Kaczynski. Like Kip Kinkel—fifteen years old, from Oregon, kills his parents, two school friends, wounds twenty-two others. Solid families they come from. Not perfect, but good mommas, good daddies, people who care about their kids. But also overindulge their kids. All that permissiveness from the sixties, thinking *any* physical discipline is child abuse, no matter how infrequent or judicious. Creating well-educated monsters who see humanity as one big Christmas stocking, full of goodies they can demand—"

"Doc," Carter argued, "I don't see it. Tesche didn't blow anybody away. He got others to do his dirty work."

"Smart lady, this FBI agent," Doc said. "Yes, *cher.* Unlike Kinkel and the Unabomber, Tesche discovered the art of finesse. He has charm, patience. He makes people bombs. His desire to even the score with an old college mate sits on a shelf in his mind. Until the right moment. Then he wraps Avery Banning in his web and moves in. Not for the kill. For control. *My* question, Mayor—" Arceneaux stopped to pencil a note on the unpainted drywall. "What terrible injustice did you do to Mr. Tesche?"

Everyone in the room had followed Doc's explanation with rapt attention. Now they turned that attention to Banning. From Tesche's files at The People's training center, which were still being examined, they knew he had studied cult mind-set and had added that tool to his arsenal.

The Mayor wiped a bead of sweat from his cheek. "A kid named Beagle . . . no, his real name was Joe Brickle, but we gave him the nickname because he was such a loyal dog. Joe wanted so damn bad to belong. So we pushed him. '*Do this, Beagle, do that . . . you can make it, Beagle . . . no, that's not right, try harder, you can do it.*' Only Joe Brickle *couldn't* make it. He was a screwup . . ."

Banning shot a glance at Arceneaux. "I overheard his last session with Jay, and I've relived it in my nightmares ever since. '*Beagle, the only way a screwup like you will ever achieve greatness is postmortem,*' Jay told him. '*Like soldiers who charge a line of fire and die in action. Dying takes courage. You have that kind of courage, Beagle. You may never achieve anything else significant, but you have that kind of courage.*' Later that night, Beagle climbed to the top of the highest building on campus and jumped."

In the silence that followed this, a gust of air brushed the polyethylene against Dixie's shoulder and fanned the room with paint fumes.

"You're talking mind control," Carter said.

"If you've never experienced it, *cher*, sit in on a snake handler's revival meeting. I defy you to stay immune to the magnetism these people have."

The Mayor sighed. "Jay Tesche chose his students with intense care—men who were low in self-esteem, impressionable, desperate to believe in something. From there, he simply figured out what each one wanted and provided it in carefully measured doses."

"You knew all this, yet you went along with him?" Carter's voice sharpened.

"I was impressionable. Hell, in college, isn't every kid ripe for changing the world?" When no one commented, Banning continued. "But I turned Jay in. Later, I needed to understand, and I backtracked everything Jay had studied. He was brilliant, so some of what he did was over my head, but it included a lot of fringe techniques that were theoretically debatable—sleep deprivation, sub-audial and subliminal commands, positive and negative reinforcement—" Banning looked around and seemed to notice the mass bewilderment.

Arceneaux waved him silent. "Take a young man—woman—who's never excelled. Who's starved for approval. Pick a skill he's good at and praise him. Pick another—something he's not so good, but maybe could do with practice. Praise him, he'll improve. First time he messes up, take away approval. 'You let me down, hey? I trusted you, believed in you, look how you repay my trust—by not living up to what I know you can do.' He'll walk through fire to regain your approval. It's a classic method for handling unruly adolescents."

"Doesn't work with my kids," the junior agent muttered.

"You're not Jay Tesche," Banning said softly.

"What happened?" Carter asked. "Tesche was kicked out of school?"

"He agreed to leave. You see, I had no proof, only my word. Joe Brickle wasn't drugged. He climbed to the roof alone and dove off in front of half the school."

"And what happened to your . . . *elite clique?*"

"After Jay left, the group broke up. Grades fell off. Athletes who excelled while we were together lost their edge. Some dropped out before graduation. Jay was the magnet that pulled us together and the inspiration that made us excel. Without him, we had little in common . . . except shame."

Without him, what would happen to the women who found solace at The Winning Stretch, a.k.a. the Church of The Light? Angela with her woman-child mannerisms? Rose, locked in her private room? Would she ever come out? Had Tesche stockpiled enough cash to support the self-contained Church over time?

"So, let me get this straight," Carter said crisply. "To retaliate for your turning him in nineteen years ago, Tesche organized three bank robberies, engineered police shootings of two women, then assassinated two officers and the Police Chief. Wouldn't it have been easier to just shoot *you?*"

Banning shrugged. "I suppose he wanted to see me drummed very publicly out of office. Humiliated, as he was all those years ago."

"Revenge." Doc wrote the word large on the wall, then struck through it. "You're getting hung up on it. But that was only lagniappe to Tesche. To him, the whole charade was all a game."

A game, a con. Mike Tesche had fooled everyone. Dixie figured that should make her feel better about being sucked in. Maybe in a hundred years it would.

Chapter Seventy-three

The Suds Club on a Monday offered precisely the level of raucous anonymity Dixie needed. Owned by a former prosecutor who, like Dixie, had seen the justice scales tipping the wrong way too often, the club attracted lawyers the way a scab attracts fingernails. They came here to drown the day's miseries, hoping to see their courtroom cohorts and opponents soused in even greater misery.

The familiar scent of yeast from the ninety-nine varieties on tap and soap suds from the adjacent laundromat engulfed Dixie as she entered. A rock-and-roll goodie, recorded by a local band called "The Convictions," all current or former prosecutors, played on the Wurlitzer. Dixie found her usual corner booth, ordered a Shiner Bock, and unplugged the vintage Pabst sign lighting the niche. She wanted no company tonight.

"Antisocial?" Belle slid her classy rump on the opposite seat.

"Can't you take the hint?"

"And miss out on an opportunity to needle you?"

"Domestic socialite like you should be home with the hubby and kiddies."

"Go ahead, take shots at the good life, Flanni. You could have it, too, if you weren't so damned hardheaded." Belle twirled her wineglass on a bar coaster and dropped the barb from her voice. "From what I hear, you eliminated the blind lady from the equation today."

"A defense lawyer's supposition. My hands were nowhere near the garrote that ended Mike Tesche's life. And Philip Laskey will survive to stand trial. I gave him your card."

"Can he afford me?"

"You might find deeper pockets among the twenty-seven accomplices. But I think maybe this one's worth saving. You'll work it out."

Belle twirled the glass some more. "What happened out there?"

"If I knew that, I wouldn't be sitting here." She related the string of disasters that ended at The People's training center. "Mike Tesche could read people as easily as you and I can read this beer label—"

"The one you've almost destroyed."

"He picked up on vulnerability and knew exactly when and how to draw you in. Dammit, I *liked* the guy! What does that say about my judgment?"

"Maybe that you're more human than you like to let on."

"Tesche was scary, Ric, but not the only manipulator out there waiting to pounce." In the past week, Dixie'd been played for a sap emotionally, financially, psychologically, and she wasn't even sure she liked her new hairstyle. "How do we protect the people we care about from predators?"

"Protecting everybody you care about sounds like a big job to take on."

"Barney would say, 'It's the tough jobs that make us, lass.' "

"Didn't your sainted father also say, 'Experience is the best teacher—if not always the gentlest'? Maybe it's not your place to shoulder everyone's experience."

"What's that supposed to mean?"

"From what you told me, Edna decided to renew her life. Met a number of new friends, enjoyed new experiences even before she met Tesche—"

"Some of those new friends were cons."

"Or just businesspeople. Would you have denied Edna the new clothes? The day spa?"

"Of course not."

"You admit that Terrence Jackson checked out fine. And the astrologer-slash-shrink *did* help Edna lose weight."

"If you're trying to reason me out of a funk, forget it. It's been a damn rotten week." Dixie signaled the waitress to bring another Shiner and another glass of wine for Belle.

The lawyer's shrewd gray eyes leveled at Dixie. "Did you and Parker have a clash before you went to see Tesche?"

Dixie's pager had recorded two messages from Parker and the usual from Amy and Ryan. Dixie had returned the calls to her sister and nephew.

"I'm not sure what's going on between Parker and me. He beckons with one hand and pushes me away with the other." Their drinks came. When the waitress left, Dixie raised her bottle to Belle's glass. "To the freedom to funk."

Belle drank to the toast but smiled thinly. "Flannigan, I once defended a poet who talked about love. You meet this soul mate, he said, this person your heart knows is perfection, who completes you, who fills you with song. Life is so good you could die right then and be forever grateful for a few days of bliss. Then, with time, you notice the rough edges. She slurps her coffee. She nags you about smoking. She talks too loud with your friends. You make suggestions, smooth out the parts you don't appreciate. Then you see a few shallow spots—she doesn't feel as deeply about certain things as you do. You begin to whittle and reshape this soul mate to fit an ideal in your mind, the same person your heart once knew was perfection."

"In other words, I'm a stubborn fool. What did you defend this poet against?"

"Killed seven women. Claimed he was madly in love with every one of them."

Chapter Seventy-four

Tuesday

Dixie's students had heard her name in the news again. She spent most of the first hour explaining how it felt to be shot. She couldn't talk about Mike Tesche yet; they seemed to respect that. She ignored Joan's fresh bruises and, toward the end of class, finally got in some instruction.

"How's your son?" she asked Lureen on the way out.

"Little pissant wants to be a *cop*." A grin illuminated the woman's face. "*One week* the other side a them effin' bars, seeing uniforms on the free side. Tell me it don't matter who they hang wit'."

Dixie hugged her. She'd been giving out a lot of hugs since she took the garrote from Philip Laskey's hand. Give one to get one. *Cows going to slaughter.*

Dixie left the center without glancing into Mike's empty classroom. All the way down the hall she could swear she heard the muted sounds of Mozart. Or maybe it was Bach.

Pointing the Mustang toward Amy's house, she dialed her number on the cell phone.

"I'm fine," Dixie told her sister, before she could ask. "No broken bones, no bullet holes." The crease in her arm didn't count. Luckily, the full details of Mike's death hadn't been released yet, so Amy wasn't as panicked as she might've been. "Is Marty around?"

The copied pages of Edna's journal lay on the passenger seat, topping a handful of mail from Dixie's post-office box. Marty would find some of his mother's words painful. But others, Dixie knew, would surely grant him the peace he'd desperately sought for so many years.

"Marty went to see Belle, then he's flying back to Dallas. Last night, he sprinkled Edna's ashes in her garden. He's going to be all right. He said to tell you that Ashton agreed to sign a partnership agreement. Dixie, have you talked with Parker?"

No. She hadn't returned his calls, but she'd listened twice to his messages on her voice mail. "Don't worry, Amy, I'll call him. First I want to talk to my nephew. Is he around?"

"You just missed him. He rode his bike to the park."

This time Dixie had a notion at which park to find Ryan. She spotted his scrawny, T-shirt-clad shoulders and eased the Mustang out of sight at the curb. His bicycle was slanted against a tree, a dirt bike close by. Ryan sat at a picnic table. A man—sandy hair, tattoos, black tank top—sat on top of the table, booted feet on the seat, arms resting on his knees.

As Dixie aimed a directional microphone, she recalled the King Pin posture Ryan had taken as he traded porno with his peers. The man on the table sat in command, despite his casual pose. Dixie hadn't liked Ryan's big-man-on-campus posture, but his subservience to this guy chilled her.

"Did you look at those last photographs before you sold them?" The man spoke low and secretively, his voice husky.

Ryan shrugged, that familiar lazy roll of his narrow shoulders. "Sure. I mean, you know, sort of."

"You knew those were models, didn't you? Posing like that. Not really doing what it *looked* like."

"Really?" Ryan clearly hadn't known.

"Looked real, though, didn't it?"

"Yeah."

"Kids make a bundle, modeling like that."

Ryan didn't say anything.

"Takes a good-looking kid like you to make the big bucks." Then he stared out at the park. "Nice town you've got here, but kinda slow. You travel much?"

"No. It's okay here."

"Yeah, real nice. But like I said, kinda slow. You said there's an arcade? Any girls there?"

Ryan shrugged. "Sometimes."

"You're not into girls? I mean like *into*?" He laughed and punched Ryan's arm. "Bet you've got something they're hot for." He laughed again. "Hanging down to your knees, I bet."

Ryan's weak chuckle sounded embarrassed.

Dixie dialed HPD Vice Division. She knew someone who would handle this the way it needed to be handled, to take this slimeball off the streets—and off the Internet.

But she also knew he might make them as cops. Leaving the microphone positioned and a recorder going, she strolled casually across the grass, behind Ryan's line of sight, as if headed to the water fountain. When she was close, she veered and straddled the guy's dirt bike.

"What the shit, bitch—?"

"Nice wheels," Dixie commented.

"Aunt Dix?!"

"I've been listening to your conversation with my nephew."

"Me and the kid were just talking." He slid off the picnic table and started toward her.

Dixie casually exposed the .38, holster unsnapped for quick access. He stopped walking.

"You didn't tell him what happens to young studs after a couple years, when they get too old to be in your kiddie shows. The 'big bucks' are all gone, into your pocket for their clothes, food, a place to stay, and the drugs you manage to hook them on. After that, the kids are out on the street, too ashamed to go home to family, too young to earn money any way but hooking. But I'll bet you can help them out there, too?"

A car from HPD Vice had arrived, and Dixie let them take over. Remembering Doc Arceneaux's comments about discipline, Dixie'd thought seriously about arranging for Ryan to spend a few hours in juvie lockup, give him a dose of the real world his small-time porno racket could lead to. *I turned the little pissant in.* But Ryan wasn't as street smart as Lureen's fifteen-year-old son, and maybe Dixie wasn't as strong as Lureen. She decided a personal jail tour would do the trick.

Back in the Mustang, she watched the Vice unit turning a corner toward downtown, Ryan's porno supplier scowling out its back window. Ryan might not speak to her until he turned thirty.

After dropping her nephew and his bike at home and providing a lengthy explanation to Amy and Carl, Dixie headed gratefully, wearily toward home. On the way, she phoned Parker.

Listening to the rings at a stoplight, she shuffled through her mail . . . a box of new checks and deposit slips, with all new account numbers . . . some bills . . . a payment from the bonding company for bringing in Voller . . . a letter from Atlanta State Bank . . .

Parker picked up on the fourth ring.

"Got your messages," she said. "But I was . . . tied up."

"Guess that's why I heard your name in the news again."

"Guess so."

"Thought I'd cook steaks tonight." Parker's voice slipped into the sexy zone, the one that always turned her to mush. "Thought maybe you and Mud could join me . . . maybe bring an overnight bag."

She considered it. A week ago, she'd've raced to take him up on such an offer.

"I have a different idea," she told him. "How about if I order pizza and *you* bring an overnight bag?"

He hesitated, but only an instant. "Sounds good to me."

Before hanging up, she said, "Parker? Thanks for worrying about me." She ordered the pizza—half with extra cheese for her, the other half with extra mushrooms for him—then she studied the letter from Atlanta State Bank. She didn't *know* anybody at Atlanta State Bank. She ripped it open.

RE: #70005466789

Dear Ms. Flannigan,

Your account has been closed due to numerous unpaid insufficient funds statements issued to the address you provided. Please contact us immediately . . .

Shit!

ABOUT CHRIS ROGERS

CHRIS ROGERS lives in Houston, Texas, where she is at work on her next Dixie Flannigan novel.